ESCAPE FROM MEDIA

WHERE MAGIC IS FORBIDDEN
AND
LOVE IS DANGEROUS

by

BRANDY STOKER

Library of Congress : 1-14906883191

ASIN: B0F3FHMKP8

ISBN:

eBook 979-8-9928152-0-7

Paperback 979-8-9928152-1-4

Hardcover 979-8-9928152-2-1

Content Warning

This story contains themes of alcohol consumption, references to drug use, violence, war, emotional trauma, child endangerment, authoritarian control, and romantic intimacy. Scenes may include battle sequences, injuries, references to loss and grief, and sensual content between consenting adults.

Reader discretion is advised. Recommended for readers 18 and over.

Disclaimer

This is a fiction work. All incidents and dialogue, and all characters, businesses, and locations are products of the author's imagination and are not to be construed as real. Any resemblance to person or persons living or dead is entirely coincidental.

To stay informed and be eligible for giveaways and sneak peaks of upcoming novels, go to www.brandystoker.com. From here you can sign up for my newsletter. In return, you will get a free short story to give you more to this story.

Read – Liberators of Media for backstory into why the city is doing what they are to people with magic.

DEDICATION

I have some of the most supportive friends and family I could have every asked for. This book is dedicated to the people who have helped me to find my dream of being an author.
There are too many to list individually.

To all the readers who have reached out to me, to tell me how much they appreciated the book. It is because of you that I have found the energy and desire to keep going on my journey. It is because of you that I feel like there are people out there to write for.
Thank you!

Book Cover – by Anglee Van Allman
Map by Ben Cole
Publishing Support by Brandy Over 40
Formatting by Brandy Jones

Review Help by:
Sebastian Probas
Mary Tilghman
Alomary Luna

CONTENTS

MAP OF MEDIA

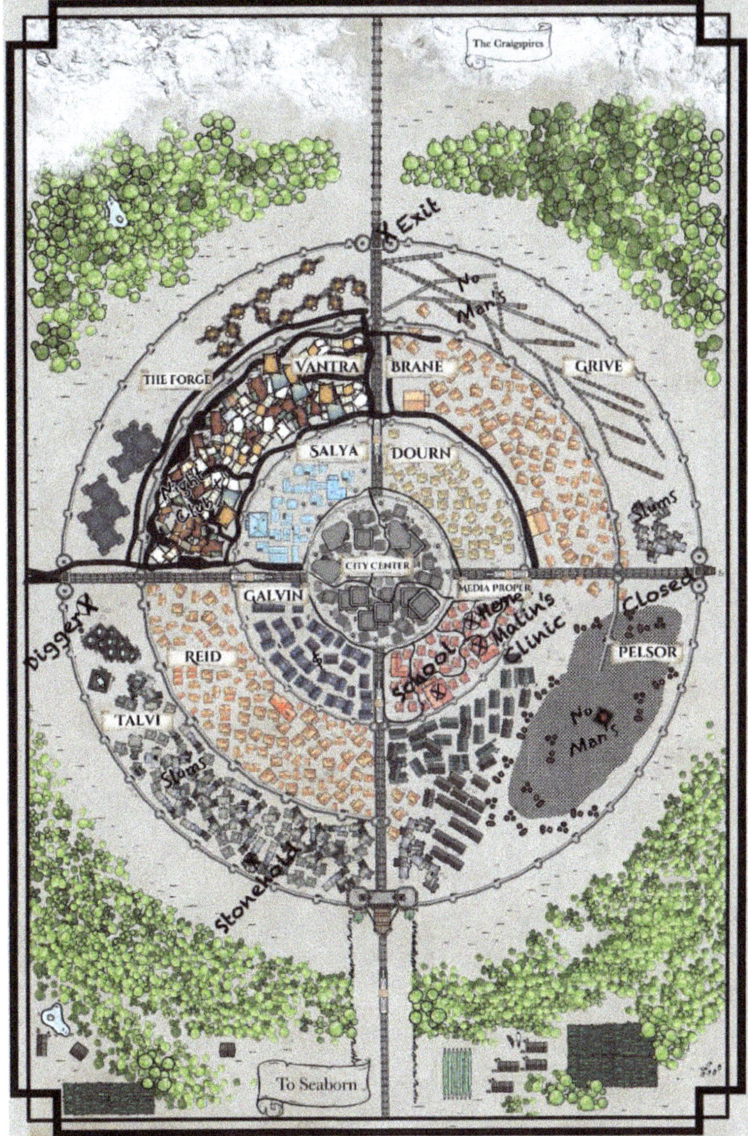

Special Thanks to Ben Cole for his Brilliant Map!
https://www.upwork.com/fl/~01b2a6d0874b771bae

Chapter 1 — Spark of Rebellion

Will felt the spark tickle his fingers before it snapped, like biting a penny. He yanked his hand away just in time, laughing as Layla glared up at him. He flinched just in time, grinning as his sister, Layla's fingers fizzled with tiny bolts of static.

"Hey!" she squeaked, her whole face scrunching into a glare that should've been scary if it weren't attached to his five-year-old sister with pale blonde hair and a stuffed rabbit dragging behind her. "Will! That's mine!"

The chocolate bar was half-melted, sticky and warm against his palm; body heat and the muggy air trapped inside the shack made everything sticky. He broke it clean, giving her the bigger piece 'cause she was only five. He was careful not to drop crumbs on the threadbare rug, handing her the bigger half.

"Layla, you gotta earn it," he said with his crooked grin. "You zapped. That's cheatin'. You gotta *sneak* if you wanna win."

Layla stomped hard enough the shack gave a tired groan, the walls shivering like they might fall in. Sparks popped from her knuckles, and he took a cautious step back, stuffing the other half of chocolate in his pocket. He loved playing like this with her.

"I sneaky!" she huffed, nose crinkling. "But I little. You ten. That's big."

just in case she decided to throw more at him.

She lunged, clumsy but quick for her size. Her sleeve snagged the edge of their crate-table, her feet scuffing across the dusty floor. Will slipped left, let her grab empty air, and spun to face her.

"Almost," he said, breath steady. "Next time, no noise. Watch yer pressure, I can feel it. Don't let the dust know you moved."

Layla beamed, the sparks in her hands cooling, but the ones in her eyes still burning bright.

The shack around them creaked and sighed with every gust from the factories. Oil dripped from the busted heater pipe, a steady *plink, plink,* that never stopped. Their two-room box wasn't much, walls gray with soot, curtains made from rags, but Will knew every board, every crack, every hidden hole like it was stitched into his skin.

And Layla?

Ma always told him how proud she was of how he watched after her and Da always liked how well he taught her to pocket.

"We did good today," Will said, glancing toward the small haul bagged by the door. "One cubit, decent veggies, and a full bar o' chocolate. Da's gonna lose his mind when he sees all we got."

Layla's face lit up, chocolate already forgotten. "And we still go to da movie 'night, right?"

"Yep. Long as we finish chores. And you don't shock nuttin'."

She dashed off, dragging the broom twice her size behind her. "I like the movies," she said, sweeping in wide, messy circles.

pants."

Will snorted. "Yeah. Fancy pants. Best part."

But he didn't tell her the real reason they went, to sit in the back, watch the crowds, and learn how to disappear.

It was school.

Their kind of school.

Layla paused, lifting a hand toward the busted radio. A spark danced from her fingertips. The radio crackled once, then fuzzed to life.

"I wish I could use ma powers outside," she whispered. "It's hard to keep 'em in."

Will knelt beside her, resting one hand on his patched cargo pants. "You know why you can't," he said gently. "You seen what happens."

Layla stared at the floor, the spark in her hands fading. "But is' me," she whispered.

He ruffled her hair, feeling the static snap. "Exactly why you gotta protect it."

Her grin was crooked and fierce. "Tonight's gonna be magic!"

Will laughed, but it caught in his throat.

If she could believe in magic for one night, maybe that was enough.

He grabbed the broom, sweeping in slow, careful strokes beside her.

"I just like when we're together," he muttered.

was bigger than this broken place.

They hadn't gone out as a family like this for months. Ma and Da been working double shifts. They really wanted to get out of this place and move them to Media Proper. They been saving for years and they said they were close.

But for a little while, they could pretend they were already there, already safe, even if it was just for a few hours.

Will stared at his sister, her small hands still buzzing faintly with leftover energy, and felt a strange hollowness.

Sometimes he wished he had magic like hers, bright, loud, impossible to ignore.

His gift wasn't like that. It lived quiet in the corners of his sight, letting him catch the shimmer of heat inside people, the pulse of anger or fear before it ever showed on their faces.

No sparks. No fireworks. Just shadows on skin.

Nothing anyone would ever notice.

"Mine's boring," he muttered, brushing his fingers against the rough sweep of the broom.

Layla giggled, a high bright sound that cut through the heavy air. "You don't gotta hide it!"

Will ruffled her hair, her fine blonde strands crackling softly under his hand. "Yeah? Well, maybe someday it won't be bad to use magic."

Before she could answer, the door creaked open.

fear but readiness. He recognized the weight of the steps on the threshold. The shape of her shadow through the curtain.

His mother.

Elara stepped inside like the wind pushed her. Her shoulders drooped. Her jumpsuit was stained with oil down the front, and her boots left soft scuffs on the concrete. The smell hit first, metal and sweat, from a day of hard work.

"Ma," he said and moved before she could. He slipped between her and the room, pulling the heavy tool belt from her waist. It dragged low in his hands.

She tried to smile and almost managed it.

Will took a damp rag from the corner and reached up to wipe the smudge from her cheek. Her hazel eyes caught him. He saw how tired she was but still lit with something warm. Something that said she saw him.

"Thanks, love," she said, brushing his shoulder with her callused hand.

She inhaled slowly, enjoying the smell that filled the air. "Did you cook?"

"I started something," Will said with a smirk. "And we got a treat."

He tossed a look over his shoulder. Layla sat with her knees pulled up, eyes wide with delight. Will reached into his pocket and held up the last piece of chocolate.

"Saved it for you. Layla earned it."

The door opened again. This time, heavier.

looked like bricks, creased and stained and too big for the narrow hallway. But his face lit up when he saw Ma.

"Elara," he breathed.

Just that. One word. But Will caught everything in it.

They stood there for a beat, just touching foreheads, leaning close while looking deeply in each other's eyes. Her hand brushed his. His shoulders dropped an inch. That was how they said I love you, in the space between aching backs and bruised hands.

Will stood still and watched it. Quiet. Careful. Memorizing the shape of it all.

This wasn't the kind of love you read about in books or watched on the theater reels. It wasn't shiny or loud. But it was real. Built on every day they'd come home, something Will treasured seeing every day.

And for a moment, just one, the factory noise faded. The shadows in the corners pulled back. And the little shack on the edge of the world felt like the safest place there was.

This brief reprieve set the stage for the evening's adventure, a venture into the cinematic world that promised a temporary escape from their reality. As dusk deepened, casting long shadows across the Talvi District, Will's parents transformed before his eyes.

Will stayed quiet, tucked near the curtain, watching the transformation. His parents became the people their real selves. The time in the factories and processing yards were the masks they wore. The parents in front of him were the real versions. The ones he wanted to be when he was older.

lit by a stub of candle. She wiped a damp cloth slowly across her cheek, revealing soft skin beneath the factory soot. Her hair was already down, spilling over her shoulders in pale waves that shimmered faintly in the warm light, like moonlight caught in a current. She was usually all tied up and smudged with grease by this time. But tonight was different.

She didn't rush.

She moved like someone remembering how.

Will memorized the way she traced a finger along her temple, as if she were reacquainting herself with someone she hadn't seen in a while. She tugged gently at the collar of her dress, the blue one with the tiny white stitches at the hem. The one she always saved for these rare nights, the ones where they had to look like they weren't from the slums. When she noticed him looking at her, she smiled.

He drew in a breath when she did so. It wasn't the tired kind she gave him after a long shift. She looked… almost happy.

Beside her, his father stood over the water basin, scrubbing factory grime from his arms. The water turned dark fast, curling with soot and oil. His movements were slow but certain, the kind of carefulness that came from years of doing everything with purpose. Every wash, every scrape, every breath measured.

Will could see the old burns and scars along his forearms. He knew where most had come from, he'd heard the stories over dinner or whispered through walls. Machines that bit back. Work that didn't stop. But tonight, his father didn't carry himself like a man shaped by machines.

He dipped his head, running a hand over his face, then combed his fingers through his thick brown hair, darker than Will's, but with streaks lightened by sun and smoke. Will noted how his jaw

searched the mirror, not for dirt, but for something... decent.

He reached for his good shirt. The blue one with buttons that were always fastened a little crooked. It smelled faintly of cedar and clean water. He smoothed the fabric over his chest, slow and precise, like putting on armor.

Will watched the reflection shift. His father wasn't a factory man anymore. He looked... tall. Steady. Like a storybook version of himself, but real. He imagined himself standing there, side by side to him in the future.

Elara and Tomas stood side by side now. Not just parents. Not just survivors of Talvi. They looked like something more. Will was proud of his parents, whether in rags or their fine clothes, but he was extra proud of them tonight.

And for a moment, just one flicker of time, Will saw not what they had endured, but what they were still fighting to protect.

He tucked the image away, deep in his mind. Because someday, he'd want to remember it exactly like this.

The night air was a strange kind of sharp, cool against Will's cheeks but thick in his chest. There was something in the air that carried too much weight to breathe easy. The scent of the slums trailed them even as they left Talvi's borders behind, laced with the bitter smoke that always clung to factory fires, no matter how far you walked.

The Hawksons moved like shadows themselves, slipping through the maze of alleys beneath the skeletal sprawl of the elevated train lines. Will led the way, counting each corner, each echo, each eye that lingered a little too long. He knew these routes, knew how the light spilled from streetlamps in predictable patches and how the neon signs flickered in them. It was a living thing, humming, watching.

Layla held Ma's hand tight, her little fingers twitching every few steps. Excitement, nerves, he couldn't tell. Maybe both. Her free hand kept sparking, barely noticeable unless you were looking. Will kept glancing back, watching the flares. Watching her.

She looked up at the theater lights like they were magic. She wasn't wrong.

Elara didn't speak, but Will saw the shift in her face. The way her jaw unclenched and her eyes danced. The low light helped her look younger, almost as she used to before the factories hollowed her out. For now, at least, the weight had slipped off her shoulders, just for a few blocks.

The back alley behind the theater was narrow and quiet. The rusted side door creaked open with the same tired groan it always gave, and Will caught it before it slammed, slipping inside like breath under a locked window.

Inside, the world changed.

Darkness swallowed them up, velvet-lined and musty. The smell of old popcorn and cheap upholstery clung to the air. Rows of red seats were lit only by the flicker of the screen. A golden hero in shining armor blasted across the screen, casting bursts of light into the gloom.

Perfect cover.

They melted into the theater like ghosts. Will's fingers worked automatically, soft touches to coat linings, swift nudges of handbags angled just right. Loose coins. Snack credits. He didn't even need to look. His hands knew what to find.

Layla sat stiffly beside him, her little legs swinging, her big eyes glued to the screen. She didn't laugh. Not even when the cartoon

her tiny shoulders. The way she pressed her lips together.

Onscreen, the past marched forward, shining towers, beautiful people glowing with power. Magical elites flying above crowds, sneering down. The fall. The revolution. The rise of the "just."

The lie of it.

Will glanced at Ma. Her jaw was tight again. Her hands were clenched in her lap. This story was older than him, older than Layla, but it still cut deep. Magic had been blamed for everything. Now, the stories were retold to scare people into compliance.

Layla shifted. He felt her hands tremble and saw the glimmer of light between her fingers before she shoved them under her thighs.

"Is' just a story," he whispered, leaning close. "Is' not real."

She didn't answer, but she nodded.

Ma leaned over and, with the elegance of someone who'd done this before, swiped a full bucket of popcorn from the couple beside them, dropping it in Layla's lap with a wink. Butter and salt filled the space between them. Layla smiled for the first time since the opening credits.

Then, the PSA came on.

Will's stomach tightened the moment the screen went black. No music. No warmth. Just that cold, gray logo and the voice, the one every kid in Media knew by heart. Calm. Icy. Absolute.

"Magic is a danger to unity. Untested individuals must report to reeducation centers. Citizens with information are encouraged to come forward. Rewards will be provided."

felt it, like a current running through the row. Her fear was loud to him.

He reached for her hand and wrapped his fingers around hers. She didn't look at him, but she didn't let go either.

The screen faded to black. The emblem of Media blazed across it.

Around them, polite applause.

Will didn't move. He couldn't.

Ma exhaled slowly beside them, brushing Layla's shoulder like a signal: We're still here.

They were still here.

But for how long?

As the Hawksons slipped from the hush of the theater into the raw night, the air felt colder, thinner. They emerged into the alley like smoke from a snuffed flame, their shared warmth already peeling away under the chill.

Grime slicked the bricks around them, the usual smear of soot and city sweat clinging to every surface. The smell of burnt oil rode the breeze, mixing with the acrid stink of rust and metal. Distant machinery drummed like a slow heartbeat, echoing through the narrow lanes of the Talvi District.

Will felt Layla press close. Her tiny hand slipped into his, cold and tight. The joy from earlier had evaporated, and in its place: silence. Parents ahead, murmuring low, too low to hear, but not low enough to hide the tension threading between them.

Then, snap.

A spark jumped from Layla's fingertips, quick and sharp against his skin. Will flinched, not from pain, but from what it meant.

it lit up a torn propaganda poster, "Magic Is Treason." Her light had caught it, thrown their shadows into stark relief.

"Careful, Layla," he hissed, too late.

The boots hit the cobblestones, heading towards them with malice.

Four guards.

Their boots clicked too loudly on the stone, even before Will saw them. Guards. Four of them. Thick uniforms. Sharp eyes. He didn't need to look; he felt it. Their attention slid over his skin like a blade, cold and hard.

"Keep walkin'," he whispered. He gripped Layla's hand tighter. She gripped back, but he could feel that her sparks were gone. Nothing tingled. Just sweat and her racing pulse under his fingers.

Ma's hand landed on Layla's shoulder, soft but steady, holding them together.

"Evening," one of the guards called out. Friendly. Too friendly. Will didn't look right at him. Just a flicker of eye contact. Enough to be polite. Not enough to make it worse.

"Good evening," Da said, calm as ever. Will didn't know how he managed that, how his voice could sound so steady when the whole alley felt like it was holding its breath.

"Enjoy the film?" another guard asked, his words slick and sticky, sliding through the space between them.

"Very good," Da replied, smooth and relaxed, like this was just another walk home. Will wanted to believe it.

Ma's voice cut in next, all honey and steel. "Is there a problem, officers?"

"We observed some... concerning activity from your daughter," he said, already reaching out.

His gloved hand landed on her coat with a squeak.

Will's chest tightened. The world got too small, too fast.

Ma moved. "Let her go." Her words were sharp, cold, ice cracking across a frozen lake.

Another guard pointed at her. "Come here."

Will couldn't move. His arms stayed locked at his side. His legs shook. His brain screamed do something, but his feet were made of stone.

"Sir, I think I see a bulge in the boy's jacket, and maybe one in the man's. I think they need a pat-down," the guard announced to the leader.

Upon hearing this, each of them was patted down, a pile of pouches, wallets, and other stolen items dropped in a pile.

The guards performed a pat down and reached into Will's coat.

No warning. No words.

He dumped the pouch on the ground. Coins clinked. A button. A necklace. Two old wallets. The other pouches revealed similar.

The sound echoed, sharp and loud, like a dropped pan in a silent room.

"Thieves," the guard said, cold as the wind.

Ma didn't blink. Her mouth twitched, but she kept her voice even. "They're just children."

"Silence," the guard snapped.

Will's ears rang.

as it connected. Cold light glowed on their faces, turning them ghostly.

Will squeezed Layla's hand tighter. She was shaking now. Her breath came fast, and she had shallow, little gasps. He could see that she was trying not to cry.

"Judge Harrow," a voice said. Flat. Dry. "Four detainees. Confirmed unauthorized magic use by the girl. Suspected in others. Theft charges confirmed. Requesting directive."

The judge's voice came back like steel wrapped in ice. Apply experimental suppression chips. If they're magical, we'll know. If not, no harm done. Parents: reassigned to penal fields. Children to re-education."

Will's stomach twisted. His throat burned. His knees buckled, but he didn't fall. He couldn't.

"No," Da said. Just that. One word: Loud as thunder.

He stepped forward. "Test it on me first," he begged. "The chips have killed people."

The judge's reply was a dagger. "Your concern is noted. Proceed."

The guards opened the black cases.

Inside there were silver tubes. Small. Round. Sharp edges. Will had seen one once, in a junk dealer's stash in the Talvi markets. People said they made you forget who you were. Sometimes, they stopped your heart.

Ma tried to move in front of Layla as the guard quickly pointed the gun at Layla's arm and fired. It happened so quickly. Layla's face froze, and Ma knelt in front of her.

"Only me, okay?"

Layla's lips were trembling. Her spark was gone. Her face was pale.

Will couldn't look away.

Layla gasped, her body jerking.

Then nothing.

She dropped like a rag doll.

Will lunged, catching her before she hit the ground.

She felt… wrong. Too light. Too still.

"Layla?" His voice broke on her name while Ma screamed a banshee's scream.

Her head rolled against his hand. Her skin was ice. Her eyes were open but wrong. Glazed. Empty. Her mouth hung slightly open, the shape of that last breath still there.

"Wake up," he begged, pressing his forehead to hers. "Please…"

It wasn't a word. It was pain. The kind that tears holes in the world.

As the guard with the chip gun headed toward Will, Ma rushed forward, but the guards blocked her. They didn't flinch. They were walls, and she was not going to be getting through.

Da's roar followed hers, ripping through the alley.

"You will NOT touch them!"

He moved like something wild. Something broken. His fist cracked into a helmet. Metal dented. A guard stumbled back.

Ma followed, her nails slashed across a guard's face. Blood burst in thin red lines.

Then:

Bang.

The gunshot.

Everything froze.

Ma jerked. Her body twisted. Her eyes locked on Will's, shocked, soft, and then… gone.

She dropped right beside him. He watched her favorite bracelet fall beside him. He quickly reached forward to secure it in his pocket. He would give it to her later, after they got out of this.

Not like someone falling. It was as if she were someone cut loose.

She hit the ground. A soft sound. A final one.

Will screamed. Or maybe just heard it. Maybe both.

She lay there. Still. Her dress was soaked in red, spreading out like a flower. The smell hit him: blood, iron, and heat, sharp as metal.

Layla in his arms.

Ma on the ground.

He couldn't hear anything except the rush in his ears. It was as if waves of noise were hitting him, distant and wild.

Boots moved. Someone kicked the pouch aside. Voices muttered.

Da was still fighting, fists wild, but it wasn't enough.

It was never enough.

His cheeks burned with tears. His throat ached, raw and tight, as if he'd swallowed fire.

They'd come for control.

But what they'd done… was ruin everything.

Then the alley cracked open.

A man burst through the smoke, huge, loud, unstoppable. His shoulders came close to scraping the alley walls. His fists swung hard, crashing into guards. They dropped, arms flailing, helmets bouncing, no match for him.

"GET AWAY FROM THEM!" he roared.

It wasn't just a shout. It split the air. Shook the world.

Will turned toward Da, just in time.

A guard slammed something against Da's neck.

A hiss.

Da jerked. Eyes wide. Muscles clenched. But he moved anyway. He yanked the device from the guard's hand. The chip gun crushed in his oversized fist, cracking sharp and final.

Then his body seized up. Knees folded. Back arched. He dropped fast and hard, all the strength gone at once.

Not a faint. Not a fall.

A break.

"No!" Will's voice broke open. "Da!"

Gorek didn't stop. He kept swinging, sending guards flying. But it didn't matter.

Layla wasn't moving.

And now Da.

The sirens wailed, shrill and endless. Red and blue lights flashed against the brick, making everything stutter and blur. The air stank of smoke, metal, and something colder, something sharp in his nose and tongue. Magic, maybe. Or fear.

"Come." The big man's voice cut through everything. Gorek. He grabbed Will's arm and pulled him up.

Will's legs gave out. They folded under him like paper.

Gorek scooped him up, easy. It was as if he weighed nothing.

Will's face bumped against Gorek's shoulder as they ran. The wind stung his cheeks. His mouth tasted like pennies. Blood.

He didn't cry. He couldn't. Crying would snap him in two.

After a while, Gorek slowed. He set Will down.

"Stay close. Run with me."

Will ran.

The ground was wet. The air smelled like oil and garbage. Everything echoed: boots, breath, sirens still whining somewhere behind them.

The city pressed in around them. Tall, sharp buildings. Wires overhead. Pipes hissing, causing steam to rise.

"Keep moving," Gorek said. He didn't sound tired. Just focused.

Will nodded, his breath hitching. His feet thudded against stone. He ran like that was the only option available to him.

Then they burst into a wide street, not so dark, not so tight. And there it was:

The wall.

Covered in signs and bolts and black cables that pulsed with faint blue light.

Beyond it... Will didn't know.

But it had to be better than here.

They ran toward a tunnel. Dark and dripping. Like a throat waiting to swallow them.

Will looked back once.

The alley was gone. The lights. The noise. Just shadows now.

"We're almost there," Gorek said, low and rough. "Stay with me."

Will nodded.

They slipped into the tunnel. The air turned cold. Water dripped from somewhere above. The ground was uneven and smelled of damp metal and dirt.

Gorek led them, turning without hesitating like he knew every twist.

Will followed.

And then, the edge.

The line.

Behind them: the city.

Ahead: the dark. The wild.

Will stepped over the edge.

He didn't look back.

He couldn't.

The city faded behind them, swallowed by trees and sky and distance. But Will felt it. All of it. The empty space where his

carved a hole there and left it wide open.

He kept walking.

Because there was nothing else to do.

*T*he woman's scream split the early morning stillness, raw and jagged like glass dragged across stone. It echoed through the skeletal expanse of the warehouse district, bouncing between corrugated metal walls and rusted loading cranes.

Will Hawkson, known in whispered circles as Hawk, was already moving before the sound had faded, boots silent on the slick concrete, his breath tight in his throat. He had been back in the city for almost a year, but the weight never left his shoulders. Not since he was ten. Not since the night he watched the light go out of his family's eyes. That was the moment the city stopped being home and became something else entirely for him. It became his battlefield, a promise, and a reason for going on. Gorek had helped him find his place in the resistance, and Will had made a vow. A vow that he would do anything he could to help protect those like he was, who needed help. He would hurt who he must make sure no kid ever had to watch what he had.

Will was shadow, draped in black, more ripple than man as he slipped between pallets and scaffolding. A shard of ice detonated against the wall beside his head, spraying frost. He ducked, pivoted, and vanished into the gap between dilapidated shipping containers.

"Freeze, caster!" a voice barked, sharp with adrenaline.

Will's muscles coiled. He tugged his mask into place, gliding soundlessly across oil-slicked concrete. The warehouse loomed like a mausoleum, cold and vast. Familiar terrain. He was a ghost here.

Then, the sound.

His stomach clenched. Memory crashed into him...Layla. He moved faster.

Through a cracked panel, Will slipped inside. His eyes locked instantly on the scene: a baby, swaddled and wailing on the concrete. A woman knelt nearby, cuffed behind her back and gasping, crawling as close as she could to comfort her baby. Her eyes blazed with fear and fury. And beside her, a guard frozen mid-sneer, literally. Ice encased his body, face locked in final disbelief.

The air was bitter with magic. Frost still crackled in the air, tangled with the scent of blood, rust, and burnt oil.

She fought hard, Will thought. But not hard enough to keep them all away.

Two more guards circled her.

"She's cuffed with suppressors, Garsa," one muttered. "Stop shaking. She's ain't gonna freeze you too."

"Don't get close to her hands!" the other snapped. "You saw what she did to Mikael. Those suppressor things fail sometimes. Remember what happened to Cook last week."

Will crept closer, rage simmering. You should be scared, he thought.

Scar-Jaw, the bigger one, lifted a comm. "Judge, we've got another caster. She defended herself with Frost magic. Orders?"

Static. Then, the Judge's voice was flat and clinical:

"Death to a guard is immediate execution. Confirmed. Execute. Method at your discretion."

The words settled over Will like ash.

Then:

"What about the kid?" one guard asked, nodding at the crying infant.

"Standard protocol," Scar-Jaw said. "Strip the magic. Mold the mind. If it lives, send it to re-education."

Will's fingers twitched at his side. Rage kindled fast and hot. Layla.

This wasn't just a rescue to Will.

This was personal.

One guard stepped in, yanked the baby from the ground. The small infant wailed louder, tiny fists beating against the armor that held it. The guard immediately pulled out the chip gun fired, as they walked toward the far door.

"Get that thing to the car," barked the other. "I can't think with it screeching."

Will shifted position, tracking every step, every movement. The moment the guard passed through the door with the child, Will's inner clock started ticking. The baby was almost gone, but the woman might still be saved.

He had to move.

Another breath. Another choice.

Two guards. One near the mother. One a few steps beyond.

Will flexed his jaw.

Now.

He launched from the shadows, striking like a predator on the guard farthest from the woman. His fist slammed into the first guard's jaw. The man staggered, stunned, but Will was already

paused... the other guard leveled the gun, at the woman and fired.

A flash of silver.

The woman was lifeless on the concrete, spurring Will to action.

His blade penetrated the guard's chest, the one with Will's arm wrapped tightly around his neck. Will twisted the knife and pulled it out. The guard grabbed his chest, gagged, and dropped to the ground when Will released him.

One down.

The other turned to Will, but too slowly.

Will struck again. Silent. This time his blade penetrated the small gap between the jacket and the helmet, he had learned that if the blade was angled just the right way, it would angle up over the neck guard of the jacket, hitting the jawline, then the brainstem. Clean.

Both guards collapsed, their cruelty severed mid-command.

Will bolted to the warehouse door. But the vehicle was already gone, baby inside.

Too far. Too fast.

He slammed a hand against the metal frame and let out a roar of frustration.

Too late.

He pulled out his radio and brought it to life. Radio static crackled. He growled. "Hawk to base. Package is lost. Baby's enroute to re-ed." In frustration he added, "This cloak-and-dagger shit wears thin. How did they get here before us?"

"We will get the baby."

Will didn't answer at first. Just let the ache settle in his ribs.

"...I didn't sign up to go through all the trouble of finding candidates only to have them get captured or worse before I can get them out," he muttered at last, voice low. *Maybe I should try the next one without them*, he thought. With that thought in his head, he instead decided to make it a promise.

He turned back toward the fallen guard. Same height. Narrower build, but close. The knife hole through the front of the dull white and black of the uniform was far too noticeable. Damn, he couldn't use this one either. His prior attempts to buy a uniform had ended with too small or too large. Will crouched beside him, breath hissing through clenched teeth.

He didn't want the uniform, he needed it. With his height, just a tad over 6'4", he tended to tower over most. After years of hauling bodies, climbing rooftops, carrying blades and burdens alike had built muscle the standard cut didn't account for and gave him fairly muscular build. It was tough to find uniforms with similar enough shape and size, as they were quite fitted.

Will caught his reflection in the darkened window and frowned. The angles of his face were too sharp to disappear into a crowd, the high cut of his cheekbones, the way his jaw set when he was thinking too hard. Even his eyes gave him away, too light, too watchful, too hard to forget. People remembered faces like his. Sometimes that helped. Other times, like today, it was a damn inconvenience. Blending in would've made this easier. So, he could access a guard facility. But neither was happening anytime soon.

Before setting off, he glanced down at himself. His hands were still covered in blood. The sun-gold skin, earned from too many missions under open skies, coated in a slightly sticky red film.

getting the majority off, he removed the black hair covering, to dry them, revealing a long mop of longer, curly dirty-blond hair. He kept the sides short for comfort. He shoved sweat-darkened strands that clung to his brow aside, to no effect.

Let it look untidy, he thought.

As he searched the guard's belongings for anything that he could use or sell, he considered going back to being a transporter, so he could get away from this city, he hated it here. He missed the days when the danger he faced was of his choosing, when he transported people who had been able to get out of the city for the resistance, smuggling those with magic to safety through the treacherous month-long journey to Aloria. Dangerous, yes, but it had been his path and one he was good at.

He'd left that behind to make a bigger difference. To go from ferrying hope to offering hope to those who may not be aware there is a way out. He wanted to be able to use the gift he had of finding people with powers, so that they would know that they have options for freedom, besides... there were other issues with transporting that would make going back to that tough.

As he stepped out into the blinding morning light, the cold air hit him like a slap. His breath fogged as he exhaled, the chill clinging to his skin beneath the layers. His heart drummed a jagged rhythm, a rebellion of its own.

The city, the Talvi District, loomed around him. Buildings stacked one on top of the other, stretching upward and burrowing downward. Their steel guts hummed with power. Talvi was a beast made of metal and industry, where he grew up, and a place where many people's dreams went to die. The vibration of Media's tech was everywhere, a hum beneath his boots, a tremor in his bones. The conduits running along the

like veins through the city's mechanical skin.

He could feel it, Media's heartbeat, thudding through concrete and wire, seeking to smother every spark of real magic.

The air reeked of rust, of oil and ozone, of the burned edges of magic that had been smothered too long.

Will lifted the radio, "I'm heading to No-Man's Land for a bit. I need a recharge. Need to get away from the tech."

"Acknowledged. Keep us posted," the other side responded.

He turned a corner; boots splashing through a shallow puddle of some black chemical and began his journey toward the ruins.

Officially, the area was still called Pelfor District. But it had been years since anyone had used that name. Not since the dragon strike leveled it, followed soon after by a series of electromagnetic bombs that rendered all tech useless in the zone. Will had been there when the fire rained down. Had felt it in his bones. Something in that blast, whether magic, metal, or some cursed blend of both, had changed the very air in that district. A district filled with warehouses, filled with supplies for the city. Now, warehouses were divided among several of the districts, the slums were mostly in Talvi, though some Grieve held some mixed in with the trainyard. The concentric rings of the city separated the districts with elevated train cars, three rings around the city center. Transportation in and out of the city was highly regulated.

Nothing stayed online in No-Man's. Drones shut down. Surveillance fizzled. Even personal comms could not work reliably.

especially when he could get close to the wall there. He typically found security was tight on the perimeter, but once you were there it became easier, as long as you avoided the guards. They liked to use the place as their private shooting range, and the order to shoot on sight was in place.

He picked up the pace, dodging between rusted fences and overgrown alleys. The magic in him pulsed faintly, weak here, under the city's eye, but he could feel it stirring. As if it were embers waiting for breath. Out there, past the ruin, he could breathe again. Maybe even find someone else, another stray to guide home.

But he wasn't naive. Talvi and No-Man's Land weren't forgotten. They were watched constantly. He was convinced the city left them as they were for a reason. A trap. A test.

The final culling grounds for magic folk who had nowhere else to run.

His gaze shifted toward the imposing wall that surrounded the city, a bastion against the encroachment of technological tyranny. The city wall rose like a cold monolith, casting long steel shadows. Beyond the barrier of the tall wall, the forest called to him, promising a refuge where his abilities could stretch and breathe, unencumbered by the oppressive everything of Media. He knew that past those walls lay a whole world still kissed by magic, huge lands where his kind were not hunted like vermin in the shadows. A surge of yearning propelled him forward, each step a silent vow to reach that haven again.

He stopped for lunch to reflect on his life choices in a quiet sanctuary he had found, out of sight, yet access to the sun and close enough to the wall to feel the pull of the trees and magic beyond. His table was a slab of rubble, his chair a twisted piece

depths of the bag at his feet. Under the sharp gaze of the afternoon sun, Will crouched low and unfastened the satchel at his feet. Unremarkable in appearance, the satchel belied the enchantment woven into its fibers. A seemingly endless void contained within supple leather.

His fingers brushed over objects that should not have fit: a coil of rope, gleaming vials of potions, and a slender grimoire bound in dragonhide. The bag drank them down like water into sand, bottomless, silent, an echo of his own craving to be unbound. He pulled out a wrapped parcel of dried meat and bread, letting the soft, pulsing magic that spilled from the trees beyond washing over him like sunlight after rain.

With everything secured, he hoisted the bag over his shoulder, the weight negligible yet grounding. By the time his lunch was finished, and he felt more in control of his magic, the afternoon light glinted off the twisted, melted metal. He began his long walk back toward the small flat he was provided by the resistance. It was in Media Proper, so the middle-class area was a suburb where the middle class lived in neatly arranged homes, working steady jobs. His place was only a bathroom and a place to lay his head, he rarely spent time there, but at least it wasn't in Talvi.

Outside, the air tasted of change and the faintest trace of rebellion. A sound attracted his attention, the echo resonated like a call to arms.

Ahead, an old movie marquee sagged over a crumbling building. The letters were faded, but he could still make them out: "Liberators of Media." That was the last movie he had watched with his parents and sister before they died. A movie about the liberation of the people against their slave owners, against those born with magic, painting them as tyrants rather than victims of history. Will's thoughts imagined what life would have been like

the very heartbeat of the world. He remembered hearing tales of grandeur, when mages shaped reality with mere gestures and conjured marvels from the ether. Those were the days when his ancestors roamed freely. Now, the ones who once shaped the skies were caged like beasts beneath it. The pendulum had swung too far. Justice had twisted into control. Now, those with the gift concealed their abilities, hunted down as though they were vermin by decree.

His tactical mind understood the revolution's roots, he wasn't blind to the sins of the old world. But this? This was something else. The old world had its own sins, when the non-magical were enslaved and the ruling class wielded power unchecked. He could not deny that the revolution had been justified. But he doubted the original rebels had ever imagined their fight for freedom would birth an oppression just as ruthless.

His nails dug crescents into his palms as he contemplated the plight of his magical kin, forced to hide, to deny their very essence or worse have it ripped away, in a fear-driven world. The ache in his hands was nothing compared to the burn in his chest, a grief so deep it had long since hardened into resolve.

A sudden chirp broke through his reverie, slicing the silence like a well-aimed dagger. The resistance radio in his hand came to life, a subtle vibration accompanying the sound. The battery was almost dead, with the time in No-Man's land. Will's fingers curled around the device; his grip firm yet reverent as if it were a lifeline threading through the darkness of oppression. He brought it close, the static crackling softly against his ear before a gruff voice emerged.

"Report, Hawk. What's your status?"

"The day is still young. I'll keep looking. I haven't found anything yet," he replied, his voice a low thrum that mirrored the quiet promise in his words, a vow that his mission was far from over, that every dawn brought new chances to mend or mar the world.

"Just so you know. Several days ago, we intercepted reports of someone with magic seen in the No-Man's Land/Media Proper area, but no details. Reports say they are ramping up efforts to find them, so we should too. It would be great if we could find them first. I figured you'd want to know," the operator continued. "We got the baby. She is safe. Stay sharp." Will then exhaled slowly, allowing the relief to settle in his chest for only a moment.

"Thanks. I'll check it out," Will assured, the radio's chirp dying as he slipped the device into a pocket hidden within the folds of the uniform. He moved with purpose now, his tall frame casting long shadows on the ground, a specter of what once was, perhaps a herald of what might yet be.

With the city of Media sprawling behind him and the unknown stretching ahead, Will Hawkson pressed on, his resolve as unyielding as the wall itself.

Despite the burgeoning day, shadows clung to him like persistent specters. With each step, he felt the echo of the woman's desperation, the baby's cries haunting the recesses of his mind. The warehouse encounter had been a stark reminder of the stakes at play, a grim warning of what awaited those who dared to defy the rigid order of Media government.

Will pressed himself against the sun-warmed bricks of an alleyway, the radio transmitter in his hand buzzing quietly as he waited for the signal. The relentless afternoon sun cast harsh shadows in the alley where he crouched, clutching his stolen radio as he scanned the crowd, searching for traces of magic. It was his calling.

He reached out with his powers to check the surroundings. He could feel something, then the thought that he didn't feel like risking anymore lives by allowing the resistance to get in his way.

"Negative," Will said, "No signs of activity. I'll meet you later at the rendezvous."

"Keep your eyes open, Hawk. We need your help."

A ripple of energy brushed against him, electric and wrong in all the ways that made the hair on his arms stand up. Not wind. Not noise. Something older. Quieter. Deeper. It was someone with intense power not far from here.

But Will was already gone, mentally and physically exhausted. The radio hung loose at his side; his attention now fixed on the buildings around him. Media's brutalist skyline loomed overhead, concrete stacked on concrete, humming with hidden conduits and surveillance. But beneath the machine hum and footfalls, there was... something else.

A flicker. A vibration. Magic.

Not loud, not overt, but present. It slid along the edge of his perception like a blade against cloth. Faint but unmistakable.

And someone, somewhere, was using an immense amount of power.

It was pure and potent, a raw surge of power clawing at the city's meticulously constructed facade of normalcy. Whoever wielded such magic was either blissfully ignorant or dangerously defiant of the laws that kept Media in its vice-like grip.

source of the magical disturbance, he felt unlikely anyone had seen him. It beckoned him, a siren's song woven from the very essence of rebellion, and he could not resist its pull more than stop the beating of his own heart.

His boots pressed against the cracked pavement as he navigated the maze of shadow-draped alleyways. The city's heartbeat was muffled here, reduced to the distant hum of technology and the occasional clink of patrolling enforcers in their mechanical armor. He moved with purpose, his instincts sharpened by years of evasion and conflict, guiding him through the oppressive gloom.

The pulsating magic drew him like a lodestone, leading him deeper into the labyrinth of Media's forgotten corners. His ability to sense others' powers had a decent range of about half a mile. He had been on the outskirts of his power and had traveled some distance, but he was zeroing in. His breaths came out in visible puffs against the chill that clung to the air, mingling with the metallic taste that pervaded the city. His hazel eyes, usually filled with a guarded warmth, now narrowed in concentration.

As he rounded a corner, the source of the disturbance took shape before him. He noticed a flicker of movement, a distortion in the light. There, amidst the tangled vines of rebar and concrete, stood a young girl, her silhouette quivering with the strain of phasing from sight. The magic was raw, unbridled; it spilled from her like sunlight piercing through storm clouds. Hidden from prying eyes, as she struggled to control the dual forces of invisibility and levitation, it painted her in shades of sorrow and splendor. If not for his power to track her powers, he might have missed her completely. Rock fragments hovered around her, orbiting like miniature satellites caught in the gravity of her will.

his chest, a pain that bloomed fresh and vivid. It was as if he were staring into the past, glimpsing once more the untamed brilliance of his sister: her laughter, her defiance, and ultimately, her demise at the hands of those who feared her. Even the young girl's blonde hair was the same shade as his sister's had been.

Her magic was wild and untrained, leaking out in ways that would get her noticed, fast. Invisibility flickered like bad wiring, and objects floated around her with a clumsy kind of grace. Will watched with a sinking feeling. She didn't even know she was painting a target on her back. Not yet. But chances are good Media would find it clear as day.

A jolt of protectiveness hit Will hard, fast and familiar. He'd felt it the day his family died, and it hadn't let go since. He knew exactly what happened to people caught with magic. Adults were usually executed, well chipped, but that usually ended in death, more often than not. It was worse for the kids. Kids had a better chance of survival, as the magic was still forming and gathering. The kids and adults who survived chipping were sent to re-education, which was a form of brainwashing, where they were mentally stripped down until there was nothing left but an echo. If the magic ran deep, the process shattered them. If it didn't, they just became something else.

"Careful," he whispered to no one, the word barely a breath in the chilled air. But the sentiment lingered, reverberating through the space between them, imbued with a silent promise, a pledge etched into the marrow of his bones. He would not stand idle while another life was extinguished for the crime of existing beyond the boundaries of fear and ignorance.

Will watched, rooted in place, as the blonde figure shimmered, her presence ebbing and flowing with the invisible tides of her power. It was a dance of light and shadow, a testament to both the strength and fragility of the magic that thrummed in her

seen adults who had practiced for years struggling to phase fully, much less wield a second.

He was in awe. His own second skill, sensing heat, was limited to thirty or forty feet in distance, and he could make a feather float if he focused hard enough.

And though he was but a stranger cloaked in the stolen garb of her oppressors, Will felt the inexorable pull of destiny weaving its intricate web around them both; two souls cast adrift in a city that sought nothing less than their annihilation.

The specter of the past clung to Will like a second shadow in the dim alleyway, its tendrils constricting around his heart as he beheld her raw power. It was an echo of a tragedy long buried, a sister's laughter silenced too soon by the merciless decree of cold metal and colder hearts. The memory surged within him, a tempest of rage and regret that now found a new purpose: protecting this girl who knew nothing of the danger she faced with every flicker of her magic.

The girl was oblivious to the storm raging within the man watching her. The stones danced at her command, suspended in a testament to her untamed potential. He was in awe of her concentration, it was absolute, a fortress of solitude shielding her from the world's prying eyes, so far beyond his abilities at that age. It was dangerous, and he had to help keep her safe.

llie Neldoreth crouched behind the crumbling wall of the old factory, breath hiccupping in her chest, legs aching from the long run that had brought her here. The city loomed behind her, all sharp steel and cold concrete, glowing faintly in the distance like it was watching. Always watching.

She'd run nearly two miles—*two miles*—and her legs still tingled from it, muscles twitching in protest. Her heart thudded hard and fast, not just from the effort but from the electric rush that came with being here.

The Talvi edge was broken and quiet, full of collapsed metal and scorched brick. Dragon-fire had torn through this place years ago, and now it felt... forgotten. Or ignored. Either way, it was hers. The air smelled like rust and old heat, the kind that never quite left the stone. Somewhere close, a drone buzzed, a low, mean hum that sounded like hunger.

Ellie ducked lower, and her heart skipped. She held her breath until it faded into the distance.

It wasn't her first time coming here, not since Nanna had told her about it. Nanna always said this place was special, that it helped magic stretch and breathe, away from all the city's heavy noise and watching eyes. And out here, Ellie could *feel* that truth humming in her skin.

She crept farther into the shadowed space and spotted her practice rocks, still there, just like she had left them. A smile tugged at her lips. She slipped her fingers out, trembling a little, and whispered to the magic in her chest. *Come on, play with me.* Nanna said the powers liked that. They get bored if you don't.

them around a bigger one, trying to make it spin like a tiny planet. Sweat beaded at her temple. Her arms shook. Her heart pounded again, but this time with excitement. When the big rock finally shuddered upward, her grin bloomed wide and wild.

Yes!

Next came the trickier part.

Ellie closed her eyes. *Be mist,* she told herself. *Roll like fog. In and out. Light and quiet.* The magic in her body perked up, eager. It surged through her veins like music, spinning in her head, lifting her off the ground just a little. She glanced at the shiny metal panel she used as a mirror. There she was, flickering in and out like a strobe. Her heart leapt.

She was doing it; **both** magics at once.

But it hurt. Her head buzzed. Her arms felt like they were floating too far from her body. The air around her shimmered like heat on pavement. She clenched her jaw, trying to hold it, to be strong like Nanna said.

Then, her vision blurred.

The big rock wobbled. Her body snapped fully visible. The magic sizzled and fizzled out.

Ellie gasped, hunched over, and dropped to her knees, the sudden stillness making her ears ring. Her lungs burned. Her chest heaved like she'd been underwater too long. Her fingers dug into the dirt to keep her from tipping over.

Too much. It was too much.

But still... she smiled. *I did it.*

seen. She wanted to show someone. Someone other than just Nanna.

The rock clunked back down beside her, and she let out a slow, shaky sigh. She stayed low, still phasing in and out a little, the magic playing tag under her skin.

Then…

The hairs on the back of her neck stood straight up.

She froze. That prickly feeling meant something. Something bad.

Slowly, carefully, she looked up.

A figure. Tall. Dressed in black. Staring straight at her.

Her magic shattered like a dropped plate.

Her heart kicked so hard she almost choked. Cold panic flooded her belly.

He'd seen her.

He saw me.

Ellie's body moved before she could think. She shot to her feet, legs barely holding her up, and ran.

Ellie's gaze locked on the figure in black. He was staring right at her.

A jolt of terror slammed through her chest like lightning. Her breath vanished. The magic inside her collapsed with a snap, her phasing blinking out completely.

Nanna warned you. Never get caught.

She thought she was safe. She'd been so sure.

wild, animal, and before she could scream, she was already moving.

Her boots skidded on the gravel, her body twisting into motion. She launched herself down the broken path, heart pounding in her ears like a war drum. The old streets of Talvi stretched ahead, a shadowy maze of collapsed scaffolding and twisted rebar. The echo of her footfalls slapped back at her like they were trying to catch up.

Don't think. Run.

She knew the path. Nanna had drilled it into her. Left at the broken pipe. Through the split wall. Past the green-tagged dumpster. *Go. Go. Go.*

But her legs were so tired.

The edges of her vision blurred. Her lungs burned with every ragged breath. The sweat on her skin turned cold in the wind as her magic flickered, weak and sputtering like a candle in a storm. She phased for half a second, just long enough to dart through a crack in the wall, but by the time she flickered back into sight, he was still there. Gaining.

He's not supposed to see me. How is he seeing me?

Her heartbeat thudded harder, wild and erratic. A stitch stabbed in her side, sharp and mean, but she forced herself to push through it.

She veered into an alley, nearly tripping over a rusted pipe. Her shoulder slammed into the brick wall. Pain exploded down her arm, but she didn't stop. Couldn't.

She was invisible again, but just for a blink.

She risked a glance behind her.

Still turning when she turned.

Still gaining.

He can't be. That's not possible.

Her thoughts tangled with fear. Her breath came in shallow gasps. Her magic was failing. Her body wanted to quit.

But her will didn't.

She gritted her teeth and pushed harder, forcing her legs to move even as they screamed to stop. The city blurred around her: twisted buildings, broken signs, flickering lights. Her vision tunneled down to just the next turn, the next breath, the next heartbeat.

Don't stop. Don't let him catch you. Don't die.

The city blurred.

Ellie didn't know how many corners she'd taken or how many narrow alleys she'd squeezed through. Her lungs burned now; each breath was raw, torn from her throat like pieces of her soul. The pounding of her boots on pavement had blurred into a constant rhythm—*thud-thud-thud*—but even that was starting to slow.

She wasn't sure if it was the magic flickering in her blood or the straight fear pumping through her veins that kept her upright. Her legs were jelly. Her vision swam. A strange buzz filled her ears. It felt like half wind and half panic.

She darted into a crooked alley between two half-standing buildings, the bricks blackened from some long-ago fire. Behind a broken dumpster, she phased again. It was brief and dropped low, clutching her knees to her chest.

Her breath came in gasps.

Too loud.

Too fast.

Too close to breaking.

She strained to listen.

Silence.

Her heart pounded in her ears; each beat was a tiny explosion. But no footsteps. No heavy breathing. No more turns echoed behind her.

Is he gone?

She didn't trust it. Not yet.

Still crouched, she crept along the back of the alley, keeping low, staying invisible when she could manage it, even for just a few seconds at a time. Every flicker took something from her. Her magic wasn't infinite; it came in waves, and this one was crashing fast.

When she finally reached the edge of the alley, she peeked around the corner. A familiar cracked sidewalk. A burned-out streetlamp she'd passed a hundred times.

Home.

Or close enough to feel like it.

Her legs nearly gave out from the relief.

She slipped out of the alley and crossed the street, walking instead of running now, keeping her hood up and her head down. She was still invisible, sort of, but it wavered like a bad reception.

heartbeat slowed. Her breaths stopped scraping the inside of her throat like glass.

She could see the edge of her neighborhood. The rooftops she knew. The twisted tree in the yard of the house next to hers. The cracked cement slab where she always tied her shoes before school.

Close. So close.

She ducked behind a bush, just for a second, letting herself collapse onto her knees. Her fingers dug into the dirt.

A tear slipped down her cheek. She didn't even know why- relief, maybe, or leftover fear that didn't know where to go.

She pressed a hand to her chest. Her heartbeat was still fast but not wild anymore. She could feel her magic settling, curling inside her like a sleepy cat.

You made it.

But even as she knelt there in the shadows of familiar streets, something inside her still whispered:

You were seen.

ill's breath caught as the girl disappeared, her form vanishing like static blinking off a screen. His legs moved before thought kicked in, instinct burning under his skin. This wasn't just about her anymore. It hadn't been since the first flicker of her power.

She was fast, as if she were panicking. She was slipping through the edges of No-Man's like she knew the route well. Will kept pace, boots hitting pavement in practiced rhythm. He was lithe and agile in his worn linen shirt, black leather and soft-soled boots that made him quiet and stealthy. The kind of shadow no one notices until it's too late.

He caught a pulse of her heat, small, sharp, vanishing fast, and homed in. Her trail flickered through the dry air, still charged from the magic she'd pushed too hard. That kind of raw energy was hard to miss. It had weight to it.

"Wait!" he called out, voice low but cutting through the space between them with a mixture of despair and determination. She didn't stop. She was phasing again, on instinct, not strategy. He muttered, more to himself than her now, "I can see your heat. Save your energy. You'll burn out and get seen."

She didn't hear him.

He pushed forward, weaving through the shifting maze of alleys and debris. The closer they got to the edge of the district, the more people there were. Not enough for full crowds, but enough to complicate the chase. He had to change his stride, still quick, still quiet, but careful now.

Will swore under his breath, catching brief flashes of blond hair ahead, but no magic. She was smart. Dangerous, but smart.

Not just because she was the target but because she reminded him of Layla. The way she ran. The desperation in her movements. Like someone who'd already lost too much and knew what came next if she got caught.

This was no longer just a mission. Not for Will.

This was the line between who he'd been... and what he refused to become again.

This wasn't just another mission. Not anymore.

The crowd pressed tighter now, shoulders brushing against Will as he pushed forward. People instinctively gave him space; maybe it was the way he moved or the intensity on his face, but even that wasn't enough. She was slipping away.

He spotted her with just enough time to see her shoulder brushing too close to a vendor's stall. The jagged edge of metal snagged her shirt. The fabric tore. She flinched. For half a second, she turned.

Their eyes met.

Blue, wide, afraid.

The moment cut through him sharper than any blade.

Will shoved forward, trying to close the distance before she vanished again. The crowd swelled, a living barrier that slowed his momentum. Street noise rose around him: horns, shouting, the dull thrum of machinery, and somewhere in it all, she disappeared.

One second, she was there. The next, gone.

Too fast. Too small. And clearly, she knew the area.

He stopped, catching his breath, eyes scanning the street signs. He needed to reorient. The chase had blurred the edges of his

deep breath. The sounds of the city faded into the background, a dull mix of traffic, conversation, and distant footsteps.

In his hand, he realized he still held the torn scrap from her shirt.

Not nothing.

He turned in place, cataloging the layout. The girl knew where she was going. That wasn't the panicked run of someone desperate. It was practiced. Controlled. She knew when to drop her power and when to blend into a crowd. That kind of awareness didn't come from chance.

She must be local. A student, probably. Will's jaw tightened. That narrowed things down.

He scanned the rooftops and corners, noting the line of surveillance cameras tracking lazy arcs across the street. Media's eyes. Always watching. Always recording. He moved quickly, ducking his head and slipping into a cluster of pedestrians, letting their bodies mask his.

This wasn't over. Not by a long shot.

He didn't know who she was yet, but she was sharp, trained, and carrying power that could turn the tide of a battle if she survived long enough to choose a side.

He tucked the fabric scrap into his coat pocket and kept walking, slipping into the city's rhythm. He'd find her again. And next time, he'll be ready.

alin had just returned from a grueling day at the infirmary, her body weary, her mind thrumming with the day's caseload. She expected to find Ellie, as usual, chattering away at the kitchen table, but the house greeted her with silence. She made a note to call Daniel's house if she didn't get home within thirty minutes or so. After slipping into more comfortable clothes and fixing a quick meal, she settled into the plush embrace of an armchair, the quiet a stark contrast to the relentless pace of life just outside their door in Media.

As she was about to dial Daniel's house, the door creaked open. A head crowned with unruly blonde waves, damp with sweat and shimmering with subtle hints of magic, peeked in. At the sight of Ellie, relief washed over Malin, melting her tired features into a gentle smile. She stood, the rays of the setting sun catching the elegant twist of her blonde hair. With a grace that masked the weight on her shoulders, she met her daughter halfway across the room. Her movements mirrored the gentle sway of the sea, and she planted a soft kiss on Ellie's cheek, her icy blue eyes thawing into pools of warmth.

"Welcome home, Ellie," Malin said softly, her voice barely above a whisper. "I was worried when I didn't see you. You usually don't stay out so late. Everything ok?"

Ellie shifted her weight, her gaze flickering away for a split second before meeting her mother's. "Hi, Mom. Sorry, I was at Daniel's. I didn't want you to worry, so I ran back," she said. "

It was then that Malin's gaze sharpened, catching the jagged tear on Ellie's shirt. Gently, she lifted the torn edge, her fingers deft and careful, scanning the skin underneath for any sign of injury.

remained on Ellie's unusual expression.

Malin's voice was gentle but firm, "What happened here, sweetie?"

Ellie hesitated. Her eyes flickered down, then over to the side, before offering a too-casual shrug. "It's nothing," she said. "Just some bullies at school being... well, bullies."

Malin's jaw tightened. Not again.

She thought back to the half-dozen messages she'd already sent Headmaster Grell, the increasingly frustrated tone in each one. And every time, the same deflection, the same hollow assurances. Of course, Grell wouldn't do anything, his own son was one of the ringleaders. There was never a consequence, never accountability. Just empty words and bruised feelings.

She reached over and tucked a curl behind Ellie's ear, offering a soft smile, but her mind was already spinning. Maybe it was time to stop playing nice. If Grell wouldn't protect her daughter, someone else would.

I will.

She made a mental note to reach out again, one last attempt before escalating it higher. The Education Board had teeth, especially with the right strings pulled. And Malin's mother had more than a few strings wrapped around her fingers, being a Chancellor on the Council of Elders. If anyone could get results, it was Elowen Neldoreth. Even if she wasn't on good terms with her mother, surely her mom would want to do something to help.

Something had to be done. Ellie deserved better.

bring it up to the school board if the principal isn't doing anything. You know I'll stand up for you if you are doing the right thing. Are you okay?"

"Yeah, it's fine. But not Armond this time. Two of his friends were picking on another girl in my class." Ellie's tone was matter-of-fact and sounded much older than a fifth grader.

Malin's maternal instincts flared as she checked Ellie for any injuries, relieved to find none. The sharp sting of worry twisted in her gut as she voiced her thoughts aloud. "It bothers me how often these things keep happening." Despite her own fears and concerns, Malin's calm demeanor and unwavering trust in Ellie's abilities remained unshaken. The lack of alarm in her voice was a testament to the strong bond between mother and daughter.

"I did tell you that you were allowed to defend yourself, but you don't need to be a superhero. I don't want you to get hurt," she assured. "You know your limits, just don't press them without understanding the consequences."

Ellie shook her head. "It's fine, really," she insisted, trying to ease her mother's concerns.

Malin sighed, brushing Ellie's shoulder in silent reassurance. "Okay. Well, let's get ready for dinner then. I'll warm it up," she said before heading to the kitchen.

She watched as Ellie retreated upstairs, listening to her daughter's soft footsteps as she went. A sigh escaped her. She knew the delicate dance of motherhood well, the fine line between holding close and letting go. Her own mother had been distant, and though Malin felt she turned out fine, she wanted to offer Ellie something more. Space, yes, but also a friendship a child really needs when growing up. A friendship she had missed from her mother.

Malin's modest living room. Awelyn's laughter rang out, familiar and comforting, echoing from the sleek apartment she'd made for herself high above the neon-spattered skyline of Media City. Her dark curls were pinned back in their usual effortless style, and she wore a sharp plum blazer that hinted she'd come straight from court. Classic Awelyn. She always had one foot in glamor, the other in battle.

"Malin, you simply must come out with us for my birthday! It's not every day your best friend turns another year wiser," she teased, eyes gleaming with mischief over the video call.

Malin smiled. Just seeing her face pulled up a hundred memories: shared textbooks and smuggled wine, all-night study sessions turned into philosophical debates. They'd been roommates at the university. They were polar opposites who had somehow become inseparable. Awelyn had pursued law while Malin pivoted from politics to medicine, but the friendship endured, no matter how chaotic life had become.

Lira's voice chimed in off-screen, before she ducked into view with a grin that nearly split her freckled face. Her blue hair was cut short and swept stylishly to one side, framing eyes that sparkled with unspoken plans. Lira had been the third in their tight-knit trio back then. She was brilliant, chaotic, and fiercely loyal. She now worked in applied tech and whispered corners of the innovation sector, always dancing close to the edge of what was legal.

"Tell her I already reserved the table, so if she bails, I'm sending a very expensive guilt basket to her house," Lira said, pointing a dramatic finger at the camera.

Malin laughed softly; heart warmed by the sound of both of their voices. They knew how to brighten a day.

our wild side, Malin. Plus, it's a night of dancing and the best street food Media has to offer. You'll have plenty of time to prepare. We are going on Friday. How can you resist?"

Malin's lips twitched into a reluctant smile, touched by their insistence. Social outings weren't her thing, but celebrating her best friend's birthday was a must. "For you, Awelyn, I'd brave even the fiercest dance floor," she replied with mock solemnity.

Their laughter bridged the miles, echoing years of shared secrets and spontaneous adventures. Lira's expression softened, teasing but gentle. "Who knows? Maybe we'll even find a charming dance partner for our dear Malin."

Shaking her head, Malin let amusement flicker in her eyes. "I'm quite content with Ellie and our quiet life, but thanks for the effort, Lira. I don't need any more complications in my life."

As they finalized plans for the birthday weekend, Malin felt a stir of anticipation mixed with her usual reservations. Yet, Awelyn's joy was infectious, and for her, Malin found herself looking forward to a night out in the vibrant heart of Media.

Their triumphant grins flickered through the grainy signal, a reminder that some bonds held steady no matter the distance. "You'll have a great time, Malin. We'll make sure of it!" Lira's voice carried a lilting of promise, her words weaving through the virtual space as if the scent of street food was almost tangible through the screen.

"You need to start living your life, Malin. It's been twelve years," Lira said gently. It was a truth that landed like a soft knock against the door Malin rarely opened.

The memory of her fiancé, lost before he could even learn of his impending fatherhood, surfaced briefly. "I know. It's hard to

murmured, her voice a whisper of resolve beneath the sorrow.

Lira immediately softened. With a tone of regret, she said, "I'm sorry I brought it up, but it has been too long, and you know Caelum would want you to be happy."

A small, involuntary smile touched Malin's lips. These friends, her chosen family, always knew how to breach the carefully guarded walls of her heart. "All right," she murmured, a quiet surrender to the affection tethering her to them.

Their cheers filled the room, bursting forth with warmth and excitement. "Remember, we'll be by your side," Awelyn assured. "You won't stand alone in the crowd."

"Thank you," Malin replied, her gratitude threading through the conversation like a silk.

With a final click, she ended the call. The laughter faded, leaving a haunting echo in its wake. She sat still, the laptop's pale glow outlining her features in stark contrast to the warmth that had just filled the room. The sudden quiet was profound, wrapping around her like a familiar shawl.

Malin closed her eyes for a moment, allowing the last traces of sunset to surrender to the deepening dusk. Behind her lids, the darkness felt softer than the city's ever-present glare, a brief and welcome reprieve.

Working at the local clinic instead of the hospital had always been her preference. It lets her connect with patients on a personal level, face to face, name to name. But it also meant confronting the reality most of Media's citizens, especially the upper class, like her own parents, chose to ignore.

older than six, eyes swollen shut from a riot control gas the enforcers swore they no longer used; a young woman dragged in unconscious, her wrists raw and bleeding from the suppression cuffs that dug deeper with every magical pulse. Then there were the routine injuries: broken ribs from "compliance encouragement," dislocated shoulders from being wrenched too hard during identity checks.

They never said the word "torture." Media didn't tolerate that kind of language. But Malin had stopped pretending long ago.

She'd cleaned wounds while pretending not to hear the whispered pleas from patients begging her not to report them. She'd memorized the enforcer patrol schedule just to find safe windows to discharge patients before they could be taken again. Healing had always been her purpose, but lately, it felt like patching holes in a sinking ship while the regime kept punching more through the hull.

Here, in the quiet of her mind, she sought the sanctuary of her true self, a place no authoritarian regime could touch.

When she opened her eyes again, the room felt changed, subtly, inexplicably. Logic was her compass, the tool she relied on to navigate every crisis, every decision. But tonight, her gut whispered something softer.

Logic told her the birthday celebration would be a mistake. She didn't like noise or large groups, and she had known Awelyn and Lira long enough to know that this would likely be an episode of 'Speed Dating', where she would have an assortment of men thrown at her, none of whom she was interested in. But something deeper, less rational, clung to the idea. Maybe she would at least have fun, she hadn't allowed herself to do that in a long time.

sounded like a period at the end of a long, unfinished sentence. The echoes of the past mingled with the promises of the future, settling into an uneasy truce within her. Moving from the comfort of her routine into the unknown felt like the beginning of something, a shift in her carefully constructed life.

Her gaze drifted to the empty chair across the room, and for a fleeting second, the ghost of another time brushed against her consciousness. But she pushed it away, focusing instead on the present, where the air still held the lingering warmth of laughter and the subtle thrill of anticipation.

The silence in the room was a blank canvas, waiting for the next brushstroke of her life to color its pallid expanse. She reached for her phone, the sleek surface cool against her skin, a small jolt of reality in her otherwise weightless thoughts. The chill was a stark contrast to the quiet warmth building in her chest at the thought of calling Andrew.

She let herself linger in the memory of the day she'd moved in, cradling a fussy, red-faced baby Ellie on one hip and trying to juggle boxes with the other. Andrew had appeared in the doorway within minutes, sleeves rolled up, keys still in hand, as if he'd dropped everything just to be there.

And maybe he had.

That was nine years ago. In that time, they'd built something real: a friendship layered with late-night conversations, quiet dinners, shared glances across their balconies, and the kind of loyalty that didn't ask for attention. He was the one who fixed her heater in the dead of winter, who picked up medicine for Ellie when Malin was stuck on shift, who brought dinner when he knew she hadn't eaten.

He never asked for anything in return. But lately, something shifted.

silences that almost said more than their words. A glance held just a breath too long. A smile that felt like it meant more.

Malin stared at the phone in her hand, her thumb hovering over his name. The warmth in her chest stirred again; comfort and confusion braided together.

"Hey, Andrew," she said, her voice carrying the kind of appreciation only true camaraderie could foster. "Would you be able to watch Ellie next Friday night?"

His response came without hesitation, a steady current of reassurance flowing through the line. "Of course, Malin. You know I'm always here for you both." The way he said her name was almost reverent.

She could almost see his smile through the phone, the way it would reach his warm brown eyes and crinkle the corners just so. The familiarity of their exchange wrapped around her like an invisible blanket, softening the edges of her solitude.

"Thanks, Andrew. It means more than you know. Awelyn and Lira are dragging me out for Awelyn's birthday. It's a birthday request, so I have to go," Malin admitted, the honesty in her voice as tangible as the low hum beyond her window.

"Of course, it's no trouble. As I said, anything for you and Ellie," he said, his voice steady and sure, like the slow comforting cadence of a heartbeat. "We can talk more about it on our Monday night game night. I think we left off with you in the lead. I feel confident I can take the lead back. I'll just pick up the usual. Right?"

"Should I cook or takeout? I can always count on you," Malin said, a smile threading through her words.

"I'll bring takeout. Your favorite from that fancy place in City Center with those dumplings you love," he offered.

Their laughter mingled, light and familiar, yet beneath the ease of their banter, something unspoken lingered. It was a routine they had fallen into, a weekly ritual that had become the cornerstone of their friendship. Buried beneath the comfort of it all, there was something Malin wasn't ready to name. Not yet. This was another time when her gut told her to take her time.

"Looking forward to it," she managed, her tone betraying nothing of the quiet turmoil that sometimes whispered through her thoughts. For now, the safety of their established camaraderie was a harbor in which she willingly anchored herself, even as the tides of change shifted around her.

Monday evening brought a chill that clung to the windows, the kind that made the whole house feel quieter than usual. Malin had just finished some cleaning when the doorbell chimed, followed immediately by the soft click of the front door opening. No knock. No pause.

Only someone familiar would enter like that.

It was their weekly game night, so she knew it was Andrew.

His arrival always shifted the air in the house, subtle, but unmistakable. Like the weight of a storm pressing just beneath the surface, changing everything without a word.

Malin turned with her usual grace, gliding into the living room. Her smile reached her eyes, lighting them into warm, blue pools.

"Andrew," she said, her voice laced with comfort and maybe something else.

He looked up, his breath caught just slightly. "Hey, Malin."

back, but the way he looked at her made her feel like she had. His warm brown eyes lingered with that familiar softness, and she had to look away before the heat reaching her cheeks gave her away.

"Come in," she said. "Ellie's in her room playing games with Daniel; just us again. I got everything set up for the game."

She gestured toward the living room where their weekly ritual awaited. He stepped inside, bringing with him the quiet comfort that always seemed to settle the edges of her solitude.

"So… Awelyn's birthday?" Andrew asked, stepping over a stray slipper.

"Yep. She's got a whole night planned, but I doubt it'll run too late." Malin rolled her eyes. "You know how much I love those things."

"I wish I could come with you," he said, a little too earnestly.

"If only." Malin's smile faltered. "Awelyn has… girl plans."

She didn't say the rest. Didn't say that Awelyn didn't like Andrew and didn't want him to be their buzzkill for the evening.

With a glance that said more than dared to, they sank into the rhythm of the night.

Hours passed, the game stretching into soft laughter and shared memories. The last rays of sun painted the room in gold as the scent of dinner lingered in the air.

"Your move," Malin murmured, studying the board.

Andrew reached for a piece, his fingers brushing hers, just barely, just enough. His touch was light, but the pause that followed carried weight.

them. They didn't speak of it, didn't have to.

Laughter came easier after that, but Andrew's had a wistful edge. Like he knew something was slipping through his fingers.

As Malin recounted an old win, she caught Andrew watching her, not just with affection, but with something deeper. Something quieter.

The game carried on, pieces clicking gently against the board, but they both knew it wasn't really about the game anymore.

When the final piece fell into place, Malin leaned back against the cushions. The golden light of the room wrapped around them like a memory, not urgent, not loud. Just real.

She breathed in deeply, savoring the familiar mix of scents: the warm spice of their takeout, Andrew's woodsy aftershave, and the faint comfort of old leather and paper from the game board. A soft sigh escaped her lips. This was the kind of evening that didn't ask anything in return. The kind that felt like home.

Candlelight danced along the walls, casting flickering shadows. In a world driven by noise and tech, moments like these anchored her. Quiet. Ordinary. Precious.

"Another win for you," Andrew said, his voice a blend of mock defeat and something warmer.

"Next time, I'll let you win," she teased, her tone light, though her mind spun with more than the game.

Their eyes met briefly, but the pause lingered. A glance charged with unsaid things, with years of shared spaces and moments where nothing happened, yet everything lived between them.

Andrew began gathering the pieces, his movements careful, as though the game deserved reverence. Malin watched him, a soft ache stirring behind her ribs.

"Always a pleasure," he replied, smiling, but it didn't quite reach his eyes. He paused before leaving, drawing her into their usual goodbye hug. This time, he held on just a little longer.

"Malin…" His voice was quiet, almost unsure. "Would you ever consider going on a date with me? Thursday night, maybe?"

She froze, caught off guard. "I… um…"

"We get along so well," he said quickly, trying to fill the silence. "Ellie adores me. It just makes sense."

She pulled back gently, her arms slipping free. "I don't think I'm ready, Andrew. With Caelum and everything… he was my everything. I can't imagine finding that again."

Andrew's face faltered. "I get that. I do. I'd wait forever if I had to. But… I think what we have is just a different kind of love. I love you, Malin. And I know I can make you both happy."

She turned, moving to put the game away, needing the distance. "Let me think about it. It's just… a lot."

"Take all the time you need. Look into your heart. You know we're good together," he said, his voice steeped in quiet sincerity. He held her gaze for a moment longer, as if willing her to see the truth he felt.

Alone now, Malin wrapped her arms around herself, the lingering warmth of his presence still filling the room. The silence felt heavier, pressing in like an unseen weight. She moved slowly, her footsteps a soft, rhythmic echo against the quiet. With each step, the boundaries between past and present blurred, tangled in the uncertainty of their conversation. The ghost of what once was tugged at her heart, while the shadow of what could be lingered just beyond her reach.

ruining it by taking their relationship to a place her heart wasn't
pushing her toward?

ill Hawkson slipped into the alley like a knife between ribs: quick, quiet, and dangerous.

The moon hung low, a pale crescent over the rooftops, casting just enough light to make movement dangerous. He leaned against the cold frame of a delivery hatch, eyes scanning the alley. The city never truly slept. It just changed its shape after dark.

Footsteps. Soft. Familiar.

"Hawk, did you find anything on patrol?" Thane's voice crackled through the comm, his voice was low, clipped, and professional.

Will didn't respond right away. He kept his eyes on the alley's shadows, posture still taut. Thane was his handler, the Resistance's point man for field coordination. Will rarely checked in unless something was expected. Or something had gone wrong.

"I found a family of brownies, but... they were safely relocated," Will murmured, keeping his tone even. "Didn't see anyone else. But that doesn't mean we weren't seen."

"Damned brownies. Little mouselike pixies," Thane hissed through the device. "We risk exposure every time they pull these stunts. One of these days..."

Brownies were unpredictable, skittish, nocturnal, and fiercely territorial. No taller than an ankle, with quicksilver movements and fur-tufted ears, they had a habit of showing up in places they didn't belong. Most humans dismissed them as rodents, but those who knew better understood how dangerous their mischief could be. They didn't mean harm, but their magic flared

of light. All it would take was one frightened brownie triggering a glow near a security drone, and the whole district could go into lockdown.

Will cut in, voice low. "Whatever happened with that bigger guy I flagged last week? Carlito was running point."

Thane's voice crackled back, "No good. They got to him first. Same story. Wife and kids too. Carlito said the guy made it through the chipping, but his wife didn't. Kids got sent to re-ed."

Will's stomach turned, but he kept his expression neutral.

"They think it's a new tech, some device that spots power before it manifests." Thane's voice dropped even further. "But... I dunno. It's almost too fast. Like they knew exactly where he'd be."

Will's spine prickled. That theory again. New surveillance tools? Maybe. But his gut said otherwise. Too many close calls. Too many *coincidences*. Either they were being watched... or there was a spy in their group. He needed to do some work without the rest of the resistance knowing for a bit, to see if his theory was right.

"I'm stepping back. For a while." Will lied. "I need space. To think."

Thane blinked. "Stepping back? You mean a vacation? Where to?"

Will's eyes flicked toward the edge of the city, where the skyline broke into the wild. "The forest. I need to recharge. Tech here's been chewing at my magic. I can feel it. I've been in the city for almost a year. Maybe I should move back to transport? I think I just need a break."

have been one of our best. I know leadership won't like it."

Will hesitated, then shook his head. "No plan. Not yet. Just instinct. I've been working for the resistance for over twenty years, and this is the first break. I think they will understand. Or at least they better."

"You've been pushing yourself," Thane finished. "Yeah. I get it." His gaze sharpened. "Be careful, Hawk. If there's something wrong in the network, we can't afford to lose you."

"I'll be careful." Will offered a tight nod. The radio squawked as the connection ended.

He didn't look back as he slipped into the dark, the shadows swallowing him like they'd been waiting.

The acrid stink of the city filled his lungs, but beneath it, something sharper tugged at him with scents of pine hanging on the breeze. Faint, wild, and real. It stirred something ancient inside him, pulling him toward the edge of the city, toward the places where magic wasn't hunted, where he could breathe.

But not yet.

A few hours later, Will had a plan. A good one, maybe even clever. She was school age, so all he needed to do was check the schools. He needed to figure out which school she was in.

He'd narrowed it down: only two schools in Media Proper District fit the right parameters. With powers like his, sensitive to magic like a lodestone, he could usually pinpoint a caster nearby. All he had to do was walk the perimeter and feel. After one pass, he was sure: Central Academy was the one.

Thanks to the city's chronic teacher shortage, getting in wasn't hard, they had openings in janitorial, or teaching. He wasn't a

position. Forging the credentials took less than an hour. Media's standards for substitutes were a joke. He was grateful that Lysa had insisted he attend high school and the lure of people to con, steal from, and save at college had him live on the local college campus also. He never got a degree, but at least some parts of the credentials could be confirmed. He'd used his real name, mostly because it was clean, without any of his many charges that some of his other alias's held. Somehow, despite everything he'd done, it had never been tied to a single charge. Gorek used to call it "impressive luck" with a look that said otherwise. Still, clean was clean. It cleared the school's background check without needing resistance help. Not ideal, but good enough.

His boots echoed through the polished halls of Central Academy, a harsh contrast to the silent shadows he'd lived in for so long. The place smelled of disinfectant and dust, but under it, something else lingered: chalk, paper, static. Life. He moved with purpose, scanning faces, watching for the one that would shift everything.

Between classes, the corridors swelled with sound: laughter, footsteps, lockers slamming shut. So many kids. He couldn't remember the last time he'd been around this many at once, let alone seen them carefree, joking, safe.

Teaching was a tactical grind. Papers to grade. Every period, every hallway, he searched. Still no sign of her.

Frustration crawled beneath his skin. He'd trained himself to wait, to outlast danger, to endure. Years of surviving on his instincts and silence had forged his patience into steel. But this wasn't just survival anymore. It hadn't been for a while.

Every time he closed his eyes, her face surfaced, not the girl's, not the target, but Layla's. Always Layla and always in that

changed forever.

His lodestone sense told him the girl was here. Somewhere. Close. But the signal was faint, like trying to hear a whisper in a storm. Still... if she was hiding her magic that well, especially under the stress of school life, that meant she was strong. Stronger than most.

And that made her worth finding.

It was Thursday at the school. He was starting to learn his way around better, at least. The teachers' lounge smelled faintly of stale coffee and burned-out ambition. Will leaned against the counter, sipping a cup of something that barely qualified as tea. The bitter taste didn't bother him, he had to drink much worse while on the journey to Aloria. It gave him something to focus on.

Two teachers stood near the window, voices low, casting glances in his direction that cut off the moment he looked their way. Will suppressed a smile. Gossip always traveled faster in confined spaces, and it didn't take a lodestone's pull to know who they were talking about.

He approached with easy confidence.

One of the women, Ms. Arden, a fifth-grade teacher with an easy laugh and eyes that missed nothing, had helped him navigate his first few substitute assignments. Petite and sharp-featured, she wore her dark hair in a pixie cut that suited her playful energy. The other, Ms. Callen, slightly plump and polished, had salt-and-pepper hair pulled into a neat twist and a gold wedding band that gleamed against her no-nonsense blazer. The corners of her mouth twitched with quiet amusement as Will approached.

smoothly, "I'm beginning to think you've conspired to keep all the well-behaved classes for yourself."

She chuckled. "You should've seen my first year. I think I had a kid set a desk on fire."

"Impressive," Will said, taking a slow sip. "Tell me, though... A friend of mine's daughter goes here. He told me to look for her. She is blonde and maybe nine or ten. Quiet."

Ms. Arden tilted her head. "A ten- or eleven-year-old child would likely be in the fifth grade. Fifth grade is a big grade this year. As far as finding a quiet blonde girl, do you have a name?"

Before he could press further, the door swung open, and Headmaster Grell strode in like he owned the air. He was tall, though not quite Will's height, with the kind of posture that tried too hard to command a room. He had pale skin, and his thin black hair was slicked back with too much product. His greasy smile, eyes with red lines, make him look creepy. The gold pin on his tie flashed under the lights, it was all shine and no substance, authority worn like costume jewelry.

He zeroed in on Ms. Arden immediately.

"Sarah," he said, letting the name linger far too long, "you look... radiant today. I hope you're not planning on hiding behind that desk all day."

She stiffened; her smile disappeared. "Thanks, Mr. Grell. Just grading papers."

Will's jaw ticked. He set his cup down slowly. "Mr. Grell," he said with a roguish grin, stepping forward as if joining the conversation casually, "is that your subtle way of asking for extra tutoring? I hear Ms. Arden gives brutal pop quizzes."

to keep morale up." Just then, Will caught the waft of mothballs emanating from Grell's direction.

Will raised a brow, his tone easy. "Well, you're certainly keeping everyone on their toes."

Grell's smile twitched, as if unsure if he'd been complimented or cut. Without another word, he muttered something about meetings and disappeared out the door.

Ms. Arden gave him a grateful glance but said nothing.

Once the door shut behind Grell, Will murmured, "Sorry about that," his tone low enough to draw Ms. Arden a step closer. "Sometimes I forget I'm supposed to blend in."

She tilted her head, eyes glinting with interest. "You don't strike me as someone who blends in anywhere."

He flashed a crooked smile. "That's the trick. Be forgettable when it counts."

She leaned a little against the counter, arms crossed. "Well, if that was your attempt at being forgettable, I'm afraid you're failing miserably."

He let out a quiet laugh. "Noted. I'll dial it back... unless it's working in my favor."

Ms. Arden bit her bottom lip in her crooked grin, "That depends. What are you after, Mr. Carver?"

He met her gaze with a playful glint. "Information. But I'm told bribery is frowned upon in school."

"I guess it depends on the bribe," she smiled, raising a brow. "What kind of bribery do you have in mind?"

friend's daughter is here. Blonde. Quiet. Nine or ten. I said I'd look in on her."

Ms. Arden let the pen trace her lips thoughtfully, drawing his eyes to her. "Fifth grade is packed this year. That narrows it down to maybe half a dozen."

"I can work with that," Will said, licking his lips, offering his most disarming smile. He leaned just slightly. "I've got excellent instincts."

"Oh, I bet you do," she said with a soft laugh. "But instincts don't get you class rosters."

"Hum," he tilted his head, voice low and playful, "Then I'll just have to charm the information out of you. Purely for professional reasons, of course."

She gave him a long, amused look. "Of course."

Ten minutes later, he walked out of the teachers' lounge with a list of students. It cost him the promise of a date with Ms. Arden, but charm and information always came at a price. Some are easier to pay than others.

Will considered handling Mr. Grell himself more than once but repeatedly decided against it. The man practically dripped malice disguised as charm; the lingering looks, the too-convenient brushes against younger teachers, the way his compliments always walked the razor's edge of inappropriate. Every time Will saw it, his fists itched.

But he couldn't afford to make a move. Not yet.

Not until he found the girl.

lodestone magic had grown stronger, sharper. She was close; he could feel it in his bones. And that meant time was running out, as his substitute assignment would only last so long.

As the final bell rang, the building erupted in chaos. Doors banged open like gunshots, and a wave of students flooded the halls, shouting and laughing. Lockers slammed in an uneven rhythm, echoing the restless beat of Will's heart. He rounded a corner, the weight of leather-bound books under his arm offering little comfort against the tension coiling in his veins. He watched the halls until there were only a handful of students, then gathered his belongings to leave for the day. His lodestone power showed that the person with strong power was still in the area, but he would have to move around to get a better lock on the location.

Ahead, in the dim corridor behind the gym, a dark-haired girl stood frozen, cornered and trembling. Two older boys loomed over her, eighth or ninth graders by the look of them, both tall for their age and built like they had something to prove. One had a sharp buzz cut and a smirk that never reached his cold eyes. The other, stockier, kept tossing a tablet between his hands like it was a game of keep-away.

Armond. Will recognized him instantly. Son of Headmaster Grell. Entitled, smug, and mean in that performative way that only came from knowing he'd never be punished. He wore a branded academy jacket two sizes too big and carried himself like a king among cowards. The other was his usual lackey, mop of greasy hair, cruel laugh, already clutching the dark-haired girl's school-issued lunch credits.

Their words were poison.

shoving her shoulder hard enough that she stumbled. "Bet your folks can't even afford replacement. We're doing you a favor."

"She's gonna cry," the sidekick cackled. "C'mon, cry a little. Maybe then you're worth lookin' at."

Will's fingers tightened around the books in his hands. His knuckles went white. Every instinct told him to step in and end this fast. He could do it without taking a chance that Headmaster Grell would end his assignment early. But he didn't move. Not yet. Not when drawing attention might jeopardize the real reason he was here.

The air thickened like the world had taken a breath and refused to release it. Will's muscles coiled under his coat. He could see the dark-haired girl flinch, trying to cover her face, her back against the wall. Too small to fight back. Too smart to think anyone would help her. Not here.

Then Armond shoved her.

She hit the floor hard, landing on her hip with a small yelp. The tablet clattered beside her. The boys laughed with power over the weak.

"Enough," a voice snapped, slicing through the corridor like a blade.

A blur of motion followed. A girl, younger, small, but fast and *fierce.* She launched herself from the far end of the hallway. Blonde hair tied in a ponytail; eyes focused like a predator's. She didn't hesitate. Didn't speak again.

She flew in a rage.

Her foot struck the stockier boy square in the chest with a high kick that sent him crashing against the lockers with a metallic *clang.* He went down hard, wheezing, stunned.

The girl spun, pivoting low as Armond lunged. She ducked under his arms and caught him off balance, driving her elbow into his ribs. He gasped. She stepped into his space, wrapped her arms around his waist, and with a practiced twist of her hips, and *threw* him.

He landed with a thud that echoed, the air rushing out of his lungs in a single, humiliating wheeze.

The entire fight had lasted less than ten seconds.

She stood over them, shoulders squared, chest heaving once. Calm, collected and untouched.

Will realized he had been holding his breath and allowed himself to breath again.

That's her.

The girl he'd been searching for.

He was amazed. She showed no hesitation, no panic, only precision and intent. He didn't know where she learned it, but he knew what it meant.

She was powerful and not only with magic.

The boys stood. One clutched his arm, the other rubbed his ribs, both suddenly unsure of themselves. Their bravado crumbled, and with muttered curses, they retreated.

Will watched, his eyes widening slightly, a flicker of unbidden admiration surfaced. She was skilled, far beyond any girl he had ever known at that age, even in the slums. Each movement had been executed with an elegance that spoke of endless practice, of discipline honed over years. He found himself silently cheering the short-lived battle on. The fact that those boys would have to know that they were not just bested by a much

he would have been able to provide without losing his position.

Will remained still, shrouded in the dimness of the hallway, his silent approval hanging in the space between them. The girl turned to help the younger girl up, her cascading blonde hair catching the glow of the lights that lined the hall.

Will's breath caught in his throat.

Seeing her again, he was starting to think it was his imagination that had made him picture her as Layla, but no here she was, the girl he had been searching for and his memory had served correctly.

A slow, quiet pride stirred in his chest, not just for her victory but for the unwavering courage she had shown. The memory of his sister surged within him, raw and bittersweet. The same defiance, the same fire; he saw it in this girl.

The tension in his body eased, giving way to something else entirely. Curiosity. As this blonde little girl helped the dark haired one dust off her clothes and gather what was left of her stuff, he walked over.

"Quite the display of skill," he remarked. "You handle yourself well."

The blonde girl was startled, turning to face him fully. He took in the icy blue of her eyes; even in the dim light of the hallway, they were noticeable. She looked up to meet his hazel gaze with a cool appraisal. After all that, her breath was steady, her stance still poised, as though she waited to see if she were in trouble before bolting. As soon as the dark-haired girl was able to, she left the scene.

"I only did what I needed to," she said. "They were going to hurt Anne."

unexpected stirred within, something beyond duty. The sight of her, the fire in her stance, the quiet strength in her voice… it captivated him.

"My mom used to say that sometimes, necessity is the mother of bravery," Will observed, keeping his distance but holding her gaze. "You stood up for what was right when it mattered. That counts for something in times like these."

"Thank you. I'm Ellie," she acknowledged, allowing a small smile to grace her lips. Her guard remained up, yet there was warmth in her words, a recognition of his understanding, perhaps even gratitude. "But who are you? I haven't seen you around here before."

"Mr. Hawkson. Will Hawkson," he introduced himself, extending his hand. She hesitated for only a moment before shaking it. "I'm here as a substitute teacher, replacing Mr. Haney for a week or so."

Ellie tilted her head slightly as if weighing his words. "A substitute teacher," she echoed, skepticism lacing her tone. "Well, those bullies have been beating up little kids all school year for their lunch money and more. I told the headmaster, but Armond is his son. He ignores it." She sounded far older than she looked.

Will allowed himself a half-smile, his tone edged with something close to amusement, "In that case, it's probably best if I don't report what I saw. I don't tolerate that kind of behavior, but as an adult, I don't have the luxury you do. Maybe it was better to let you handle things your way." He nodded toward the now-empty hallway. "Bullies shouldn't win, and they did look the part."

"Yep, they are," Ellie agreed.

do I have the pleasure of addressing?" Will asked as they walked out of the building, hoping to find her name on the list he had gotten from Ms. Arden.

"Ellie. Ellie Neldoreth." Ellie replied politely.

"Stay safe, Ms. Neldoreth," Will added, his watchful eyes following as she turned away. He allowed her to leave, then he easily followed her from a distance on her path home.

As Ellie walked, Will trailed behind just far enough that he could hear them talk, his presence a silent shadow at a distance. He hadn't expected to feel so protective of her, but after watching her stand up to the bullies, it had become impossible not to. There was something about her, something quiet, strong, and unshakably good.

At a street corner, Ellie turned and waved to a boy about her age jogging toward the corner. Dark hair. Hoodie in warm weather. Watchful eyes. Her face lit up with a brightness that tugged at something in Will's chest.

"Hey, Daniel!" she called, her voice carrying clearly in the still air.

Will slipped into a position where he could still hear, careful to remain out of sight. When he met up with her, they began walking again. Ellie launched into a breathless recounting of the bullying incident, how she had stepped in to defend Anne. Will noted how she glossed over his involvement, as if uncertain about him or unwilling to give him credit. He couldn't tell if that was caution or calculation. Maybe both.

A moment passed between the kids, where they spoke of school, games, and shows, and then Daniel seemed to remember something.

out a small, silver badge that gleamed in the late afternoon sun. "I got accepted into the Guardians of Order."

Will's breath caught. He tensed instinctively.

Ellie's voice sounded weaker. "Isn't that the group that hates magic?"

Daniel hesitated. "Well... not exactly," he said, clearly choosing his words. "It's more about protecting people. They teach us how to keep the community safe from magic. You know, the dangerous kind. We help stop problems before they start." The way he said it, it was as if he were remembering words off their booklets.

Ellie didn't answer right away. Will could see the way her shoulders stiffened, and her fingers curled into her sleeves. She was calculating how much of herself to hide.

"I always thought most people with magic were good," she said at last, her voice careful. "If everyone has a little good in them... then maybe people with magic do too. What if they teach you that all magic is bad? What about those who use it for good?" Ellie pressed. Will imagined she must be thinking that her friend being indoctrinated with fear and suspicion towards something so integral to her identity would be a problem.

Daniel turned to look at her with gentle concern. "There's no such thing as good magic. We all know that eventually, it corrupts. It always does. That's what my dad says, and he's seen it firsthand. Remember that fire-starter a few years ago? Burned people alive. This club teaches us how to stop things like that before they happen."

He tucked the badge back into his hoodie. "They're not hurting anyone, Ellie. They are just putting magic suppressors in them

It's for safety."

Will clenched his jaw. Suppressors. He'd seen too many kids suffer under the lie of safety.

Ellie said, "Just... be careful, okay? My mom always says there are two sides to every story."

"I will," Daniel promised. "I just want to help people. Like my dad. His unit just got an award for the most captures this month."

Will saw the change in her, Her world was shifting beneath her feet, and even at her age, it looked like she could feel the shift in their friendship.

They chatted quietly, the easy rhythm of childhood friendship pulling them forward. At the end of the street, they split; Daniel toward his house, Ellie continuing alone.

From his position, Will watched her go with a knot tightening in his chest. She hadn't said anything, not yet. But a moment of misplaced trust with the wrong person, one little slip, and it would all be over.

He couldn't let that happen.

Ellie continued down the street toward her home, a quaint white house with a bright red door. She was greeted with a warm hug by what could only be her mother. He observed the striking resemblance between them. Ellie was practically a miniature version of her.

The vibrant colors of the flowers in the garden seemed to smile at her as the mother checked the mailbox for any new letters or packages. She handed Ellie a small package to carry inside. The moment was simple, domestic, but it spoke volumes.

mousey brown hair lingered on his front steps, clearly trying to catch the mother's eye.

"Hey, Malin," the mousey man said. Will noted the way his face lit when she finally turned to acknowledge him.

"Andrew, are we still on for tomorrow night? Awelyn is really looking forward to taking me dancing," Malin said, adjusting the mail in her hands.

"Of course, Malin, you can always count on me," Andrew replied enthusiastically. Then his tone softened slightly. "Have you done any thinking about my offer?"

Will narrowed his eyes as he studied her reaction. Her posture remained polite, but there was no excitement in her expression. She hesitated before answering. Andrew walked over to where she stood.

"Thanks. I'm still thinking about that part, but it is a big decision for me," she said as he reached for her hands, filled with mail.

"Maybe it would help if we talked about your concerns. You mean so much to me; surely, we can discuss it," Andrew pressed.

With furrowed brows and a contemplative expression, she finally replied. "We have such an amazing friendship. I wouldn't want to ruin it. I know it has been so long since Caelum died, but he was my everything. What I had with him was so amazing, and although I think you are fantastic, I just don't feel that same way I did with him." At his dejected look, she continued, "That is why I want to keep thinking about it. You know how I am with decisions. It takes me forever to figure out which game we should play next. I just need time to think things through."

This seemed to be an answer he could accept. He released her hands and took steps toward his door, then said, "You can count on me for tomorrow night."

just lock up. With you so close, it should be fine. I don't expect to be out late, but I'm riding with them, so…" she said, breathing a sigh of relief that he handled it so well.

As Malin and Ellie made their way into the house, Will watched intently from his hiding spot. He knew he needed to come up with a plan to follow Malin the next night when she went out; after all, as he had found, the best way to get to someone, especially a child, is through their loved ones. He had previous assignments convincing children, and the best results had all been when he could get the parents on his side. And he could tell that Malin was certainly someone who cared deeply for her daughter's well-being. The mother was his best bet.

Malin stood in front of the old mirror her mother had insisted she keep, its carved edges flickering with the soft bedroom light. She smoothed the silken folds of her midnight blue dress, her fingers brushing over invisible wrinkles with a nervous precision. The gown clung in all the right places, elegant, unfamiliar, and far too aware of itself. She hadn't dressed like this in... years. Not for anyone. Not even herself.

Height had always been a challenge, and the black strappy heels she'd reluctantly chosen added even more. The dress, borrowed from Lira, had looked modest on its original owner, falling just to the knee. On Malin, it stopped at mid-thigh, a fact she'd pointed out to Awelyn more than once. But Awelyn had waved off her concerns, insisting it was "perfect." Malin wasn't so sure. She already knew she'd spend the entire night tugging at the hem.

Awelyn had insisted on the braid, some kind of trend she'd seen online. Malin had nearly laughed it off, but now, seeing the tiny crystals catching the light, she couldn't quite bring herself to undo it. Tiny crystal strands woven through the braid caught the light as she moved, glittering unpredictably. The effect was striking, almost magical, and matched the earrings, bracelet, and necklace Malin had unearthed from a long-forgotten jewelry box earlier that evening. She'd had to brush off the dust before opening it, the quiet symbolism not lost on her.

It had been over a decade since she'd gone out for anything other than duty. Everything about this felt wrong. Too tight. Too bright. Too much. And yet... the woman in the mirror wasn't a stranger. That's what scared her most.

"Mom, you look amazing!" Ellie's voice rang out, bright with excitement. The eleven-year-old bounced on the bed, eyes sparkling like she'd just unwrapped a present. "Like a fairy tale princess!"

Malin's lips curved despite herself. "Thank you, sweetheart. Awelyn and Lira spent hours getting me ready. I'm not even sure I remember how to do all this anymore."

She reached up to adjust the intricate silver hairpin tucked in her braid, but her fingers trembled slightly. It wasn't the hair, or the heels, or the dress. It was the quiet knot of unease curling low in her stomach.

"You're going to have *so* much fun, Mom," Ellie said, leaping to her feet. "Can I borrow your sparkly eyeshadow sometime?"

Malin chuckled softly. "When you're a little older, maybe. Now, shouldn't you be getting ready for bed?"

Ellie groaned dramatically but nodded. "Okay, okay. Andrew isn't going to make me *hang out* with him, is he? I just want to play games with Daniel."

"You can, as long as your homework is done."

Ellie flung her arms around her, warm and weightless. "Goodnight, Mom. Love you! I'll see you in the morning and you *have* to tell me everything."

She disappeared in a blur of energy, leaving behind the scent of shampoo and the echo of laughter.

"Love you too," Malin whispered after her, her voice softening into the stillness.

Silence wrapped around her like a familiar shawl. Malin turned back to the mirror. Her reflection looked... foreign. Not the

Someone braver. Someone softer. When was the last time she'd gone out like this?

She moved toward the closet for her handbag, but her fingers brushed against something hidden in the back.

A photograph.

Time slowed. Her breath caught.

She pulled it out gently, like it might disintegrate under her touch.

A younger version of herself smiled back, radiant in a crimson dress, caught mid-laugh. Beside her, Caelum, all sharp cheekbones and dark, laughing eyes, his arm slung around her waist like it belonged there.

The memory hit like a whisper and a punch all at once. The memory of his scent came back first. All musk and spice, then the feel of his warm skin pressed against hers. The music, the candlelight, the thrill in her chest when he knelt.

Her throat tightened.

"Oh, Caelum," she whispered, fingertips grazing his face in the photo.

But then, the ache. The memory that always came next. The knock at the door. The officer's face.

"I'm sorry, ma'am. There's been an accident."

She remembered the floor tilting. The numbness. Her hand on her still-flat stomach.

"No," she'd whispered. "We're going to have a baby."

The sympathy in the officer's eyes had nearly broken her.

And just like that, her future had turned to ash.

promises to a baby who would never know their father. Love, laughter, the life they were building, all of it vanished in one heartbeat.

Malin closed her eyes now, steadying her breath. The grief never fully left. It lingered like a ghost in her ribs.

Awelyn would murder her if she ruined her makeup.

She slid the photo back where it belonged, her hand lingering on the fabric beside it.

"It's just one night out," she murmured aloud, her voice barely above a breath. "Caelum would understand."

She picked up her handbag and turned to the mirror. The dress clung in all the right places. The braid crown Awelyn had insisted on was still perfectly pinned. The makeup, smoky and a little too bold for her taste, made her look more like a stranger than herself.

And just behind her reflection... the ghost of her past stared back.

The sound of the front door opening snapped her attention to the present.

"Malin?" Andrew's voice called from the front. "You ready? Looks like they just pulled up."

She smoothed the fabric over her hips and stepped into the hallway.

When Andrew saw her, his eyes widened. "Wow," he breathed. "You look absolutely stunning."

A flush crept up her neck. "Thank you," she said, keeping her voice even. "It's... different, that's for sure."

heads tonight."

She offered a small smile, feeling uncomfortably visible under his gaze. "Awelyn had a whole theme planned. This is one of Lira's dresses. She wanted us all to match her aesthetic, apparently." She reached for her shawl, letting the moment pass.

As she stepped past him, Andrew reached out to hug her. She shifted just enough to guide it into something brief, polite.

"Ellie's playing online games with Daniel in her room," she said, adjusting her bag. "She's eaten, since you are next door, I don't see much need to stay the whole time, just make sure to keep check on her at bedtime. She can stay up a little later."

She paused.

"I may be back later than I'd like. I'm riding with them."

Andrew nodded. "Of course. I've got it covered."

Then, more softly: "You really do look amazing. And if you have a good time... maybe I could take you back another night?"

Outside, the night air touched her skin like a warning: cool, sharp, unsettling.

She wasn't sure she was ready.

The guilt hit before she reached the end of the walkway. Andrew's hopeful expression lingered in her mind. She had known how he felt for years. She'd tried to feel something more. She really had.

But she couldn't force a heart that refused to open.

Not since Caelum.

known his shape before they'd even met.

And nothing had ever felt like that again.

The glimmering silver limousine out front looked like it had rolled straight off a government commercial: sleek, smooth, and soulless. Its chrome surface caught the streetlights like it was trying too hard to shine. Malin hesitated, her fingers brushing the sleek metal, as the limo driver held the door for her. It vibrated faintly with the engine's low hum, too silent to be natural. When she ducked her head inside, she saw Awelyn and Lira, both adorned in elegant gowns and sparkling jewels, pouring champagne.

Lira leaned over to hand her a glass with a dramatic flourish, her eyes sparkling. "Well, well. Look who's finally ready to paint the town!"

"You look incredible," Awelyn said gently, sensing her pause. "Come on, the night awaits."

The doors sealed shut with a soft hiss. As they glided through the neon-lit streets, she found herself lost in thought. *When was the last time she'd done something like this?* The years seemed to melt together, a blur of work and motherhood.

The club pulsed with electric energy, a pulse of flashing lights and pounding bass. Holographic dancers shimmered in and out of existence, their projections flickering like fireflies against the dark walls. The air was thick with scents of perfume and spice-laden drinks.

Malin stepped inside, momentarily overwhelmed by the sensory overload.

all in.

Lira laughed and looped arm through Malin's, walking her to their private table in the corner. "Welcome back to the land of the living, darling. Let's get you a drink."

As they wove through the crowd, Malin couldn't shake the feeling of being completely out of place. The music throbbed through her, each beat a stark reminder of how long she'd distanced herself from this kind of life. Around her, patrons tapped glowing wristbands like it was second nature, their drinks materializing in thin air seconds later. Malin watched one glass shimmer into existence, the liquid inside glowing faintly purple. Efficient. Impressive. Completely impersonal.

Nothing in Media was magic. It was just math wrapped in spectacle; everything was engineered, controlled, and perfected.

"What do you think?" Awelyn shouted over the pulsating rhythm, gesturing to the spectacle around them.

Malin hesitated, searching for the right words. "It's certainly... different," she replied, her analytical mind struggling to process the onslaught of light, sound, and movement. "I'm not sure I remember how to do this anymore."

Lira pressed a fizzing, neon-blue concoction into her hand. "That's why we're here, love. To remind you how to *live* a little."

Malin took a tentative sip. The drink was unexpectedly sweet, decadent, and delicious. She lowered the glass, catching sight of herself in the mirrored surface by the bar. For a moment, she hardly recognized the woman staring back at her. Was this really the same person who spent her time pouring over medical journals and reading bedtime stories?

"To new beginnings," Awelyn declared, raising her glass.

tugging at her lips. "To new beginnings," she echoed, though she wasn't sure she truly believed it. In that moment, she decided to let go and attempt to enjoy herself.

Hours passed in a haze of music, dancing, laughter, and drinks that shimmered with unnatural hues. Malin had moved herself to a seat off to the side of the bar, more observer than participant. Awelyn and Lira had joined a lively group of Awelyn's friends, their laughter bursting through the air, rising above the pulsing rhythm of the music like sparks from a fire.

At the center of their table sat a half-eaten cake, its frosting catching the shifting lights in glossy, pastel swirls. Around it, an assortment of half-finished drinks in every conceivable color formed a kaleidoscopic ring, abandoned in favor of dancing or louder conversations.

Malin's buzz had long faded. She didn't want to ruin the night by overindulging. And despite the chaos, the noise, the lights, the unfamiliarity, she realized she was enjoying herself.

Lira's voice cut through the din. "Oh, Malin! Come meet Jaxton!"

Suppressing a sigh, Malin turned just as Lira approached with a tall, well-dressed man with perfectly coiffed hair in tow. Jaxton's smile was perfect in a way that didn't feel human, teeth a little too white, skin too smooth, his pupils dilating just a second too slow. Malin clocked the subtle hum of augmentation in the base of his voice. Bio-tuning, probably. It explained the overly smooth cadence.

"Jaxton, this is my brilliant friend I was telling you about," Lira gushed. "She's a doctor at the infirmary."

superficial interest. "A doctor? How fascinating. You must have the *most* thrilling stories."

You have no idea, Malin thought, and forced a polite smile. "It has its moments," she replied, keeping her tone.

Jaxton launched into a monologue about his latest business venture, his voice smooth, rehearsed, and utterly self-absorbed. She nodded at appropriate moments, but her mind was already drifting.

His nostrils were tinged with a faint pink flush. Eyes slightly dilated, and didn't constrict when the overhead light flickered. His jaw worked a little too tightly, and his speech pattern had a faint tremor underneath the confidence.

Stimulants. Or sleep deprivation. Or both.

She tracked the symptoms almost absently, the way someone else might people-watch for fun. It was second nature by now, diagnosing strangers mid-conversation.

'Is this what I've been missing?' she mused internally. 'Shallow conversations and forced pleasantries? Maybe solitude isn't so bad after all.'

"...and that's how I doubled my net worth in just three months," Jaxton finished, flashing another blindingly white smile.

"How impressive," Malin said, carefully selecting her words that neither encouraged nor insulted. "If you'll excuse me, I need to freshen up."

She turned away before Jaxton could respond, catching the flicker of disappointment in Lira's look. A pang of guilt surfaced. She knew her friends meant well. She felt like they had orchestrated this night out not only for the birthday but to help her meet someone.

Malin weaved through the pulsating crowd, the bass thrumming through her chest as she made her way to the bathroom. As she turned toward the restrooms, she caught her reflection again, this time on the polished surface of a drink cooler. The woman staring back wore borrowed glamour, sparkling in borrowed light.

She looked... fine. Even beautiful.

But she didn't look like herself.

She didn't look like Ellie's mother.

The moment she stepped inside, the music became a muffled heartbeat behind the door. She leaned against the cool sink, savoring the brief respite from the sensory overload outside.

Her reflection stared back at her from the holographic mirror, her icy blue eyes betraying a hint of weariness. She took a deep breath, the scent of lavender freshener mingling with the faint traces of synthetic alcohol. She debated staying with her friends or calling the cab to head home.

When she left the bathroom, she noticed the dizzying lights and the overwhelming music. It only served to remind her how much she'd changed. No amount of drinks, dancing, or charming strangers could bring her back to the person she used to be.

'I don't belong here,' she thought, longing for the quiet comfort of home, her daughter's laughter, and the predictable rhythm of her life. She had enjoyed herself for a little while, but she felt the need for some air.

"Just a little longer," she whispered to herself, straightening her posture as she took an empty seat at the bar in eyesight of her friends.

Tall. Confident. Too confident.

He didn't even glance around for attention, he didn't need to. His presence drew it like gravity.

The line of his jaw was sharp beneath a dusting of stubble, too rugged to be accidental. His shirt, loose black linen, shifted with his movements, revealing the edge of a tattoo creeping across his collarbone. The kind of detail that would be interesting if she were the kind of woman to care about that sort of thing.

She wasn't.

He was clearly built like someone who worked with his body. The kind of man her younger self might have called trouble, with a capital T. His tight black leather pants clung to his muscular legs, emphasizing the strength beneath, while polished black boots grounded him with quiet authority. They were not the latest fashion, like the others she had met. These had a worn and comfortable look to them, as if it hadn't occurred to him to do anything more than clean them up.

He pushed a tousled strand of light brown hair from his eyes, the longer curls falling in a soft curtain while the shorter sides framed his high cheekbones, sharpening the already dangerous charm of his features.

Malin tensed. Not visibly, she hoped but enough to notice. Great. Another walking cliché.

"Is this seat taken?" His voice was deep, smooth, carrying an easy confidence.

She glanced up, prepared to brush him off, meeting a pair of warm hazel eyes. "My friend dragged me here. I'm obviously not as young as I used to be. I used to enjoy places like this. I just

rowdy group near the center of the bar, a rueful smile on his lips.

She blinked. Not a pick-up line. At least not an obvious one.

"No," she said slowly. "I don't think anyone is sitting there."

"I'm Will. Will Hawkson," he extended his hand, large and strong, though not calloused. They weren't the hands of an office worker either, as they were not well manicured.

She hesitated. A doctor's habit, measuring before acting. But curiosity edged out caution. "Malin, Malin Neldoreth," she replied, shaking his hand.

He didn't hold it too long, another difference from most of the men who had hit on her through the night.

He settled onto the seat beside her, his presence calm but assured. "So, Malin," he said, settling in like this wasn't unusual at all, "what brings you to this corner of solitude in a sea of chaos?"

A strange thing to say. Almost poetic.

She felt the corners of her mouth twitch. "Chaos can be a bit... overwhelming. She hesitated, then added with a touch more edge, Just so we're clear... I'm not the type who meets people in bars."

Will chuckled, leaning slightly toward her. "Good. Neither am I."

His gaze flicked back to the crowd. "They're trying to make up for my missed social nights by introducing me to every woman they know, and a few they don't. I think they believe I'll just fall into the right arms if they throw enough women at me."

She tilted her head, mildly amused. "You too?" she asked before thinking. The words slipped out on their own.

boyish.

It caught her off guard.

She took a sip of her drink to cover the pause, watching the bioluminescent liquid swirl in her glass. The glow shimmered across her fingers.

"The problem is that they keep sending women who are vapid and clueless. I'd leave this place alone if they wouldn't be so upset about it."

"I know what you mean," Malin smiled. Her first real smile of the night.

She was smiling. Not forced or polite, but real. Where had that come from? Maybe it was him. There was something... disarming about Will. Like he wasn't trying so hard.

"I suppose there are worse ways to spend an evening," she replied, surprising herself with the hint of playfulness in her tone.

Will signaled the android bartender, and Malin felt a subtle shift in the atmosphere. The music pulsed in the background, but it faded. Or maybe she'd just stopped paying attention to it. She swirled the iridescent liquid in her glass, watching as its bioluminescent glow cast a soft shimmer on her fingers.

"So, Will," she began, rolling his name on her tongue to test how it felt, "Which District are you?" she asked, assuming he would say Galvin or City Center, as many of the others in the club had. Galvin is the upper-class District where she grew up, where you could raise a family, if you had money. City Center was the seat of politics, as well as a mass of high-rise facilities where you could live, work, and play and never need to leave the area. It was the area of highest luxuries, filled with pompous snobs.

space between them feel intentional. "Just moved to Media Proper from Seaborn. I got a teaching position. I'm substituting at Central Academy until a full-time spot opens up."

"My daughter goes there." That got his attention. "Ellie. She's in Ms. Rife's class. It's a good school, but the headmaster runs it like his personal throne room."

Will chuckled, pushing his curl behind his ear. "Yeah, I got that impression, too. I'll keep an eye out for her. I bet she looks just like a miniature version of you." His eyes flicked over her again, quick, appraising, not predatory. "Teaching's a challenge. But it matters. Kids are... well, sometimes nightmares, but mostly great."

The words lodged somewhere deep. She understood that, devoting yourself to something hard because it mattered. Her throat tightened for a beat.

"She'd like that," she murmured. "Her name's Ellie, and she's... a handful. But she's worth it."

Will shrugged. "Most of the women I've met tonight ran the moment I mentioned I was a teacher." He grinned again, one-sided and sincere.

She smiled, pushing a lock of hair that had fallen from the braids behind her ear.

He let out a small laugh. "Since we are just talking, that probably doesn't matter."

"Good thing we are just talking then," she echoed, laughing softly.

She hesitated before adding, "I'm a doctor. I work at the clinic in Media Proper."

Just out here saving the city."

The absurdity made her laugh. It bubbled up before she could decide whether to let it.

And somehow, just like that, the conversation found its rhythm.

As they talked, the bar around her seemed to lose its harsh edges. The flickering lights, too bright when she first arrived, blurred to something softer, like reflections on water. Even the sharp scent of disinfectant and recycled metal faded beneath something warmer.

Masculine. Especially when he leaned closer to catch her words over the pounding bass.

Sandalwood. Vanilla. A thread of spice.

It enveloped her slowly, curling in quiet waves. Familiar, though she couldn't place why. Something grounding. Calming. Like stepping into a memory, you didn't know you had.

"What about you, Malin?" Will asked. His tone was easy, but not dismissive. Curious in a way that didn't feel performative. "Have you always called Media Proper home?"

She nodded, catching herself before offering more than she should. "I moved there when Ellie was just a baby. It was shortly after medical school, one of my first placements. I stayed. Some of my patients… I've known them their whole lives."

His posture shifted slightly. Closer, but not demanding. He had presence. Not the heavy, dominating kind, more like gravity. A quiet pull.

"And have you ever thought about leaving?" he asked, and this time, his voice dipped lower. He leaned close, his words

else would hear.

She felt her smile falter. Just slightly. Most people wouldn't catch it. But she did.

"You mean Media?" she echoed softly, choosing her words like steppingstones. "I've never left."

She hesitated, then added, "When I was younger… Caelum, Ellie's father, and I had plans to see the world together when we were in college. He traveled for work while I finished my medical school. We were going to get married when I got my first assignment." Her voice thinned. "But he died. While he was traveling."

A pause. Then, quietly, "I'm so sorry," he said, and rested his hand over hers.

His hand was large, warm, and steady. Surprisingly soft. No calluses.

Not a laborer's hand. Not an office worker's, either.

The contact was electric. Not just warmth, energy. Like something dormant inside her shifted, reached toward it.

His eyes shifted, like he'd remembered something just then. "It *can* be scary," he admitted, his grin edging toward rogue, but not reckless. Then he leaned in again, closer than before, lips almost grazing her ear.

She felt his breath warm against her skin, and a shiver raced up her spine.

"But it's also beautiful," he said, voice pitched for her alone. "And with the right person… safety isn't so hard to find. I spent most of my youth on the road, with a merchant crew. There are places where magic isn't hunted, where it moves alongside tech like they were made to work together."

too long folded. A flicker in her chest, *noticing* she'd stopped thinking.

Not analyzing. Not diagnosing. Just *feeling*.

Excitement. Or maybe longing. It surprised her.

He wasn't speaking anymore, but he hadn't pulled away. He stayed close, as if waiting. Her mind spun, not with worry, but with proximity. With possibility.

She turned toward the lights instead, as if they could provide answers. "That sounds… dangerous," she murmured. "Even talking about it feels dangerous."

His voice dipped even lower, drawing her in until she leaned closer—*if that was even possible.* For a second, she thought his lips might've actually brushed her ear.

A promise, just below a whisper: "Maybe. But danger's often just the beginning. Sometimes it's the only way to get to something better."

And then… he stopped.

The words hung between them. Soft. Weightless. Like an open door.

He didn't push it open. Just… left it there.

She should've been analyzing everything: his posture, tone, the dilation of his pupils under low light. All signs. Clues. That's how her brain usually worked. Quietly, instinctively.

But somehow, she hadn't noticed when that part of her switched off.

Or maybe, she realized with a jolt, it hadn't. It had been occupied. With him. Not just observing but reacting. Feeling.

Overthinking, party of one.

And still, the warmth didn't go away.

At some point, she hadn't even noticed when her hand had remained in his. His other hand had joined the first, between sips of his drink.

She blinked down at their hands. His touch was warm. Natural. Not possessive. Just... there.

His thumb moved in slow circles across her skin, drifting now and then to brush her wrist, gentle, almost absentminded, but somehow intentional too.

She should've pulled away by now. But she didn't.

As the night wore on, she felt it. The shift. Not sudden. Just... easy. Her walls, which usually stayed solid no matter how she smiled, softened under the gentle weight of his attention. A little at a time.

There was something about Will. Steady beneath the charm. Safe, somehow. Even if her rational mind kept reminding her, he's still a stranger.

She turned to him, the words slipped out before she could decide whether to say them. "I didn't think I'd enjoy myself tonight. It's been... years since I've let myself have a night like this. Just for me. Before you came over, I was halfway through planning my exit. But... you made this a good night."

Will didn't grin this time. His smile was quieter. Uncomplicated. "I know what you mean. Life sneaks up on us like that. Sometimes the moments we don't plan for are the ones we need the most."

in her chest, warm and unfamiliar. Like breathing after holding, it in too long.

The music still thumped behind them. Laughter rang out from the dance floor. Lights spun overhead like a galaxy on repeat.

But between her and Will, the noise fell away. Like they'd stepped into some softer, quieter space that only existed between them.

They kept talking. One story sparked another. Time blurred at the edges until she couldn't remember the last moment, she'd felt this… seen.

Malin spotted them before they saw her, Lira's dramatic arm gestures, Awelyn's off-balance strut, and the way they practically vibrated with mischief. The moment she made eye contact, her stomach dropped.

Oh no. She knew that look. She'd known these women too long not to.

Whatever came out of their mouths next was going to be mortifying. Malin didn't need to check the ornate wall clock to confirm what her body already knew, late. Her feet ached in her heels, and the buzz of the bar was wearing thin.

They were drunk. They led three friends with them who had obviously also had too much to drink. "I hate to cut this short," she said, and meant it. "But I should probably head home. My friends are on their way over, and I've got an early shift at the clinic."

Will nodded, his expression understanding. "Of course. Time does have a way of slipping by when you're in good company."

we meet, it won't be because I'm in injured."

Malin laughed softly. "I'd prefer that too."

She wanted to stand, but something in her resisted, like her body hadn't agreed to end this yet. The moment felt threaded with something delicate. Unfinished. The hum of the bar's music and chatter rushed back in, reminding her of the world outside their conversation.

"It's been... unexpectedly nice," she admitted, a small smile playing at the corners of her lips. She hesitated, then added, "I'd enjoy meeting up again. Maybe for a coffee or something, sometime?"

Will's hazel eyes warmed. "I'd like that. Media may be a big city, but fate has a funny way of bringing people together."

He stood, pulling her chair out for her, prompting her to stand. It was a small, effortless gesture, but it caught her off guard. Only then did she realize how tall he was. At almost six feet, she rarely had to look up at anyone, even in heels. But Will was easily four inches taller, forcing her to tilt her chin slightly just to meet his gaze.

She forced down the flutter rising in her chest, unwelcome, ridiculous, and stepped aside just in time for the incoming storm of perfume, glitter, and high-octane fruity cocktails. Their personalities were always bold, but tonight, emboldened by alcohol, they were practically on fire.

"Hellooo," Lira drawled, eyes widening as she looked Will up and down. "Who is this tall drink of sin? Yummy. I'll have one of those straight up."

Awelyn leaned in with a conspiratorial grin, clearly delighted. "Malin, if you ever finish sipping on Mr. Tall-and-Tempting, pass

and could keep me busy all night."

Malin blushed a deep, unmistakable red, her eyes widening in horror as Awelyn's words landed with her subtlety of a drone strike. She risked a glance at Will, only to find him wearing a broad, amused grin; clearly entertained, and just as clearly aware that her friends were thoroughly drunk.

He arched an eyebrow, biting back a laugh. "Are they always this subtle?"

Malin groaned and buried her face in her hand. "I swear they're usually... slightly more civilized."

"Awelyn, Lira," she said through a tight smile. "Please meet Will."

The two women offered exaggerated waves and drawn-out greetings, nearly knocking into one another in their enthusiasm.

Will smiled, gracious and unbothered. "Pleasure to meet you both."

Even with the room spinning into chaos, flashing lights, high-pitched laughter, a swirl of perfume and alcohol, she was still aware of him.

The heat of his presence. The way he shifted slightly to stay near her without crowding. He had dropped her hand, but her skin felt like it remembered his hands anyway. Ridiculous.

"I'll walk you out," he said, and she nodded, grateful for the escape, and maybe something else she didn't want to name.

As they stepped into the cooler air near the door, his hand settled gently at the small of her back. The warmth of it soaked through the fabric, fingers brushing just at the edge of her hip. Not possessive. Just enough to be felt.

spine, just a small one. Not worth mentioning. Not worth thinking about. Definitely not.

"Ohhh no, no, Malin," Lira interrupted, her tone syrupy-sweet with mock innocence. "We need to drop these three off first in Galvin," she said, gesturing with dramatic flair toward a trio of barely upright partygoers being propped up by androids. "You should ride home with this tall, broody gentleman? I mean, it's efficient. Practical, even."

"Very practical," Awelyn added, jabbing Malin with her elbow. "Environmentally responsible, even. Who knows? Maybe you'll get another ride when you get home."

The group howled at that, dissolving into laughter and high-pitched giggles.

Malin stared at them, wide-eyed, her entire face burning. "You're all absolutely unhinged."

Will chuckled low, clearly enjoying every second. "Birthday. Huh. I'm betting they won't remember much of it."

"Only when they're drunk," Malin muttered, casting him a look that was part apology, part please don't run.

He grinned. "Well, in that case, I consider myself lucky to have caught them on such a good night."

Malin sighed, pressing her fingers to her temple as the heat crept up her neck. "I see the two of you are clearly just fine."

Lira winked. "Oh, we're better than fine. The limo got us. We fantastic. You, my dear, are glowing. Now go. Let the man take you like the gentleman he clearly is."

"I live just off Monroe Street."

"Oh, I didn't mean a cab…," she and Lira broke out laughing, tickled at her reference.

Malin blinked; he lived barely three blocks from her.

Awelyn gasped, then let out a delighted giggle. "Yes! She would love that!"

Malin shot her a sharp look, but Awelyn stumbled forward, wrapping her in an exaggerated hug and whispering in her ear, "It's my birthday. Come on. Let me be your matchmaker. He's adorable, and you need fun."

She hugged Awelyn back anyway. What else was she going to do, throw her into the fruit punch fountain on her birthday? Malin blushed, her protest melting as she hugged her friend back. "You're lucky it's your birthday."

"Damn right I am," Awelyn whispered, grinning into her shoulder.

At the exit, Will held the door open, and a cool breeze swept past, brushing her skin like a whisper. The night air still carried the city's familiar tang, but beneath it, faint, something else. Green. Alive. Like the world beyond Media was pressing up against its edges, trying to breathe through.

"It's still chilly," Will said, voice low, "but it's the kind of night that makes you want to wander just a little longer."

He turned toward her, catching a sliver of light in his eyes. "Thank you," he said. "For making a newcomer feel like he belonged."

half-smile.

"You know... we don't have to share a ride," she offered. "I don't mind going on alone if you'd rather not."

Her voice came out steady, almost too steady. The lie sat within her chest, tight.

Will smiled. It was slow and easy, as if he knew. "And miss the chance to make sure you get home safe? That'd be criminally unchivalrous of me."

He stepped beside her and, with just enough flourish to make her laugh, offered his arm.

"Besides," he added, grinning, "I'm told it's environmentally responsible to share rides. Who am I to argue with the science?"

She slipped her hand into the crook of his elbow and tried not to notice how solid he felt.

As they walked toward the waiting hover-taxi, she let herself glance back, one last time. Awelyn and Lira were attempting to herd their entourage into the oversized limo. One friend was bent over a trash bin, another doing her best impression of a newborn giraffe trying to climb inside.

Yes. She was absolutely fine with her decision.

Will reached the taxi first and turned back, offering his hand. She hesitated for only a moment before taking it. His touch was warm, steady. Intentional. He helped her inside without a word and closed the door behind her.

Her pulse hadn't settled by the time he slid into the opposite seat.

The night had taken a turn she hadn't seen coming.

And something told her... it wasn't over yet.

driver cut a sharp turn that threw her sideways. She caught herself instinctually, one hand braced against Will's solid chest.

Bare skin. His shirt had shifted, and her palm landed right where the fabric parted. His skin was warm. Firm. Ridiculously smooth. Muscle beneath, lean and coiled.

Controlled power.

"Sorry," she breathed, but he only chuckled.

"No complaints here," he murmured, voice threaded with amusement.

The driver turned up a bass-heavy track, the music swallowing any chance of conversation. But silence didn't stop her from noticing that his arm had come around her. Reflex at first, maybe, but now it lingered. Easy. Protective.

Her body was hyperaware. Every inch of her dress seemed to register the heat of his body. She could feel the slow, steady rhythm of his heart, completely unfazed, while hers felt like it was trying to rewrite its beat entirely.

Her thoughts spun, loose and weightless. Solitude had always been her anchor. Ellie. Her clinic. Stability over desire. Rational over risky.

She'd told herself what she had with Caelum was once-in-a-lifetime. Unrepeatable.

But sitting here, pressed against Will, she wasn't so sure anymore.

She glanced up, gaze catching the line of his jaw, the smirk tugging at his lips. A knowing one. Like he could hear the questions she hadn't spoken.

warm, watching her without pressure. Just… there.

What would it feel like, she wondered, *to have his hands on her skin? His mouth on hers?*

The thought hit low and hard. A slow ache curled in her belly.

Her breath hitched, escaping with a sound she didn't have time to catch, half sigh, half something more.

Will's gaze dropped, locked on hers. Something flickered behind those calm, steady eyes.

Then the taxi slowed to a stop in front of her home, Ellie's bike laying by the front door.

Disappointment bloomed before she could reason it away.

They'd arrived.

She inhaled, grounding herself in the rush of cool night air as the door opened. "Thank you for your chivalry," she said quietly, stepping out.

Will held the door, then followed, closing it behind him. The taxi lifted off the second the door sealed, disappearing into the city's glowing grid.

"Well," he said, watching the taxi disappear into the sky, "guess it had better places to be."

He turned back to her with a soft smile. "I'm just a few blocks away, I'll walk. Really, tonight was great. I'm glad we ran into each other."

Malin hesitated, tucking a strand of hair behind her ear that didn't really need fixing. "Would you… maybe want to grab coffee Sunday?"

morning. Well… technically *this* morning."

"I'd like that," Will said, voice warm. Then, after a brief pause, he tilted his head. "Would it be too bold to ask for a kiss goodnight?"

Her breath caught. "Well… I… um…"

Will stepped closer, slow, deliberate, leaving space for her to stop him if she wanted.

She didn't.

Her pulse thudded in her ears as he closed the space between them. He searched her eyes, like he was waiting for her to pull away.

She didn't.

And then he kissed her.

It started soft, barely a brush. Tentative. Testing.

His lips were warm, patient. Like he was asking a question with his mouth, not quite sure she'd answer.

She did.

Her lips moved with his, shy at first, then more certain. A slow pull built between them, something that coiled low and tight in her stomach.

He tasted faintly like spice and something darker—bourbon, maybe—and the edges of heat. She felt his breath, his focus, the way he didn't rush. He was reading her, waiting for her cues, letting her set the rhythm even as he deepened the kiss by degrees.

Her hand found the front of his shirt before she realized it, clutching the fabric like it could steady the flutter inside her.

he pulled her fully against him. Her breath caught, but she didn't pull away. Couldn't.

There was no space left between them.

Her brain, so good at tracking vitals, patterns, warning signs, was completely, uselessly quiet.

She wasn't thinking. Just heat and pressure and the feeling of being wanted in a way that didn't ask her to be anything but *here.*

The kiss shifted. No longer careful. No longer a question.

It was an answer.

Malin gripped the front of his shirt, her thoughts dissolving. She wasn't thinking anymore. Just *feeling.*

The kiss was heat and history, want and wonder. It said all the things neither of them had dared.

And just as she melted fully into him, ready to chase that fire wherever it led, he pulled back.

Breathless, she blinked up at him. Lips parted. Stunned.

Will's smile turned slow and wicked, mischief flickering in his eyes like a secret he wasn't quite ready to share.

"That was…" he murmured, voice low, "even better than I imagined."

She was still catching up, heart racing, knees barely steady, when he leaned in again, close enough that her breath stalled.

"I don't want you too tired for work," he said, rough and quiet. "But if I wasn't trying so hard to behave… I'd keep you up for hours."

The words landed like a jolt.

to form anything resembling language.

She couldn't think. Not clearly. Not with *that voice* still in her ears and the ghost of his mouth still on hers.

He stepped back, gently guiding her fingers toward her key.

When she didn't move, he leaned close again, almost whispering. "You should probably go inside… before I stop pretending I'm a gentleman."

That grin: boyish, smug, and completely disarming, struck her like a second kiss.

She didn't trust her legs, but somehow, she made it to the door.

Hands trembling slightly, she unlocked the door and stepped inside.

The scent of him clung to her. Warm sandalwood. A hint of spice. It wrapped around her like he'd followed her in. She paused at the window, watching him.

He waited until she'd closed the door. Only then did he turn, tossing her a quiet wave over his shoulder, unhurried, like he knew she was still watching.

Malin leaned against the door, the cool wood pressing into her spine.

Her mind replayed everything: the first unexpected hello, the hover-taxi, the kiss that short-circuited her brain.

The chemistry was undeniable. But she told herself it was probably just a spark. A fluke.

She'd know by Sunday. Coffee would be the test.

At least, that's what she told herself.

her. Something familiar, but unknown. Like a dream she'd only partially remembered.

She barely registered kicking off her heels before collapsing onto the couch, her body finally syncing with the emotional storm she'd been riding all night.

With a long sigh, she closed her eyes and breathed in deep, hoping the quiet might settle her.

But even as she tried not to read into it, her heart betrayed her.

That flutter. That warmth that refused to fade. It was *familiar.*

It felt like Caelum.

That same breathless pull, the tilt of the world, the quiet certainty that something had shifted.

She brought trembling fingers to her lips, still tingling.

It wasn't the same. The man was different. The sensations were new.

But the feeling...

That spark. That terrifying hope.

It was exactly the same.

And that scared her more than anything.

The afternoon sun cast Malin's home in a warm, golden wash, too peaceful for how fast Will felt his heart beating. He slowed his steps as he reached the door. *Why do I feel like a teenager showing up for a first date? He asked himself.*

He knocked - three steady raps - and listened to the sound echo into the quiet Sunday air. A second later, the door creaked open to reveal Ellie.

She looked like she'd been wrestling gravity itself. Her curls were damp and wild, her workout clothes clinging to her small frame, her cheeks flushed from effort. She blinked at him, recognition blooming across her face like a sunrise.

"You! Yeah! Mom's been all gaga all day," she blurted, eyes bright. "She thought you ghosted her. She told me it was Mr. Hawkson from school. I told her you didn't seem the ghosting type."

Will almost choked on a laugh. That was direct.

"She home?" he asked, trying and failing not to smile.

Before Ellie could answer, footsteps approached from inside. Malin stepped into the doorway. Her cheeks were a subtle shade of pink. She tugged at the hem of her worn, sweat-covered, t-shirt, clearly trying to make herself look less like someone caught off guard and completely failing.

Their eyes met, his hazel, her ice blue, and something passed between them. He couldn't name it. He couldn't tell if she was thinking of slamming the door in his face or asking him in.

He felt it too.

Ellie's laughter broke the tension wide open, bright and loud and fearless. Will glanced down at her, grinning, bouncing slightly on her toes, and for a second, it was easy to forget the walls, the guards, the ever-present eyes of the city.

He exhaled and gave a sheepish smile, shifting his weight slightly on the doorstep.

"Sorry for just showing up," he said, rubbing the back of his neck. "After... the other night, I realized I never got your number. And I had no idea which infirmary you work at."

Will noticed how beautiful Malin looked when she blushed, color rising from her cheeks to the tips of her ears. She stepped aside with a quiet grace, her movements instinctive, like she was used to making space for others while never quite lowering her guard.

"Come in, Will. Sorry. When I hadn't heard from you yesterday about our plans, and Ellie and I always train on Sunday afternoons," she said softly, her voice warmer than he expected. He noticed a smile tugging at the corner of her lips, like she was trying to fight it and failing.

As he stepped inside, the shift in air hit him: sweat, rubber, a hint of citrus cleaner... and something distinctly hers. A clean, soft scent, like wildflowers and tea leaves. It lingered in the room like a signature.

The living room looked like it had hosted a small war; martial arts pads were scattered across the floor, along with water bottles and towels that hadn't quite made it to the laundry basket. But it didn't feel chaotic. It felt used. Lived in. Real.

Ellie stood in the middle of it all, practically vibrating with pride. Her cheeks were flushed, her curls sticking to her forehead, and she wore her sweat like a badge of honor.

Will from school. He saw me take out Armond."

Then, without missing a beat, she turned toward him, already bouncing into motion. "Watch this, Will!"

Before he could respond, she launched into a series of strikes and blocks: quick, clean, and confident. No hesitation, no wasted movement. Each action came sharp and smooth, like she'd been born knowing how to fight.

Will watched, caught between amusement and awe.

The kid had fire. And discipline.

Clearly, Malin didn't just patch people up; she trained them to survive.

He didn't need to guess who had taught her.

Malin stood nearby, arms crossed loosely, watching with the kind of pride that didn't need words.

Will took it all in the thump of feet against padded floors, the steady rhythm of breath, the undercurrent of strength that pulsed through the room. This wasn't just training. It was survival. A mother teaching her daughter how to stay alive in a city that would chew them up if it could.

He wasn't used to witnessing this kind of softness carved from steel. It stirred something in him.

A strange, quiet sense of trespass.

He wasn't just in someone's home. He was in their haven. Their shield. And the fact that he'd been let in at all…

That meant something.

and confidence in Ellie's movements. She had real skill. What struck him more, though, was Malin's quiet presence in the corner, calm and alert. Not hovering. Not instructing. Just watching with the kind of protective stillness that could only come from a mother who'd taught her daughter how to survive.

Sunlight filtered through the windows, catching in dust motes and glinting off sweat-slicked skin. The scent of the room was sharp with effort, rubber mats, dried sweat, a hint of citrus soap, but beneath it all was the warm, earthy trace of Malin. Like sun-warmed skin and something sweet he couldn't name. It hit him in the chest harder than he expected.

He leaned against the back of the couch, arms crossed, watching Ellie snap into another round of kicks.

"Your form's solid," he said, breaking the rhythm of her strikes. "You've got control and power. That's a rare combo."

Ellie beamed. "Really? What kind did you do?"

Will glanced at her and Malin, noting the subtle curiosity in both their eyes. He cleared his throat. "Bit of a mix. Grappling, throwing, whatever worked at the time. Learned a lot working on ships. Every port had its own flavor of trouble."

His gaze drifted to Malin. "Let's just say I didn't always train for sport. Sometimes it was survival."

That earned him a look. Subtle but sharp. Ellie didn't notice. She was already bouncing again. He had a feeling he'd be getting more questions later. That's what he was hoping for.

"Can you show me something?" she asked, practically vibrating with excitement.

Will grinned but didn't answer her right away. He turned to Malin instead.

Malin's expression softened, but there was a line of steel beneath it. "I don't usually let strangers spar with my daughter."

Her words weren't cruel. Just honest. Measured. Protective in a way he could respect.

"Fair enough," he said, giving a respectful nod. "I could show you a few things. Let her watch."

She considered it, and he didn't push.

"Maybe later this week," she offered.

Before Will could answer, Ellie burst in. "Tuesday! You should come for dinner on Tuesday!" She spun toward her mom, eyes pleading. "Can he? Please?"

Malin froze, clearly torn. Her hand smoothed over her shirt like she needed something to do with her fingers.

"Ellie, I'm sure Will has other plans…"

"No," Will said, too fast. He locked eyes with Malin with a crooked grin. "Tuesday works."

She took her time looking away. And for some reason, that stuck with him. Not what she said. Not what she did. Just… that she didn't look away.

"Great!" Ellie announced, blissfully unaware. "It's a date!"

Will chuckled softly as he watched them, this hurricane of a kid, and the calm in the eye of her storm. It felt good to laugh. Really laugh. He realized he hadn't done that in… longer than he cared to admit.

It brushed up against something he hadn't let himself feel in ages.

Not just interest.

Longing.

To belong. Even just a little.

Ellie chattered at full speed about dinner plans, something involving sweetbread and sauce and a dozen other things he couldn't follow. Will nodded, letting her talk, but his thoughts were drifting. Not aimless, just... pulled.

He hadn't expected this. Not her, not Malin. Not the quiet hum of comfort inside these walls. They weren't just surviving; they were living. Somehow, in a city built to smother people like them, they'd carved out a life that felt human.

It shook something loose in him.

He realized he was starting to kid himself about thinking that there could be any more to any of this. He reminded himself why he was here. This was just a job. Nothing more. He didn't belong in spaces like this.

And yet.

The promise of Tuesday's dinner hung in the air; it was not just a meal but a step closer to a ledge he wasn't sure he should go near. He leaned against the doorframe as the late sun poured across the floor, watching Ellie land another sharp, perfect kick.

"She was pretty impressive after-school last week," he said, voice low as he turned to Malin. "She's got good instincts."

Ellie lit up, practically bouncing on her toes. "Really? Did you see the spinning kick? I nailed it. Wanna see again?"

She launched into an animated recap of her entire day, complete with exaggerated moves and sound effects.

hopeful.

Will looked toward Malin. He noticed her hesitation, brushing down her workout top again, her hands slowing like she was buying herself time to decide.

He couldn't read her eyes as they met him, they were so cool and stormy. There was a flicker of something unspoken.

"We've got plenty," she said at last, voice even. But there was a softness there that hadn't been before.

"You sure?" Will asked, still not sure if she meant it. The words came out easily, but he felt the weight behind them.

"Absolutely," she smiled. Small, controlled. But it reached her eyes.

When Malin and Ellie slipped down the hallway to change, Will stayed behind, hands tucked loosely in his pockets. He let his eyes wander slowly at first, then with more curiosity than he wanted to admit.

The place wasn't polished, but it had weight. Like every item had been chosen, not styled.

The couch had seen better days, with faded cushions and a sag in the center where someone curled up often. There was a soft blanket tossed over the arm. The arm of the couch was smooth from use. A couple of Ellie's books sat half-stacked on the coffee table, next to what looked like a cracked ceramic mug holding colored pencils.

The walls were painted a warm neutral, chipped in places near the baseboards. On one side, a shelf held mismatched photo frames, some crooked, one missing its glass. He stepped closer, careful not to overstep. One photo showed Ellie, younger, arms crossed, a smile tugging at the corner of her lips.

A faint scent hung in the air, something spiced and earthy, maybe clove or nutmeg, wrapped around something sweeter like vanilla or citrus peel. It didn't smell like perfume. It smelled like someone lived here. Someone who cooked. Someone who cleaned because they had to, not because guests were coming over.

There were signs of both structure and softness: a set of laminated daily routines stuck to the fridge, a training schedule half-wiped on a small whiteboard by the door… and near it, a single drawing in bright crayon pinned to the wall. A house with three stick figures. Two tall. One small.

He stared at it longer than he meant to. He noticed that jealousy had him wondering who the third figure was.

This wasn't just shelter. This was home. Not polished, not perfect, but real. Every corner told a story of effort. Of survival. Of love, even when unspoken.

And somewhere in the middle of it all, he was standing. Wishing he could belong.

He didn't, and it occurred to him that if he did his job right, all of this would be lost.

But for the first time in longer than he could remember…

He wished he could.

He heard the padding of bare footsteps walking down the hall toward the kitchen. He turned to see Malin, her towel-dried hair tumbling around her face, Will looked up and nearly forgot what he was going to say.

to himself, "I know it sounds like a line, but it's not. Really, I like this version of you better than the one with heels and lipstick. This feels like you."

Color bloomed on her cheeks as she tucked a damp strand behind her ear.

"Thanks," she murmured. Then, quieter: "Just so you know, I don't usually allow strange men into my home. There's just... something about you. You feel familiar. Like I've known you forever."

She gave a sheepish laugh. "Sorry. I have this... condition where I say exactly what's on my mind."

Will grinned, the right side of his mouth tugging higher, his dimple flashing before he could stop it.

"It's refreshing," he said. "Most people make you work for every honest word. You're different."

He hesitated.

"You remind me of my mother," he added, the words slipping out before he could put up the usual filters. "She always said what she thought, too. Drove my father crazy. He used to say that was the reason he fell in love with her."

He hadn't meant to say that part. It wasn't part of the plan.

But the thing was, there wasn't a plan anymore.

At least not one he wanted to follow.

Ellie beamed, practically glowing, and Will didn't miss the way she glanced between him and her mother like a kid watching a story unfold in real time. Her joy filled the space, bouncing off the walls, weaving into everything.

plates, the low hum of the fridge, the occasional scrape of a drawer. It was quiet but not empty. It was the kind of quiet that came with comfort.

Will found himself standing closer to the center of it than he ever expected.

His gaze drifted to Malin. Her brow was furrowed in concentration as she carved the roasted chicken. Her movements were careful and efficient. The scent of rosemary and thyme rose in slow curls from the cutting board, rich and earthy. It mingled with something faintly citrusy in the air, something that clung to her skin and felt maddeningly familiar now.

Ellie chattered nonstop between bites, her mouth full half the time as she recounted her training. Will didn't catch every detail, but the sound of her voice, light, unfiltered, and real, made him feel relaxed.

The table was a little mismatched. Nothing fancy. One plate had a hairline crack through it, another was clearly from a different set. But it didn't feel careless. It felt like history. Like these things had lasted because someone wanted them to.

He couldn't remember the last time he'd sat at a table like this and felt... steady.

By the time dinner was over, the awkward edges between them had softened. Not gone but faded. Replaced by something warmer.

They drifted into the living room. Ellie immediately seized the remote and claimed the biggest cushion, her voice bubbling with

favorite show, something involving heroes, heartbreak, and time travel. None of it made much sense to Will, but he didn't mind.

Malin took the middle cushion. Will sat beside her. Their knees brushed, just lightly, but neither pulled away.

"Watch this part, it's the best!" Ellie grinned, pointing at the screen as the music swelled into a sweeping orchestral battle theme.

Will leaned back, eyes flicking toward the screen, though his focus kept slipping sideways to the quiet shift in Malin's posture, the way her body instinctively curved toward her daughter.

Ellie's energy began to wane. Her words slowed. Her eyelids fluttered.

Soon, he noticed her head tip gently into Malin's lap.

Watching Malin stroke Ellie's hair, reminded him of when his mother would do that with him. The love she showed looked slow and soothing, as if it were an unconscious gesture that spoke of years of comfort and care. He knew it wasn't for show.

Something tightened in his chest, not painful, just... sharp. Familiar and yet entirely new.

He didn't know what unsettled him more: how natural it felt to be here, how guilty he felt about having to pull them away from this, or how badly he wanted to stay.

Seeing Ellie fast asleep, Will stood, his movements quiet and deliberate. He scooped her into his arms, holding her with a gentleness that felt natural, even though most people wouldn't expect it from someone like him. She murmured something he

into the fabric of his shirt.

"Her room is just down the hall," Malin whispered, gratitude threading through her voice.

He nodded, his footsteps soft on the wooden floor as he walked past a series of photographs, snapshots of birthdays, school plays, and sleepy mornings. Little glimpses of Ellie's life. Of Malin's love.

He pushed open the door to Ellie's room. It was soft and quiet, painted in pastel shades with stuffed animals lining the shelves like sentries. A gauzy canopy hung above the bed, as delicate and magical as a dream.

He laid her down carefully, tucking the covers around her with steady hands. She didn't stir. A stray strand of hair had fallen across her forehead, and he brushed it aside. A plush dragon, its stitched scales catching a shimmer of moonlight, rested near the pillow. Most kids were taught that dragons were monsters, scary things to be feared. It made him smile, seeing the toy given a place of honor here. He tucked it beside her, imagining it as a little guardian to keep the nightmares away.

As he walked back toward the kitchen, where he heard Malin moving around, something shifted inside him. She wasn't like the women he'd known before; there was no pretense with her, no masks. She was honest. Caring. Open.

He was here to convince her to leave the city. That was the mission. Get them out. Keep them safe. Fast.

His charm had built him a reputation; people tended to trust him, maybe like him, but that was a tool, not a truth. He'd used it to survive. To protect the ones who couldn't protect themselves. He wasn't just some rogue who liked to flirt for fun.

without letting her get too close. And if she ever found out who he really was, that he'd never held a proper job, that he'd grown up in back alleys and underground tunnels, would she still look at him the way she did?

He wasn't on her level. He knew that.

And if she ever found out, there was no way she'd fall for someone like him.

He still had a job to do.

The scent of the evening meal still lingered in the kitchen, a warm blend of herbs and spice that wrapped around him like memory. Malin stood at the sink, hands deep in soapy water, her movements steady, precise. The quiet clink of porcelain echoed off tile. No other sound.

Will stepped toward the old wooden speaker perched on the counter and tapped it. A gentle stream of music flowed out, soft and slow, curling into the air like sunlight through a window.

He moved closer to her, smiling, boyish, and hopeful. "May I have this dance?" His voice came out low, careful. Not a joke, an offering.

She looked back at him, blinking once in surprise before her expression slid into something unreadable. Not no. Not rejection. Just... cautious.

"We were talking all night Friday," he added, quieter. "I kept meaning to ask you. During one of those slow songs."

She dried her hands on a towel and turned to him. In the warm glow of the overhead light, her eyes found his, and something settled. "You may."

His hand slid to the small of her back. The motion was muscle memory by now. He'd learned to dance as a tool, something that got him closer to secrets, slipped him into galas and private clubs where the wrong people said the right things after enough drinks. Twirls, dips, posture, it had all been part of the act.

But this wasn't an act.

Even with all that training, this felt different. Easier. Like he wasn't performing. Like maybe he'd done this with her before, in some other version of life he couldn't quite remember.

The kitchen faded, noise and edges falling away as they swayed. His other hand found hers, and their fingers laced together without effort. They fit. Like that space between them had always been meant to close.

She felt stiff at first. He could feel it in the line of her shoulders, the tension in her spine. As if she was not used to this kind of closeness.

He didn't push.

Just moved with her, steady and soft, letting the music carry them until something in her gave a little. She eased into him. Not all the way, but enough. It was enough.

Inside, he was a mess. No rhythm, no grace. Just heat, guilt, and want, all twisted together.

Was this fair? To her? To Ellie?

He was supposed to be protecting them. Helping them leave. That was the plan. That had always been the plan.

But right now, with her breath warm near his neck and her fingers still laced with his, the plan felt far away. And suddenly, it was not so simple.

At the end of the song, he spun her once, then drew her in, close. Too close for thoughts to finish forming. Her body folded against him, wrapped tight in his arms. Their hearts pounded against each other's chests, fast and in sync.

His eyes met Malin's, and in that stillness, he felt a shift. Like the night had turned a corner and they were standing on the edge of something neither of them could take back.

"Malin," he said, his voice low and rough-edged. "I know this is too fast. I thought… there'd be more time. A slower buildup. But there's something about you. About Ellie. I don't know how to explain it, but it feels so right here, with you both."

He paused, searching for words that felt real, not rehearsed. "I know it sounds crazy. Maybe it is. But I've never wanted anything like this before."

He could see her studying him, reading every flicker of his expression, weighing it. He didn't know what she'd find. But he hoped it was enough.

She was tall; taller than anyone he'd ever been with. He barely had to tilt his chin. Her lips were parted, like a breath caught between hesitation and something more. Her mouth was right there, the perfect angle. So, he kissed her.

Soft. Slow. Just enough to make contact.

He didn't expect the heat of her response, the way her tongue slipped past his lips first, bold and sure. It set something off inside him, something primal. A rush of fire shot through him.

But it wasn't just heat. It wasn't just hunger.

This burned deeper.

and filled with flames. He knew this feeling. Not exactly, but close.

He'd felt it carrying Ellie to bed, that fierce instinct to protect, to guard, to *stay*. And now, holding Malin, it hadn't faded. If anything, it had rooted deeper. Stronger. More certain.

He barely knew her. But it didn't feel new. It felt ancient. Familiar. Like the magic that lived in his blood.

For a moment, the world beyond the walls, the regime, the magic ban, all of it, felt like a distant shadow. Right now, it was just them.

"Will," she whispered back, voice low and unguarded, "I don't know what the future holds. I'm not like this. It's been a long time... But tonight, this moment, it feels right."

And for now, that was enough.

The kitchen's soft light wrapped around them like a fragile cocoon. Their dance had blurred into something slower, closer, then something far more urgent. The space between them vanished, breaths mingling, shared and sharp. The slow rhythm gave way to heat, the steady burn of something that had been building since the moment they met. Their hands roamed, learned, and explored as they stood their ground in the middle of the kitchen.

He lingered in the feeling of her hands on his body, as she pushed her hands under his shirt, and the feel of her breath on his face mere inches apart from her, teetering on the brink of whatever awaited them next. Will's hands explored the gentle curves of her body, his touch both careful and yearning. Her fingers wove through his hair, drawing him closer with a fervent pull. He cupped her breast, teasing the sensitive peak, reveling

He ached to see what other places made her squirm like that.

The music that once filled the air had long since faded into silence, leaving only the echo of its melody lingering in the corners of his mind, as if guided by an ancient, primal rhythm. Before he realized it, their footsteps had traced a path from the warm, cozy confines of the kitchen to the inviting embrace of the couch, led by the unspoken language of desire. His shirt hung loosely open, the fabric barely clinging to his shoulders, revealing glimpses of his tattooed torso with intricate designs that seemed to dance in the dim light, while her top lay discarded, showcasing her ample, smooth breasts, untouched by any ink.

His pants were a poor barrier against the potent arousal that surged through him, one of the most intense he had ever felt. With a seamless, graceful motion, he lifted her effortlessly, her body fitting perfectly against his as he carried her toward the sanctuary of the bedroom. The door closed quietly behind them, a gentle click in the otherwise silent house, ensuring that little Ellie remained undisturbed. He laid Malin down softly on the bed, allowing a moment for the heavy anticipation to saturate the room, thick as the night air.

With deliberate care, he began to remove her remaining clothing. Each garment slipped away slowly, one by one, revealing the allure of her skin beneath, as the intimacy of the moment enveloped them both, drawing them deeper into its embrace.

With a deep breath, they began to explore each other's bodies thoroughly; hands moving over every inch of skin, mouths tasting and claiming one another.

Will's tongue traced tantalizing circles around Malin's nipple before enveloping it with his lips and suckling gently. A moan

pants, unbuttoning them hurriedly to free the throbbing erection contained within.

Her hand wrapped around his shaft, stroking him slowly but firmly as they continued to kiss. He groaned at the touch, feeling both a need for release and a desperate longing for more intimacy.

Before she could push him past the point of no return, he reluctantly stopped her movements. He wanted – no, needed – to prolong this breathtaking experience and savor every delicious second. With practiced care, he parted her legs to unveil the delicate skin of her inner thighs. Will peppered soft kisses there, each lingering like a whispered confession of affection. His fingers delved deep inside her velvety warmth while his thumb expertly teased her swollen clit, sending quivering ripples of pleasure through her core. He elicited at least three orgasms, before he decided it was time for his own needs to be met.

As he moved between her legs, he could feel the warmth and wetness that spoke volumes of their mutual desire, a tangible testament to the passion they shared. Will entered Malin slowly at first; they both gasped at the sensation. He would stroke into her, driving her to heights, then he would stop, holding her there while he felt her squirm with need. It took every ounce of strength not to give into the pleasure, but he knew what he was working toward.

He gradually increased his pace, each deep thrust drawing moans as they spiraled together toward ecstasy. Their bodies moved with perfect sync, driven by raw instinct and overwhelming need. Guided by passion, anticipation curled around them, hot and electric.

burning too intense to control. Every push and pull, every gasp and breath, were pieces of something greater, a tapestry of connection they hadn't dared imagine until now. He didn't need to hold back any longer, as they were both on the pinnacle. He climbed toward that final edge, lifting her with him. Together, they gathered wildly, tightly, building toward something far brighter than he could have believed possible.

Will lost sense of time. All that mattered was Malin in his arms, and this fierce and primal need to finally claim what had been promised from the beginning, maybe even before. He belonged to this. He belonged to her. And when release came, it left his soul shaking.

They collapsed, shaking and breathless. They lay there within one another's arms, the heat of their climax echoing through the silence. He barely remembered his name. He barely remembered hers. And still, it was the most real he had ever felt.

Moonlight slanted across the room in thin silver lines. Everything outside these walls disappeared. They lay there naked, her spooned within his arms. She was asleep, feeling so right.

This wasn't supposed to happen.

He was here with a purpose. He was supposed to keep them safe, convince them to leave, and use whatever charm he had left to make her trust him. That was the plan. That was always the plan.

But somewhere between Ellie's quiet breath against his shirt and Malin's fingers in his hair, that plan had started to feel like a betrayal.

His eyes noticed the backpack, slouched near the door, a small, ordinary thing. But it hit him like a weight. School. Mornings.

heartbeats.

He moved to get up, she stirred, smiling as she turned to face him, pressing her still naked body against him, with a sleepy relaxation in her eyes.

He pulled back, barely, his lips brushing hers one last time with something that tasted like regret.

"Mind you, my body thinks I'm insane," he murmured, voice rough with everything he wasn't saying. "But I feel like the right thing to do is to go."

He forced a smile, thin and tired. "Ellie's got school in the morning."

Malin studied him, her expression unreadable in the low light. He thought he saw a flicker of disappointment, but maybe that was his own, reflected back at him.

She nodded, slow and composed. "Of course. We both have responsibilities."

She wrapped herself in a robe, while he dressed. Then, moved with him to the door, close but no longer touching.

Before she opened the door, he pulled her close. "You know that I want nothing more than to make you moan like you did earlier at least once more tonight, but I'm thinking that you and Ellie might be much more important to me than I can put in words right now and I don't want to screw this up between us by rushing something, more than we've already rushed things."

Their final kiss was soft and unhurried, but it left something behind an ache, a question, a promise not yet spoken.

welcomed it. Breathed it in. Let it anchor him. The air in Media always had a strange taste, metallic and sterile, but tonight it felt like a slap.

A low groan escaped him, raw and unfiltered. He scrubbed his hand down his face.

He'd let this go too far. Or maybe, for once, not far enough.

He strode down the path with a casualness that didn't match the rush of his heartbeat or the weight sitting in his chest. Longing clung to him, heavy and bright. At the sidewalk, he paused and looked back.

The house glowed softly behind him, a warm, quiet light in the middle of all this gray. A beacon, if he let himself be poetic about it.

Then the door shut, closing off the glimpse of Malin's silhouette, and he turned away.

That's when he saw Andrew. Malin had told him about the neighbor, who had always been such a good friend. The one from the drawing he had been concerned about.

The man stood at his window, face partially lit, unreadable in the shadows. But Will could make a pretty good guess. The sight made him grin, just a little.

Without hesitation, he lifted a hand in a casual salute and followed it with a quick wink. Just enough to acknowledge what they both knew, even if it remained unspoken.

Andrew's head jerked slightly, a stiff nod that might have passed for angry or bitter, or both. Will didn't need to read his mind. The way Andrew melted back into the dark was the answer he needed.

thrill of what had just passed stayed with him, curling through his chest, but so did something sharper. Unease. Guilt. A reminder that none of this was simple.

The cold air helped. He let it bite at him, steady him. He was glad it was there.

The schoolyard buzzed with the noise of recess: laughter, squeaky shoes, the clang of a tetherball chain. Will leaned against the cold playground fence, the ghost of a smile still lingering from the night before.

His eyes scanned the crowd until he spotted her, Ellie, mid-laugh, spinning in a circle with a group of girls. She looked up and spotted him instantly.

"Will!" she called, darting away from her friends, sneakers slapping the pavement.

He straightened, already raising a hand. "Easy, kiddo," he said, ruffling her hair just enough to make his point. "Let's keep it professional. Eyes everywhere, remember?"

She caught on fast. "Got it," she said with a little grin, then tipped her head. "Are you and Mom… dating?"

The question hit him harder than he expected; it was so simple, so loaded. "Ah, we're… seeing where things go," he said. "It's not always simple for grown-ups. But yeah. I'd like that."

Ellie nodded like she understood. She probably did more than most. "What kinds of stories do you like?"

Will smiled, a little crookedly. "Fiction. The kind that lets you imagine something better."

like us reading that," she whispered.

"No," he agreed softly. "They don't. Especially not the ones about what's past the barrier."

Ellie leaned in. Her eyes widened. "We're really not supposed to think about that."

Will dropped his voice lower, conspiratorial. "We'll keep that between us."

She beamed at him, and it did something to his chest, made it ache in a way that felt right. They talked a little longer, about stories, about magic, about things she dreamed about but couldn't say aloud in class.

Then he said, quietly, "Before I came here... I lived beyond the barrier. In a place called Aloria. The sky's wide there. The air smells like freedom."

Ellie's eyes lit up. "That sounds amazing!"

The recess bell rang, slicing through the moment.

"Next time," Will promised, hand brushing her shoulder before she turned to run back toward the building. He watched her go, heart full and raw, already thinking about what he'd tell her next.

Then...

He froze.

Across the yard, beyond the fence, a figure stood.

Still. Watching.

Not a parent. Not a teacher.

Someone in a dark coat, too far to see clearly, but unmoving in a way that prickled every instinct Will had honed on the streets.

the glint of something metal at the collar. A chip reader? A comms link?

Gone.

The figure slipped between buildings like smoke.

Will's pulse kicked up. The smile faded from his face.

The cold had nothing to do with the sudden chill in his spine.

If they were watching now… then they already knew. He prayed there didn't know who they were looking for. It was only a matter of time before they found her though.

Will's scent still lingered in the hallway. He'd been disappointed when she told him she already had plans tonight, but he was coming over tomorrow after work.

It wasn't strong, just a trace. Sandalwood, warmth, that subtle spice she still couldn't name. It clung to the air like a memory, faint but undeniable. She'd walked past that spot three times already, pretending she wasn't looking for it.

Ridiculous.

She shook her head and turned back to the laundry, folding a towel with more precision than necessary.

Focus.

The laundry wouldn't fold itself, and she had just enough time to finish before Andrew arrived for game night. Their usual rhythm: takeout, board games, and familiar company.

Safe. Predictable.

Ellie had already disappeared into her room for a night of virtual games with friends, and the house had settled into a peaceful hum. Malin padded barefoot across the hardwood, the boards cool beneath her feet, and her muscles finally started to relax.

Then the front door opened.

She startled, body tensing on instinct.

Too early.

Andrew should still be at work. Maybe he'd left work early.
Andrew should still be at work. Maybe he'd left work early.

A low thud followed. The door closed much harder than normal. It was almost a slam.

Something in her gut twisted.

She walked toward the living room.

Andrew stood just inside the doorway, shadowed by the fading light. The sunset behind him threw streaks of color across the hardwood, but his broad shoulders, rigid, imposing, blocked them. A bouquet dangled from his right hand, stems crushed in his grip, red petals wilted and torn at the edges.

She registered the details automatically.

He was a wreck: hair disheveled, shirt wrinkled, buttoned wrong, second too far down on the left, the collar sat uneven on his neck, as if he'd yanked it on without checking the mirror.

Her steps slowed.

His eyes, normally soft amber, had hardened to flint.

"Who's the guy who left here late last night?" Andrew's voice cut through the air, tight, brittle. No hello. No smile.

Malin froze in place. His hair was a mess, pushed back in uneven ridges like he'd been raking his hands through it nonstop. That alone was enough to set off alarms.

How does he know about Will?

She kept her expression still, her voice calm. "I don't see why that's your business."

shifted, subtly blocking the path, creating an invisible line that would help her decide if she needed to escalate or not.

She caught the sharp edge of his cologne, clean citrus and wood, but it hit her differently tonight. It was joined with the distinct smell of alcohol. She had never known Andrew to drink more than a glass or two and never so early in the day. It hung in the air like something rotting beneath perfume.

Andrew's jaw clenched. His eyes went hard. "Don't play dumb, Malin. I saw him. Leaving your house. Extremely *Late* last night."

The whole scene felt... off. Controlled tension barely holding.

She considered her options, weighing each word before speaking. "Andrew," she said evenly, "I don't owe you an explanation about who I spend time with."

His nostrils flared. A vein ticked at his temple. The bouquet twitched in his hand. One of the crushed flowers slipped free and landed on the floor between them. "We're friends, aren't we? I thought we told each other everything."

The hurt in his voice was palpable, but there was something else there too; a possessiveness that made Malin's skin crawl. The air shifted. Her breath caught the lavender from her hand cream, a small detail anchoring her.

"We *are* friends," she said gently. "But that doesn't mean..."

"Did you sleep with him?" The question came out fast, sharp enough to slice through the air.

Malin's patience began to fray. She straightened her spine, her icy blue eyes hardening. "That's none of your business, Andrew. I think you should leave."

But he didn't move. If anything, he stepped closer. The shadows framed him now, longer and darker across the floor. His frame invading her personal space, crossing that invisible line she had created as he tried to push farther inside the house. The scent of his cologne, once comforting, now felt cloying and oppressive.

"Malin. You're better than this," he hissed. "You don't know anything about that guy."

Malin's frustration bubbled over. The air in her lungs turned tight. Her chest rose slowly, controlled. Deliberate. "And you don't know anything about my relationship with Will," she snapped, her voice rising. "You have no right to question me like this."

He scoffed, sounding bitter. "*Relationship?* Already? Couldn't even agree to a date with me. One date. And now some stranger, you're already calling it a relationship?" He was heated.

Heat flared beneath her skin. Her cheeks flushed, not with guilt, but fury. Her pulse pounded at her throat, loud and insistent.

Don't escalate. Don't trigger. Defuse.

She leaned into the part of her that was trained for pressure. The part that made her a doctor. The part that kept breathing even when everything else started to slip.

Her heart pounded fast, loud, too close to the surface. Heat flushed her cheeks, tightening the skin across her chest with every shallow breath.

She wanted him to go. Out of her house. Out of this space where Ellie was just down the hall. Raising her voice would only make things worse.

She had to control this. She had to control him.

"Andrew," she said, her voice calm, low. Deliberate. "I understand you're upset. But my personal life is mine. I think we should reschedule game night."

"So that's it?" he spat. "You're choosing him over me?"

Her restraint snapped like a taut wire under pressure.

"This isn't about choosing," she said, sharp and controlled. "It's about boundaries. And I don't think you understand mine."

She took a steady breath. "You've had too much to drink. I don't want to upset Ellie, so maybe we can talk more about this outside or at your place." She calmed herself to encourage him to walk with her to the door.

Her voice lowered, firmer now. "I don't feel safe with you in my house. Not with my daughter here. I want you to leave. *Now.*"

As they reached the doorway, her fingers closed around the handle. Her mind raced: Ellie, their friendship, the delicate balance she'd built, everything suddenly tilting, off-center.

He was walking with her, and she let him think she was following him out.

Just before he crossed the threshold, he shifted, stepping back toward her.

Only slightly.

She moved to shut the door.

He spun fast, and his hand clamped around her wrist.

The grip came hard and suddenly. *Too tight.*

Pain flared, white and hot, shooting up her arm. She gasped, breath catching in her throat. Her eyes snapped to him, wide with shock.

"Andrew. Let go." Her voice dropped sharp with warning. Controlled. Cold.

something desperate, was no one she recognized.

"Malin, please. Just…just listen…"

Something in her cracked.

Or locked into place. She knew it had to be the alcohol talking. He would hate himself for his behavior in the morning, but it wasn't something she could accept. It had to stop.

The clinical side of her vanished. Her body took over.

Training. Instinct. Pure reaction.

She twisted sharply, breaking his hold, stepping into the motion. Her other hand struck fast, a solid, practiced palm to the center of his chest.

He stumbled backward, thrown off balance, breath knocked from him.

"Malin, I…"

"Get out." Her voice trembled, not with fear, but fury. Adrenaline crackled through her limbs.

She advanced, every nerve alert. Ready.

He backed up fast now, eyes wide, hands half-raised in surrender. Maybe the hit had knocked some common sense loose also. The energy had shifted; whatever had been boiling in him drained away, replaced by confusion and something close to shame.

She didn't care.

He crossed the threshold.

And she slammed the door behind him. The sound cracked through the house like a gunshot.

of the door.

Her breath came in short, shallow bursts. Too fast. Too sharp. The silence inside the house roared around her.

The room felt bigger without him in it. Emptier. Like the tension he left behind hadn't decided whether to follow him or stay behind and watch her.

Her wrist ached, a dull, pulsing throb beneath the skin. The spot where Andrew had grabbed her felt raw, like it still carried the imprint of his hand.

She didn't move until Ellie's footsteps came running down the hall.

Malin turned just in time to see her daughter's wide eyes, panic rising behind them.

Ellie had seen it. Or at least enough.

Malin crouched quickly, wrapping her arms around her. "I'm okay," she whispered, pressing her lips to Ellie's hair. "I promise, baby. I'm okay."

It took time - too much, maybe - but eventually, she calmed Ellie, guiding her gently back to her game, back to her little world. Safe.

Alone again, Malin stood in the quiet hallway, staring at her phone. Her thumb hovered above the screen.

Awelyn and Lira were both working tonight. She could call them, but what would she even say? That her oldest friend had turned into someone she didn't recognize?

They'd never liked Andrew. It would be all '*I told you so*', whether they said it or not.

That she felt like she'd just escaped something she hadn't fully processed?

Her gaze landed on Will's name.

Her finger froze.

She shouldn't. It was too soon. Too intense. She didn't want to be that woman, the one who collapsed into the arms of the next man because she didn't know what else to do.

You barely know him.

But even as she thought it, her brain offered a counterpoint: *You knew Caelum even less.* That had been a one-night stand her freshman year of college; that night had rewritten her entire life from that night on.

"This is ridiculous," she muttered, dragging a hand through her loose blonde waves.

But still... she hit the call button.

One ring. Two.

"Malin?" Will's voice came through, warm, alert. Already on edge.

"Hi, Will," she managed, her voice catching in her throat.

"Is everything okay?" Concern wrapped around the question, immediate and sincere.

She exhaled, her eyes fluttering shut at the sound of him. "I hate to bother you, but... can you come over?" Her voice wavered, softer than she intended. "I just... I need to talk to someone."

"Of course," he said without a beat. "Let me wrap something up, and I'll head over."

"Thanks," she whispered.

at the floor.

She didn't move for a long time.

The knock was light. Almost playful.

She blinked at the sound, surprised by how quickly he'd arrived. Three blocks weren't far, but he must have dropped everything.

When she opened the door, Will stood under the porch light, broad-shouldered, casual, his smile soft and careful, offering comfort, not pressure.

His eyes locked onto hers. The moment he saw her face, something in his expression shifted.

He knew.

Her gaze flicked to Andrew's house.

The blinds twitched.

He was at the window. Watching. *Still.*

She turned away and stepped back to let Will in.

"Hey," he said softly.

He wrapped her in an embrace, and she moved into it without hesitation, as if his arms had been waiting for her all night. The air in the house shifted with him inside, pressure easing, something loosening.

She closed the door behind them. The latch clicked too loud in the quiet.

"Thanks for coming," she murmured, folding her arms across her chest.

already blooming. His jaw tightened, but he didn't speak. He reached for her hand slowly, giving her a moment. When she didn't pull away, his touch skimmed the inside of her wrist, light, steady. Calming.

"Tea?" he asked. The word sounded like something solid to stand on.

She nodded. Her throat felt tight. Tea was simple. Tea was manageable.

Will guided her to the couch, gestured for her to sit. "Feet up," he added gently.

She did as he said, tucking her legs beneath her, feeling the stretch of sore muscles and emotional whiplash catching up all at once.

Will moved through her kitchen with quiet familiarity. Not intrusive, just *there*. Present. Steady.

She sat numbly, letting the moment hold her. Letting herself be held by it.

He returned with two steaming mugs.

Without a word, he set them down on the end table, then lifted her legs so he could sit beneath them, settling her across his lap like it was nothing unusual. After pulling her close, he reached over and placed one mug in her uninjured hand.

With the other, he carefully took her bruised wrist, his fingers featherlight.

"You don't have to tell me," he said gently. "I'm happy to just be here."

He paused, then added, "But if you want to talk..."

pressing. Not pitying.

His thumb brushed the inside of her wrist, slow and steady.

And for the first time since the door had slammed, she felt herself breathe.

Malin cradled the warm cup in her hands, inhaling the soothing aroma of chamomile. "It's... complicated," she said, her voice barely above a whisper. "Andrew showed up, and he was... different. Angry. He grabbed me, and I..."

"Andrew?" Will's brows lifted. "The neighbor friend?"

She nodded once.

"I'm guessing you handled it," he said, quiet pride laced in his voice, but his eyes still searched her face.

She nodded, taking a sip of tea to steady herself. She paused in thought. "I've never seen him like that before. He had been drinking. He saw you leaving last night. It was like... like he wasn't himself."

Will leaned forward, his elbows resting on his knees. "Andrew isn't Ellie's father. Right? I thought I remembered it was Caelum."

She laughed at the thought, "No. We are just friends. I've just never been drawn to him. He's always been so sweet and nice to us. I don't know what I would have done without him. He's just a neighbor. He's always been such a good friend. I guess I always knew he had a crush, but..."

"So, you two never..." Will arched his eyebrow as he asked.

"No!" She defended. The thought appalled her.

He let out a sigh of relief. "Ok. So, since he isn't her father, that will make things easier. He's past tense now."

think you said he had passed," he asked. She recognized attempts as de-escalation of panic attacks by bringing up better memories.

"Caelum passed...," she gasped, her voice shaking with emotion as she struggled to form the words, "the day I found out I was pregnant with Ellie, only weeks after he had proposed." Will's arms wrapped tightly around her, providing a sense of security amidst the pain. The sound of his steady heartbeat and the familiar smell of his cologne were the only things keeping her grounded in that moment. "He was on travel with work, but I never really knew what he did. I'm still haunted by not knowing what work he was doing or how he died. All I know is that he was gone, just like that."

She hadn't opened up about this to anyone for years but sharing it with Will brought a sense of relief and closeness unlike anything she had felt before.

"I can't even begin to understand the weight of your loss. But I'm here for you now and always will be," Will whispered, his hand gently stroking her hair as they held each other in a tight embrace. She finally felt safe enough to let herself break down completely, knowing that he would catch every shattered piece of her heart.

Malin sniffled, wiping away the last of her tears. "I'm sorry, I just get so emotional when I talk about it."

"No need to apologize," Will reassured her. "It's good to let it out and not keep it all bottled up inside."

He reached for her hand, squeezing it gently. "So, do you have any other family in the area?" he asked gently.

She shook her head. "Just my parents. We were always a tight-knit family, but after Caelum's death, my dad and I became even

the times they had spent together, whether it was fishing at the lake or watching old movies on lazy Sunday afternoons.

"I was always daddy's girl," she admitted, feeling a sense of warmth at the thought of her father.

"What about your mom?" Will asked cautiously.

Malin's expression darkened slightly at the mention of her mother. "We've never been as close as my dad and I," she explained hesitantly. "There always seemed to be a strain between us, ever since I was a little girl." She paused for a moment before continuing with a sigh. "They are together, but it almost feels like they are only together because it is convenient. I don't feel the affection. I can't even imagine staying a relationship like that."

Will nodded understandingly, his fingers still intertwined with hers.

"But my dad is more than enough family for me," Malin continued with a smile, grateful for his presence and understanding nature.

"Your dad sounds like an amazing man," Will commented sincerely.

"He truly is," Malin agreed wholeheartedly.

Their conversation had drifted into lighter topics: books, bad coffee, the cracked roads near Galvin. With every laugh and shared memory, Malin relaxed more than she had in years. It was strange how natural it felt. Like they had known each other forever instead of mere days. She hadn't felt this kind of connection since Caelum... and even that had never settled this deeply into her bones. The thought sparked a flicker of guilt, but it faded under the quiet warmth of the moment.

something else. Something intentional. Charged.

Will swirled the last of his tea, then looked at her, eyes too thoughtful, and she braced herself for whatever question he was holding back.

"Malin," he said carefully, like each word had been weighed before release, "has anyone in your family ever... shown any signs of magic?"

Her cup paused halfway to her lips.

The question hit like a match dropped in a dry field. Magic? Knowing how taboo magic is to discuss, she tread carefully. She didn't have anything to hide, but why was he asking that now? Of all things?

She blinked, her heartbeat stuttering just enough to be noticeable. "Magic?" The word came out thinner than she meant. She felt like her voice was controlled, but barely. "Why would you ask something like that?"

He didn't flinch, but she saw the flicker. He was watching her reaction.

"Just... curious," he said with a shrug that was too casual to be casual. "You've got a sharp mind. Strong instincts. Sometimes that runs deeper than training."

Her instincts flared. He was probing for something. This wasn't casual conversation anymore. It bothered her, but... she didn't have anything to worry about. It wasn't like anyone in her family had magic.

She set the cup down slowly, deliberately, her gaze narrowing. "That's not something most people just bring up over tea."

"No," he admitted, voice quieter now. "It's not."

Or a warning. The air between them felt still, not threatening, but not entirely safe either. She crossed her arms and leaned away from him.

"My sister," he said after a beat. "She had magic. Only five when someone found out. They chipped her, back when the chips were still experimental, but... she didn't make it."

His voice cracked, grief slipping in like a blade between the words.

Malin felt a ripple of sympathy cut through her wariness. That made sense then. He had seen the consequences of those chips. It was a polarizing conversation in the clinic.

"When I see Ellie sometimes, it brings me back to my sister. It feels so good," he added. "Makes me feel like she's right here, looking after her."

That landed differently, so the question about magic was about Ellie. She turned slightly toward him and rested her hand on his. "I'm so sorry. I'm glad Ellie can bring you that kind of comfort."

Then, another shift.

"Have you ever had Ellie tested?" Will asked.

There it was again. That careful tone. Still gentle... but now pressing.

"I honestly hadn't even considered it." Her answer came quickly. "I don't think anyone in our family has ever had magic." She shook her head, trying to sound firm, but even to her own ears, it lacked certainty. "I highly doubt it though. My father works for Masoncore, they are the company that designed the chips, so it is doubtful. Why do you ask?"

person without magic liking dragons like that." So far, his questions on this subject had all been innocent.

She blinked, thrown. That was an odd detail to focus on. Was he serious? Or was that a metaphor?

"It was one of the rare presents my mother sent," she said, her tone shifting slightly as her brain tried to recalibrate. "Ellie said it was from a story Grandma told her when she was little. As far as I know, they barely talk, so... it must have been some talk, for her to hold on to it so tightly."

Her words trailed off. She found herself staring at nothing in particular. Her mind was racing, threading connections between old gifts, bedtime stories, Will's pointed questions, and the strange truths Ellie sometimes seemed to know before anyone told her.

Something wasn't adding up. And she hated when things didn't add up.

Still almost sitting on his lap, they sat in silence for a moment on the couch, both drinking their tea. She stared out into space, but she could feel his eyes on her as he sipped his tea. She leaned her head against his, nuzzling against his neck, filling her lungs with his musk.

Damn he smelled good, she thought, inhaling his scent, then swallowing her last drop and putting the cup aside. With the cup gone, she wrapped her arms around him to pull him closer.

He put his cup down on the coffee table, providing him with two free hands to hold her.

She felt his hand under her shirt first, as it traced the curve under her left breast, sending shivers down her spine. She

hands provided so much pleasure.

Will lifted her chin gently, and his gaze met hers with an intensity that seemed to light a spark between them. In that charged moment, an electric energy ignited, drawing her irresistibly toward his lips as though they were the gateway to his soul. Time blurred; whether the kiss lasted minutes or hours, she couldn't tell. Her lips, raw from the graze of his stubble, met his as their clothes brushed against each other, creating a friction that sent shivers down her spine. She could feel his hands roaming her body, exploring every curve and contour, pausing to trace the rise of her breasts and the firmness of her hips before lifting her gently from the couch and carrying her to the bedroom.

Once he had her settled on the bed with the door closed, he removed his shirt, revealing his nearly bare chest adorned with tattoos. His deep, commanding voice broke the silence: "You can take your clothes off, or I can, but those clothes need to go," leaving no room for misinterpretation.

"Of course," she purred, "you should have the honors," before adding teasingly, "but first...I have plans for you." With a wicked smile, she reached for his pants.

His smile broadened with delight at her bold move, as her hand gently grasped him through the fabric, she could feel his size and strength. Her eyes widened with desire as she slowly unfastened his belt, unzipped his fly, and released his arousal into the open air. She marveled at it, hard and throbbing. She had few experiences in high school, but Caelum had been her first time. Will was not Caelum. She had felt him the last time, but it had been completely dark, and they had not explored in this way.

around him, sliding it up and down at a slow, rhythmic pace. She had been impressed with his size before she began her motions; the movements made him even harder and larger.

With her hands busy, he pulled her t-shirt up, reaching behind her to unhook her bra, pulling it up and out of the way so he could fondle her breasts while she worked. He stopped her motions and lifted her arms, pulling the shirt and bra out of his way. With her naked breasts on display, she could feel a shiver of excitement running through him.

He moved to lie next to her. She felt his caress as he reached out to explore her curves with soft, deliberate touches, his fingers caressing her skin as they moved over her body. He cupped her breasts, gently massaging her nipples until they hardened under his touch. She released a soft groan of pleasure and couldn't stop herself from arching closer to him.

Returning her attention to him, she reveled in the sensation of eliciting small pulses of pre-cum when she touched his manhood in just the right spots. She could see how her touch awakened his visible need. She pushed him on his back, straddling his chest, as she leaned forward, taking him into her mouth, savoring his taste as he moaned softly with each movement. One of his hands grabbed at her hip pulling her close to his lips, the other used its fingers to tease her clit. It was hard to concentrate on her efforts on his cock, with the combination of tongue, lips, and fingers providing her pleasure.

At one point, she had to stop, her enthusiasm almost reaching a peak. He surprised her by abruptly shifting their positions, flipping her over so that her stomach pressed against the bed. He tugged at her hips, causing her to slip off the edge of the bed, before kneeling behind her. With intense care, she felt him

his tongue, then alternated. She tried to move, but he held her to the bed in that position. She writhed with mounting intensity, each near climax halted by him at the last moment.

At one point, Malin released an unabashed moan that nearly filled the room, a sound so rich and vibrant that it seemed to ripple through the stillness, nearly waking Ellie in the adjacent room where moonlight softly filtered through the curtains. The sound teased the silence, drawing them both into shared laughter that enveloped the room with warmth and intimacy. After that, Will playfully silenced her with a light press of his hand or with his lips, curbing any further noise. That laughter lingered like a cherished melody, drawing their hearts ever closer in that tender instant.

Overwhelmed by desire, she felt she might shatter under the intensity of her need. After nearly reaching climax twice, she shifted her position. Though he tried to hold her in place, her martial arts training lent her the advantage, she used his momentum to flip him onto his back. Lowering herself onto him, she locked eyes with him as she moved rhythmically, their breaths growing quicker and shallower with each passing second.

Sensing that the familiar surge was building, he warned, his voice a near whisper, husky with lust, "I'm coming."

With a knowing smirk, she pulled away just before he released a torrent of cum that burst forth in a fountain, cascading over his abdomen.

After his climax subsided, she leaned over him and used the remnants of his arousal to reach her own peak, their bodies uniting in a final burst of ecstasy before dissolving into blissful oblivion.

dawn gradually crept over the horizon. Malin lay nestled in Will's arms, a deep sense of contentment washing over her like a gentle tide. She couldn't recall the last time she felt so utterly consumed by another, both physically and spiritually. His touch had ignited a fierce blaze within her, illuminating every hidden corner with a warming light she never knew existed. Each caress sent delightful shivers down her spine, awakening a deep, smoldering fire that she surrendered to completely, a river of overwhelming sensation carrying her away on an emotional tide. Just the memory of it made her wet and eager once more, even though they both needed sleep. Turning to him, a small, serene smile graced her lips as she embraced a long-forgotten peace and warmth.

She was chaotic in her decision-making, wrestling with the weight of her newfound knowledge, but his presence and their profound connection made her thoughts clear.

alin awoke slowly, still groggy and sensing her lack of alertness. Her mind had been reeling over all the options and decisions she had to make, especially about her feelings. She noticed Will stir beside her; she saw the chance to speak when he might be more forthcoming, and she continued.

"Okay, here goes me trying to be open…" Malin murmured, still curled beside him. "It's been twelve years since Caelum, and I don't think I've ever felt this kind of connection. Not even with him."

She hesitated, her fingers fidgeting at the edge of the sheet.

"I don't want to scare you off. I just…wanted you to know how I really feel."

Will's hand skimmed slow circles across her bare shoulder. The warmth in his touch matched the softness in his eyes, making it hard for her to think.

"I feel it too," he said quietly. "It's been a long time since I had these feelings again. A little over thirteen years. I was going to marry her… I had the ring and everything. Then one day, she just…left. No note, no goodbye. I never found out why. I've had other relationships, but nothing like that and never like the way I feel about you. I can't explain it, but it is as if I have known or seen you before, and my body is constantly reaching out to you."

They lay together in silence, her head tucked into the crook of his shoulder, the quiet stretching warm and safe between them.

His fingers wandered, light, aimless. Drawing shapes across her skin. She sighed, content, letting the rhythm settle into her.

His whole body tensed.

She felt it before she saw it.

Will sat up, slowly, like something had just clicked into place.

Her eyes snapped open. "What is it?"

He blinked, looking down at her, not scared, exactly. More... startled. Careful.

"I just... noticed," he said, voice low. "I don't want to scare you, but did you realize you have a suppressor under your skin?"

The words didn't make sense.

She sat up fast, dragging the sheet with her, holding it to her chest like armor.

Her heart kicked into overdrive.

"A suppressor?" she echoed, icy blue eyes locking on his. "What are you talking about? That's not possible."

"Malin, it's not that uncommon. Please don't worry..."

"A suppressor?" Her voice rose, sharp and defensive. "That's absurd. I'm a doctor, Will. I would've noticed something like that."

The walls of the room felt like they were closing in, warmth replaced by a creeping chill.

Will didn't move closer. He just sat calmly, his voice even. "It's designed not to be noticed. That's the whole point."

She shook her head, blonde waves falling around her shoulders. "No. You don't get it. I don't have magic. I'm just, me."

Her breath came faster. She wrapped her arms around herself, suddenly unsure of every cell in her body.

hide your abilities. Even from you."

Panic rose fast in her chest, sharp and hot, pushing her breath up into her throat. The room tilted, just a little, but enough to make everything feel unstable. Her bedroom, once warm and safe, now seemed foreign. Like the walls were watching. Closing in.

She closed her eyes and pressed the heels of her hands to them, trying to slow it down. Breathe. Just breathe. Find the logic. There had to be a rational explanation.

This isn't real. There's no way this is real.

She closed her eyes and tried to regulate her breath. Counted silently: *In. Two. Three. Out. Two. Three.*

"Malin," Will's voice came gently, anchoring her. "I know this is a lot. But I'm here. We'll figure it out. Together."

She opened her eyes.

He was still sitting there, his expression unreadable except for the quiet intensity in his gaze. Not pity. Not fear. Just... presence.

And still, it unraveled something inside her.

"How?" she asked, her voice barely audible. "How can you be so calm about this?"

Will offered the barest smile. "Because I've seen this before. More than once. Discovering magic doesn't change who you are. If anything, it makes you more yourself."

His words landed like a stone in her stomach.

And I know that discovering your true self, your magical heritage, can be beautiful and empowering. It doesn't change who you are at your core, it actually makes you so much more."

trying to punch through the fog.

"You've seen this before?" she asked, searching his face. "As a teacher?"

He nodded. "Not always a teacher," he said gently. "Before that, I helped people through transitions like this. Helped them figure out what to do and how to stay safe. If you want, I can help you too."

Her heart kicked harder. She wanted to dismiss it. Pretend the conversation had never happened. Just go back to the part where she felt safe, tucked beside him in the dark.

But she couldn't unknow this. And her mind, trained to solve, analyze, predict, was already spiraling through possibilities.

"I... I don't know what to think," she whispered, her voice small in the dim light. "I've been a doctor in this town long enough to know how this goes. The choices are bad either way." Her fingers gripped the blanket. "If I ignore it, I'm burying part of myself. I've seen what that does to people. It breaks them."

Her throat tightened. "But removing it? That's dangerous. People die from that. Or worse, they live and get hunted for what they are."

When Will reached out slowly, she didn't flinch. Their hands met.

She glanced at the faint scar on her arm, the one she'd always assumed came from a childhood accident. But now...

A cold flush crawled down her spine. Her skin prickled, her hands numb. Her heart pounded.

"They wouldn't have done this," she whispered. "My parents... If I was pregnant with Ellie, they'd have told me. Right?" But even as she said it, the doubt hit like a stone.

If they'd thought it was dangerous? Inconvenient?

She pushed off the bed and grabbed her robe. Her skin felt too tight.

"Malin, wait," Will said quickly, his voice calm but firm. "Look at the wall. What color is it?"

She blinked at him, caught off guard. "Gray."

"Right. You're here. Just here." He gave her a small smile. "Sorry. Old trick. Grounding."

She stared at him for a long moment, then looked away. "You should go," she said, still flustered. "You have school tomorrow. You need sleep."

"I thought you knew," he said quietly. "I wouldn't have brought this up otherwise."

"I don't know anything," she snapped. "That's the problem."

She moved toward the door, but he caught her gently, pulling her into his arms. She stiffened.

"I'm sorry," he whispered into her hair. "I shouldn't have said anything, not tonight."

She froze, then let herself breathe into the warmth of his embrace. And that was it, the dam cracked.

Tears spilled, hot and fast. The truth of it all broke her wide open: the scar, the secrets, the fear of not knowing who she really was.

Will held her, solid and quiet, not trying to fix it, just steady.

Eventually, he helped her back to bed. She lay down, not because she wanted to, but because there was nowhere else to go. He curled behind her, a quiet weight that kept her anchored.

flickering, suppressor. scar. Ellie.

Morning came with the smell of coffee.

Rich. Familiar. Grounding.

Malin blinked against the light and saw the steaming mug beside a small crocus, freshly picked.

Her chest tightened.

She sat up, cradling the mug in her hands. The ceramic was warm. The heat seeped in like a tonic to her system.

Her mind replayed the night: the scar. The panic. Will's voice. His arms.

Then she heard Ellie's laugh from the other room.

"Good morning, Mom!" Ellie barreled in, curls bouncing. "Guess what! Will made pancakes, and he's taking me to school!"

Malin blinked.

Will looked up from the couch, freshly dressed, damp hair, his grin too smug for this early in the morning.

He stood as soon as he saw her, like she was the only thing in the room that mattered. That smile again, conspiratorial, warm. When he kissed her, Ellie giggled behind her hand.

"Good morning, beautiful," he murmured.

Then, near her ear, a teasing whisper: "Hope you don't mind. Figured you'd want Ellie off to school. And I happen to be heading that way…"

She laughed despite herself. "You really have made yourself at home."

was buying it.

"Best. Day. Ever!" Ellie crowed out loud. "He made pancakes!"

Malin narrowed her eyes at him. "Well. That's it. She's yours now."

And, of course, he'd made her pancakes too. Golden, fluffy, and still warm. Of course, they were perfect.

Before he left, he crossed the room to her, his gaze suddenly serious.

"If you need anything," he said softly, "just say the word."

He hesitated.

"We still need to talk. Really talk. About everything. But..." He smiled gently. "You and Ellie, you're it for me. I'm in. No matter what you decide."

He kissed her once, briefly but certain.

And then he was gone.

Malin called out sick from the clinic.

She didn't even leave a long message; she just tapped out the words quickly and sent the message before she could second-guess it. Guilt scratched at the back of her mind. They were already short-staffed. But the thought of stepping into that sterile, fluorescent-lit space, pretending to be fine, to be normal, made her stomach twist.

She couldn't do it today.

The house felt too quiet. Not peaceful, vacant. She moved on autopilot, making tea she didn't drink, tidying things that didn't need cleaning. Her fingers kept drifting to the inside of her arm,

the truth lived now.

The word lodged in her brain like a splinter:

Suppressor.

She didn't know how long she stood at the sink, hot water rushing over her hands. The light outside had shifted. Afternoon, maybe. Or nearly. Through the steam rising from the faucet, she caught her reflection in the kitchen window.

Pale. Eyes shadowed; lips parted. She looked like someone waking up from a long sleep and not liking what they found.

What else didn't I know? she thought

The question echoed inside her like a warning bell.

Her heart began to pound.

She dried her hands and grabbed her phone. Stared at the screen. Her thumb hovered, then moved.

It rang twice before he answered.

"Malin?" Her father's voice was warm, full of that usual casual concern. "Everything alright?"

Her father was head of one of the largest technology manufacturing companies in the city, Masoncore, he spent countless hours on work activities, but every time she called, he immediately answered, no matter what. He made time for her, checked in on her every other day, and made it a point to invite them over for dinner regularly. She knew that she could always count on him. This new information didn't seem logical.

She didn't answer right away. Her voice felt like it had to crawl up her throat.

"I need to talk to you," she said at last. "It's important."

She sat at the edge of the kitchen chair, the wood cold through her leggings.

"I found out about the suppressor," she said.

Silence.

Long enough that she pulled the phone away to check if the call had dropped.

It hadn't.

"Oh, Malin." His voice had changed, lower and slower. "I was hoping… we wouldn't ever have to talk about that."

"Why not?" Her grip on the phone tightened. "You implanted something in my body and never told me."

"It's not that simple," he said softly. "It goes back to before you were born. Our family, your mom's and mine, we've always had strong magic in our bloodlines. But after what happened to your aunt…"

"What happened?"

His breath caught. "She was taken," he said. "By the government. Media authorities. No trial, no charge. Just disappeared one day. Your mom never forgave herself for not stopping it."

Malin pressed a hand to her chest. Her heart was hammering again.

"So, you decided to do what? Hide me from myself?"

"We did what we thought was safest," he said. "We had the suppressor implanted shortly after you were born. It was the hardest decision we've ever made."

She stared at the scar again. It suddenly looked deeper. Angrier.

decide. Especially when I got pregnant with Ellie. I should've known."

There was another pause. A heavy one.

"Your mother made sure Ellie was chipped," he said quietly. "At birth."

Her vision blurred.

"What?"

"You were in recovery. She didn't want to frighten you. She just… we did what we thought was safest."

Malin shot up from her chair, the legs scraping sharply against the tile.

"You chipped my baby? Without my permission?"

"Malin…"

"She could've died. Do you have any idea what that means?"

"I do," he said. His voice broke slightly. "I've lived with that fear for years."

She pressed her palm flat to the table, grounding herself, trying not to scream.

"You both made decisions for us," she said. "Not with us. For us. You stole that choice."

"You don't understand," he murmured.

"I do understand," she snapped. "I'm a doctor. I've seen what suppressors do to people. What happens when they malfunction? When they fail. You didn't save me, you silenced me."

Silence stretched between them again.

174

treatments. Safer chips, ones that don't have the same issues. And support. I can schedule something at. We have people who…"

"No," she said quickly, her voice as hard as glass. "Not your company's doctors. I'll figure it out myself. I am a doctor."

He sounded small now. "I'm sorry. I really thought we were protecting you."

"I know you did," she whispered. "But you didn't protect me. You erased a piece of me."

There was nothing more to say. Not yet.

"I need time," she said, her voice trembling. "Please."

"I understand," he replied, barely above a whisper. "I love you, Malin."

She ended the call without answering. Not out of cruelty. Just survival.

The silence that followed was louder than anything else.

She set the phone down on the table like it was radioactive.

And then she just stood there, staring out the kitchen window again. Her reflection stared back: unblinking, uncertain, undone.

Malin gripped the cool edge of the counter, its solid presence the only anchor in a reality that wouldn't stop spinning. She stared into the sink, watching the water swirl down the drain: chaotic, endless, ungraspable. Her gaze drifted to the window, where the sun hung low on the horizon, casting long shadows across her familiar yard. Everything looked the same. And yet, nothing was.

Not with the weight of magic pressing in on her.

Not with the truth unraveling behind her ribs.

She didn't question it. Somehow, his presence didn't feel like an intrusion; it felt like reinforcement.

Ellie had curled up on the couch, watching her favorite show while Will helped Malin finish the meal. They moved around each other easily in the kitchen as if they'd been doing it for years. Her body knew how to lean into him now. Her mind hadn't caught up.

By the time they sat down to eat, the sun had dipped below the skyline, shadows stretching long across the kitchen tiles. The warmth of the moment settled around her, quiet, almost safe.

Then Ellie spoke.

"Do you think we'll ever leave Media?"

Malin froze mid-motion, the serving spoon paused above the mashed potatoes. The question hit like a static shock. Small. Quiet. But jarring.

She blinked at her daughter, unsure how to answer. Before yesterday, she wouldn't have considered it a real option. Leaving Media wasn't just taboo; it was dangerous. Suicidal, even.

But after today...

Malin sat slowly. "Where did that come from?"

Ellie twirled her fork through her peas. "One of the kids at school got taken today. I heard an older boy say he's getting chipped." Her voice dropped. "Some of the others say... he's not coming back."

Silence settled over the table.

Malin felt the air shift. The walls felt closer somehow.

to the center. For re-education."

Malin's stomach turned. She glanced at Will. His face was unreadable, but he gave a subtle nod. The story was true.

Ellie turned to him. "You've been outside Media, right? You could help us. We could stay together."

Malin swallowed hard.

"I talked to Grandpa earlier," she said carefully. "He said there's nothing to worry about. Nanna had you chipped at birth."

She hadn't expected the flood of relief that came with saying it. The knowledge that Ellie might be safe from detection had to mean something. One small mercy.

She pulled Ellie into a tight hug, pressing her cheek to the top of her head. Her daughter still smelled faintly of lavender shampoo and the outdoors, sun-warmed hair, dusty playground, and the faintest trace of crayons. Familiar. Innocent. Safe.

"You don't have anything to worry about," she murmured. "I'd want you to be happy and healthy no matter what. I'll protect you, no matter what that looks like."

Ellie looked up at her glassy eyes. "Well... I don't think what Nanna did worked."

She held up her arm.

And then it disappeared.

Gone. Like smoke. Like light passing through air.

Malin's breath caught. Her body went ice cold.

No...

"Ellie," she whispered.

gone anywhere. But it had. It had.

She looked at Will, trying to read his expression. He was calm. Too calm. An unsettling stillness in his eyes.

"How long have you been able to do that?" Malin asked, her voice barely there.

Ellie shrugged, suddenly shy. "A while. Nanna has been helping me learn how to control it."

Malin's knees gave out, the chair catching her just in time. Her knuckles whitened on the armrests. Her whole world shifted again, tilting.

Ellie looked nervous now. Scared.

Malin forced a breath. Then another. She reached for steadiness and found it in her voice. Barely.

"That's amazing," she said, forcing her lips into something close to a smile.

Will locked eyes with her, gentle but direct.

"You're not surprised," she said to him.

"I can sense gifts," he replied. "One of mine. It's probably what drew me to you. And to her."

Before Malin could respond, Ellie's eyes lit up, and a glass from the counter floated through the air and into Malin's hand.

Her mouth went dry.

She darted to the window, snapping the curtains shut.

Will cautioned with quiet urgency. "Ellie," he said gently, "you really should try not to use your powers like that here. Not inside the city limits. Strong gifts can be traced, and you have some of the strongest gifts I've ever seen."

questions crashing into her. Then, out of nowhere, an old memory surfaced. One she hadn't thought about in years.

Her mother. In the kitchen.

Stirring a pot without touching it. A spoon swirling on its own.

She'd thought it was a trick at the time. Her mother had smiled, said it was "just a little talent," and made her promise never to tell. She hadn't.

She remembered the flicker of fear in her mother's eyes when she said it.

They'd always kept the gifts hidden. It had been the rule. The only rule that mattered.

And now her daughter could vanish.

Malin stared at Ellie, then at Will. Everything inside her felt both hollow and full, fear and love, awe and dread crashing into each other.

The rest of dinner passed in a blur. The food tasted like paper. Her thoughts were static.

Later, Will washed the dishes while she helped Ellie with homework. Words moved across the page, but her mind wasn't really there.

When she tucked Ellie in, the weight of everything sat heavy on her chest.

"I don't want you to go away either," she whispered, brushing a strand of hair from Ellie's forehead. "I don't know how to leave Media, but... you're right. We may need to do something. And I think Will can help."

Ellie smiled, already drifting.

of her chest.

Magic. In her daughter. In her bloodline.

In her.

She turned out the light, heart aching with questions and no answers yet.

About an hour later, with the dishes done and the house still, Malin lay back on her bed, heart pounding against her ribs like it was trying to claw its way free.

Will lay beside her, solid and warm, his presence a strange mix of comfort and electricity. She curled into him, resting her head on his shoulder, one hand pressed lightly to his chest. The air between them buzzed with something unspoken. Not fear. Not entirely. Something closer to inevitability.

She had spent the entire day thinking through this decision, turning it over and over in her mind like a scalpel under light. The risks. The unknowns. The part of her that had been trained since childhood to fear magic, to avoid it, to report it. That voice still whispered to her from somewhere deep and old, tucked behind her ribs like a memory passed down in blood.

But it couldn't outweigh what she knew.

Ellie had magic. That was a fact. And if she stayed in Media, she'd be hunted. That was a fact too.

Malin had spent years treating chipped patients, men and women who came in broken in ways no scan could explain. Anxiety. Depression. Disassociation. The look in their eyes complaining, *"It's like something's missing. Like I'm not me anymore."* She'd seen the charts. She'd seen the suicide rates.

And now she knew why.

version of herself edited by someone else's fear. But taking it out… that meant owning the unknown. It meant facing whatever was waiting inside her.

"I need to do this," she said finally, voice barely above a whisper. "For Ellie. For me."

Will shifted beside her, his fingers ghosting along her arm until they found the faint scar near her elbow, the place where everything had been hidden from her. Where everything had been stolen.

His touch stilled there, gentle. "Are you sure?" he asked again, soft but weighted.

She nodded; her throat tight. "Yes," she said. "I'm ready."

"There are risks to removing the chip," he murmured, eyes locked on hers. "Real ones and I can't promise it'll go the way you want. I can't even promise it'll go safely."

"I know," she said.

"And if it doesn't, if the process overwhelms you…"

Malin cut him off gently. "You'll protect Ellie."

Will swallowed, his voice cracking. "With my life."

She nodded. "Then I'm ready. When I've seen it in the past, there were always 2 people performing the procedure. Once the chip is lifted out, someone needs to cut the ties to the body."

He hesitated one last time. "I know. I've done this a time or two. You're trusting me with something irreversible."

"I already have," she said.

sharp blade gleamed in the lamplight. She didn't ask how he knew what to do, just closed her eyes and focused on breathing. On not shaking. On staying still.

She was a doctor. She'd cut into flesh hundreds, if not thousands of times. She knew anatomy. But this wasn't another body on the table. This was hers.

When the knife touched her skin, cold and precise, her body jerked reflexively. She gritted her teeth and held herself still. The numbing agent dulled the sharp edge, but it couldn't dull the idea of it, what it meant to be opened.

Will worked quickly, hands steady but his voice soft.

"It's hooked into your nerve matrix. Just breathe."

Pain flared, hot, deep, ripping along her arm like fire chasing bone. Malin bit down a cry, her jaw aching from the tension. Her vision blurred as Will used tweezers to work the suppressor free.

Then, something changed.

The pain didn't fade, it exploded outward. Replaced by something deeper. Larger.

Pressure bloomed in her chest, thick and unfamiliar, like something ancient unfolding inside her. Her spine arched. Her fingers clenched the sheets. Her mouth opened, but no sound came.

Then...

Light.

Not light from the lamp. Not anything in this world. A glow surged behind her eyelids, through her skin, pulsing like a second heartbeat. She gasped, eyes flying open...

Everything was too bright. Not blinding, but alive. Radiant shapes spun in the air around her, colors she didn't have names for. Power raced through her veins, singing through her blood like liquid flame.

She turned her head.

Will was there but changed. Or maybe she could finally see what had always been. Threads of magic shimmered around him, golden and violet, wrapping gently through the air between them. She could feel her threads tied to his.

"Malin?" His voice sounded far away. Muffled. Like underwater.

She reached for him, their fingers brushing, and sparks leapt between them, dancing across her skin in tingling bursts of energy.

"I can feel everything," she whispered, tears slipping down her cheeks. "It's… incredible."

The world was alive. Breathing. She could sense the hum of power in the walls, in the floor beneath her, in the roots of the trees outside. The magic curled around her like recognition, like welcome.

And then, all at once, it became too much.

Voices pressed in, layers of thought not her own. Her pulse roared in her ears. Her body trembled with the weight of it. Every sense overloaded.

Her vision fragmented.

Light. Sound. Pressure. Power.

Then darkness.

ill caught Malin just as her body went slack, the blade slipping in his grip. It sliced across his forearm, hot and sharp, but he barely registered it.

She sagged against him, weightless and too warm. He lowered her gently onto the bed, careful not to jostle her body, careful not to panic.

The sting of the cut flared again. He pressed the heel of his hand against it to slow the bleeding, but his gaze never left her.

Her breathing was shallow, rhythmic, but every second felt like an eternity.

The air in the room had shifted. Denser. Electric. He could taste it, like ozone and iron. Magic was blooming beneath her skin, thick and pulsing, the pressure building in waves that made the hairs on his arms rise. The glow began at her fingertips, a faint iridescence tracing the veins beneath her skin like bioluminescent ink. It shimmered in bursts, like something inside her was knocking. They painted the air like ribbons.

Will's chest tightened. He had seen this before, but never like this.

Magic didn't just *wake up;* it fought for space. And Malin's body wasn't just waking. It was *calling* out to the magic in the world and offering it a home. Standing next to the bed, he laid his hand as close to her as he dared.

He stood back from the bed, his pulse hammering in his ears. He didn't move. He couldn't. He was afraid even a breath might shatter the fragile tether holding her here.

steady pulse of her skin. Each flicker of light threw shifting shadows across the walls, elongating, warping. It looked like the room itself was holding its breath.

She twitched once. A jolt through her shoulder. Then stillness again.

His own breath hitched.

Will had always prided himself on his calm. On control. Years of conditioning, of watching transformations like this unfold with detachment, like a sniper holding his breath just before the trigger.

But now?

His palms were slick. His throat was dry. The smell of sweat and blood hung faintly in the air, sharp as the blade that had triggered this change.

He reached out, fingers hovering just above her arm. The skin was hot beneath the glow, her pulse fluttering rapidly beneath it. He could feel the energy radiating from her, wild and uncontained. His shirt suddenly caught fire. He quickly smacked it out, garnering slight burn marks on his skin, but it became extinguished just as quickly as it started.

Gods, please.

He didn't even know which one he was talking to. He'd seen too many in too many places as he traveled, so he decided to prayed to them all.

Maybe one would heed his call. Media had banished all religions, as they seemed too much like magic. He'd given up on faith long ago, and still... he prayed.

She was beautiful. Even now, in the middle of all this chaos. Her hair spread across the pillow like a halo. Her lips parted slightly.

And still she fought.

Fought for control. Fought to survive.

Will's hands curled into fists at his sides.

He had no idea what she'd unlocked. This wasn't standard. He had never seen a reaction to this level, and he had sat through hundreds of these. His only guesses were that her bloodline had to be stronger than anyone guessed; that the suppressor hadn't just dulled her gift, it had *caged* it. Now the bars were gone, was it calling in reinforcements.

The magic didn't trickle in, it **poured**.

It was pooling in her chest, lighting veins like lightning bolts across her skin. Each pulse of power ran through her like a live wire. He could almost hear it, a low-frequency hum beneath the silence. Her body arched over and over again, muscles tensing against an unseen current, her breath catching like she'd forgotten how to inhale.

He wanted to touch her. Anchor her. But he didn't dare. He had heard all the warnings about how touching someone going through the change could affect the transformation.

The wound from the blade on his arm reminded him of reality. The bandage was soaked through now, sticky and warm. He didn't care. His eyes were locked on her, looking for any signs of movement.

"I'm here," he whispered. His voice cracked. "Please…"

The room trembled with tension.

He didn't realize he'd been holding his breath until her fingers twitched, just once.

Then again.

Will's knees nearly gave out.

"Malin," he breathed, falling to his knees beside her. His hand found hers, still too warm, still glowing faintly. But alive. **Present.**

"I can't lose you," he whispered, forehead to her hand, voice barely holding.

"I stopped believing I'd ever find someone like you. Stopped thinking I could deserve it. But now that I have…"

His voice broke. "I still don't think I'm enough. But a world without you in it?"

He paused, the thought cutting too deep to finish. He shook his head. "I don't know how to go back."

Will noticed that the glow on her skin began to fade, but something else remained. "Runes," he muttered. It was half curse, half prayer.

The markings on her skin were delicate, almost ghostly, etched along her arms like silver threads pulled from some ancient loom. Not ink. Not scars. Not anything he'd seen before. They shimmered faintly, alive with a pulse that wasn't hers alone.

It was like the power inside her had risen to the surface, carving itself into shapes, a language older than words. Living runes.

Will swallowed hard. He'd seen a lot of magic in all its violent, beautiful forms, but never this. Not in himself and not in anyone else.

As the last of the glow ebbed from her skin, Will felt the shift, the magic settling, the transformation nearing its end. He hesitated, then made his choice.

Warm and Solid.

Alive.

She was here and it looked like she might have passed the climax of the transformation.

He could feel the energy pulsing from her. He could feel it reaching out to him and something within him reach right back.

"Malin..." he whispered, the sound raw in his throat.

She didn't stir.

Panic clawed at the edges of his control, but he forced himself to breathe, to stay grounded, for her.

Whatever this was... it wasn't normal. He'd never seen anything like it. Not in himself. Not in anyone. And that made it worse.

"You're not just powerful," he murmured, voice catching. "You're changing."

His gaze returned to her face, still, peaceful, too still. He didn't care what the markings meant. Not yet.

He just needed her to open her eyes.

Holding her hand, as if it was his lifeline, he sat and waited.

"I love you," he said. He hadn't meant to say it, much less out loud. Not yet. At least he was thankful she couldn't have heard. They spilled out, unshaped, unasked for, raw and real.

The air in the room finally shifted. Lighter. Like something had passed.

He didn't move.

He just held her hand and watched her breathe.

Will shook himself awake when he realized he had fallen asleep with her hand in his, on the edge of Malin's bed. Her fingers began to twitch, the glow had all but faded, and her breathing was soft and even. He concentrated on watching the rise and fall of her chest, as it steadied something in him.

She was still here.

He let the truth settle in his bones, just long enough for the storm inside him to ease. Then the shift came, automatic and relentless. His thoughts locked into motion, clicking through contingencies like weapons laid out on a table. Whatever came next, he would be ready. The risk of staying within the city limits was too high. Ellie and Malin couldn't afford that exposure, not now. Not ever.

They had to leave. That much was clear.

The only thing left was figuring out how.

Option one.

Let someone else in the rebellion take over. Walk away. Cut ties before they tighten even more.

He dismissed it before the thought had fully taken shape. He couldn't do it. He couldn't leave Malin or Ellie in anyone else's hands, not even the rebellion's. They weren't assets. They were his. And that truth settled in his gut with a weight he didn't try to deny.

Option two.

Stay hidden. Blend in. Disappear in plain sight until they were strong enough to protect themselves.

worked, if Media weren't a steel trap wrapped in glass. Reflective. Inescapable. All it would take was one miss step. One wrong breath. If they were flagged... re-chipping, re-education – if they lived, he'd seen what that did to people. And Malin? She might not survive it. Not with what was inside her now.

Neither would Ellie.

Option three.

Escape. Fast. Quiet. Before the city even noticed she'd changed.

He could see it. A break in the western wall. A deal with the right handler. A mentor waiting on the outside who owed him too many favors to say no. It was possible. Risky, but real. And the farther they got from Media, the less likely Ellie would be tracked.

He could take them to the border. Drop them off. Vanish.

But the thought of letting go of Malin's hand, now that he knew what it felt like, made something in his chest twist sharp.

And then there was the fourth path.

The one he'd tried not to consider.

Aloria.

It wasn't just a myth, or a rebel fantasy. It was real. He'd been there. The difference in the air felt, how magic thrived in the soil, the sky, the blood. They could start over there. Safely. Together.

If he stayed.

If he didn't disappear.

damp hair filled with sweat. Even now, the faintest shimmer of runes traced across her skin like ancient promises.

He brushed his thumb along the back of her hand, careful not to wake her.

Every hour he spent with them made leaving harder.

He thought he'd buried that part of himself, the part that craved connection. That believed in a life outside missions, outside loss. He'd done it once, long ago, and the price had been unforgivable.

He'd told himself that kind of love wasn't worth the risk. But Malin had made him question that with a glance. Ellie had made him question it with a laugh.

And now, he couldn't imagine a future without them in it.

He squeezed her hand gently, only this time... she squeezed back. That was what he was waiting for. That was the sign that told him that she would come out of this, and she was safe.

"We have to leave," he whispered, barely audible. "Soon."

Because the choice had already been made.

Will had chosen her.

Malin's eyelids fluttered, the faintest twitch of lashes catching the low light. Will leaned in, every muscle poised, every breath held. The stillness around them buzzed with energy. It wasn't the ambient kind, but hers: raw, volatile, alive.

She was awake.

"Easy," he murmured, his voice a low thread, meant only for her. The air still hummed with the residue of her transformation, but it was her face, those delicate features knit with confusion and effort, that anchored him now. He moved as close as he could to her, touching, caressing, and checking that this was real.

"Welcome back." The words came softer than breath.

He picked up the water glass and touched it gently to her lips, watching as she stirred, her brow furrowed. She drank a little, then blinked up at him like she was surfacing from somewhere deep.

Her eyes darted, unfocused. Slowly, as if pushing through water, her hands rose. Fingers trembled, then sparked. Flickering arcs of light jumped between them, erratic and electric, painting the room in flashes of fractured color.

Not just magic. Wild magic. Untamed, untrained, answering only to instinct. He had never actually witnessed it.

The aurora of power danced through her, painting streaks of green and violet and molten gold across the ceiling and down his arms as he reached for her. It was beautiful, and deeply dangerous.

"What's happening to me? I feel like I got hit by a train," Her voice cracked on the edge of panic.

"Your body and mind are meeting your powers," He said it as gently as he could, but the truth carried weight.

He knelt beside her bed, his body already angled to shield, to ground. "Breathe with me," he said, catching her hand, warm, buzzing with kinetic force.

The moment they touched, another cascade of light pulsed from her palm. His skin tingled. But he didn't let go.

"Focus on something real," he said softly. "Your breath. Mine. This room. You're here. You're safe."

Her chest rose. Fell. Again. He matched her rhythm, slow and steady.

The flares at her fingertips dulled into a soft glow. No longer lashing out, just… there. A quiet pulse. Like a second heartbeat beneath her skin.

"You're doing beautifully, Malin." His thumb brushed over her knuckles. "You're not lost in it. You're in control."

Her eyes met his, storm blue, fractured with light. The fear hadn't left, but something else had joined it. Trust.

Around them, the air still shimmered faintly. A current passed between them he couldn't name, only feel. It coiled through his

thread pulled tight.

In that moment, the world outside their walls, Media, with its cameras and concrete and quiet threats, ceased to exist.

There was only her.

Moonlight sliced through the blinds, casting a lattice of shadow across the bed. The room had gone quiet again. Malin's glow faded, her energy spent, her body slack with exhaustion. But Will's attention never wavered.

Will's heart had slowed from a gallop to a wary trot, but his body still pulsed with tension. The kind that settled behind the sternum, right where instinct made its home.

Run.

Protect.

Strike.

Not from her. For her.

He sat still, legs aching from hours in the same position, the weight of everything they'd just done pressing into his spine. The room was quiet now, but not peaceful. It was the silence that followed a storm, charged, humming, waiting for the next blow.

He'd thought the transformation would be the worst of it.

It wasn't. It was this.

The after.

The waiting.

The knowing.

lightning strike. He could feel it crackling faintly against his skin, the hairs on his forearms still raised. The air smelled scorched, like copper, ozone, and beneath that a distinct waft of sweat combined with lavender, distinctly her.

Malin slept beside him, the soft drag of her breath the only sound breaking the stillness.

She was alive.

But rest wouldn't be enough.

Magic that strong didn't just wake up quietly. It announced itself. And someone would have felt it, the flare of power, the rebirth, the ripple through the threads that tied gifted people together like spider silk.

Her gaze wandered down to her arm, blinking slowly at the faint glow of symbols that had begun to shimmer along her skin, thin lines etched like delicate filigree, pulsing softly in the low light.

She lifted her wrist slightly, eyes narrowing.

"I got tattoos in my sleep?" she rasped, her voice dry, the faintest smirk tugging at her lips. "That's... new."

Will exhaled a half-laugh, tension breaking just enough to let him smile. "Better than a hangover and a bad haircut."

"Debatable," she murmured, letting her hand fall back to the bed, but the humor flickered warmly in her eyes. "Did you know I would get them?"

"No. As usual, you are unique. This is the first time I had ever heard of someone getting tattoos because of a transformation," he clarified.

Some might not know what they'd felt yet. But soon, they would.

flushed from strain, but calm now. There was still a faint warmth to her skin, like a low-burning coal under ash. He didn't know what that meant. But he knew what it cost.

She closed her eyes, but he could tell she was heading to improvement.

The clock was already ticking.

The city would notice.

And when they came, they wouldn't come to talk.

He exhaled slowly through his nose. The air tasted like dust and old metal. His throat was raw, dry. But his mind was clear.

He bent toward her, voice just above breath. "We must leave this place, and soon."

Her lashes fluttered open. A slight shift of breath, acknowledging that she heard him.

"We need to be gone today," he added, watching her blink herself awake.

Her gaze searched the room, then settled on him, unfocused, drowsy, trying to catch up. He brushed the damp hair from her temple. Her skin was still too warm.

"Your rebirth…" He hesitated. The words felt too clinical. "It was stronger than I expected. Someone felt that. They might not know where, but they'll be looking."

Her brow furrowed. "That wasn't… normal?"

He almost smiled. It was so her, asking the question like a doctor reviewing a case file.

gently. "You and Ellie… I've never seen anything like you."

Pride flickered in his chest, unexpected and full. It ached, the way love often did when it came too fast.

"I want to see what you can do." He let the words land softly, then added: "But not here. Not yet."

The room dimmed around them, moonlight glinting off the edge of the window, tracing pale lines across her sheets. The heat of her transformation had finally bled away, leaving behind only sweat-damp linens and a faint prismatic shimmer clinging to her skin like dew.

He stood, stiff joints, and crossed the room in a few quiet strides.

"How quickly can you be ready?" His voice was steel now, low and sure. "I can get you both out of Media. I have contacts. Routes. We'll be gone before they know where to look."

She rubbed her temples. Still too pale. Her voice was soft.

"I have patients… Ellie has school…"

Will crouched, his knees creaking against the wood floor, and laid a hand on her leg, steady.

"Not anymore," he said gently. "Unless you're willing to risk being found. Risk them finding you, taking her…"

Her face changed then, understanding dawning like a slow sun behind storm clouds.

"Oh."

He nodded. "I want to take you to Aloria. We will be safe there."

eyes widened slightly.

He stood and moved to the closet, crouching low to pull out a large backpack from the top of a closet, dusty but strong. He tested the straps automatically, fingers moving by rote. Always prepping. Always planning.

"Sleep," he said, turning back. "I'll take care of everything. Ellie's bag. Your med kit. Rations. Trade goods. We'll need coin. Warm clothes. I'll handle it."

She nodded once, her body already giving in to exhaustion. He watched her eyes fall shut again. Her breathing evened out.

He reveled at the knowledge that she was here. Still alive. Still here.

He turned to the window and stared at the city's lights, glittering like cold stars in the dark.

"Aloria," he said aloud, letting the name roll off his tongue like a vow.

It wasn't just safety. It was a second chance.

A life where Ellie could be free. Where Malin could be powerful without hiding. Where maybe... maybe, he could finally stop running.

But as he stood there, packing their escape into a single, quiet promise, he knew one thing with unsettling certainty.

The longer he stayed near them, the deeper they got under his skin.

And for once, he didn't want to cut them out.

arm sunlight spilled across her blanket, but it didn't feel like any other morning. Something had shifted. Even in sleep, her heart seemed to know. Fingers, careful but insistent. A voice, low and familiar, but not one she expected to hear.

"Ellie?" She heard Will's whisper like a thread pulled tight. "Ellie, I need your help to find some things."

She blinked her eyes open, sticky with sleep. Will stood over her, backlit by the pale morning light leaking through her curtains. His hair was messy, his face tight, not with anger, but something else. Worry?

Still fuzzy with sleep, she mumbled, "Is it time to get ready for school?" Her voice came out dry and small, like it hadn't caught up to the rest of her yet.

She looked around her room. Everything looked like it was the same: her blanket, the soft pile of clothes on her chair, the morning light creeping across the rug. But Will was here. In her room. Why?

"Ellie, I know this is a lot to take in, but I trust you'll understand how important this is," Will said. His tone wasn't sharp or loud, but serious in a way that made her sit up straighter.

She blinked a few times and gave him a sleepy nod.

"Remember how you were showing your powers last night?" he continued. "Well, things have changed. Your mom and I decided we need to leave the city. Today."

sleep-hazy brain, but the idea of it stirred something in her chest. Leaving. Adventure. Her heart gave a small flip. "We can go to that place you told me about?" she yawned, the excitement starting to win over her tiredness.

"Yes, honey. But first, you need to get dressed and pack this backpack. Clothes and just a few important things. I'll have breakfast ready by the time you're done."

His voice didn't sound like a teacher's voice. It sounded like Mom's voice in the mornings when something really mattered.

She rubbed her eyes again. Was this a dream?

Maybe not.

With a sigh, she sat up and padded to the bathroom down the hall. The cold floor stung her feet just enough to convince her this was real. She didn't totally understand what was going on, but her teachers always said that when a grown-up tells you to do something important, you do it.

She heard Will in the kitchen opening cabinets. She wondered where Mom was. *Why didn't she hear her too?*

Ellie opened her dresser drawer and ran her fingers across the tops of her shirts. The soft cotton felt cool under her fingertips. She picked her favorite one first, the striped one, bright and cheerful, like a popsicle, and then the one with little flowers stitched along the hem, the petals slightly frayed at the edges. That one made her feel fancy.

She folded them carefully, the way her mom liked. One edge, then the other. Tuck. Smooth. Into the backpack they went. But

low in her stomach. Something about it felt... final.

She turned to her desk, grabbing her sketchbook. Its cover was soft and bent in the corners, smudged with graphite fingerprints. She ran her thumb across the edge before slipping it in beside her clothes. The tin of colored pencils came next, the lid loose, the colors worn down and stubby from so many afternoons drawing in her room. She set them in with the same care she'd use to carry glass.

Then her doll, Beatrice. A squishy, lopsided thing with one button eye slightly bigger than the other. Mom had fixed her so many times. Ellie pressed her nose to its yarn hair. It still smelled like bedtime, blankets and dreams and the vanilla lotion Mom used. She nestled it on top, patting its soft belly. "You're coming too."

Now for shoes.

Her favorite sneakers, easy. Scuffed from the playground, paint-splattered from that one art day at school. They slid right in. Then her sandals, still dusty from the park. But the boots... her boots were bigger. Stiff. They made her feel strong on rainy days.

She tried turning them sideways. Pushed. Wiggled. Sat on the bag. It wouldn't close.

"Will?" she called, her voice catching. "What if they don't fit?"

From the kitchen, his voice floated back, warm but firm. "Then they'll need to be left behind, kiddo. Just the essentials."

Ellie stared down at the boots. She'd had them forever. They were part of her.

Her throat tightened. Slowly, she pulled them out. The backpack zipped with a loud scratch. The sound was sharp in the quiet

floor, like they were waiting to be picked anyway.

But they wouldn't be.

She hugged her backpack close to her and stood. It felt heavier than it should, like she'd packed memories, not clothes.

Gripping the straps of her backpack, Ellie stepped into the living room, then into the kitchen where a plate was waiting for her. There were pancakes, warm and fluffy, with steam curling into the morning air. She slid into the chair and took a bite. Maple syrup. Just the right amount. Somehow, Will had known.

She watched him move around the kitchen, back and forth like he was chasing thoughts he couldn't catch. He smiled when he saw her looking. That smile made her feel steadier. Safer.

Her mom had told her once that her dad had died before she was born. Sometimes she imagined what having a dad would've felt like. Not someone loud or strict, just someone kind. Someone, who smiled and did things to make her happy. Someone with a smile like Will's.

But something about him seemed off this morning. His movements were sharp around the edges. His forehead kept wrinkling when he thought she wasn't looking.

Where's Mom?

The thought made her glance to the hallway. Her stomach gave a little twist. "Where is Mom?" she asked, trying to keep her voice calm, even though her chest felt tight. Mom was always up before her. Always. Even when she was sick.

"She's in bed," Will said, pausing mid-step. He turned toward her, his face softening. "Can you come sit for a second? There's something really important I want to talk to you about."

Ellie slid off the chair and padded to the couch, sitting down beside him. Her heartbeat faster.

"Why is she still sleeping?" she asked quickly. "Doesn't she need to get ready too? She's coming, right?" Panic crawled up the back of her throat. The idea of leaving without Mom was unthinkable.

"We'll get her up soon," Will said gently. "She's definitely coming with us."

Relief swept over Ellie so fast she nearly sagged into the cushions.

"How do we get there, then? Do we take a car? Or a train?" She pictured the place he'd told her about, Aloria, wasn't it? All shining towers and green trees.

Will sighed, his shoulders dropping like he'd been carrying something heavy for a long time. "No, Ellie. We won't be taking a car or a train."

He paused. His mouth moved like he was looking for the right words.

"Last night," he said finally, "your mom and I made a big decision. We removed something from her arm, a magic suppressor chip. It was stopping her from reaching her powers."

Ellie blinked, letting the words settle. A strange mix of shock and hope bloomed in her chest. "Mom has magic too?"

"She does," Will said, his smile returning, this time softer. Like he was happy, too. "Just like you."

Ellie's excitement surged. She wanted to run down the hallway and throw open the door. But before she could move, Will stopped her.

"She's resting right now. The process took a lot out of her."

okay? I mean... how did you do it? Taking the chip out?"

"It wasn't easy," he admitted. "But she's strong. Stronger than anyone I've ever known. She's okay now. I promise."

Ellie nodded slowly. Her head was full of questions, but one rose above the rest.

"You're telling me the truth?"

Will looked her right in the eyes. "Always."

Then he hesitated, his expression shifting just a little. "Since we're sharing... maybe I should show you something too."

Will held out his hand, his brows knitting in concentration. For a second, nothing happened, then the small paperclip on the coffee table trembled, lifted, and hovered in the air like it was caught in a secret breeze.

Ellie gasped. Not loudly, more like her breath got lost in her throat.

"My telekinesis isn't nearly as strong as yours," Will said, still focused, "but I can see wavelengths. Like heat ripples, or sound shadows. I can sense magic in others."

Ellie's eyes darted from the floating clip to Will's face. Something in her chest felt lighter. Brighter. "You have magic too?" she whispered.

"Yep," Will chuckled, lowering the paperclip gently back onto the table. "We all have our gifts, Ellie. Yours are just... a bit more spectacular." He smiled, softer now. "I think your mom might have some like yours."

stay still. Magic wasn't just hers anymore. It was something she shared. With her mom. With Will.

For a second, the room didn't feel like the apartment she'd always known. It felt like part of something bigger, something secret and glowing just beneath the surface of the world.

"So, what happens next?" she asked, her voice quiet but sure.

"We wait for your mom to wake up," Will said. "Then we leave. All together. It's going to be a big adventure."

He reached for her hand and squeezed it. Not hard. Just enough that she knew it was real.

Ellie nodded. Her heart was still thudding with worry for her mom, but the glow inside her refused to dim. Everything was different now. She was different. And maybe that was okay.

Will stood and moved toward the counter. "Ellie, can you do something for me? We'll need snacks for the trip. Think you can pack us some?" His voice had that teacher-tone again, gentle but serious. "And while you're at it, can you tell me where your mom keeps the medical kit?"

"Mom keeps it in her room," Ellie replied, shifting into her focused voice. "By her dresser. In the black bag." She stood straighter, like a helper now instead of just a kid. "I'll pack the snacks."

As Will disappeared down the hallway, Ellie turned to the pantry. She opened it slowly, blinking at the rows of familiar boxes and jars. Her hands found the chocolate-covered almonds and the bag of dried mango slices, Mom's favorites. She added a sleeve of crackers, a half-full container of trail mix, and a roll of hard candies, stuffing them into one of the sealable bags.

Her fingers shook a little. She clenched her jaw to steady them.

Will set the medical kit on the counter. "Ellie? Do you know where the matches or lighter are?"

She paused, tapping her chin. "Utility drawer, I think. I'll go get them."

The floor felt cold under her feet as she crossed the room and came back with the box, holding it out carefully.

And then it happened.

A sound, soft and strange, cut through the quiet like a ripple through water. A moan. From the bedroom.

Ellie froze; her hand still outstretched with the matches.

Will turned toward the noise at the same time she did, both caught in the stillness.

"Mom's Awake?" Ellie said excitedly; running down the hallway.

cacophony of voices, a swirling sea of sound, flooded Malin's mind. Her body ached with a deep, consuming pain like she'd been hit by a truck. She couldn't tell if the voices were speaking or singing. The language was unfamiliar, but the cadence was... ancient. As she tried to lift her head, the room spun wildly, a carousel of distorted shapes and colors.

The ceiling twisted above her, then crashed back down, too close. Her awareness flickered like a faulty lightbulb. She felt herself slipping, pulled out of the present by waves of pain and confusion. The voices rose and fell, haunting and rhythmic, pulsing with the beat of her heart. She drowned in sound, memory, and something too vast to name.

A small, choked breath escaped her lips, and the world went black.

When she opened her eyes, Ellie stood in the doorway, clutching the frame with small, steady hands. Behind her was **Will**, eyes wide, the kind of joy on his face that stole Malin's breath.

She blinked. A lazy smile tugged at her lips, unbidden. "Hey there. My two favorite people," she murmured, voice scratchy. "Why are you both looking at me like I just came back from the dead?"

"Mom!" Ellie's voice was electric. "You have powers now? Like me?"

Malin pushed herself upright slowly, wincing. "I... I guess I do. But there are all these voices in my head, and I can't make them stop."

"They're just getting to know you. You have to learn how to talk to them."

Will stepped closer, his tone light but grounding. "Ellie, since your mom's awake, maybe we should let her move around a bit, huh? We've got a lot to do."

Ellie gave her a fierce hug. Malin's arms wrapped around her daughter in return, and something flickered beneath her skin. Not just warmth. Recognition. A spark of something ancient, familiar. Magic, maybe. Shared. Alive.

Ellie bounced off. "I'll get you coffee!"

When she was gone, Will stepped in, arms wrapping around Malin before she could even stand. He pulled her close, firm, steady, as if reassuring himself that she was real. There was a tremor in his voice.

"I really thought I was gonna lose you." A beat passed. "What do you remember?"

"Not much," she admitted. "Bright light. Pain. Then... nothing."

Will nodded, gently pulling back. "It was a long night. But you're safe now. That's all that matters."

Ellie reappeared with a half-full mug of coffee, practically vibrating with excitement. "We're going on a trip!" she announced, pointing to the bags by the door. "Will told me this morning. I'm so excited!"

Malin blinked, heart skipping. "The magic," she whispered, memory threading back through her like a seam. "Yes... I remember now."

Ellie edged closer, hopeful. "Do you feel different? Like something inside you... whispering?"

what they're saying."

"That's the magic!" Ellie beamed. "You have to really listen. Not with your ears, with your whole self. Like... when music moves through you, but you don't know the words yet."

Malin closed her eyes.

Silence stretched. The city outside fell away. Her breathing slowed. And there it was, a hum, just beneath her skin, soft and wild and waiting.

When she opened her eyes, they shimmered, not with power, but with wonder.

"It's beautiful," she whispered. "I can hear it. Like a song. Does it always sound like this?"

She didn't expect an answer. The sounds in her head had grown louder. The voices were overlapping in a symphony of ancient languages, layered and alive. It wasn't painful exactly, but it wasn't peaceful either. It was awakening.

And it was only just beginning.

Just then, Will shifted, drawing Malin's eye to the white bandage wrapped around his forearm. Concern flickered in her chest.

"Will... your arm?"

"It's nothing," he said quickly. "Just a scratch from last night." But the wince that followed said otherwise.

Before she could think better of it, Malin reached out. Her fingers brushed the bandage, then pressed gently.

A warmth bloomed beneath her skin. Soft. Golden. Real.

Light unfurled from her palm, delicate and radiant, spilling over the cloth like the slow spread of dawn. Ellie's breath caught

due to astonishment, partly something deeper. When she finally pulled her hand back, Will slowly peeled the bandage away.

No blood. No wounds. Not even a scar.

Will met her gaze, stunned. "Well. Maybe we don't need that medical kit after all."

Malin blinked, caught somewhere between disbelief and amusement. "All those years of medical school," she teased, a smile tugging at her lips.

But as she looked down at her hands, the humor faded. "How... is that possible?"

"It's who you are now," Ellie chimed, gently taking her hand. "You're like me, Mom. We're the same."

Malin's throat tightened. "How did you get so smart?"

Ellie beamed, practically bouncing. "Nanna helps me. Even from far away. She says she has to stay hidden, so no one suspects."

Malin's brows pulled together. "Nanna? My mother?"

Ellie nodded. "She talks to me in my head. Like the voices you hear, but quieter."

Malin's heart thudded. That couldn't be true. Her father had told her... had insisted... that Nanna didn't know. That she had suppressed Ellie's magic after she was born, just in case.

But that clearly hadn't happened.

So, what else had he lied about?

She barely noticed Will's voice at first, the words registering a beat too late. "Ellie, go finish the snacks," he was saying. "I need a moment with your mom."

questions unraveling fast.

She looked at Will. "I need to talk to my mother. Not over the phone. In person."

Will's expression sobered. "Malin… your parents live in the Galvin District. That's toward danger, not away from it."

"I know," she said, folding her arms. "But I have to. If she's been speaking to Ellie, if she's known this whole time…"

Will hesitated, then nodded slowly. "I can angle us in that direction. If you can convince her to meet us closer, maybe near Talvi, I know someone who can get us through the barrier. Quietly."

She nodded, already calculating. "I'll try."

He gave her a look that was almost apologetic. "Go take a shower. It might be the last hot one you get for a while."

Then he was gone, already moving on to the next task.

Malin stood in the quiet room, the silence settling like dust around her. She didn't feel different, but she knew she wasn't alone in her body anymore. Something lived there now, quietly humming beneath her skin.

She reached for the bedside candle, her fingers brushing over the matchbox, then paused, surprised to find a flicker of heat roll down her finger like a spark. She giggled like a little girl when the flame popped out of the tip of her finger.

Her eyes drifted to the half-packed bag Will had left out for her. She flipped it open, checking for what he might've forgotten. Her hand brushed silk. She lifted the fabric, Lira's ridiculous gag gift from her last birthday.

A negligee.

She smiled to herself and tucked it back in the bag. She'd ask him about it later. She headed for the shower, disrobing after turning on the water.

A pressure stirred behind Malin's eyes, a strange warmth blooming at the back of her skull. Then, like a breath against her cheek that wasn't really there, she heard a voice. Not aloud. Not in the room. But *in her head.*

"Malin. It's me. Your mother."

Her breath caught. A chill prickled up her arms. She looked around the room, heart thudding, but nothing had changed.

Mom? she thought, unsure if it would reach.

"Yes. Just think your thoughts. I can hear you. It's part of my gift," her mother's voice answered, soft and matter-of-fact, as if this were the most normal conversation in the world.

Malin's skin flushed hot, then cold. She quickly grabbed a towel and wrapped it around her, suddenly feeling too exposed. *What's going on? Why didn't you ever tell me?*

There was a pause, and then, gently: "I wanted to. So many times. But your father, his work, his loyalties, I couldn't risk it. He was always watching, always asking questions. I didn't know where you stood, you have always been so close with him."

You thought I'd turn you in? To Dad? The thought did not make sense. Her chest ached, raw with disbelief.

"I didn't know what you'd believe. You were so close to him. I had to protect you both in my own way."

Malin leaned against the vanity. The cool air brushed against her bare legs. She clutched the towel tighter around her, her fingers vibrating.

There have been some changes around here. I met someone, she thought, slowly, choosing each word. *His name's Will. He's helping us leave the city. We're leaving today. You'd probably like him. He... he has powers too.*

There was a beat of silence before her mother answered.

"You waking up from your powers does accelerate plans. Understand. I'd like to help. I'm needed here, or I'd go with you, but maybe we can meet on the way. I had already started making some plans to get Ellie and I out, and likely trying to convince you to go with us, but this adjusts those plans."

Malin blinked hard. The air felt heavier now, like the pressure before a thunderstorm. *Preparing? For what?* The weight of it all was crashing down on her: secrets, years of silence, and now this voice in her mind like a ghost she didn't ask for.

Why isn't Dad included in anything? How come he thought Ellie was chipped? You have powers. Other than us, what do you have keeping yourself here?

"Rude," her mother quipped dryly. "Just because I'm older doesn't mean I'm helpless."

Malin's eyes narrowed, jaw clenched.

"I'm part of the resistance. I've been helping people like you and Ellie escape. Underground routes, safe houses. I've kept my distance for years, but I've been watching. Helping. Ellie's power is growing, and she needed guidance. I couldn't sit back any longer."

Ellie? The word burst from her chest like a kicked door. *You've been training her? Without telling me? You planned for her to leave... possibly without me?*

come with us. But I couldn't count on it. I had to make sure she survived. There wasn't time to wait for you to be ready."

Malin winced, a sharp pulse spiking behind her eyes. Her thoughts felt too loud, too vulnerable. *Do I even get privacy in here anymore?*

"You'll get used to it," her mother's voice teased. "Think of it as a magical version of me dropping by for tea. I'll knock next time."

A phantom knocking throb at her temples made her smirk, despite herself. *You're unbelievable.*

"You always said so," her mother replied, with a flicker of warmth. "Ellie's more than you realize. And you, your power runs deep, from both sides of your family. This is only the beginning. I'm sure you haven't been able to access much, as you haven't learned how to communicate with it, but you will. You choosing to go through that was hard, but it is a wish come true for me."

Malin let out a slow breath, grounding herself in the feel of the blanket's weight in her lap, the distant hum of the streetlights beyond the window, the faint lavender-scented candle on the dresser, already burned low. The whole room felt unfamiliar now. Like waking up somewhere that used to be home.

I was going to stop by your house before we left, she thought carefully. *But Will says it's too risky. He wants us to head toward Talvi instead.*

"He's right," her mother replied without hesitation. "Tell him to meet me at Stonehold on Fourth Avenue. The shopkeeper there knows how to find me."

There was a long pause. Then her voice softened.

Malin. I've always loved you. And I'm so glad you're awake now. I just wish I could have been there for you the way I was for Ellie."

Then the pressure lifted.

The silence that followed was sharp and still, like the air after a lightning strike. Malin sat unmoving; her hand pressed to her chest. Her pulse thundered beneath her fingers.

She was fully awake now, no trace of sleep left in her blood. Only adrenaline. And magic.

The cool water hit her skin like a wake-up call, drawing a small gasp from her lips. Malin stepped fully into the stream, letting it pour down her back in steady rivulets that made her shiver, then sigh. The water warmed quickly, steam curling upward as the tension in her shoulders began to melt.

She closed her eyes, tipping her head back into the cascade. The scent of the lavender soap, familiar, comforting, blended with the faint tang of metal from the old pipes. Her muscles ached, a dull reminder of everything her body had just endured. And still, beneath it all, her skin hummed with something new. Magic. It lingered in her bloodstream, alive and restless.

How do I even begin to understand this?

The day's revelations circled in her mind. A mother who could speak in her head. A daughter with powers she'd hidden like secrets folded into a storybook. A man she barely knew, yet trusted, with all of it.

She ran her hands through her damp hair, letting out a long, slow breath. "I might not get this again for a while," she murmured to herself. "Hot water. Quiet. Time to think."

And then a gentle knock on the door.

"Yes?" she called, her voice a little breathier than intended.

"Ellie's fully locked in on her show," he said with a smile in his voice. "I think we could start a fire in the living room, and she wouldn't look up."

Malin smiled, warmth blooming behind her ribs. "What's she watching this time?"

"Something with creatures and human companions. She's fascinated with how they connect."

That tracked. "She's always wanted a pet. I never let her have one."

She let the water rinse over her face, grounding herself in the moment. The realization of what she had just been through and how much this man, essentially a stranger, had done to help her and Ellie, it struck her how much he meant to her.

"Will," she said, barely above a whisper. "Thank you. For being here. For all of this."

There was a long pause. Then, thick with emotion, "Always, Malin. Always."

The words curled around her like the steam, warm and sure. She closed her eyes again, letting herself feel it.

And then, softer this time, his voice cut through the spray. Lower. Rougher.

"I'm really surprised you are up and looking so rested. It must be your healing power. I expected to see you barely dragging through today." He paused, then added with a husky tone in his voice, "I completely understand if you aren't up to anything and I'm completely okay with just enjoying being next to you in

you... Mind if I join you?"

Her breath caught. The air in the bathroom suddenly felt heavier, hotter.

She hesitated; her heartbeat fluttered in her throat. *This is crazy. Isn't it?* But her body answered before her mind could make a case.

"I... yes," she said, a little stunned at her own voice. "Come in."

She didn't turn right away, letting the rush of water cover her skin and letting the moment expand. She heard the rustle of clothing and the soft shuffle of bare feet against tile. Her nerves danced with each sound.

When she finally turned, her breath snagged in her chest.

The door clicked open. Will stood there, fully nude, steam coiling around him like mist clinging to marble. His body was strong, familiar now in a way that surprised her. A ribbon of runes and glyphs, inked in black and something faintly glowing, traced the contours of his spine, from the base of his neck down to the dimples at the small of his back. He stepped in, and the shower enclosure, though oversized for one person, was quickly filled by his towering frame. The shower head was far too low for his height. He had to duck his head to wet his hair.

Her gaze dropped to her own forearm. One of the symbols there matched his. Not just similar, *identical.*

She blinked, the connection clicking in her mind like a lock turning.

"Will... this symbol," she whispered, reaching out to touch it gently on his back. "It's the same as mine. Right here."

He turned, brow furrowing as he followed her finger.

"But I've had the others for years. They're... markers from before the city. From Aloria."

"But this one, this exact glyph. It's new to you?"

He nodded slowly, brow tightening with thought.

Malin looked back down at her own arm, at the shape now glowing faintly beneath her skin. The warmth there pulsed gently as if responding to his touch.

Something was happening. Something *more*. And neither of them could explain it yet.

But in the water and steam, with only inches between them, they both felt it.

Not just heat.

Connection.

Malin swallowed hard, trying to keep her eyes on Will's face, but they drifted. Her cheeks warmed, and she hoped the steam would disguise it.

"This is... new," she said. Her voice was barely audible over the shower.

He stepped closer, water cascading over both of them now. "Is this okay? I know you have been through a lot, so I have no problem just standing right here, enjoying you."

She nodded; words were suddenly harder than they should be to form. He was here. Real. Solid. Close. And somehow, it felt natural. Like her body had decided before her brain could overthink the situation.

"It's been a while since I've done this," she murmured, the honesty falling out before she could second-guess it. She could feel a lump in her throat.

I know you've just been through a lot. I think I know how to find the cold water," he teased.

She smiled weakly at his comment. It did help her nerves, but her body wasn't going to allow this opportunity to pass by either. Malin reached for the shower gel, his fingers slightly trembling. "May I?"

He turned his back. She poured a small dollop into her hand, the citrus and pine scent grounding her. She placed her hands on his shoulders, spreading the lather over muscle and skin. Her fingers found a scar, then another.

"Your back is a whole story," she murmured, enjoying the feel of the muscle and sinew. "What do these runes mean? I especially like this one that looks like mine."

"Some I chose. Some... chose me," Will said quietly. "I wasn't aware there was one there that looked like yours," he nodded toward the one that matched hers. "That's new. That one has me at a loss. It does feel pretty incredible when you touch it, though."

She felt the magic again, humming beneath her skin like a live wire. His warmth and presence weren't just physical; they were tuned to something deeper.

Will turned, facing her now. His eyes searched hers, not hungry but open. He reached for her gently.

"Malin." His voice was low and husky. "Open your eyes."

She hadn't realized she'd closed them. When she opened them, she met his gaze, and something cracked open inside her. There was an intensity, a craving, that pulled her from her core.

Then his lips were on hers.

hands found his hair, and her body pressed into his without a thought.

A rush of heat flared between them. Not just want, but something *else*. A resonance. The same thing she'd felt when she healed him, now magnified. It buzzed in her fingertips, surged through her spine, and drove her wild with need.

"Will," she breathed, pulling back. "I can feel everything. Your heart, your breath, it's like we're connected."

He nodded, forehead resting against hers. "I feel it, too. I don't know what this is; I've never experienced this before..." he groaned deeply. A guttural groan hit her to her core and made the fire within her burn. "I don't want it to stop. You need to decide. I'm not sure I can be in here for too much longer without turning that cold water on if you don't feel up to things."

His breathing was getting shallow, and his erection was building quickly. She reached down to touch him, wrapping her hand around him. She reveled in the sharp intake of his breath as she slowly moved her hand to his tip.

They stayed that way, pressed close under the water, breaths syncing, skin slick and warm. For once, Malin didn't try to name it or analyze it. She just let herself feel.

"I didn't expect this," she whispered.

"Me either," Will murmured, his arms tightening around her. "But I don't want to run from it."

And for the first time in years, neither did she.

Water cascaded down their bodies, steaming and relentless, as their lips crashed together in a frenzy of need. She felt his tongue trace her lips, asking for access, which she welcomed. It plunged into her mouth, pulsing in and out. It spurred her memory to

shower wall, leaning into her while she writhed in his arms. She let out a soft moan, the sensations building within her. Her hands clawed at his back while her breasts pressed against his hard chest, pebbling and aching for his touch.

He pinned her there, the cold tiles a sharp contrast to the heat of their bodies. His mouth trailed down her neck, teeth grazing her skin as he sucked and bit, leaving marks that would linger for days.

"Will," she gasped, a whisper into his ear. His cock was so hard, throbbing against her thigh, touching her entrance, while they rhythmically pushed against each other. She gasped as he slid his fingers into her. First, teasing, then bringing her to heights of passion, almost to climax. When he moved his hand, she felt a void that needed to be filled, an aching that called out to him. Arching her back and rocking in his arms, she cried out as he thrust into her, an answer to her unspoken request.

He was so hard; it made her gasp. His hands gripped her hips, holding her steady as he pounded into her with a ferocity that left her breathless. The water poured over them, mingling with their sweat as they moved together in a rhythm that was as old as time.

"Harder," she implored, her nails carving fiery trails down his back. Her voice, almost foreign in its urgency, escaped her lips, "Fuck me harder, Will." She saw his eyes widen with a flicker of surprise, yet delight danced within them as he eagerly complied. The feel of him pulling her down on his shaft with each pull drove her crazy. He immersed himself in her, his solid chest pressing insistently against her own, while she savored his mouth voraciously claiming hers, their lips locked in a fervent dance.

punctuating the symphony of her escalating pleasure, making her tighten around him with every stroke, each desperate grip drawing a groan of sweet torment from his throat. Knowing she had such control over him gave her such a sense of pleasure, especially given how he had a similar control over her.

His breathing was ragged, each inhalation a struggle, as he growled, "You feel so good." His lips crashed onto hers once more in a blistering kiss. "I can't get enough of you."

With each thrust, an intoxicating crescendo built within her, like a symphony reaching its peak. He seemed crafted for her, seamlessly finding every hidden note, propelling her ever closer to the precipice. Her body quaked, the first tremors of ecstasy cascading through her like an unstoppable tide.

Sensing her impending release, he stifled the scream rising in her chest with another kiss. Her orgasm tore through her in a cataclysmic wave, her nails embedding deeply in the sinew of his shoulders. His hips faltered as he reached his peak, his essence surging within her, thrusting with one final, powerful drive. She clung to him, legs quivering as they weathered the aftershocks together, her back pressed firmly against the cool, unyielding wall.

When he finally lowered her to the water-slicked ground, they both panted, breathless and utterly spent. The water, now tepid, did little to quell the warmth of their entwined bodies, and all she desired was to remain nestled close to him, enveloped in the aftermath of their shared passion.

Malin traced slow, distracted patterns across Will's chest. When she noticed her nail marks, she began to heal them. He stopped her, "No. I want those right there. I'm yours and I have no problem with your mark of claim." The deep rumble in his voice sent a shiver through her.

mother's voice still echoed in her mind.

"Will," she said, tone soft but steady. "I talked to my mom. I need to tell you something."

He turned toward her instantly, the relaxed ease from a moment ago gone. "You talked to her?"

Malin nodded. "She reached out. Mentally. She said she'll meet us at a place called Stoneholds, in Talvi."

His muscles tensed beneath her fingers. Not obvious, but enough for her to notice. He repeated the name carefully.

"She said the shopkeeper there would take us to her," Malin continued. "And she... she told me she's been working with the resistance. That she was planning to get Ellie out. Without telling me."

Will's eyes flicked away. His hand on her hip had gone still. "She said Stoneholds?"

"Will," she asked, a chill crawling up her spine, "do you know her?"

He didn't answer right away. The silence stretched between them like a thread pulled too tight.

"What's her name?"

"Elowen. Elowen Neldoreth. You probably recognize her name because she is a Chancellor on the Council of Elders," she explained.

Something shifted in Will's face. Not surprise exactly. Recognition, maybe. Worry. She wasn't sure. But it was enough to set off alarms.

"Will," she pressed, her voice a notch sharper, "what aren't you telling me?"

her eyes. "It's… complicated. I need to check in with my contacts. We'll need to make some adjustments in our plan now."

Malin didn't move, but every part of her felt like it was leaning forward, trying to parse the space between his words.

"I promise I'll explain soon," Will added, leaning in to kiss her. It was soft, but something about it felt like a goodbye.

"Thirty minutes," he said quietly. "Be ready."

And then he was gone, towel around his waist, leaving a trail of damp footprints and unanswered questions.

Malin stood frozen under the cooling spray, staring at the door.

Was it her mother that had set him off, or Stoneholds? she wondered.

She turned off the water and stepped out, grabbing a towel. Her movements were sharp, her brain already switching gears.

She dressed quickly, braiding her damp hair back with precise fingers. She added items to the *"Essentials"* that Will had prepared for her, things he might not have thought she would want.

If her mother was part of the resistance… if Will knew more than he was saying… What part of her life did she really know?

"I feel so much more like myself now," she whispered to herself, getting herself dressed. "How is that possible?"

ill wrapped Malin tightly in his arms as he swung the front door shut behind them. The soft click of the lock echoed louder than it should have, final and hollow. Malin didn't flinch, but she buried her face deeper into his neck, her breath warm against his collarbone.

Beside them, Ellie stood close, one hand clutching her doll, the other patting her mother's back like she wasn't sure how else to help. Her eyes were too wide, too still for an eleven-year-old, flicking between her mom and the waiting street.

He knew it would be hard for them. Leaving this house, this life. It had been their sanctuary. Even for him, after just a handful of days, it was hard to walk away. But staying? That was no longer an option. Not now. Not with what had awakened with-in Malin. Not with what was coming.

The weight of their escape settled on Will's shoulders, mirrored by the heavy packs strapped across his back. Malin's slender frame was burdened by a bag that looked out of place against the elegant twist of her sun-kissed hair. The soft clink of the chopsticks hidden in those waves caught his ear, a quiet, poignant reminder of the life they were leaving behind.

Ellie's fingers gripped her doll tighter, white-knuckled now. She didn't cry. She didn't complain. But he could see it, the fear and excitement braided tightly together in her chest as she clutched her doll to her chest. Twelve years old, standing on the edge of everything changing.

Will lifted Malin's chin gently. Her eyes were glassy, red at the edges. He brushed a tear from her cheek with his thumb and pressed a kiss to her forehead.

best," he whispered into her hair, not because he was certain, but because he needed her to hear it.

The crisp morning air met them with a chill, carrying the false promise of calm. The taxi idled at the curb, its engine a quiet rumble beneath the tension. It looked ordinary. Harmless. But Will's eyes lingered on it too long, scanning for anything that could be a threat. Too many years of surviving in the trenches made him doubt every shadow.

Then a voice shattered the stillness from the doorway of Andrew's house.

"You haven't been responding to my messages. I'm guessing I really screwed something up the other day. I know I'm not supposed to drink like that..." then it looked like he noticed the bags and Will, "Leaving so soon?" he ventured with a warm friendly tone, the hesitation in his voice betraying his inner turmoil. "What's the occasion?"

"The parents," Malin replied quickly, echoing the story they'd rehearsed. "We're visiting them for a few days."

"Odd," Andrew said, tone dipping darker. "I spoke with your father this morning. He was worried. He asked me to check on you. Funny...he didn't mention that."

He felt her body stiffen and a tremor of concern rippled through. It was subtle yet unmistakable. She looked at him in a silent conversation, he nodded in understanding. He placed a gentle kiss on her cheek, his offer that he trusted her to deal with this and his promise that he would do whatever it took to back her up if needed.

by something harder. Jealousy, hot and sharp. The storm brewing under his skin broke with a flare of anger.

"Malin," he said, his voice high with disbelief, as though seeing her in Will's arms had scrambled his thoughts.

He stepped toward them, a disheveled silhouette in sweatpants and a wrinkled shirt, uncombed hair, face pale and drawn. His eyes flicked from Ellie, gripping her doll, to Malin, tucked into Will's side, and then to Will himself.

"Wait," he said, breath hitching. "Please. Just... wait a second."

Malin hesitated, then stepped out of Will's arms and moved toward him.

Will didn't follow but shifted subtly, placing himself in front of Ellie without making it obvious. Whatever this was, an apology or a desperate plea, it wasn't going to be simple. But he knew Malin could handle herself.

Andrew extended his hand to her as if to shake in apology. Andrew pulled Malin into a sudden hug. It was clumsy, too quick, and she immediately pushed him away. She took a step back, firm now, her spine straightening as she returned to Will's side and looped her arm around his waist.

Will remained motionless, even though every muscle in his body wanted to launch himself at him and beat him to a bloody pulp for the marks that had been on her wrist. He waited for Malin to decide his next steps.

Facing Andrew, Malin's voice cut clean and calm. "Andrew, I appreciate the apology. But drunk or not... You did show me who you are." Her words landed like stones. "I'm with Will now."

make Andrew visibly pale. The moment carried the ring of finality.

His gaze noticed the bags. Confusion flickered across his face, followed by suspicion. The pieces were starting to connect.

"Bye, Ellie," Andrew said, his voice suddenly too sweet, too controlled. It sent a ripple of unease through Will.

Ellie clutched her doll tighter and shrank behind him.

Andrew stepped forward, too fast.

Will moved to block him, but before he could act, Ellie's foot shot out and caught Andrew solidly in the knee.

He yelped as he crumpled to the ground, groaning in pain.

Will loomed over him, calm and cold, eyes narrowed. He was already calculating what might happen next, what Andrew might try, what he himself might be forced to do.

"Maybe we should get in the cab," he said low, his voice tight with restraint. "I don't think Ellie would like to see what I will do next if he tries something else."

He touched Malin's back lightly, guiding her.

She didn't move right away. Her gaze dropped to Andrew, still kneeling.

"Maybe next time," she said, her voice like frost, "you'll remember my life is mine to live. And who I let into it, who I let stay, is my choice. Consider this the end of our friendship too."

With that, she turned and walked to the car.

Will caught the change in Andrew's face as she left, the cracked facade, the wounded mask giving way to something colder, darker. Resentment burned behind his eyes.

of his mouth and finished with a sharp look when he got in the car. It said everything he needed to.

Will sat stiffly in the back seat; eyes locked on the side mirror. He noticed that Malin hadn't said a word in minutes.

The cab pulled away from the curb, its tires slicing through the wet pavement with a hiss. They didn't speak. No one needed to. The silence was too full, tight, wired, dangerous.

She sat angled toward the window, one hand loosely gripping the edge of Ellie's coat, the other resting in her lap, fingers clenched so tight they were white. He caught the way her chest rose and fell just a little too slow, the way she blinked harder than necessary. She was holding it in. Barely.

Ellie leaned against her mother's side; doll clutched tight in her lap. Her eyes were wide, but not with fear. She looked ready. Like this was another adventure. Will didn't know if that made it better or worse.

He tracked the city as it slipped past the rain-streaked windows. Streetlights flared in streaks of gold and red, bleeding into puddles, then vanished behind them. Every reflection could be a face. Every car behind them could be too close.

He hated this part. The quiet collapse. The silent grief of someone leaving everything behind and pretending it was fine, for the kid, for herself. For him. This time, he could not stop that quiet grief from slipping through his defenses and barriers.

He didn't trust the driver. The guy hadn't said a word beyond destination confirmation. Kept his eyes on the road. Too perfect. Too calm. Will watched his hands, his shoulders, every micro-movement.

that didn't mean much. It was early. And if someone had eyes on them, they'd wait. Follow at a distance. Play it carefully.

He leaned forward, speaking low enough not to get the driver's interest. "Just so you know, I only made pancakes because I didn't want to be accused of kidnapping *and* poor breakfasting in the same day."

She blinked. Turned slightly toward him, her lips twitching like she wanted to smile but didn't quite have the air for it.

"I take my charges seriously," he added, tapping Ellie's doll. "Although I do worry, she's plotting to overthrow me. She hasn't blinked once." This drew the giggle out of Ellie he was hoping for.

That got a small, real laugh out of Malin. The sound was quiet, but it was there. She reached over and rested her hand briefly on his knee.

"Thanks," she said, voice rough.

"For breakfast?"

"For this." Her eyes flicked to the rearview mirror, then back to him. "All of it."

He checked the mirror again. A black sedan. Not close, not far. It changed lanes when they did. He filed the plate number. Didn't react. Just noted it.

The itch between his shoulder blades wouldn't leave. Too many unknowns. Too many things out of his control. They were out of the house, yes, but not safe. Not yet. Not even close.

His hand drifted near his bag. Just enough to feel the weapon stashed inside. One comfort in the chaos.

owe me thanks until I get you both out clean."

She didn't respond to that. Just turned back to the window and wiped at the corner of her eye when she thought he wasn't looking.

He was.

But he gave her the grace of pretending not to notice.

They had to make it to Talvi. And for that to happen, he had to stay two steps ahead of anyone following them.

Will kept his voice low, leaning just enough to catch Ellie's eye. "We've got a few moves coming up, okay? Gonna need you to stick close and stay quiet. Think you can do that for me?"

Ellie gave a quick nod, clutching her doll tighter to her chest. Her face was serious, too serious for a kid her age, but her eyes stayed locked on him with trust. He brushed a curl from in front of her face and pushed it behind her ear.

"Good. I knew you could," he praised. She was tracking and she was handling all of this so well. She was not the first child he had gotten out of the city, but she had surely been the bravest for her age.

Malin sat beside her, eyes fixed out the window, jaw tight. Her hand rested on Ellie's knee, but Will could see her knuckles were white. She hadn't said much since they left the house, and he didn't blame her. Every street they passed was one she'd memorized. Every turn the driver took could be the last safe one.

Will scanned the sidewalk through the streaked glass, his gaze catching on anything out of rhythm, pedestrians walking too slow, faces turning a second too long, reflections in the shop windows that didn't line up with what was outside.

entrance."

The driver gave a grunt of acknowledgment. Will watched his hands on the wheel. Steady. No tremor, no hesitation. Still, he made a mental note of the plate.

When they stepped out, the noise of the street hit hard, vendors shouting, the sharp sizzle of food carts, someone playing a metal-stringed instrument that was way too loud for how close it was. Perfect chaos.

Will leaned close to Malin as they walked. "We're switching cabs through the crowd. Follow my lead, Keep Ellie between us, and if I tap your arm, duck right. If I pull your wrist, left."

She nodded without looking at him. Professional. Calm. But her breath paused for half a second as they stepped into the crush of bodies.

Will looked down surprised. Ellie moved between them, but she had chosen to hold his hand, instead of Malin's. He smiled and made a mental note, then went back to his plan. She kept pace without being told. He tried to adjust his gait to her smaller steps. She was almost at a jog to keep up, but she was keeping up. Smart kid.

They wove through the merchant tents, past booths thick with spices, bolts of cheap fabric, and knockoff tech. Will kept his shoulders loose, but his eyes flicked constantly checking, watching for anyone who stopped when they passed. A quick handshake behind one tent got them their new clothes, a brown satchel already packed with ID cards and travel papers.

Fifteen minutes later, in a back room behind a vendor's curtain, they changed.

Malin and Ellie in the mirror. She'd tucked her hair into a cap and swapped her more fashionable navy coat for a black leather jacket with a hood and brown linen shirt, paired with a pair of black pants with lots of pockets and loops. Ellie's bright dress was gone, replaced with simple travel wear, olive green jacket over a black t-shirt, dark jeans, and boots. With the addition of a head scarf to cover her hair, she looked like someone else's child entirely.

"You're a natural," he told Ellie. "Remind me never to play hide and seek with you."

That earned him the smallest smile. Malin caught it, too, and her mouth curved just slightly before she turned away.

When they stepped out again, Will handed the old clothes to a clerk who was part of the resistance and would ensure they got donated to help others.

She had always heard of the Shadows, as the Talvi District was known as, but she'd never imagined she'd be riding a grimy train straight into its heart with her daughter tucked at her side. When they boarded, Will ushered them to the back corner seats while he stood next to them facing out, surveying the train car and mastering the art of looking menacing.

As they sat in silence, Malin swept her gaze into the stream of workers and early risers. Oil-streaked uniforms. Bandaged hands. Hollow eyes. The scent of sweat and metal lingered like a second skin. Burns, old fractures, missing fingers, she saw them all, her diagnostic instincts already cataloging injuries she couldn't treat. Not here. Not anymore.

She'd passed Talvi often enough, heard the stories, maybe even listened to a few, but they'd never *felt* real until now. Until she was sitting shoulder to shoulder with people broken by the very city that had once coddled her. How could the city allow this to continue like this? She felt a sense of shame for not having ever considered their situation, taking the luxuries of her life for granted.

With the lull of the train and feeling protected, she was lost in thought. Her thoughts drifted to Caelum.

He would've been furious. No, *righteous.* She could still hear his voice in heated debates with her parents, passionate and relentless. Fighting for the lower districts. Advocating everything from healthcare to food access, and better protection.

help the poor in Talvi and Grive Districts on their off time. How differently would her life have been if he hadn't died?

She blinked hard, grounding herself back in the present. The train hummed beneath her feet. The car rocked slightly as it picked up speed. And just ahead of her, Will stood like a wall between them and whatever might come next.

She looked at him, at his back, broad and steady, and felt the echo of what she'd once known with Caelum. But also, something new and so much stronger.

It was the way he kept one hand on Ellie through this whole trip. Not gripping. Not restraining. Just... *there*. A tether to help share his strength, knowing that she would need it.

Ellie had been reaching for him more than her. Not out of fear but comfort. Trust. It warmed something in Malin, even as it stung a little.

He trusted Malin's instincts. If she veered off plan, he adjusted without question. He shielded, not smothered. Led, but never pushed. He was protective without being possessive. It was more than she'd known how to ask for, but here it was, in every gesture.

Even now, when the four men in piercings and layered leathers looked toward their corner, Will didn't flinch. He shifted his stance just slightly, splayed his feet, and squared his shoulders. Maybe even flexed a little.

The message was clear.

You want them? You go through me.

They didn't speak. Didn't need to. Malin slid her hand under the edge of her shawl and found his. His fingers closed around her

position.

It was enough. A wordless reassurance.

They weren't out of danger.

She already knew.

The train rattled on. Four stops down. One to go. The crowd had thinned, but the tension hadn't. She kept her gaze low, watching Ellie's fingers fidget with the edge of her doll's dress. Still calm. Still collected. Malin brushed her thumb gently over Ellie's hand and felt her daughter squeeze back. There were only a handful of passengers left. She prepared herself for what to expect. She had only heard rumors of Talvi.

She heard that the buildings were so tall that some streets were in shadows all day, every day, hence the name the Shadows. It was over-congested and there were poor living conditions. A whole district that was forgotten about. It was a tangled web of industry and secrecy that stretched its fingers toward them.

At the next stop, the doors opened to a wall of heat, metal, and something else, thick in the air, sharp on the tongue. Not rot, exactly. More like exhaustion baked into brick. It was a combination of scents: old grease, rust, and too many years without rest. In Media Proper, you only caught a trace of it in the wind. This was the source and the smell was so strong it made her gag.

The sound of machinery pulsed through the district, deep, rhythmic, and unending. A mechanical heartbeat beneath the city's skin. As if crossing an invisible threshold, Will adjusted without a word, his steps shifting with the kind of ease that said he'd walked this path before. He stopped as they moved away from the train station and the crowd.

their surroundings, "Make sure to cover up." His words were soft yet urgent; she understood them for what they were, a command woven with protective intent.

She complied without hesitation, her movements deft as she concealed her blonde hair beneath the dark fabric, masking the ethereal blue of her eyes. Ellie mimicked her, clutching her doll tighter against her chest, the small figure was a beacon of innocence in a world that no longer promised safety.

Will's voice was tight but steady. "The Shadows are thick with pickpockets. Keep Ellie between us."

Together, they stepped into the labyrinth.

The streets narrowed into crooked alleys flanked by leaning brick and rusted steel. Warehouse walls rose like cliffs on either side, some draped in sagging banners for companies long since dissolved. Above them, scaffolds and catwalks crisscrossed the sky, dripping shadows onto the uneven cobblestones.

"Stay close," Will murmured without looking back.

She did. So did Ellie, tucked carefully between them. They moved together, her hand on Ellie's shoulder, Will just ahead, his stride measured and watchful. Every few seconds, she'd catch the flick of his eyes, scanning windows, watching for movement.

Will looked, nodded once, and adjusted course. When he noticed Ellie falling behind, he picked her up. He continued his trek at a faster pace, holding Ellie, with her bag on her back, as well as his own bag on his back.

Their pace didn't slow. It wasn't a run, not quite. But it was faster than walking. The kind of movement you use when you're trying not to draw attention, but you *need* to get somewhere.

tagged the post in bright violet spray paint, **FOURTH,** with an arrow curling to the left. Her heart jumped. "Finally," she said, sighing softly.

Will led them without hesitation, clearly familiar with the directions.

The sign, hanging from a fire escape, was the first hint they were close, nothing flashy, just a roughly carved plank of wood hanging crookedly from a rusted iron bracket. The single word was carved into it in bold, uneven letters: *Stoneholds.* It swung slightly in the gritty wind, creaking as if protesting its own weight.

Malin slowed instinctively, her eyes tracing the sign as if it might say more the longer she stared at it. There was something unsettling in its simplicity. No decoration. No warm welcome. Just a name. No clue to the type of establishment, but it looked like it had been open for many years.

Then she saw the doors.

They were massive, twice the height of any she'd ever seen, thick and ancient. Clearly, it is not part of the newer construction surrounding it. The building looked like it had grown in layers over time, like scar tissue over a wound. Stone, wood, and metal, all stacked, bolted, and patched together. And those doors... they belonged to another era. Charred streaks crawled up their surface, deep gouges cut across the grain like claw marks, and thick cast iron bands sealed them together with bolts the size of her fists. Surrounding the doorframe were deep, carved runes.

Malin curled her fingers tighter around Ellie's hand. She hadn't realized she was still holding it until she felt Ellie squeeze back.

Will stepped ahead, one hand raised as he reached for the door. He didn't hesitate. Of course, he didn't.

marks, the weight of it all, and stepped forward anyway.

Stoneholds' door swung open with a creak that seemed too gentle for such a foreboding entrance. Malin hadn't known what to expect, but it wasn't *this* when she walked in.

They had barely passed through the doors, when Will's arm shot out like a barrier, firm but not rough, as he closed the door behind them and put Ellie down. Malin stopped instantly, nearly bumping into him, and Ellie froze beside her with her eyes wide with wonder. As the door closed, noise from the street fell away like a lifted veil. No more clang of gears, no shouting vendors. Just… quiet. Still. As if the place was holding its breath.

Will turned to face them fully, his expression serious, more serious than she'd seen since they left the house. His hazel eyes held hers first, then shifted to Ellie's, steady and deliberate.

"Before we go any further," he said, voice low but clear over the distant thrum of Talvi's industrial hum, "you both need to listen to me."

The air around them thickened with purpose.

He pointed just past the threshold, where a faded metal plaque was bolted crookedly to the wall beside the door. It was nearly swallowed by rust and soot, but the words were still legible if you squinted:

LOOK. DON'T TOUCH.
IF IT MOVES, TELL GOREK.
IF IT SPEAKS TO YOU — LEAVE.

Malin felt a chill crawl across her spine. Ellie's fingers tightened around hers again.

There are things inside that *look* like they're broken or forgotten... but they're not. Some are dangerous. Some are just plain mean. And if it has eyes..." He glanced at Ellie, softening his tone slightly, "Don't stare. Don't let it *stare* at you too long, either."

She could hear the tension in Will's voice, the way it tried to be calm but carried the edge of past experiences. He wasn't trying to scare them. He was trying to protect them. She appreciated the difference.

"I mean it," he added, his gaze returning to Malin with a flicker of something deeper beneath the surface. "Just follow my lead."

Ellie gave a tiny nod. She gripped her doll tighter.

Malin didn't need more convincing. She simply said, "Okay."

Will waited a beat longer, scanning their faces to ensure they understood.

Malin swallowed and nodded. "What is this place?"

"Most know Stoneholds as a general merchant shop. Those runes on the door can tell if someone has magic or not. If they don't, it glamours the shop, so it only shows them basic necessities, clothing flour, food, and that sort of items. For those of us with magic, it shows us what is really here. There are general items, but mainly it is a curiosities shop filled with magical items from around Mordovia. Gorek's family has merchant shops in all the big cities, he sent me to most of them." He paused for a moment, then added, "Stoneholds is where I grew up after my family was killed."

Malin was starting to be able to put some of the pieces together. He grew up here. In Talvi. Among this. She couldn't imagine.

shop's air was warm and thick with the scent of old paper and worn leather, comforting, oddly enough. Every shelf groaned under the weight of artifacts that practically hummed with history. Talismans. Scrolls. Vials filled with powders she couldn't identify. They reached a tall counter with no one there.

"Do you mind waiting right here? I need to check the back room."
Will's voice was low, but the underlying tension hadn't left it.

Malin nodded, and he squeezed her hand gently before brushing a kiss across her forehead, quick but intimate. It steadied her more than she expected. Then he disappeared through the heavy curtain at the back of the shop, swallowed by shadows.

The silence that followed was thick with dust and mystery.

She turned in place slowly, trying to take it all in, but there was too much. The shop was cluttered in a way that defied logic, yet everything felt... placed. Intentional. A maze of relics and fragments from forgotten ages.

Some objects sat quietly, wrapped in cloth or caged behind glass. Others seemed to breathe softly in the low light, barely noticeable but alive enough that she kept her distance.

There was a tarnished birdcage that looked empty, but her instincts told her otherwise. A mirror leaned against the far wall, covered in script she couldn't read, and when she passed it, her reflection didn't move quite in sync.

She swallowed hard.

Next to her, Ellie's small hand tightened around her doll. Her wide eyes roamed the shelves with a careful awe, taking in the sudden shift from danger to enchantment.

to her side, the way her shoulders tensed even though her face remained calm. The place might have *felt* like sanctuary, but Malin's instincts warned her otherwise.

Sanctuary didn't come with signs that said - *If it speaks to you — leave.*

Ellie's curiosity began to get the better of her and a shelf of brightly colored bags captured her interest. Having successfully explored those items, it gave her the courage to explore more.

Malin kept close behind Ellie, her eyes flicking from shelf to shadow, every instinct on high alert. The shop was unnerving enough, but the sheer volume of strange objects made it worse, some too still, some not still enough. She had just opened her mouth to call Ellie back when the girl, wide-eyed and oblivious, backed up to get a better view of something and collided into something.

Someone.

Malin's heart stopped.

The back of a man — no, a *mountain* of a man — stood before Ellie, so massive his silhouette blocked the flickering light from the lanterns above. Ellie had bumped into the tree trunk that must be one of his legs. Her head had not even come to his waist. His frame was all muscle and harsh angles, arms thick as iron bars, and shoulders so broad they dwarfed everything around him. His skin was rough and scarred, his jaw sharp enough to cut glass.

She stepped forward on instinct, one hand reaching for Ellie, the other already preparing to call Will if her voice could find its way through the tightness in her chest.

intrusion. Malin's heart slammed in her ribs, but she forced herself to stand her ground. She couldn't move fast enough. Ellie looked up, startled and small beneath his shadow.

"Watch where ye..." the man began as he turned, voice like deep, rolling thunder...

and stopped.

Malin blinked.

Something shifted.

"Sorry, sir," Ellie squeaked, her voice barely rising above the crackling hearth nearby.

Malin was impressed she'd managed any words at all. *She* was having trouble finding her own.

The sharpness in his expression cracked, a faint crease forming at the edge of his mouth, and then, unbelievably, he laughed. Deep and warm, like a sudden fire in a freezing room. Not mocking. Not cruel. Just... unexpected.

Ellie's face lit up with relief, and Malin's shoulders sagged.

"No harm done, little one," the man said, his voice softening around the edges, a kindness folded in beneath all that iron. He reached out slowly, gently, to pat Ellie's head, careful, respectful of the doll she clutched tight to her chest. His hand easily covered the whole top of her head.

Malin didn't breathe until his hand fell back to his side.

Whoever this man was, he had the kind of presence that lingered in the bones, and she wasn't entirely convinced his warmth made him safe. But he hadn't hurt Ellie. And that mattered more than anything.

he was, even he only came up to the stranger's shoulder. But there was no tension in his approach.

To Malin's surprise, the man swept Will into a crushing hug.

"Will, my boy! So good ta see ya! It's been what two years?" the mountain said with a huge grin.

As Will pulled free, he came over to her with one of those full, dimpled smiles she rarely saw.

"Gorek, this is Malin. And her daughter, Ellie," Will said, gesturing to them with a hint of shyness that surprised her. *Was he nervous about what Gorek would think?*

Gorek studied them both with that same heavy gaze. But this time, something sparked in it, recognition, old and deep.

"Da likeness is uncanny," he remarked in a rumble, the corners of his mouth twitching into a knowing smile. "Chu must be related to Elowen. Spitting images ya are."

Malin's chest tightened.

"How do you know my mother?" she asked, trying to keep her voice even.

"Aye, tha's right." Gorek gave a loose wave of his hand, though his eyes stayed fixed on the memory. "Lysa an' me, we've known her a long while now. One of our oldest, truest friends. She'll be 'round here somewhere, likely in the back with Lysa, fussin' over somethin', no doubt."

Then his attention shifted to Ellie, who gazed up at him like she'd stumbled into a fairy tale.

As they followed Gorek deeper into the sanctuary of Stoneholds, Malin's mind refused to quiet. Questions unfurled behind her with urgency.

How did Gorek know her mother? Not just in passing, but *well.* Well enough that his entire demeanor softened at the mention of her. Well enough that he wasn't surprised to see *her* here. Or Ellie.

Why had Mom never mentioned this place? Or these people? Why did Will hesitate, just slightly, when introducing her, as if *she* were the one being vetted?

And that rune. Will's rune. The one that matched hers exactly. It hadn't been there before; *he* admitted as much. So how had it gotten there? And why was she only just learning about all of this now?

Her thoughts spiraled. She wasn't sure what triggered it, but it was then she realized, *My mother reads minds.*

The moment she thought it, her mother's voice cut in, not imagined, cut gently into her spiral.

"Yes, Malin. I hear you. You're close. You'll have your answers soon. Just calm yourself."

Malin froze mid-step, her fingers curling slightly. *You didn't knock*

Of course, she heard. Of course, she'd been listening to her thoughts this whole time. Her pulse kicked up a notch, not from fear, but from the sheer weight of being seen so thoroughly. It was like trying to keep a secret from the sun. Ugh. She thought back to all those lies she told her parents when she was a teenager. Mom had pretended she believed her.

They weren't anything worse than I had done. She let out a huff of frustration that drew an arched eyebrow from Will.

She exhaled slowly, gathering herself as they kept walking.

Focusing back on their walk, this backroom was massive, Malin noticed it before he said a word; Will's jaw was tight. His shoulders were just a bit too squared. His eyes scanned every corridor they passed, every shadow they crossed. It was subtle, almost imperceptible, but she saw it. The way he angled his body slightly to the outside of their group, how he kept checking the corners like someone trained to expect trouble.

They were safe now, weren't they?

The hallway stretched ahead of them, the warm lamplight flickering against old stone and wood, but Will's steps were too deliberate, too. He hadn't said anything, but she could feel it. The way he scanned every shadow, every corridor they passed, it wasn't just caution. He was unsettled.

Malin shifted closer and lowered her voice. "What is it? You keep looking over your shoulder."

Will didn't answer right away. His jaw tensed, eyes flicking toward the high shelves and dark corners of the shop. "Just a feeling," he muttered. "Like something's off. Doesn't make sense, though. We weren't followed."

She didn't press, yet. But her mind logged it. Will didn't rattle easily. If he was on edge, there was a reason.

Then there was Ellie.

The contrast was almost jarring.

Where Will's tension radiated like static, Ellie practically *floated*. Malin was just noticing the low hum again, the strange, melodic rhythm that had followed her since she woke up changed. It

Comforting, almost.

Ellie bounced on the balls of her feet, clutching her doll with one arm, excitement buzzing off her like static. "I missed Nanna. It's been a long time since I got to see her," she chirped. "I'm so excited!"

Malin thought about how long it had been and was surprised by the time. Had it really been over three months? She hadn't even realized, though she wasn't really that close and visits to Nanna and Poppa's house were really for her to see her Dad. Her mom was there most of the time, but she didn't change plans if she wasn't available.

Ellie grinned up at her. "She said she brought those lemon drop cookies! The ones you like so much! My favorite is her dragon fruit cookies."

That pulled a smile from her, small but real. She could practically taste the tart-sweet sugar dusted on her fingertips, memories sharp and soft all at once.

"She said we're safe now," Ellie continued, tugging gently at Malin's sleeve, "and that I'm doing *so good*. She said you'd be okay too, once you stopped overthinking everything."

Malin raised an eyebrow. "Did she now?"

"What does overthinking mean? Aren't you supposed to think?" Ellie asked, completely unbothered by the tension that still curled around Will like smoke.

Malin looked at Will again, and now it made sense. He *didn't* feel safe. She could see it in every quiet defense his body had erected.

She took Ellie's hand, steadying herself. There was a strange comfort in seeing her daughter so at ease, but also a dissonance.

did *Elowen* know that they didn't?

And why hadn't she told Malin?

Malin moved briskly through the corridor, her boots clicking against the uneven cobblestone, each step a quiet echo in the heavy hush. Her fingers skimmed the rough, cold stone of the walls as they passed. They were solid, ancient, and unyielding. This backroom area was more like a labyrinth than a back room. A person would need a map to remember all the twists and turns. Her heart thudded in her chest, not just from fear but from the sheer weight of history in these walls. She drew a slow breath, trying to calm the tension coiling in her ribs, her icy blue gaze sweeping across the unknown and unfamiliar environment.

Malin glanced between them, surprised at how easily the tension in Will's shoulders eased in the presence of the hulking man. Gorek's size was still intimidating, but his tone carried an almost brotherly or fatherly warmth. Whatever history they had, it was real and recent enough that trust hadn't worn thin.

"Aye, I heard through the tunnels you're not runnin' routes as much these days," Gorek added, eyes twinkling beneath bushy brows. "Word is, you're more of a seeker now."

"Sometimes," Will replied. "Lately, I've been finding things I didn't even know I was looking for."

That made Gorek bark a laugh, full and genuine, the kind of sound that bounced around in the ribcage long after it ended.

Malin caught herself smiling, just barely. Despite everything, the fear and uncertainty, she liked the way they spoke. Like men who had walked through fire side by side and come out singed but still standing.

reflecting the flickering torchlight that danced across the stone walls. Their camaraderie was unmistakable, threaded with ease and old wounds, a quiet strength built over years of facing danger together.

She watched Will and studied Gorek, turning over their words like puzzle pieces, trying to make sense of what they'd shared, who they'd been, who they were to each other, and what that might mean for her and Ellie.

The thought made her stomach twist, not with jealousy, but with the realization that there were parts of Will's life still hidden from her. Shadows she hadn't even known what to look for. And yet, the more she saw of him in this place, his easy confidence, his silent checks on her and Ellie, his trust in this giant of a man, the more she wanted to understand it all.

"Lysa's been bouncin' 'round since first light," Gorek said, glancing over his shoulder with a grin. "Couldna stop talkin' once the message came in. Says it feels like only yesterday chu was tangled up with that wild, flame-haired mage. Chu know, da one who could set half a forest on fire jus' blinkin' too hard?"

Malin raised a brow, eyes flicking to Will.

A faint flush rose in Will's neck, his hand running through his hair in a gesture she now recognized as his way of dodging discomfort as he glanced back at her. He laughed, quiet and sheepish. "Let's just say she's safe and sound in Sarhen now. Beyond the Sea of Helm. Far, far away."

His gaze slid to Malin then, and for a heartbeat, their eyes locked. She saw it there, a brief flicker of concern in his expression, the subtle brace for how she might react to the mention of another woman.

times. But it mattered that it might matter to him. She filed that look away, a mental note to ease his mind later. She wasn't interested in ghosts.

"Speaking of being well out of reach," Will said, his voice cutting through the stretch of quiet that had crept in, "how's Lysa these days? I trust she's still keeping you sharp. I've dreamed about that fruit pie she made last time for weeks."

A laugh rumbled from Gorek's chest, low and warm, like distant thunder wrapped in fondness. "Oh, aye, she's just the same. Always stirrin' trouble one minute, pullin' me out of it the next. Been cookin' more, too, now we've got that helper around. Chu'll meet him soon. He's out runnin' errands. Wee thing's 'bout Ellie's age. Quick hands. Sharp eyes. Got a feelin' chu'll like 'im."

Malin watched the shift in their expressions immediately. The lines around Gorek's eyes softened with something like pride, and Will's smile curved without restraint. Not his smirk. Not the charming grin he used to deflect. A real smile, no dimple, but honest. Something anchored in old memory. The way they spoke of Lysa wasn't just fondness for him, and it was grounding.

"I bet she's thrilled to have someone to fuss over again," Will said, and Malin heard the admiration tucked beneath the tease.

Gorek chuckled, shaking his head fondly. "Lysa's inner glory when she got rebel business ta fuss over. Give her a mission, a list, an army of stubborn fools, and she'll ha'e it sorted 'fore supper."

The corridor ahead shimmered faintly, like heat rising from pavement but colder. It was as if a wall of water hung in midair.

"Prepare yerselves," Gorek warned, his voice dropping into a low, guttural growl that vibrated through the heavy stillness.

only d'ose wit magic can pass."

Malin's heart kicked hard against her ribs like it was trying to punch its way free. The narrow corridor felt tighter with every step forward. Her mind spun with questions. What did only those with magic really mean? What would happen to someone without it? She looked to Will with a look of concern.

"It's fine. It takes some getting used to, but it's better on the other side," he assured.

A pulse of instinct took over. Without thinking, she reached out, one hand for Ellie, the other for Will. Ellie's small fingers curled around hers with childlike trust, but Will's hand found hers with deliberate strength. His grasp was warm, steady. Anchoring. One squeeze said everything: *I've got you.*

"Stay close," Will murmured. The words brushed her skin more than her ears, quiet but absolute.

With Gorek in the lead, his massive frame unbothered by the shifting air, they stepped into the invisible wall.

Malin's breath hitched.

The first step felt like moving into a dream, not quite water, not quite air. Cool pressure wrapped around her, thick as fog. She expected dampness, maybe resistance, but the barrier gave way like mist with weight. Each step deeper was like wading through memories that weren't hers, whispers curling against her ears in languages she didn't understand.

She tightened her grip on Ellie's hand, glancing down.

She had the excitement and calm of a child going on a kiddie rollercoaster.

Of course she was.

completely unshaken. That belief, so absolute, was its own kind of magic.

The thought grounded Malin, even as her body rebelled, with her lungs straining to draw breath that didn't feel like air. Power pressed in on her from all sides, thick and electric. Beneath it, the voices stirred; they were familiar now but warped as if echoing through water, deeper and more ancient than before.

Will's hand stayed strong in hers. Steady. His calm seeped into her bones, slowing the drumbeat of her fear.

Then, suddenly, it was over.

The resistance vanished.

They stumbled through to the other side, and air rushed in dry, clear, and real. Malin gasped as if surfacing from deep water. Her boots scraped against solid stone, the cold of the passage behind them already beginning to fade.

She blinked, heart pounding in her throat, and turned back to look at the shimmer behind them.

It looked like nothing now.

Like the way back had never existed.

Will turned toward her, his brows drawing together as he scanned first Ellie, then her. "You alright?"

"That was *so* weird," Ellie whispered, eyes wide with excitement rather than fear. "It felt like walking through jelly, but like... smart jelly." Her voice was hushed, like she wasn't sure she was allowed to talk about it.

"You?" he asked, tilting her face to look at his. The concern pooled in his eyes when she didn't respond right away.

Will's hand. He hadn't let go.

She nodded slowly, her voice still missing. But her eyes said enough.

He leaned in, kissed the tip of her nose, and offered that crooked grin that always seemed to sneak past her defenses.

"You handled that like a total badass... but if you faint now, I promise to catch you dramatically. Preferably in slow motion."

A startled laugh escaped her, short and breathy but real.

Ellie grinned, hugging her doll tight. "Nanna said it would feel weird but not scary. She was right."

Malin watched her daughter with a quiet awe, the kind that snuck up on her in moments like this. Ellie hadn't flinched. Not once. She'd stepped through magic and mystery like it was nothing new, like the world had always been full of strange doors and hidden paths.

She's so much like him.

There was pride in the thought, not the loud, boastful kind, but the steady, unshakable pride of a woman watching her daughter become everything she hoped she could be. Fearless. Adaptable. Stronger than the world expected. So much like Caelum.

Will stood tall next to her, his hand brushing lightly down Malin's back, a grounding gesture.

Finally relaxing enough to look around, the contrast hit her immediately. Where the Talvi District was all steel and grime, exhaust-stained walls and pulsing machinery, this place felt like a different world entirely. The lights weren't gas or synthetic; they were crystals, softly glowing from above, casting dappled

Efficient. Enchanted. And they didn't hum. Just... glowed.

Even the air felt different. Cleaner. More oxygen-rich. Moisture clung faintly to her skin, not from humidity but from some underground reservoir or filtration system she couldn't see. Someone had put thought into this place, into how to make it livable and hidden at the same time.

Her shoulders dropped before she realized she'd been holding them tight. The tension, the city-driven hypervigilance, all bled out of her slowly. Her senses stayed sharp, but her nervous system began to believe they weren't in immediate danger. Not here.

Will walked beside her, silent but solid. He hadn't said anything in a few minutes, but she was still aware of him in every breath. His presence had become... her rock. And that surprised her more than anything.

They only walked about half a city block before they reached a door. It was tall, arched, and wooden. It was built for function first, but someone took the time to carve intricate symbols around its edges. She didn't recognize them, but they looked similar to the ones on the door of Stoneholds.

The door opened before they could knock.

A petite woman with long, pale silver hair that looked more like woven thread than anything organic stood there, wrapped in a rainbow of colors. Her movements were fast and fluid, and she carried herself with an energy that didn't match the expectations of her apparent age.

"Will!" she gasped, the name cracking like a spark in the quiet air. Her voice was high and airy, with a rasp like a laugh caught in a teacup. It was the kind of voice that invited you in for soup but could scold you to the bone in the same breath.

off guard, but as soon as she was in his arms, he lifted her off her feet in a deep, bear hug.

"My boy! I am so happy to see you." The outpouring of happiness was honest and pure. He placed her carefully back on the ground, but she didn't move far from him, his hand held tightly with both of hers.

Malin didn't miss the look on his face. Relief. Real, unguarded relief.

"Look at you," the woman scolded fondly, pulling back to examine him at arm's length. "Skin and bones. You've been living off ration bars again, haven't you? Gorek told me you have been in town for almost a year, and did you come by for dinner even once? Don't think I don't know."

Will laughed, and it was a different sound, softer. Younger. It caught Malin off guard.

I remember when you first showed up down here, all knees and elbows and too much curiosity," Lysa said, already turning toward the door and ushering them in. "Running around the underground like you had rocket boots strapped to your feet.

She'd heard Will speak of Lysa before. She was the woman who had taken him in, raised him, and helped shape the man beside her now. It was strange, almost jarring, to finally put a face to the name. Lysa wasn't what she had expected. No flourishes. No pretenses. Just presence.

Malin's gaze followed the older woman's movements. There was a sharpness to her, not unkind but efficient, like a blade honed over decades. She moved quickly and precisely, and the room seemed to respond as if it had learned long ago to keep up with her. Will clearly adored her. That much was obvious in the way

Lysa was near.

When Will turned toward her, the smile on his face hadn't completely faded.

"Lysa, I'd like you to meet Ellie and Malin. They are pretty important to me." His tone shifted, gentler, but also proud. "Ellie, Malin, this is Lysara Stonehold. Lysa raised me, basically. She was like a second mother."

Lysa went straight for Ellie.

"So... You're Ellie," she said, eyes sparkling. "I've been hearing about you since you were born. Your Nanna talks about you all the time."

Ellie lit up. "You *know* Nanna?"

"Oh, child, I've *known* Nanna since before your mother was born," Lysa said, winking. "We go way back."

Malin's brain hadn't stopped ticking the entire time. The energy here felt nothing like the city. There was no tension behind every glance. No dread hiding in every corner. Just calm. But layered beneath it, beneath the comfort, the crystals, the lightness, was something older.

She wasn't sure if that was comforting yet. But she was starting to understand why Will had brought them here.

Lysa turned to Will with a fond smile, her voice floating like soft fabric caught on a breeze. "I haven't seen that look on your face for years, all mooning about."

Malin followed her gaze and caught the subtle glimmer that passed between Lysa and Gorek, something unspoken, a long-

playful, cutting straight through pretense.

"He couldn't have picked a better one, that's for sure," Lysa said, her voice dropping with a conspiratorial lilt. "He's well and proper caught, this one."

She winked, her smile widening, and for a second, Malin didn't know what to do with the warmth that bloomed in her chest.

"Looks like he caught a fine one… finally. I've warned you away from all those others," Lysa jested, like it was a simple fact, not flattery.

Malin offered a small, tight smile in return, but she felt it. The compliment. The quiet approval tucked inside the tease. Strangely, she wanted it.

Gorek chuckled, the sound deep and dry like gravel underfoot. "She's neh wrong. Tis ben a stretch fer 'em. But…," his tone shifted, more serious now, "dere's no time fer tales of da heart. Elowen be waitin'. Bes' na make her pace."

The name hit like a quiet bell in Malin's chest. Her mother. Finally.

Before Malin could answer, Lysa stepped in close and took her hand. Her grip was deceptively strong, but there was a softness under it, a quiet strength. It wasn't just a greeting. It felt like a message wrapped in warmth and steel.

"Ye'll be fine," Lysa said, her voice lowering to something just between them. "Shame it took trouble following him home to get Will back through that door… but I'm glad it was you that brought him. It's nice to meet you as well."

Her smile curved but didn't quite settle into joy. It was edged with something older. Something earned.

Lysa had seen plenty of hardship. And she was measuring her now. Not to judge but to understand.

"They are in the parlor; let's not tarry," Lysa instructed, leading the way down the hall.

And Malin, ever the analyst, recognized the calculation.

They turned toward the rear hallway. Lanterns glowed low, casting swinging shadows across the stone walls. The air felt different here. There was a denseness and charge that felt foreign.

"This way now," Lysa said, leading them toward the door at the far end. "Answers await, and maybe more questions than you bargained for."

Malin moved to follow, but her breath caught in her throat as the door creaked open, slow and deliberate.

She stepped through, her pulse quickening, and the faint scent of herbs and earth washed over her like the first breath after surfacing from deep water.

She wasn't ready. But she was going in anyway.

alin stepped through the doorway, her pulse was drumming in her chest, hoping that if nothing else came from today, at least she might have some answers to the questions rolling around in her head. Light pooled in uneven patches along the stone floor, struggling to push back the dark that clung to the corners of the poorly lit room.

She spotted them at the far side of the room, seated casually and sipping tea, as if this was a quiet afternoon and not a reunion loaded with secrets.

Her mother exuded an air of composed elegance, as she always did, her posture a graceful dance of refined diplomacy. Her presence was like a serene painting, each movement deliberate and fluid, honed through years of practice. Yet today, there was an unexpected vivacity in her expression, a youthful glint that seemed to lift her features, making them appear lighter and more vibrant than Malin had ever recalled. Her eyes sparkled with a hint of mischief, and her lips curved into a gentle, almost playful smile, transforming her usual poise into something enchantingly lively.

But it was the woman beside her that made her breath catch in her throat, as if the air itself had thickened. Pointed ears parted the cascade of her silken hair, sharp and elegant as the finest sculpture. Malin blinked in disbelief.

An elf.

Here.

In the heart of Media.

fluidity that seemed to defy the laws of nature. Her features were so exquisitely refined, they bordered on the surreal, as if crafted by the hands of an artist with an unearthly muse. Her age was a mystery. She looked to be thirty, close to her own age. Her beauty was untouched by the passage of years. The robes she wore were a masterpiece of design, intricate patterns woven into the fabric like a tapestry of dreams. Jewels glittered in the light, casting a radiant glow that suggested she was someone of significant stature. Royalty, perhaps. Or something even greater.

Malin had never encountered an elf before, and her mind swirled with uncertainty, not knowing what to make of this extraordinary presence.

"*Nanna!*" Ellie's delighted cry shattered the stillness. She broke from Malin's side in a blur, her little feet slapping against the floor as she ran full tilt into Elowen's waiting arms.

Her mother actually dropped to one knee, wrapping Ellie in a fierce embrace. Her mother's voice cracked with emotion. "There you are my brave girl."

Malin paused, not from jealousy or anger, or even sadness. It was surprise to her mother's reaction to Ellie. She was open, loving, relaxed, and oh so different than the cold, distant mother she grew up with. She was acting the way that she had always wished her mother would act with her as a child.

It was a moment she hadn't been sure she'd ever see, her daughter glowing with joy in the arms of the woman who once felt like a stranger... and now lived inside her head.

Will's hand found the small of her back as she attempted to stay strong with the smile appropriately affixed. His contact was steady. Familiar. A silent *I've got you.*

She let herself breathe.

gently, "Lady Anariel, this is Malin, Elowen's daughter. And Will, my son."

She noticed Will's brow ticked up in surprise at the introduction, but he said nothing. The elf turned to face them, her movement fluid, precise, and almost too graceful to be real.

"A pleasure," Anariel said. Her voice had the softness of wind through chimes, light and lyrical, but impossible to ignore. Her violet eyes were flecked with silver, locked onto Malin with a quiet intensity.

"I see why your mother brought you," she said. "I can feel your magic is... it is strong."

It could have been a compliment, but she wasn't sure.

Then Anariel's expression shifted. "But something's not right."

She stepped closer. Her hands hovered inches from Malin's body. At first she thought Lady Anariel would slap her, but she was scanning, not touching, but clearly searching. They stopped at her shoulder, where her bag sat on her back.

Will moved instantly, slipping the bag from her arm.

Anariel's fingers dipped inside and plucked a tiny object no bigger than a grain of rice. A tracker.

Malin's heart fell.

"It had to be Andrew," she whispered, fury and disbelief rising together. "That hug..."

Gorek took the tracker from Anariel's hand, his expression unreadable. "Da barrier's veil will keep us hidden. They won't get ta clean read." With that, he turned and disappeared through the door.

embrace. "It's okay. Gorek will handle it."

Malin pressed her fingers to her temples. She needed to think. To *breathe*. She prided herself on her ability to handle difficult situations that was why she was so good as a doctor. With all the change and feeling like everything she knew was a lie, she could feel the beginnings of a panic attack coming.

She stepped back, planting her feet. *Colors,* she reminded herself. Ground yourself.

- Red – the rusted pattern in the rug.
- Orange – the flicker of lantern light on brass.
- Yellow – enchanted crystals glowing along the floor.
- Green – a sprig of mint in the teapot.
- Blue – the velvet of the chair by her mother.
- Indigo – the corner shadows.
- Violet – the shimmer in Anariel's eyes.

The tightness in her chest eased. Slowly.

Only then did the room come into full focus again.

Warm steam curled from porcelain cups resting neatly on a carved wooden table, set for five with an almost ceremonial precision. The air held the subtle sweetness of steeping tea, jasmine, maybe, or something floral with a hint of spice. The room itself was unexpectedly cozy, its walls rounded and smooth like they'd been carved directly from the earth. Despite its underground location, it didn't feel oppressive. The ceiling arched high above them, lined with wooden beams strung with dried herbs; they painted the air with hints of lavender, thyme, and clove.

A stone hearth dominated one wall. The fire was steady and warm. Above the embers, a black cast iron pot hung from a thick iron hook, and the aroma wafting from it made Malin's stomach

It smelled like something that had been cooking for hours and tended with care. Along the far wall, shelves were built directly into the stone and held stacks of handmade pottery, tin utensils, and jars sealed with wax and string.

Despite the room's generous size, everything was arranged to encourage closeness, no corners wasted, no space unused. It was a space meant for small gatherings, for secrets and shared warmth. For belonging.

Around them, the room thrummed with a vitality that defied the stillness. The ancient tapestries on the walls, the books with their leather-bound spines cracked from use, the myriad of artifacts that adorned the shelves. They all called her, or was it the magic within her. As Lady Anariel spoke and moved, the room seemed to react like she was the axis upon which the room turned, her every gesture a verse in an unfolding epic.

Malin's voice was quiet. "Mom."

Elowen looked up, her familiar eyes, cool blue mirrors of her own, meeting her daughter's. "Malin," she said softly, rising. "I'm so glad you made it." The words were honest and caring, not the welcome she had expected.

Before she could say a greeting, Ellie interrupted and looked at Lady Anariel. "Nanna told me about you. Will you teach me?" Ellie said, her tone laced with reverence, but there was something more here. The elven woman's eyes, ageless pools, reflected the wisdom of countless lifetimes. They met the little girl's eyes with intensity. "Yes, my child. I'm here to help both you and your mother."

"Malin, this is Lady Anariel," Mom introduced, her voice carrying a note of pride, as if presenting a treasure long kept hidden. "She has been a dear friend for many years. She was actually my mom, your grandmother's friend. She is a truly great teacher of

greatly help you when you need to pass through their lands to get to Aloria."

"It is an honor, Lady Anariel," Malin managed formally, her words feeling clumsy in her mouth, inadequate to bridge the gulf between them.

"The honor is mine. Your mother has told me you recently received your gifts. I'm so pleased the procedure went well. The power coming from you and Ellie. It's extraordinary," said the elven woman, her voice a melody that seemed to flow from the very essence of Aloria itself, rich yet tinged with a sorrow that spoke volumes. At Malin's nod, she continued, "I will join you on your journey and help you to master these gifts."

"Thank you," Malin said, unsure how else to respond. "I haven't had much chance to use it yet. I can feel it there, humming under the surface, but it hasn't really... manifested much."

"No wild magic bursts?" Lady Anariel tilted her head, a flicker of surprise in her violet eyes. "You have control already?"

"I don't know if I'd call it control," Malin admitted. "It just hasn't... happened. Will thought using it might draw attention, so I've been careful."

Lady Anariel regarded her thoughtfully, like she was taking mental notes. "What have you been able to do?"

Malin hesitated. "Healing. And I lit a candle, a small flame, nothing dramatic. I'm a doctor, so the healing didn't surprise me. It just felt... natural."

"A doctor," Anariel echoed with a nod. "Healing would find a comfortable home in you, then. But two abilities already? That's notable."

Others are drawn to a person, shaped by who they are, what they've survived. It will be interesting to see whether you've inherited any of Ellie's traits... or your mother's."

Malin's brow furrowed. "How many abilities do most people have?"

"Most? Just one. Occasionally two. Three or more is rare, but not impossible," Lady Anariel replied. "Your mother, for example, has five. Though they vary in strength, and it took her years to master them."

She didn't move, but her mind was in motion, tracking glances, weighing posture, absorbing the quiet choreography unfolding in front of her. The way her mother subtly angled her body toward the elven woman, a deference disguised as casual posture. The faint dip of Elowen's head before she spoke, like the echo of a bow that had once meant everything. Even the candlelight seemed to hesitate, casting long shadows across the elf's delicate features, as though the flame itself wasn't sure it should reveal her fully.

"Times are changing," Lady Anariel said, her gaze sweeping over Malin with an appraising air. "And with change comes new roles to be filled, new paths to tread. It will be interesting to see what happens with the prophesy. As I've said before, I still feel very strongly that Ellie is involved somehow."

"What do you mean prophesy?" Malin said worriedly.

"It's nothing. I don't think it is referring to Ellie, just some strange coincidences. We can talk about that later when there are fewer pressing issues to discuss," mother dismissed the question.

Malin was slightly stiffened by the dismissal, especially about her daughter. Though nothing explicit was spoken, Malin felt if

chance, she wanted to be aware of it.

There was a pregnant pause while Malin composed her thoughts.

"Malin," came the voice of Lady Anariel, cutting through the tension like a blade. "Although Lysa was kind enough to introduce Will, how is it that you are traveling with him?"

Her commanding tone brooked no hesitation, and Malin could almost see the disappointment etched in the fine lines around her mother's eyes, a testament to unmet expectations. She turned toward Will, the weight of her mother's authority pressing down upon her, shaping her next words with care.

"Well," Malin began, her voice steady despite the tempest raging within. "This is Will. Will Hawkson. As luck would have it, I met him while I was out with friends, and he teaches at Ellie's school." Her introduction was succinct, each syllable measured to convey both respect and necessity. She felt the need to go into more. He wasn't just a man standing there, he was someone she had come to rely on, in this little amount of time.

"Will Hawkson. Also known as Hawk, perhaps?" Elowen repeated, her inflection betraying that she may know more than had been said. It might not be magic, but Malin knew the true measure of her mother's strength: her ability to cloak emotion in layers of reserve, revealing only what she chose. It was a dance of veils and shadows, and Malin had been forced to learn the steps from birth. Now, standing before the one who had taught her, she felt the familiar pull of admiration and apprehension, unsure of which would lead in this silent waltz of wills.

Elowen's eyes were cool and penetrating, holding him in a gaze that weighed and measured. After a moment, she spoke, her voice calm yet carrying the weight of command.

years," Elowen said, her voice calm but heavy with implication. "Lysa's told me stories for longer still. I practically watched you grow up. Your exploits, though roguish and reckless, are impressive. You've saved hundreds through your work."

Her gaze sharpened. "Given *my* role as Commander in that Resistance, I'm curious... who gave you the order to get involved with my daughter? Or my granddaughter?"

The title, Commander, landed like a stone in her stomach. She turned sharply to look at her mother, whose face let nothing through. Then she turned to Will, who looked away with a look of embarrassment. Her pulse spiked.

More big secrets hidden from her. A dozen questions surged through her at once. But even as the shock rocked her, her body leaned instinctively toward Will, her shoulder brushing his. She wasn't sure where the truth started or stopped, but she knew she wanted to hear it from *him*.

Beside her, Ellie bounced on her toes, looking between the adults. "Really? Will is like a superhero, Grandma!" she exclaimed, tugging at his hand with a grin full of pride.

Will's voice came low and even. "I got no order. This was something I did on my own and was not part of the resistance."

He looked like he might explain further, but Elowen raised a hand. One small, commanding gesture. He fell silent.

"There's more to a man than his words," Elowen said, her tone clipped. "Here in the Shadows, we don't guess. We *see*." She stepped toward him. "Will Hawkson, Will you let me look. Let me see if the tales match the man. Do you consent?"

Will gave a shallow nod.

temples. The air in the room shifted. Malin's spine locked tight. Will's jaw tensed, his body held taut, and for long moments, no one breathed.

A minute passed. Then another. Malin gripped his arm, her concern flaring as he flinched—once, sharply—before going still again.

Then Elowen pulled away. Her eyes were unreadable, but that was no surprise.

Malin stepped closer and wrapped an arm around his waist, needing him to feel her presence. He gave her a quiet, grateful look. No words passed between them, but everything he couldn't say echoed in that glance.

"I'm satisfied," Elowen said at last, her expression finally softening, but just barely. "For now."

Will exhaled. "I know my past is... complicated," he said, voice guarded. "But keeping them safe, Malin and Ellie, that's all I care about. I would die for them."

Elowen nodded once. "I believe you." Her eyes flicked to Malin. "You'll be included in the travel plan."

Then her voice steeled. "But if your past brings danger to this mission, if it threatens what we protect, I will end it."

The fire within Malin burned at those words. They struck her final nerve. "If you think for one moment I would be going anywhere without Will, it is you who made the mistake. I don't care if you are my mother, Chancellor, or Commander. You do not have that call to make," Malin said, with steam radiating from her body.

"Malin. Settle," Elowen said authoritatively. "It was a warning. Not a command." Her voice gentled, and an odd calm began to

mother's magic.

Ellie, oblivious to the full weight of the moment, leaned into Will and whispered, "I still think you're a superhero." Her hand clutched his tighter. She was quiet now but watching. Listening.

Elowen returned to her chair, her movements graceful as ever, the hem of her cloak whispering over the floor.

"We proceed with caution," she said, her tone final. "But we proceed *together.* Trust is earned in action. In truth. Let's see if Mr. Hawkson continues to prove worthy of both."

The room seemed to exhale, tension ebbing as her words settled like dust. Malin felt it in her chest, a pause, not an ending. The stakes remained. But for now, they had bought themselves forward momentum.

Here, deep beneath the city, among hidden allies and flickering candlelight, trust had become the only currency that mattered.

"You depart at first light," she declared, voice carrying the inflexible tone of steel wrapped in velvet. "Lady Anariel will guide you through the forest under the protection of the elven kindreds. Zane will accompany you for protection, as well as to get safely to his family in Aloria."

A hush fell, and the weight of her words settled upon them. Will had told her that the journey was dangerous, and the forest was a perilous path, so having the help of elves sounded like it would be beneficial.

Will shifted his stance, the flicker of apprehension reflecting in his guarded expression. She noticed lines of concern between his brows before he spoke. "With respect, Commander," he ventured, the timbre of his voice betraying a hint of dissent. The

included, through contested terrain is..."

His words trailed into the charged silence. It seemed it was a challenge but drawn on from experience. Will's gaze locked with her mother, neither yielding nor wavering in the delicate dance of authority and concern.

Mother's lips pressed into a thin line, the subtle shift of her posture speaking volumes to those versed in her silent language.

"Your concerns are noted," she said, resonating with the gravity of their predicament. "But time is a luxury we cannot afford. The dawn will not wait for our readiness."

"Your first waypoint is an establishment I saw that you know, the Inn in the West Woods. You will camp for one night, then the third will be in the town of Seaborn, where you will board your ship at first light. You cannot be late. It is not an easy journey by any means, but I trust you will be able to find a way through." Will held her stare, acknowledging the unassailable truth in her words with a curt nod. The discussion was closed; the command had been given. The lingering scent of unease mingled with resolve as they all braced for the journey ahead, where the promise of Aloria called like a beacon in the night.

The air was still, with the weight of Will's unvoiced concerns. The thick walls of the ancient room held their breath as Lady Anariel rose from her chair. Her gaze was tranquil, an ocean of calm in the rising storm of doubt.

"Children, do not fret over the weaving of our path," she began, her voice harmonizing with the faint rustle of her gossamer gown. "I think you will find me an asset."

fanned like willow branches in the wind. A shimmer sparked around her, a haze of distorted air, and in a blink, she was gone.

She reappeared across the room, near a heavy tapestry embroidered with constellations Malin didn't recognize.

The room held its breath.

The display wasn't just powerful; it was controlled. There was no fanfare, no sparks or thunder, just quiet, impossible movement. It was a demonstration, not of aggression but of how she may be useful.

"Power such as ours cannot be left to chance," Lady Anariel said, her voice even, eyes sweeping across the room. "It must be trained, shaped. Without guidance, magic will shape *you*." She glanced toward Ellie, then at Malin. "These younglings carry more than talent. They carry *potential*. And if the prophecy holds any truth, they will need *all* of it."

Malin stiffened at the word *prophecy*. She felt the shift in the room, the hush of hesitation. But before any whisper of debate could begin, Elowen stepped forward.

Her figure, backlit by the flickering crystals, radiating calm and command.

"This isn't the time for stories," she said flatly, her voice cleaving the silence. "We're not here to weigh legends. We act. Because delay costs lives. The rest are prophecies or myths, stories retold over time that may never come true. They can wait."

She paused long enough to ensure her words landed.

"At dawn, you march. Not as scattered rebels, but as one."

Her gaze moved to Malin. "Your daughters will know safety in Aloria. That is my word."

guard. But Elowen's tone left no space for questions. She made a note to ask about that.

Malin inhaled deeply. The scent of moss and smoke lingered like old memories: damp stone, warm iron, steeped tea. She held onto those things to keep the moment real.

Then Elowen asked, "Are there any questions?"

No one spoke.

She continued, her tone returning to efficiency. "Lysara has a meal prepared and rooms arranged. If you need supplies or have requests, speak up over dinner. You leave early. The forest crossing is hard. Your ship departs in three days. Much of the journey will be on foot."

Then, softer, "Malin, I'd like a word before dinner. Will, can you help Ellie find her room and wash up?" Will met her eyes with a nod, smiled a half-crooked smile, and lifted one eyebrow in a look that told her he would speak with her later, and it would be okay.

Without argument, Will guided Ellie away. Lysara followed.

Anariel dissolved again into air, her magic a quiet rupture. Only Malin remained there with her mother.

Elowen didn't speak at first. She just watched. The flicker of candlelight caught her features, casting them in alternating shadow and clarity. Something unreadable lingered in her expression. Not distance, but weight. Like she was waiting for Malin to cross a line on her own.

Malin held her gaze, saying nothing. The room was quiet, only the soft drip of water somewhere deep in the stone.

fears she wasn't ready to voice. But under all of it, a fragile, steady thing glowed.

Hope.

Not the kind that burned bright. The kind that endured.

"Mom," Malin found herself speaking before she could measure the prudence of her words, her tone steadier than she felt. Words that had been building up spilled out. "There are so many questions. I just don't understand," she paused, allowing them to build within her.

"How I could have missed so many things. Daddy. Daddy must have put Andrew in my life to spy on me. Why would he have done that? I thought he loved me. How did I not know you were speaking with Ellie? How did I not know she had magic? Am I a bad mother for noticing? Why... weren't we closer?" The emotional baggage spilled out of Malin like vomit. Malin's legs would not hold her in her outpouring, and she fell to her knees, putting her head in her mother's lap, her mother's fingers running through her hair. Elowen allowed her time to process the questions and catch her breath from the tears. When she was able to continue, she said, "I feel so lost, so naive, and stupid. How did I miss so many important details within my own life?"

When her mother wrapped her arms around her, it caught her off guard. It was an act of comfort and caring that she had wanted so much for so long.

"You shouldn't feel that way. I longed to be close to you, to release your powers, and to teach you, for us to grow together. I was afraid you might not make it through the procedure, but I regretted not telling you every day. You barely made it through when it was put in. I had planned to pretend to chip you, as I was

While I was being treated, they chipped you at your father's order." She looked up to see a tear run down her Mom's face.

"You know, it was Will, who got you through that procedure. When I looked within his memories, I saw him while you were transforming. When the magic was trying to decide if it would stay or go. He called out to the magic and assured it that you were worthy. They were drawn back to you by him. I do owe him so much. As far as your father, I do feel he thinks he was doing the right thing for you. We just have different ideas of what that should be." She placed a light kiss on her forehead, as she had when she was just a little child.

The moments only lasted few, then Malin was able to gather her strength again, "I don't know the first thing about traveling outside of the city. I have heard the forests are thick with more than just elves. I'm so worried. That is how Caelum died. I can't let Ellie lose another parent."

"You should know that Caelum was part of the resistance. He died when he was found to be helping transport people to Aloria the way that Will used to transport people. He was also killed at your father's direction, before he knew you were pregnant with Caelum's child. Your father has always felt some guilt for that. I think that is why he put Andrew into your life. Andrew is your father's assistant."

She paused to dry Malin's tears. "On top of that, Will is the best transporter the resistance has. He has been doing that almost, all of his adult life and the route you are taking is one he knows well. He will take care of you. I was prepared to try to dissuade you from him, but after seeing in his mind, he may have his flaws, but I believe he is the best one for this trip." Mom's tone was honest and plain. She allowed the words to sink in; a layer of anger took over the ladened emotion before.

something about it....and what was that about daughters, plural?" Malin questioned.

"You caught that, did you?" her mom smiled. "One of my gifts is prophesy. It isn't my strongest gift, and I don't know everything, but... I have searched for everything I could about the prophesy and how it might connect to you or Ellie, and I haven't found anything. That is why I feel it is not you. While searching, I did see you holding another daughter. I can't see much else, but I know that to be fact."

Her eyes widened. "Really? Another daughter? Does it say when? Anything?"

"Sorry. No. We shall just have to see."

Mom continued, "I know you and Ellie have the power in you to make it through. I also know that your father would not allow either of you to be injured, and Masoncore has funded control over many of the guards. I expect that he would have ordered to ensure you aren't hurt, but there are people in the city who know of the prophesy, and if there were any thoughts that you might be part of it, they would want to control you."

In the silence that followed, Malin drew a deep breath, bracing herself against the tide of emotions that threatened to sweep her away. Her mind, ever analytical, began to chart the unknown waters they would soon navigate, plotting each potential course with the resolve of a seasoned captain.

"One thing I know about you, you will have everything under control, and you won't send Ellie or me somewhere we shouldn't be. I trust in your plan. I also wished we had been closer as I was growing up, but I really love that Ellie has been able to receive the love that I always hoped I could feel from you," Malin conceded, the finality of her acceptance resonating in the hush that enveloped them.

I cannot show you in other ways. It is so hard to pretend that I can't hear thoughts that it is sometimes easier to stay away from those I'm at most risk of discovery." She touched the handkerchief to her eyes, then continued, "At dawn, we move, but for tonight, let's eat. I know Lysara's cooking, and my stomach is already growling," she decreed with a smile, her voice warm.

They stood. Her mother was a bit shorter than her, but it still felt so good to feel her arms wrapped around her. She couldn't remember the last hug she had gotten from her. They stood there in an embrace for several moments until her mother pulled away.

"Now go. Clean yourself up and go settle things with Will. I know he is concerned, both about you and about how you feel about him. You have my blessing with him. He is one of the good ones." She walked her to the door of the parlor that opened to the hall and pointed down the hall.

ill pushed the door open, then froze. It wasn't danger that made him pause this time, it was memory. The soft glow of crystal light hummed from the walls, casting warm patterns over the stone. The air smelled faintly of earth and lavender soap. It was his childhood bedroom and smaller than he remembered, smaller than Malin's bedroom had been. Lysa had left everything exactly as he left it on his last visit.

Simple. Functional. Just like him.

The Queen-sized bed, longer than standard to fit his adolescent growth spurt, sat against the far wall, the same hand-carved headboard Gorek had made when he turned eleven. The shelves were mostly empty now, but one still held a few remnants he hadn't thought to hide: a carved wooden hawk, worn at the edges from being held too often. A tattered book of resistance codes and cyphers tucked spine-in like a secret. A sketch pinned to the wall, rough lines of a long-forgotten cityscape. He debated pulling it down.

He hadn't thought about the fact that he would need to bring *her* in here. In the past, when he transported some ladies whom he had gotten friendly with, those women were given their own rooms. Lysa had made a point to tell him that they should stay here. She was a troublemaker sometimes. He could still change rooms.

His boots made no sound against the worn stone floor as he crossed to the satchel by the bedside. He didn't need to check it, he'd already packed twice, but the ritual grounded him. One last sweep, one last habit he couldn't break.

Everything felt louder now. Sharper.

He glanced back toward the hallway, toward the soft footsteps that weren't far behind. He expected Malin soon. Then, he realized, with a small, unsteady breath, that he was nervous.

Damn.

It wasn't the danger that shook him. Not the journey ahead or the secrets still buried deep. It was her. The way she saw things. The way she *saw him,* with eyes that didn't flinch. Like she expected the best from him.

He wasn't sure he deserved it.

The walls hummed gently with the magic woven into the rock, a calming pulse that reminded him that this place was safe. For now. He decided he should probably go check on things and spun to leave the room.

Will stepped softly into the hallway, the stones cool beneath his feet, the low hum of magical lanterns casting golden halos along the walls.

He heard her before he saw her, Malin's footsteps, hesitant, then her shape emerging from the corridor's shadows like a vision pulled from memory.

Tears glistened on her cheeks, caught in the crystal light like stardust. Her striking blue eyes, usually sharp and calculating, shimmered now with something softer, raw, and vulnerable. When she looked at him, she smiled.

He didn't feel he deserved that look.

She crossed the last few steps between them without a word, and he wrapped her in his arms without thinking, grounding

people over the years, comforted, protected but this was different. This mattered to him.

"Will," she breathed, the word low and full of unspoken things. "I just spoke with my mom. She told me you saved me and if it hadn't been for you, I wouldn't have made it through my transformation. That she trusts you."

He stiffened. That was not what he expected.

"I'm not thrilled you lied," she added, "but I understand why. She trusts you, after seeing what's in your head. I trust you because of what I've seen in your heart."

His breath caught. A lifetime of guilt and guardedness cracked beneath those words. He pressed his lips to her cheek and pulled her in tighter, not bothering to hide how much it meant.

"You have no idea what that does to me," he said quietly.

They didn't speak for a moment, just held each other in the quiet hum of the hallway. Her head fit perfectly on his shoulder. Her presence settled something in him.

When she finally pulled back, her eyes had regained their usual spark.

"You know," she said, a mischievous note sliding into her voice, "now that I know you're into fiery women, maybe this new ability of mine makes sense. Maybe you drew it to me."

A small flame flickered to life at her fingertips.

Will arched a brow. "So, this is my fault?"

"Clearly," she said, smirking. The flame danced closer, a hair's breadth from his temple. "You light fires within me, I just happen to wield them."

burning us out of these tunnels."

"Please." She blew the flame out with exaggerated grace. "I'm the picture of control."

He stepped closer, warmth radiating between them now. "You're a menace." He smiled.

She didn't deny it. She just smiled, slow and dangerous.

Will's voice dropped. "Malin."

Their eyes met, blue and hazel, flint and tinder, and the space between them disappeared. His hand found the small of her back, her arms looped around his neck, and their lips met in a kiss that carried every unspoken truth between them.

Not a promise. Not yet.

But something close.

Will caught the sound before he saw her, small, fast footsteps down the hall. The rhythm was familiar: light but purposeful. Ellie.

He pulled back from Malin, slower than he should've, his hand lingering at her waist for just a breath longer. Her cheeks were still flushed from their kiss, her lips parted like she might say something, then stopped.

The moment broke as Ellie rounded the corner, her wide blue eyes landing on them with open amusement.

Will straightened automatically. It wasn't from guilt, but because his instincts never let him stay off-guard for long. Still, a faint smile tugged at his mouth as Ellie appeared, arms crossed like a tiny guard catching them mid-moment.

her tone a perfect mix of mischief and command.

Before he could respond, her small hand wrapped around his with more strength than he expected, threaded with that quiet hum of magic he was starting to recognize. She grabbed Malin's hand too, tugging them both with impatience.

Will chuckled, letting her lead the way. He caught the sound of Malin's laugh beside him, soft, almost surprised, and something in his chest eased.

She pulled them toward one of his favorite places in the world: Lysa's kitchen. Even before they stepped through the archway, the scent hit him. The smell of herbs, simmering stew, and something sweet baking low and slow. His mouth watered, anticipation blooming like muscle memory.

If Lysa had made *the pie*, he might actually believe the world was still worth saving.

As they entered the dining area, a tapestry of aromas enveloped them. It was a feast conjured from simplicity; root vegetables roasted to caramelized perfection, a hearty stew that simmered with notes of thyme and rosemary, and freshly baked bread that he knew would steam when torn open. Its crust would crack under the pressure of eager fingers. The golden glow from the enchanted lanterns cast a warm hue over the rustic table, laden with the bounty of harvest.

Will took his seat, the wooden chair creaking beneath him, sturdy, familiar, real. He was pleased to see Malin choose the chair next to him, rather than next to Ellie. She chose to sit across the table from them, Ellie moved with a focus far beyond her years, her telekinetic abilities on display in the casual way

Just... *her.*

Gorek sat at the head of the table, as usual and Lysa across from him. Lady Anariel sat beside Malin, closest to Lysa, who was in her element with an almost full table.

He let the moment settle, feeling it in his bones.

The meal unfolded with an easy rhythm, laughter, stories passed around like second helpings, the kind of soft chaos that only came from people who trusted one another. Will watched it all quietly, drinking it in.

He couldn't remember the last time he'd had a meal like this. Not ration bars in a safe house. Not hurried bites on the run. This was different. This had *roots.*

And for the first time in a long while, surrounded by the clatter of dishes and the hum of voices, Will Hawkson felt something he hadn't dared hope for:

Home.

Will found himself casting sidelong gazes to Malin more than once. The soft curve of her smile was genuine, unguarded. It lit something in him. That smile didn't just stop his heart; it *quieted* it, in a way that nothing else ever had.

He shifted his eyes across the table, watching Ellie nestled between Malin and Elowen. It struck him again, how alike they were, and yet how distinct. Elowen radiated composed power, all calm control and measured grace. Ellie was a flame barely contained, vibrant and bursting at the seams. Both carried the same clear, ice-blue eyes but the resemblance shifted in smaller things. Elowen's features were refined, sculpted: high cheekbones, regal bearing. Ellie, still growing into herself, had rounder cheeks, a sprinkle of freckles, and a spark that couldn't be taught.

frame, tempered by experience, softened by compassion. Three generations at one table, and somehow, they all fit. Like the pieces of a puzzle, he hadn't known he'd been trying to solve.

They ate, savored, and reveled in the momentary peace, letting the flavors of the food and the warmth of company soothe the jagged edges of their lives. The succulent bite of the stew, enriched with the hearty tang of wild game, melded with the earthy sweetness of the vegetables, creating a symphony of taste that sang of home and hearth.

Will Hawkson cradled his cup, the rich red wine within catching the flickers of the hearth's fire. The robust laughter and the clinking of cutlery filled the room with a warmth that even the chill from the outside world could not penetrate. Across the table, Gorek's boisterous voice rose above the din, his bear-like frame shaking with mirth as he recounted tales of Will's youth.

Gorek leaned back in his chair, a smirk wide across his stubbled face. "Remember when young Will snuck into the foraging tunnels? Thought he'd bring back supper for all of us, almost got himself buried in a cave-in."

Lysa groaned with affection, setting down her cup. "Oh stars, don't remind me. I nearly lost my voice screaming his name. When I found him, covered head to toe in soot with a sack of half-crushed mushrooms and that smug grin, he just looked up and said, *'Don't worry, Lysa. I mapped the whole tunnel on the way in.'*" She shot Will a look, her eyes dancing. "You were eleven."

Gorek chuckled. "Didn't have the sense to stay put but had the foresight to draw a map." He looked over at Malin and Ellie. "That's the first time we realized he didn't just have guts; he had purpose. Always trying to help us with one project or another."

wanted to be useful. To make sure no one else got lost. That's never changed."

The room seemed to lean into their words, the air thick with the scent of roasting meat and fresh herbs, anticipation hanging on the edge of each tale. Will felt his cheeks warm, not just from the heat of the fire or Malin's occasional, sly glances, but from the affectionate embarrassment of being so fondly laid bare before friends who had become his chosen family.

A small boy slipped into the room like a draft through a forgotten crack, he was quiet, cautious, and easy to overlook if you weren't paying attention. But Will noticed.

The kid couldn't have been more than twelve, maybe thirteen, with a too-thin frame wrapped in a patchy sweater that hung off his shoulders. Light brown curls flopped across his forehead, framing a face that looked like he was trying hard not to show anything, but Will recognized that kind of mask. He'd worn it once too.

Zane's hazel eyes darted across the room, landing on each of them like stones skipped across a still lake, never staying in one place too long. His movements were deliberate, shoulders tight, as if waiting for bad news or a problem.

"Zee," Lysara said gently, her voice like a warm blanket. "Come in, love. Everyone, this is Zane. He joined us a few months ago."

Will's gaze lingered on the boy. He didn't miss the flicker of fear behind those eyes, or the way Zane scanned for exits before even considering a seat. Survival instincts. Deep ones. Will knew the look well. He knew what it meant to walk into a room and expect nothing good.

was going to be traveling with him, he should know a bit about the boy. He would have to ask Lysa later.

Lysara rose from her seat, a smile lighting up her face as she crossed the room to where Zane stood hesitantly. The others at the table watched with anticipation, knowing Lysara's motherly instinct would not let the boy escape without a warm welcome.

Placing a gentle hand on the boy's shoulder, Lysara said, "He has been such a huge help around here the last few months, since he came to stay after his family...." her voice trailed off to not upset Zane.

Will offered a hearty greeting, clapping Zane on the back. Will felt a surge of protectiveness toward the boy, knowing all too well what it was like to be an outsider looking in.

Gorek leaned forward, his voice booming with a rough-hewn warmth. "How'd yer task go, Zee? Everythin' squared away, then?"

"Yes. Sir," he said softly.

Ellie asked directly, studying Zane with curious eyes. "What happened to your family?"

Zane hesitated for a moment before answering. "My parents and sister were killed when they put those suppressors in 'em. Luckily, some people were able to get me to Gorek a'fore they found me too."

There was a collective understanding around the table as they glanced at each other knowingly. They accepted him in among their chosen family.

a reassuring squeeze of his shoulder. "You came at the perfect time though. I really needed the help around here."

Zane looked down at his feet, then sat in the open chair next to Ellie.

The boy's gaze lifted toward Lysara and Gorek, and in that look lay unspoken volumes of reliance and silent pleas for stability. The love and protective bond between them were palpable, he remembered it well.

Gorek patted the seat next to him, a broad, welcoming gesture that left no room for hesitation. "C'mon now, lad. We were just swappin' tales about our brave Will here," he rumbled, the words rolling out like warm stones. "He came to us much the same way ye did, quiet, scrappy, and lookin' like he'd bite before he'd speak."

Zane slid into the offered chair, his posture relaxing marginally as Lysara placed a generous helping of stew before him. The boy offered a small, grateful smile, a rare glimpse of the child within, before he turned a pair of keen eyes on Will. In them shimmered the reflection of a past that both understood, a connection unsaid yet deeply acknowledged.

"Will's bravery is something you share, Zane," Lysara remarked. Will noticed Zee's back straighten and he lifted his eyes to actually look at the others.

"Bravery comes in many forms," Will added, addressing Zane with a nod of respect. "Often, the bravest thing we can do is simply keep going."

Zane held Will's gaze, absorbing the words, and for a fleeting moment, the room's atmosphere shifted from the light-hearted revelry to one of somber understanding. But it was a testament to the resilience they all shared, a quiet acknowledgment that

them together, each step a silent vow of solidarity.

"Zane," she began, her voice soft yet laced with an unwavering strength, "it's time for you to know about Aloria."

Will noticed the shift in the boy's posture; he stiffened, his fork pausing midway to his mouth. The lingering laughter died upon Zane's lips, giving way to a wary stillness.

"Aloria. I've already heard about Aloria?" Zane's voice was barely above a whisper.

"Yes, my dear, but it is time you know it." Lysara's hands enveloped Zane's warm and reassuring. "You have family there. They are survivors from your past. It's time for you to be reunited with them. To learn more about who you are... and who you could become."

Zane's breath hitched, a fathomless ache swirling in his gaze. Will could see the struggle playing out within the boy; an internal battle where fear grappled with burgeoning hope.

"But I... I don't wanna leave," Zane protested, his voice cracking under the weight of uncertainty. "Did I do somethin' wrong?"

"Sometimes, Zee," Lysara said, a note of sadness threading through her nurturing tone, "to find our place in this vast tapestry, we must follow threads we never expected to grasp. Here there is a constant worry about being found. Media is not a good place for a child with powers to grow up. There, you will be able to live as you truly should."

Zane's slender frame shook as he turned into Lysara's embrace, seeking solace in the azure shawl draped over her shoulders. His small hands clutched at the fabric, holding on as if it were the anchor in a storm-wrought sea.

pleaded, muffled against her chest.

"There is nothing wrong with you. You deserve every opportunity. Everything changes, sweet one," Lysara murmured, kissing the crown of his head. "But some things remain constant. Our love for you is one of them. Maybe when you are grown, you can come back and be a transporter like Will became when he left us, allowing you to be in both cities."

Will watched the tender scene, feeling the taut strings of his own heart resonate with Zane's turmoil. He understood the boy's reluctance; the thought of leaving behind the only semblance of security could chill even the sturdiest of souls. He counted himself lucky that he was able to stay with them for so long."

Yet amidst the shadows of doubt, the spark of destiny called Zane, as it did to all those who bore the gift of magic in their veins. And Will knew that regardless of the path Zane would tread, the threads of their shared past would forever bind them in ways unseen, unspoken, but ever present.

Will Hawkson stood and walked around the table to Zee, his boots silent on the worn wooden floor. The candlelight threw a soft glow over Zane's pinched face, casting shadows that seemed to quiver with the boy's fear. Will knelt beside his chair, offering a solid presence in the tumultuous sea of emotions that Zane was drowning in.

"Zee," Will began, his voice a low rumble, as steady and sure as the ancient trees that ringed their hidden sanctuary. "I've heard about how brave you were on challenges that made others quit, and you chose to do the right thing." His hand found Zane's shoulder, grip firm yet gentle, a lifeline. "You carry within you a courage that is rare, and a fierce heart. I know exactly how you feel, I was there, even younger than you. I know how amazing Lysa and Gorek are, but if you have family in Aloria, that will be

love you just as much as them. "

The air hung heavily with the scent of pine resin and the lingering warmth of Lysara's cooking, a bittersweet reminder of the safety they were about to leave behind. Will could feel the tremor beneath his fingertips, the silent battle raging within Zane, a war between the longing for known comforts and the call of an uncertain destiny.

"Lysa told me of your importance to them. As they are my family, that means you are important to me," Will continued, his gaze locking on Zane's hazel eyes that mirrored his own. "I bet your parents would be very proud of the man you are becoming."

Lysara moved into the sphere of light, her amber-flecked eyes brimming with a tender resolve. She placed a hand over Will's, her touch like a whisper of silk, and leaned down to meet Zane's gaze.

"Zane," she said, her voice a melody of comfort woven through the air, "no distance will stop the bond we have formed. We will be with you, in every sunrise that greets you in Aloria, in every star that winks at you from the velvet sky."

He watched Lysa pull a small crystal pendant from around her neck, then press it into Zane's palm. It pulsed with a soft luminescence, a beacon almost. "With this, you can reach across the miles. We can talk, and Will can help you to find your way back to us if you don't feel it is a better place for you."

Zane wrapped his fingers around the pendant, like it was a treasure. His eyes lit with a small flicker of hope and he threw his arms around her and held tight.

"Remember," Lysara murmured, her warm breath stirring the curls at Zane's forehead, "there's strength in embracing change,

wants to step back."

It dawned on Will that the choice to bring Zee would increase the complications for the four of them on the trip. Looking into his eyes and knowing that feeling of loss and knowing how important Lysa and Gorek had become to him; it felt like looking at a young version of him. He watched the exchange, a silent vow etched itself into his soul. He would help this boy and help him unlock the boundless potential that simmered beneath his skin. In the muted glow of the room, amidst the mingled aromas of hearth and home, a new chapter awaited them; a journey fraught with peril, perhaps, but also paved with the gold of untold possibilities.

Lysa stood, releasing Zee from her embrace and said, "I have pies, let me go get them." The most amazing words he could have heard sealed that moment perfectly. Since he was up, he followed Lysa in the kitchen to assist how he could.

The rest of dessert passed in easy rhythm, the tension of the earlier conversation dissolved into warm laughter and clinking utensils. Across the table, Zee and Ellie had struck up an animated conversation. The boy had introduced her to a tiny chipmunk that peeked out from his coat pocket, Felix, with twitching whiskers and twitchier nerves. Ellie was instantly enchanted. Will watched as Zee explained, a little shy at first, how he could speak to animals. Ellie leaned in, wide-eyed, hanging on every word like it was the most natural thing in the world.

The final embers in the hearth cast a soft, golden glow over the faces gathered around the table. Will leaned back in his chair, the pies had been so much better than he remembered that he ended up eating two slices. Shadows danced upon the walls of the cozy dining room, playing with the edge of reality where truth often blurred into legend.

cascading like molten gold down her shoulders. The flickering light reflected in her cool blue eyes, giving them an otherworldly luster. Her laughter, moments before, had filled the room, clear and natural, intertwining with Lysara's tales and Gorek's booming chuckles as they had done their best to embarrass him with stories from his past.

Not to leave Malin out, Elowen had shared a few stories of her daughter as a girl. Her tales that carried the same warmth and quiet pride as Lysa's stories of him. Will watched as Ellie leaned in, wide-eyed, soaking up every word about her mother climbing trees in formal skirts or sneaking cookies from the kitchen and blaming it on the cat. Ellie giggled with delight, her gaze bouncing between Elowen and Malin like she was seeing her mother in a whole new light.

Will found himself watching Malin more than the story. She had flushed at first, a bit embarrassed, but gradually relaxed into it. There was a rare softness in her eyes, a smile tugging at the corners of her lips that felt utterly unguarded. She hadn't just been strong her whole life, she'd been wild and clever and full of spark, much like Ellie. And that spark hadn't dimmed. If anything, it burned brighter now.

He realized, somewhere between the laughter and candlelight, how much he wanted to learn *all* of her stories, not just the ones her mother told.

Now, amid the gentle clinking of cutlery being tidied away and the contented sighs of a meal well-enjoyed, Will caught the subtle shift in the air. An undercurrent of anticipation, a charge that hummed between him and Malin, electric yet unspoken. He could see it in the way her lips quirked upward, a silent conversation passing through their shared glances.

with the promise of the night ahead. He stood, the scrape of his chair against the wooden floor. His movements were deliberate, the product of a life spent on alert, but tonight they carried a different weight; a cadence of desire wrapped in the guise of casualness.

"Retire, I mean," he added, the corner of his mouth turning up in a playful smirk. His eyes locked onto Malin's, and with a flicker of mischief, he winked. A single wink that spoke volumes of their connection.

Malin's responding smile was enigmatic, her eyes alight with a flame that owed nothing to her magical powers. She rose gracefully to her feet, the loose fabric of her shirt whispering secrets against her skin as she moved. They stood there for a moment, suspended in time, the air around them charged with the tantalizing possibility of what lay beyond the here and now.

As he started walking back out to the hall, Lysa stopped him and pulled him back, "Will. I need to speak with you. Maybe Malin can get the kids settled and meet you after."

The table was almost clear and most of the others had retired for the night. Gorek was washing dishes. Will felt a wave of apprehension wash over him. Lysara's request didn't sound like catching up, it sounded like there was something important to discuss.

He followed Lysara's lead as she made her way over to one of the cozy armchairs positioned by the fireplace. The flames crackled merrily, casting a warm glow over the room. Will settled into a chair next to her, waiting for her to speak.

"I'm not sure where to start. Do you remember a Felicity Stamer?" Lysara said after a pause. He hadn't heard that name is years, maybe even a decade.

almost 12 years ago. I brought her here once or twice." Will had been unprepared to hear that name again, much less out of Lysa.

"Zane is twelve years old; he looks like the spitting image of you, and when he showed up, I was given a letter from a Felicity Stamer saying that Zane would be safe with his father.... She named you as the father... Will Hawkson."

He didn't know what to say. He was sure his mouth was likely hanging open.

What do you say about something like that?

She continued. "Apparently, Zane was never told that the man that raised him was not his father, so Zane does not know. I'm not sure how to tell him. I debated on telling you. He got here almost 6 months ago. I was going to find you, but as I knew you had come to town and hadn't come to visit, I figured you had other things going on for you. Until I saw you with Malin and Ellie... It didn't even occur to me that you might be interested. The way you are with Ellie, it seems obviously fatherhood looks good on you."

"I'm... I'm a father?" Will was completely at a loss for words.

They spoke for a little longer and Lysa told her what she had learned of Felicity and the life Zane had before he came to stay with them. It broke his heart, but he was so glad to hear that Felicity had found a man who was willing to raise him as if he were his own son. They had a good life in Galvin, where Zane had gone to a great school. All the things he could never have given Felicity or Zane.

Lysara got up and gave him a big hug, "You are, and you will be a great one." She then left him with his thoughts, so she could go help Gorek with dishes.

There is no denying that Zane does look just like a young version of him. He felt at a loss. His mind flashed on images of Malin. She would be able to help him process this.

Will stood and blindly walked to the bedroom, his shock leading him to the only one he felt could quench his confusion. The only one who made him feel steady, with just her presence.

ill's face was ashen when he entered the room. She stood and met him, as he shut the door behind him. A gleam from the crystals caught in his eyes, betraying a storm within.

"Malin," he began, his voice a low rumble that resonated with a shock that concerned her. "Lysa just told me that I am Zane's father."

She wasn't sure how to react to that. She had wondered about it. They looked the same, they even had a few of the same mannerisms, both had the same crooked grin when they were laughing, the same tilt of their head when they listened, and they both found it so important to take care of others. She had almost expected to hear come out one day. *What do you say to that?*

Watching him, she asked, "What do you think about it?"

He led them to the bed, lay down, and asked her to snuggle up beside him. "I don't really know what to say. There's no denying it, I suppose. You must have noticed it too. Felicity and I..." he trailed off, lost in thought. "I was ready to marry her. We had been involved in some rescue missions and intelligence operations for the resistance. She talked about wanting to quit and settle down. I wasn't there yet, but one night, after a particularly dangerous mission that didn't go as planned, but we managed to escape, we celebrated with the crew. I intended to propose over breakfast, but she was gone the next morning. I never saw or heard from her again."

"So, you loved her," she asked.

"I think I did. We were always like oil and water, driving each other crazy, then making up. It was never easy being with her,

married, that would be enough to make her want to stay with me, but I wanted to keep working. I never got the chance to try. She left a note and was gone."

"Does this affect your plans?" she asked, her voice tinged with uncertainty. She wasn't sure how she fit into his plans, but she thought she would want to.

"That is a very good question," he admitted, a hint of nervousness in his tone. "We hadn't really discussed plans for the future. I was almost afraid to jinx things with us," he confessed, his honesty catching her off guard.

"Does Zane know? I'm guessing he doesn't based on his behavior. Would it be better to tell him after we are on the road and when he has had a chance to get to know you?" Her thoughts spilled out in a stream, and he seemed to appreciate her open analysis. She hesitated, then added, "He is already so upset about leaving. We don't know his reaction."

"Good point. I'm not sure I'm ready to say anything, either. That would be a big blow for him. Having grown up without my parents... I mean if he doesn't want to stay with me, I understand, but..." he looked as though he were plagued with bad thoughts, and she reached out to stroke his arm lightly. He continued, "Whatever we do about things, I'm kind of hoping we would do it... together."

Will's hand found Malin's, their fingers intertwining as if to weave together the frayed edges of their reality. The room, dimly lit by a single glowing crystal, seemed to hold its breath, awaiting their next breath, their next move. His touch was warm, grounding; reminding her of the fireplace they just left, so distant from the sterile chill of the city.

thrum that resonated within the walls of her heart, "I'll tell him. I'll tell Zane everything."

Malin nodded; her analytical mind momentarily set adrift by the overabundance of emotions she felt in Will's presence.

The room was thick with a tension that hung in the air like a storm about to break, the kind of heat that made the skin prickle and the lungs tighten. She lay there, her head resting on his shoulder, her body pressed against him in a way that felt like a slow, deliberate kind of tease. His breath was steady, but beneath it, she could feel the energy of something wild, something untamed, a beast waiting to be unleashed.

Will turned her face to his, his fingers brushing against her cheek with a gentleness that made her turn toward them. He drew her closer, his lips hovering just above hers, teasing, taunting, until the tension was almost unbearable. And then, finally, he kissed her.

It started softly, a whisper of a kiss, the kind that spoke of secrets and unspoken desires. His lips moved against hers with a slow, deliberate rhythm, each touch sending a jolt through her. She could feel the heat of him against her leg, the way his breath mingled with hers, and it was enough to make her dizzy.

She could feel his hardness pressing against her thigh, and it took all her self-control to resist grinding against him right there. Still, he stayed in command, moving at a slow, deliberate pace that was as maddening as it was intoxicating.

She could feel his hands as they roamed, sliding down her sides with a possessiveness that made her gasp. She could feel the hard press of his muscles beneath her fingertips, the way his body tensed as he pulled her even closer. Her shirt was the first

exposing the curve of her breasts and the soft swell of her stomach. She didn't stop him. Instead, she reached for his shirt, her fingers trembling as she worked the buttons free, each one a small victory against the growing tension between them.

His lips met hers again with renewed urgency and need. His tongue slipped into her mouth, exploring and claiming as she reciprocated with equal fervor. The kiss deepened into something raw and primal, verging on desperation. He was breathtaking, and she couldn't help but emit a soft moan as his hands drifted to her waist, deftly undoing the button and zipper of her pants before slipping his fingers beneath the waistband. In response, she freed him from his pants, taking hold, and moving her hand slowly up and down his shaft.

As her hand found his arousal once more, his own hands began to roam, cupping her breasts before sliding between her thighs. In that moment, he confirmed what she already knew: she was wet and already yielding to him.

With their shirts finally discarded, she felt the heat of his skin pressing against hers and marveled at the way his muscles rippled under her touch. Her fingers wandered along the contours of his chest, noting the firm planes and the slight dewy sheen of sweat beginning to form.

He paused for a moment, locking his eyes with hers as if silently seeking permission. Words were unnecessary; her body responded without them, arching into his touch as he unhurriedly slid her pants down her hips. The cool air caressed her exposed skin, yet it was nothing compared to the burning intensity of his gaze as he absorbed every detail of her, desire blazing in his eyes. His hands moved to his own pants, shoving them down until he was free, his cock hard and throbbing as he stood there. She could see the thickness of him, the way his veins stood out against his skin, and it made her desire wet. With both

intertwined, and the sensation of skin against skin was almost overwhelming.

His lips found hers again, silencing her moans as his fingers continued their relentless assault. She could feel herself getting closer and closer to the edge, her body trembling with the need for release. And then, just when she thought she couldn't take it anymore, he pulled his fingers away, leaving her aching and desperate.

He then pulled back, his breath coming in ragged gasps as he looked down at her. "You're so fucking beautiful," he murmured in a voice rough with desire. The hunger in his eyes was unmistakable, barely contained, which only heightened her longing for him.

Continuing his exploration, his hands wandered further. She felt the warmth of his gaze as he took in every inch of her, while his fingers brushed teasingly along her inner thighs, provoking and tantalizing her until she practically squirmed with desire.

He didn't need to be told twice. His fingers slid between her folds, finding the slickness there and drawing a low moan from her lips. He stroked her slowly at first, exploring every inch of her with a tenderness that made her heart ache. But then his pace quickened, his fingers moving with a rhythm that had her gasping for air.

He spread her leg and licked and sucked, till she was panting and close to climax. Then he stopped tracing a path of kisses up her stomach and to her nipples, where he then fondled and teased one nipple with is one hand, the other hand was thrusting in and out of her, while his tongue teased and sucked the other breast. She was writhing, her body unable to think, just feel.

"Will," she breathed, her voice barely above a whisper. "Please."

tighter until she thought she might explode. And then he added another finger, stretching her in a way that made her see stars. Her hips bucked against his hand, desperate for more, desperate for release.

He brought her to climax at least twice. But he wasn't done. Not yet.

He pulled her to the side of the bed and turned her over to her stomach, so that her legs were to the side of the bed. In a deep husky voice, he asked, "Are you ready?"

She nodded, her body quivering from her prior climaxes.

And then he was inside her, filling her in a way that made her feel whole. He moved slowly at first, giving her time to adjust to his size, but soon his pace quickened, each thrust drove him deeper into her.

She could feel the heat of him, the way his body moved against hers with a rhythm that was both primal and perfect.

She whimpered in protest, but he didn't give her time to recover. She gasped as he entered her over and over. She thought he would be touching her diaphragm from the inside as he was ramming into her. Over and over, he thrust, until she was close to climax again. He stopped, directing her to move.

He moved to the middle of the bed and waited for her to straddle him, which she gladly did. His hands held her up with her breasts. She could feel his fingers teasing her, as she moved her hips and raised herself up and down providing such intense pleasure, she wasn't sure she could focus. Occasionally, he would pull her down to him, so that he could lick her nipples. She couldn't think. The waves built until she let out a scream of pleasure. Her orgasm hit her like a tidal wave, crashing over her with an intensity that left her breathless. She could feel herself

her higher and higher until she thought she might pass out from the sheer pleasure of it. The waves crashed over and over, as he raised her up and down on his shaft until he was there too, his own release crashing over him with a force that left him trembling. He pulled her down on him, burying his face in her neck as he came, his body jerking with the force of his orgasm.

They lay there for a moment, their bodies still entwined as they tried to catch their breath. The room was silent except for the sound of their breathing and the occasional creak of the bed as they shifted positions.

Finally, he pulled back and looked down at her, a soft smile playing on his lips. "That was…" he began, but she cut him off with a kiss, a slow, lingering kiss that spoke of all the things they hadn't yet said.

The world outside faded away, leaving only the sound of their synchronized heartbeats and the heat of their connection. With each movement, they deepened their bond, weaving their souls together in the intricate dance of intimacy.

The shadows cast by the flickering lamp danced upon their entwined forms, painting a tableau of love and defiance; a momentary escape from the ever-looming threat of discovery. But for now, in the seclusion of their embrace, they found strength, and in their passion, a silent oath to protect what they had forged together against all odds.

She felt a soft kiss on her temple, coaxing her from the depths of sleep. His lips brushed against her skin, and his fingers trailed down her arm, each touch was a reminder of the night's passion, leaving an unspoken promise lingering on her skin. The scent of their union still hung in the air, blending with the freshness of the new day.

resonated in the quiet room, rekindling the desire that the night had nurtured. She reached for the warmth of his body with a gentle touch, revealing the strong, naked man beside her.

"You'd better be careful, or we'll end up delayed and lacking the energy we need for today," he chuckled in a deep, husky tone.

She opened her eyes to meet his steady gaze. Here was a man she knew so little about, yet she now depended on him for survival. Her heart fluttered, not just with lingering passion, but with the realization of their intertwined destinies. She watched with a hint of wonder as Will effortlessly gathered her belongings. His thoughtfulness was a soothing balm, allowing her to focus on the day ahead rather than the tasks at hand.

He stood, his naked body in full gaze. She took it in, every curve, every sinew, every scar. Malin's breath caught in her throat as she watched Will dress, his muscular form a symphony of strength and beauty. She couldn't help but admire the tattoos that adorned his skin, each one telling a story of his past. She looked forward to better understanding the meaning behind each one. As he pulled on his shirt, she saw the glimpse of a deep scar near his shoulder, a reminder of the battles he had fought.

She stood and walked toward him, drawn to him like a moth to a flame. Her fingers traced the design on his chest, feeling the rise and fall of his breathing beneath her touch. Will turned to face her, his eyes softening as they met hers.

"Every mark tells a story," Malin whispered, tracing another tattoo that ran down his arm.

"And every story has molded me into who I am today," Will replied, leaning in to brush his lips against hers. His touch was electric, igniting a fire within her that burned brighter with each passing moment.

"Thank you for finding me... for opening my eyes. I shudder to think what life would've been like if Ellie had been found... if I hadn't..." Her voice snagged on the edge of the unspoken horrors. She didn't need to finish.

Will gently tilted her chin up, his smile half-grin, half-confession. "Thank *you*. Honestly, I wouldn't have blamed you if you'd slammed the door in my face after learning who I really was. I've spent most of my life wearing masks and ducking the truth. I had given up on the kind of love my parents had. Figured I'd just go full rogue and embrace the legend." He gave her a sheepish look, brushing his fingers over her cheek. "Still not sure I'm worthy of you. But I'll never stop trying to be."

It hit her square in the chest, this was warm, real, terrifying. Her heart did that ridiculous flip it had taken to make every time he dropped one of those broody, sincere confessions. She blinked at him, stunned into silence.

They leaned together, foreheads touching, the moment thick with unspoken promises. He kissed her brow, so gentle and reverent, and she swore her bones turned to jelly.

Then, because he couldn't help himself, he leaned in with that cocky little twist to his smile and murmured, "As much as I'd love to throw you back on that bed and prove just how talented I am at making you moan while I'm multitasking..."

Her brows shot up, amused. "Multitasking? Is that what we're calling it now?"

"Strategic time management," he clarified, backing toward the door like the bed had turned into a live wire. "Sadly, the schedule disagrees. Marching. Monsters. Possibly a few death-defying escapes. You know, a regular day in transporting."

delayed gratification?"

"Exactly." He gave her a wink over his shoulder. "But don't worry…I'm excellent at building anticipation."

With that, she watched him walk out and close the door, leaving her wrapped in her sheet, thoroughly flustered, and grinning like a woman who'd just been hit by a particularly charming lightning bolt.

Love, she thought wryly, apparently came with banter, butterflies, and criminal levels of confidence.

Freshly dressed in her travel gear, black leather pants, a fitted linen shirt, and a dark jacket that echoed Will's usual ensemble, Malin stepped into the dining room. The scents of breakfast greeted her immediately, warm and rich, curling through the air like welcoming arms. She paused at the threshold, taking in the quiet hum of morning preparations and the comforting familiarity of the space.

Will wasn't there. Lysa, busy at the stove, glanced over her shoulder and offered a warm smile. "He's in the back, finishing the final touches on the route," she said. "Gorek's in the shop, making sure the gear's solid."

Malin nodded, absorbing the information like puzzle pieces clicking into place.

"And Lady Anariel?" she asked.

"She'll meet you in the forest," Lysa replied, stirring a pot with her usual precision. "Can't exactly have an elf strolling through Talvi, now, can we?"

Malin smiled faintly at that, the absurdity of it somehow grounding. Of course not. Magic still moved in secret, and so did they.

they watched the chipmunk scurry between them, their laughter blending into a harmonious tune that filled her with warmth.

"Chitter seems extra energetic today," Ellie noted, her eyes shining with the same icy curiosity as her mother's.

"Maybe he knows we're off on an adventure," Zane responded, his hazel eyes not showing the sadness about leaving, and she hoped Ellie had something to do with that.

"I told Zane everything I knew about Aloria," Ellie chimed in, pulling closer to bask in their shared excitement, her tone filled with the confidence of a city expert. "It's going to be incredible." Her smile was radiant. The pet chipmunk, encouraged by their friendly vibes, scampered up Ellie's arm and settled on her shoulder, its tiny paws gently tickling her skin.

"Seems like Chitter is on board with our plans," Zane commented, a grin breaking through his usual reserved demeanor. He appeared more certain about their decision today than he had been yesterday.

"Are you ready?" Malin asked, her analytical mind already mapping out their path through the challenges ahead. Yet, she allowed herself this peaceful moment, drawing strength from the children's laughter and pure joy, which she would rely on in future trials. The children nodded in agreement.

A subtle shift in the atmosphere tugged Malin's attention toward the doorway. Her mother entered, composed and resolute, her presence still commanding even in this quiet place. Yet, instead of a formal greeting, she moved straight to Malin and wrapped her in a polite but warm hug, offering a rare smile.

tight with focus.

"It's time," her mother said evenly. She held out a soft leather pouch, the weight of it unmistakable as it landed in Malin's palm. Coins.

"That's for 'The Digger'," her mother added, her tone vague.

Malin's brow furrowed. "The Digger?"

"A private contractor," she clarified. "He maintains a tunnel network beneath the city. Gorek's still working to finish an exit route from here, but for now, it only leads north, which would cost you time and put you in more danger heading to Seaborn."

Malin passed the pouch to Will without a word. He slipped it into the inner pocket of his jacket with practiced ease.

"We're set to meet him within the hour, just beyond the Talvi wall," Will said, but the crease between his brows deepened. "There are more guards on patrol than usual. My contact said security's doubled since yesterday."

"That's your father's doing," Elowen replied tightly. "I intercepted him speaking with Andrew. He filed a report claiming you and Ellie were kidnapped. It's a cover, just an excuse to deploy his private enforcers without oversight."

Malin's pulse ticked up. The weight of her father's influence stretched further than she'd realized, like a shadow that clung no matter how far she ran. It was hard to reconcile the warm, doting Daddy from her childhood with the cold strategist they were discussing now.

While she wrestled with the dissonance, Will moved efficiently, double-checking each of their packs with the quiet intensity she'd come to recognize as his brand of worry. His eyes flicked

they weren't leaving anything behind.

In the next room, Lysa and Gorek took Zee aside to give their goodbyes in private. When the boy returned, his face was streaked with drying tears, but his jaw was set. He was ready.

"I'll make sure da supplies're waitin' fer ya on da ship," Gorek said, clapping Will on the shoulder and giving Malin a firm nod. "Jest make sure ye get dere on time."

Seeing Ellie holding Zee's hand, she walked over to him, "I want you to know, I am here for you. I'm a doctor and a healer, but mostly I'm a Mom. I don't know how you feel, but I want you to know that I can help," There wasn't a good thing to say in this situation, but she hoped that helped.

"That's what I told him. We talked for a while last night. I think things will be good," Ellie said

She watched as her mother bent to wrap Ellie in a warm, lingering hug, gentle but with the kind of intensity that only comes when you know goodbye is more than temporary.

Then she turned to her.

Without a word, she stepped forward and pulled Malin into an embrace. It wasn't formal or practiced like so many of their past exchanges, it was deep and real, the kind of hug Malin had quietly longed for all her life. A shiver of emotion passed through her as her mother's arms closed around her.

I would leave with you, her mother's voice echoed gently in her mind, *but there are important votes next week, ones that could shift momentum for the cause. I plan to meet you in Aloria. You're right… with you both gone, there's nothing left tethering me here.*

The words hummed softly in Malin's head, intimate and sure. She closed her eyes and just held on.

know you'll protect our little girl. She's growing up so fast.

Before Malin could respond, before she could ask the questions blooming in her chest, her mother stepped back. One last lingering look passed between them, quiet and full of promise. Then she turned and left the room.

Lysa said her goodbyes to all of them but gave Will the longest. As they began walking, Will and Gorek led the way, with her holding the end of the line. With a deep inhale, She readied herself, allowing the warmth of the present to shield her against the dangers that were ahead.

They arrived at the magical barrier, an invisible line that separated them from the technologically choked city of Media. Going through it again, Malin was accosted by the copper smell and acidic tang that was Media. She hoped that Aloria would be more like the burrow.

Will guided the group through the labyrinthine alleyways that crossed the Talvi District. Shadows stretched like grasping fingers from between the cold, concrete structures, each one harboring the potential for betrayal.

Stopping to check that everyone was together, Will murmured, "Keep close." His voice barely heard above the clanging of distant machinery. She watched his gaze dart from one shadow to the next, alert for any sign of the ever-watchful enforcers that prowled the district.

Catching sight of a guard, she pulled the black shawl over her head, to cover her hair and got Ellie's attention that she should also. Will's hood concealed his head, though it was hard to miss his size and muscles.

The guards, clad in their monochromatic uniforms, stood on the catwalks looking down, their eyes shielded behind reflective

approached, the danger of their endeavor weighing heavily upon their shoulders. It was the first of the checkpoints they could expect. The guards changed the checkpoints regularly, so it was harder to plan movements.

Only because she was aware of his plan, had she noticed his movements, they were so fluid and natural, but with a deceptive calm, Will produced a small, intricately carved box from within his cloak and slid it across to the nearest guard. She saw the man's fingers twitched subtly, betraying his anticipation as he peaked in the lid to reveal the glint of coins nestled within. The bribe was accepted with a curt nod, the unspoken agreement hanging thick in the air like the humidity before a storm.

As they emerged on the other side of the checkpoint, a sudden movement caught Malin's eye, then she met brown eyes she recognized. There, standing at the edge of the crowd, was Andrew, his familiar brown hair tousled, his eyes wide with shock; or it could have been betrayal? Time seemed to constrict around Malin, her heart pounding a frantic rhythm against her ribcage. He was on a catwalk, a distance away to the side.

She spurred the group to walk faster and got Will's attention with a hiss, "Will! It's Andrew and he saw me." An urgent need laced her tone as she begged him to move faster. "We must hurry." They got past the group of guards, just as a large group of workers were released from their shift and flooded the walkways.

When Andrew caught her eyes, she looked to Will. She could see the realization hit him. He flashed understanding across his features, and without hesitation, he ushered the group into a brisk pace.

Panic clawed at her throat as she risked a glance over her shoulder. Andrew's figure was swallowed by the pressing

with renewed haste. Her analytical mind raced, calculating escape routes and contingencies, even as her chest tightened with the strain of impending capture.

"Here!" Will called out, gesturing toward a nondescript metal door, half-hidden by the looming skeleton of an abandoned factory.

They slipped inside just as the guards' shouts reached a fever pitch behind them, bootfalls thundering like war drums. Will slammed the door shut, then locked it. The clamor outside was replaced by suffocating silence and the echo of their own ragged breaths. The darkness swallowed them whole leaving them standing in pitch black.

Malin leaned against the cool wall, trying to slow the frantic beat of her heart. Will's hand found hers in the darkness, steady, warm, and anchoring her like it always did. Even as relief crept in, her mind remained sharp. If the guards were even remotely competent, this building would be one of the first places they'd search.

They needed light.

With just that thought, she summoned a flame to her palm. It flickered to life with a quiet whoosh, casting golden light over their small group. Shadows jumped along the cracked walls, revealing a narrow path winding deeper into the old factory. They followed it, weaving through tight corners and uneven flooring for what felt like an eternity, though she counted about 300 feet by her pace.

Finally, they reached a steel-plated door set into the wall.

Will opened it cautiously.

Inside, a small man sat in the corner, perched on a rickety chair, rhythmically tapping one foot like he was impatiently waiting.

saucers and he used his hood to avoid the light.

"We got held up," Will replied as he stepped inside and secured the door behind them. "And we might have company."

The Digger's gaze sharpened slightly, but his expression didn't change. "Well, let's get to business then."

He stretched out a hand, expectant for something to fill it.

Will passed him the leather pouch. The man opened it, fingers nimble as he sifted through the contents. Satisfied, he handed Will a rolled parchment that was sealed with a mark Malin didn't recognize.

Then, with an almost theatrical flick, he pressed a small, rusted button hidden behind a pipe.

Click. Whirr. Grind.

A metal panel on the floor hissed and groaned open, revealing a dark staircase spiraling downward into the unknown.

"Pleasure doin' business," the Digger muttered. "Stick to the path marked on that map. I've got traps that'd make an enforcer weep."

He stood, brushing off his pants, and added, "When you get down, I'll close the hatch. I won't leave this room 'til the hatch is sealed. They won't find the entrance, not unless they're better than they look. As always Hawk, don't bother keeping or destroying the map, I change the tunnels every week."

Malin glanced at Will. He was calm, with no tightness in his jaw, whatever this is, must be going to plan. She caught his eyes and smiled and he returned the look. This was it. One last descent before they were truly gone from Media. He took the first steps down the stairs, followed by Ellie, who was holding Zane's hand behind her.

metallic wheel sounds came from the mechanisms near the top and the opening closed.

The bottom of the staircase opened into a wide, damp cavern where five tunnels yawned before them like gaping mouths. A single torch flickered on the wall, its glow too weak to comfort but enough to see.

Will plucked the torch from its bracket and handed it to Ellie with a soft, "Hold this, Bright Eyes." She cradled it carefully, her small face lit by the flame. She noticed Ellie smile and look at her when she noticed the little nickname.

Malin moved beside Will as he unrolled the map. The parchment unfurled with a crackle, its surface crowded with inked symbols and delicate lines. It was a maze of Endless twists, switchbacks, dead ends. She watched Will trace his finger along the highlighted path, counting turns under his breath. She followed his movement, committing each fork and twist to memory in her own methodical way. It wasn't just for backup, it was how her mind worked. Strategic. Analytical. Prepared backup plans.

When he folded the map and tucked it into his jacket with a nod, she understood. They were past the point of decisions. From here on, there was only forward.

She glanced up. The middle tunnel. Of course it would be the one that looked the least inviting.

"Keep close," Will murmured. His voice carried no fear, but she knew his caution was earned from past attempts. The torchlight turned the planes of his face to fire and shadow, and he looked every bit the soldier the stories whispered about.

Malin's gaze dropped to the children. Ellie's hand had found Zane's in the gloom, their fingers laced tightly. It gave her unexpected comfort, how easily they fit together. Zane, barely

quiet focus. She noticed, with a flicker of affection, that he clenched his jaw the same way Will did when he was on edge. His spine straight, his eyes flicking between every shadow, they were more alike than either probably realized.

Will's eyes met hers briefly, checking, steady. Then they moved forward.

The tunnel exhaled around them, air damp and cold as it ghosted across her skin. The darkness wasn't just absence, it felt alive. Watching. Breathing. Whispers rode the stone like memories not meant to be remembered. It felt like they had been walking for hours. There was no concept of time and they had left all of their electronics at home, so they couldn't be tracked.

Malin summoned flame to her palm, a slow steady burn that required a surprising level of focus. It pulsed gently, casting golden light around her. She would have preferred to stand by his side, but she felt better knowing the children were between them. He kept checking on her, looking into her eyes to make sure she was okay.

They moved together, like one with Will leading with quiet precision, Ellie and Zane side by side, and Malin just behind, her thoughts ticking like a metronome: worry, calculation, resolve.

Their footsteps echoed in hushed defiance of the silence. The creak of boots, the whisper of cloth, the steady breath of children who'd grown up too fast, all braided into one fragile sound. A rhythm of survival.

The tunnel stretched endlessly ahead, winding like a serpent. They climbed uneven stones, crawled carefully over jagged rocks, and slid down moisture-slick slopes where the walls closed in tight. Every turn carried the threat of ambush, yet every step forward whispered promise.

earth. A door, a torch sconce, and a silent moment that settled over them like a held breath.

Will placed the torch into the mount, then pushed against the heavy door. Its hinges groaned softly, a sound that somehow seemed reverent.

Light poured through the opening.

Malin blinked.

The last vestiges of darkness clung to their clothing as they emerged from the tunnel's embrace, a noticeable difference to the vibrant tableau that unfolded before them.

For a heartbeat, her brain refused to accept what her eyes showed her.

A forest. Not the ornamental trees of Galvin or the artificial gardens of the upper districts, this was *wild*. Untamed. Alive.

She had seen it on maps. Dreamed of it. But she had never stood among trees that stretched so high that it whispered secrets in a language older than stone. They could barely make out the wall in the distance of the trees.

Sunlight filtered through a lush canopy of leaves, casting a gentle, dappled light that painted the forest floor with shifting patterns of gold and shadow. The vibrant green above was so intense it seemed almost otherworldly, as if the forest had been plucked from the pages of a fairy tale. The scent enveloped her senses first, a rich blend of loamy earth that smelled of ancient soil, crisp, clean air that felt like a refreshing breeze on a warm day, and the subtle perfume of wildflowers whose names eluded her but whose fragrance was as sweet as honey. It was an intoxicating aroma, a heady cocktail of nature's finest, and her lungs eagerly absorbed it.

the very light between the trees, was Lady Anariel.

Malin felt the group still around her, a breath held collectively. Even Will, usually unreadable, had a flicker of surprise across his face. The elves hadn't just arrived, they'd *been* here, unnoticed, part of the forest itself. That mastery overshadows and stillness sent a shiver up her spine.

Lady Anariel stepped forward, her presence like moonlight given form. Her armor, crafted from something resembling leather but flowing with the ease of silk, shifted with her movements, hued in woodland tones that made her seem an extension of the trees themselves. Tiny crystals were woven into her long hair, catching what little light filtered through the canopy, glinting like stars on the edge of dawn.

"Welcome," she said, her voice a song, soft and resonant, like water over smooth stone. "You are under our protection now."

Beside her stood two elven warriors, still as carved stone. One was pale as silverleaf, his long hair almost glowing, features sculpted into something too flawless to be real. The other was darker, with skin like polished mahogany and eyes that gleamed like obsidian, his presence grounded, watchful. Different as dusk and midnight, but both radiated that same ageless grace and barely veiled power.

Malin's breath caught. For a heartbeat, she forgot the danger they'd just escaped. She wasn't just looking at other people, she was looking at legends. And while their welcome felt warm, the air still hummed with tension.

Because beauty could be deadly. And peace, especially now, never came without its shadows.

gradually slipping from Zane's grasp as if entranced by the scene before her. She reached toward the shimmering golden light as though trying to capture its ethereal brilliance in her hands.

Malin's gaze darted to her daughter, and a deep ache resonated within her. That sense of wonder and unbridled freedom... she had nearly denied Ellie this experience. Nearly kept them both locked inside a city of shadows instead of standing here, breathing clean air, seeing real sky.

Beside Ellie, Zane stood in silent reverence, his mouth slightly open, hazel eyes reflecting the golden haze. He didn't speak, didn't move—but something changed in his expression. A flicker of belonging. A spark of something close to peace.

And then Will.

Malin turned to him just as he gave her that stupid, lopsided grin. "What?" she asked, arching a brow. "Do I have a bug in my hair or something?"

He shook his head, stepping closer until his hands found her waist. "No. I just... I forgot how it felt. Seeing it for the first time. Watching you now—I remembered."

Her heart thudded. For the first time in days, the tight band around her chest loosened.

She caught Will's eye. "We made it. We're out."

His smile faltered. "Yeah," he said quietly, voice dropping. "But we're not safe yet. Not this close to the wall. Drones patrol these edges. Some on foot, some worse. We'll need to move deeper before full light."

Not safe. Not yet.

But this?

Then — *crack.*

A sharp *snap* of a branch echoed from the trees behind them. Not far.

Will's arms tensed instantly, releasing her as he dropped into a half-crouch. His hand flew to the blade at his side.

Malin turned, scanning the trees.

Another sound. Heavy. Rhythmic. *Bootsteps.* In the distance but heading their way.

Not one. Several.

Will's voice was low, urgent. "Move. Now."

And just like that, the forest wasn't wonder. It was cover.

Will led the way deeper into the forest.

They had been walking for over an hour in silence. The kids were clearly fading. They'd gotten far enough from the walls that Will wasn't worried about patrols now, though danger in the forest had a way of being... less predictable. Still, it felt like the right time to rest.

He spotted a shallow stream ahead, flanked by mossy rocks and a few fallen logs that would do well enough as seats. "Let's stop here," he said, nodding toward it. "Stay close. No wandering."

As if they had the energy.

He dropped his pack and leaned against a wide pine trunk, letting his legs stretch out. The forest swayed softly above them, whispering in a language only the old trees knew. Ellie and Zane collapsed by the water, giggling over a shared biscuit, sitting side-by-side, their laughter carrying like sparks in the wind.

Speaking of sparks.

Malin was near the stream, bent over, splashing water on her face. The droplets clung to her lashes and collarbone, her wild hair loose around her shoulders. She turned, met his gaze, and started toward him. No hesitation. Just quiet confidence.

She flopped onto the rock beside him, her knees drawn up, arms looped around them. Her cheeks flushed from the hike, her boots scuffed, her jacket rumpled, and she'd never looked more radiant.

A little firelight in the forest gloom.

"Sparks," he muttered quietly, just low enough that she could hear.

call me Sparks?"

He shrugged, smirking. "Well... you're quick, hot-tempered, and entirely too good at lighting me up."

"Ugh." She rolled her eyes but didn't hide her smile. "That's the worst nickname I've ever heard."

"I could go with 'Your Fiery Highness.' But that feels a little formal, unless I'm on my knees," he said in a low husky voice pulling her towards him.

"Sparks it is," she deadpanned, stealing his canteen.

He caught her. She tried to smother a grin and look shocked, but he could see it. She liked it. He liked having something that was just theirs, that they didn't have to share.

He gave her a quick kiss, then released her, heading toward the stream. Some nice cool water would help, as he didn't think it was the walking that was heating him up.

Will caught Malin's voice beside him. "Lady Anariel... I just realized we never formally met your friends."

Anariel inclined her head. "These are my guards, Nar and Khelek Warden. My tribe communed with whispering leaves in the groves near the Draconian Mountains. We are Mellyrn. We are stewards of starlight, guardians of balance between nature and magic. Our traditions include training some of the fiercest warriors among the elven nations. That path is what led me to Media. These two are brothers, bound by vows to serve and protect me. Few can match their skill, especially when they fight as one."

Will had already been sizing them up.

elite, they were something more. Specialized. Dangerous.

Nar was wiry and tall, all fast-twitch muscle and economy of motion. His deep crimson hair caught slivers of light like sparks off a blade. Braided down his back, but loose enough at the temples to obscure sharp cheekbones and eyes that didn't reflect anything. It almost looked like they absorbed. His robe moved like shadow, but underneath, Will spotted the glint of steel, daggers everywhere. Chest, thighs, boots, wrists. A knife fighter. Close-range. Fast. And judging from the way the heat shimmered around him, he barely kept his fire magic restrained.

Khelek, on the other hand, was built like a siege tower. Massive frame, pale skin that shimmered faintly under the filtered sunlight. Midnight hair flowed down past his shoulders like a curtain of ink, and his armor was tight, engraved, and enchanted. It was built for impact. Deep silver and cobalt tones rippled across the runed surface. The sword on his back was absurd in size, but the way he carried it seemed balanced and controlled, with ice crusted the hilt.

Fire and ice. Speed and force. Assassin and enforcer.

They were opposites in every way, but perfectly balanced. Will recognized that kind of brotherhood. That kind of discipline.

And then there was the vow to consider. Elves didn't take oaths lightly. With lifespans that spanned centuries, maybe longer, swearing loyalty was no passing pledge. It wasn't just a lifetime of protection; it could be millennia. That said more about Anariel than it did about them.

He was damn glad they were allies.

Because if they ever came for him? He wouldn't survive both.

Will stepped forward. "Were you able to get that intel I asked for?"

neutralized."

Khelek's eyes locked with his. "Orc raiders are shifting south. Probably hunting supply caches. If that's your path, we'll meet them head-on. We could take them, but I wouldn't bet on everyone walking away."

Nar added, "I would recommend we angle west, then turn south. More distance, but better odds."

Will exhaled through his nose, jaw clenched. Just once, he wanted a clean run.

"And surveillance?"

"Three drone passes before dawn," Nar said. "No engagement. Yet."

Will nodded once. "Seaborn lies southeast. A few routes lead there, but it sounds like our best bet is west, then swing back south. Harder march, but worth it if it keeps the kids safe."

It was then that Will's heart tightened, a prickling sensation crawling up his spine. His eyes snapped to a shadow ahead, just beyond the bend in the trail, a darkness too still, too dense, even for the forest's thick canopy.

Something was wrong.

He shifted closer to the group, hand drifting toward the hilt of his hidden blade. Every instinct, sharpened by years of running, surviving, screamed that there was *danger* coming.

The elves noticed it too. Will caught their eyes. One sharp look exchanged between them was all it took, they sensed it. They vanished into the trees, melting into shadow with the ease of

if needed.

He turned to the children, voice low and taut.

"Find cover. Now. Something's coming."

No hesitation. Just the wide-eyed flash of alarm as they scanned the trees and obeyed.

He guided them to a massive fallen tree, its trunk hollowed by rot and time. There was just enough space for them if they curled tight.
"Inside," he whispered, steadying them with a firm hand, his touch as much reassurance as command. He crouched low, helping pull-in Ellie's bag, tucking her hair beneath Zane's arm.

Malin had already moved, clever and quiet, ducking beneath a rocky overhang and drawing her shawl up to mask her hair. Will took up a post between them, sliding into a thick cluster of bushes where he could cover both flanks.

And then they waited.

The forest held its breath.

A faint whir.

Then louder.

Closer.

After what felt too long, he spotted it, a surveillance drone, hovering roughly fifteen feet above the forest floor. Sleek. Mechanical. Watching.
What the hell is a drone doing this far out?

The buzz of its rotors mingled with the rustle of leaves, turning the forest's natural song into something sinister. Will stayed frozen, watching through gaps in the branches. Its red sensor swept across the trees in slow arcs, scanning for movement.

himself over Ellie, shielding her.

Will felt a knot tighten in his chest, equal parts pride and terror. *That instinct, that's what matters. That's what saves lives.*

The drone hovered, uncertain. Will didn't move. Didn't breathe.

Then, slowly, it veered off, climbing higher into the trees and drifting away toward the east.

Silence reigned again, broken only by the whisper of leaves and the slow, painful release of held breaths.

Will let his hand fall away from his blade. His fingers curled into the moss-covered bark of the fallen tree as he finally exhaled.

"Clear," he murmured.

A rustle behind him, Zane helped Ellie out of the log, brushing dirt and debris from her cloak. Will met his gaze. The boy's eyes shimmered with adrenaline, but there was no panic now, only resolve. Will nodded once.

A warrior's nod.

An acknowledgment.

He's got the makings of an amazing protector.

With the drone now just a malignant memory, they emerged slowly, brushing off bits of bark and forest from their clothing, as if shedding the last few minutes of silent fear. Lady Anariel stood tall, violet eyes catching the final rays of sunlight. She lifted one hand, elegant and deliberate, motioning for them to gather close. Her voice followed, a soft thread of ancient song, braided with purpose and quiet authority, wrapping around them like the ivy above their heads.

carpet of fallen leaves. The light had grown thin and amber, the forest filtering it through latticework branches. The scent of moss, loam, and something faintly magical clung to the air, *a memory of what once was... and what still might be.*

Will kept to the front, senses taut.

"The Telebrook Inn's our stop tonight," he called back. "Still a good stretch ahead. Let's keep moving. Everyone good?"

A few weary nods. No complaints.

He respected that. More than they knew.

His gaze never stopped scanning. A twitch of underbrush, a gust of wrong wind, he filed it all. The forest hummed with energy. It was familiar, living, but not always friendly.

They'd been walking for hours. He could feel it now, *the pull.* A hum beneath his skin, faint but growing stronger. People with magic up ahead. The Inn. A waypoint. A place to sleep... and maybe be seen.

It was both haven and hazard.

Media guards stopped there too. Watched. Waited. Picked fights they couldn't start inside the city.

The last light drained from the sky as the forest gave way to deeper shadow. Roots tangled across the trail, and the path narrowed between moss-slick stones and sloping hollows. Will slowed his pace, just enough to glance back.

Zane's shoulders were high and tense, jaw clenched. Ellie rubbed her eyes with the back of her sleeve but kept walking. They were fighting it, but exhaustion clung to them like fog.

He exhaled through his nose.

legs. Hydrate."

He crouched beside a fallen log, muscles loosening, *partially.* One hand resting on his thigh, the other close to the blade strapped to his hip. *Relaxed* was never an option. Not this close to the city.

He caught Zane's glance, brief but telling.

Relief, flickering behind a mask of control.

Too young to look like that, Will thought.

He'd worn that same expression once.

Still did.

"Zee," Will said gently, crouching beside the boy. "I knew your mother, Felicity. She had a fierce spirit. Brave, kind. She was... amazing. I'm sorry you lost her."

Zane's hazel eyes, so much like Will's own, snapped up to meet his surprise flickering behind practiced calm.

"You knew my mom?" His voice held a careful edge, guarded but hopeful.

"I did." Will nodded, keeping his tone soft. "We were rebels together, fighting the system before it got this bad. She talked about wanting a family someday. About being a mother. You meant the world to her, even before you existed."

Zane looked down, fingers tugging at the hem of his shirt. "I remember... she used to say I had to be strong. For the people who couldn't be."

fighting. It's kindness, loyalty, and protecting people, like you did for Ellie today."

The boy's chest rose slightly, a flicker of pride softening the line of his shoulders.

"I try to be like her," Zane whispered, barely loud enough for the wind to catch.

"Then you're doing exactly what she would've wanted." Will placed a hand on his back. "She'd be proud. I know I am."

He hesitated, then added, "Last time I saw her was about thirteen years ago. She vanished one night. I never found out what happened. But now, knowing she had you? It means she had joy before the end."

Will noticed Zane blink rapidly, fighting tears. So, he gave him space, rising smoothly.

"I'm gonna check on Malin," he said, casually. Ellie immediately slid over and wrapped her arms around Zane's shoulders. Good timing. Good heart.

Will crossed to Malin, needing her quiet strength like a balm.

After a while, he clapped his hands softly.

"Alright. Not far now. Let's move out."

As they walked, Zane sidled up beside him.

"My mum made everything feel like an adventure," he said, voice drifting like smoke.

Will smiled. "Then she lived with joy, even when the world was dark. That's rare. And powerful."

There was silence, then...

"Did you know my dad, too?"

proud of you, though."

Zane grinned faintly. "He used to say we were nothing alike. We didn't look anything alike; we didn't even act similarly. But he taught me to ride a bike and never missed a ball game."

"Sounds like a good man," Will said, quietly. "And sounds like you had love in your life. For all of us, it doesn't matter if it came from blood or bond, you make family by your actions."

They walked in silence for a stretch, not awkward, but companionable. Will filled it with light chatter, stories of far-off markets, wild food combinations, magical pranks pulled by fey vendors. Zane listened. His eyes were bright and interested.

Eventually, the trail began to widen. The canopy above thinned.

"Hey," Ellie said, suddenly. "Today was good."

Will chuckled. "Yeah. It really was."

They emerged into a twilight-draped clearing. The Telebrook Inn nestled among the trees, lanterns glowing warm and welcoming. Smoke curled from its chimney. Outside, a group of dwarves threw axes at a splintered post. Sparks danced where the blades struck wood. Ellie gasped.

"Whoa!"

Will smiled at her awe.

Just then, a handful of Sprites darted through the air. Ellie reached out to one with a delighted laugh.

"Careful," Will warned too late. "Most of 'em bite." Just as he said that she yelped as it *bit* her.

Will watched Ellie jerk her hand back, a sharp squeak escaping her lips as a sprite zipped off into the trees. Zane glared at them like he was memorizing their faces for later. Too late. Ellie

finger.

Will chuckled and muttered to himself, "They don't have their humm worms yet."

"Excuse me. Our what?" Malin's voice rose beside him, sharp and suspicious.

He turned just as she narrowed her eyes at him. "Humm worms," he said with a casual shrug. "Tiny little creatures. You put one under your tongue. It burrows up through the ear canal and settles in your auditory nerve. After that, boom… instant translation."

Malin's expression twisted into something between horror and disbelief. "That is the most disgusting thing I've ever heard."

Will grinned. "I mean, sure, when you say it like that."

"Because there's a *better* way to describe willingly swallowing a worm that climbs into your head?"

"They're not slimy. Kind of dry and wriggly. Like… crunchy rice noodles."

She gave him a withering glare. "Will."

"Okay, bad example." He lifted both hands in surrender. "But they're the best way to understand when the other races speak. They'll help more than you think."

"And you just expect me to, what? Pop one in and smile while it takes up residence in my brain?"

"Technically, your ear," he said, tapping the side of her head, "but yes. After dinner, maybe. When you're in a better mood and less likely to stab me."

either learn all these other languages or let this little worm in my head."

Will grinned as he walked backward toward the inn's entrance. "Welcome to the resistance, Sparks."

As they reached the large double wooden doors, Will paused, casting a glance over his shoulder to make sure everyone was still with him. The kids looked worn but alert, Malin kept close, and even Anariel looked oddly at ease in her forest-toned armor under the fading light.

"An interesting assortment of clientele," Malin muttered beside him, voice low. He didn't need to answer, just quirked a smile and pushed open the door.

The familiar scent hit him first, but the ration bars he ate earlier with the fruit had left him quite hungry. The smells of roasting meat, damp wood, and spiced tea were making his mouth water. The Telebrook Inn always smelled like memories.

Inside, the inn was a patchwork of comfort and mystery. Shadows flickered across aged wood beams, thrown there by hearth fires that crackled in stone-walled corners. The air was thick with the hum of conversation, the occasional clang of tankards, and the soft strains of a bard's lute. Above, trinkets and weapons dangled from the rafters, enchanted or not, Will knew more than half of them were fakes. He'd tried to swipe a few when he was younger and stupider.

His gaze swept the room instinctively. Always first the exits, then the crowd. Nothing set off alarms, no uniformed enforcers, no twitchy bounty hunters. Mostly tired travelers, hunched over plates and mugs, too worn out to care who else came in from the cold.

subtle widening of their eyes, the way they leaned slightly forward. Wonder, thinly veiled. He couldn't help the flicker of pride that came with watching Zane instinctively step in front of Ellie without even thinking. Good instincts. Growing fast.

Malin's voice drew him back. "Over there," she said, nodding toward a half-shadowed alcove near the back. She moved like someone who'd been hunted, quiet, deliberate, always clocking sightlines. Will approved. She is another with a good eye for protecting.

"Good spot," he said, following her lead. The tension in his shoulders began to ease.

"Lady Anariel, Nar and Khelek decided to head up to their room. They said they would meet up in the tavern in the morning," she said as she made room for her.

He was about to sit down at the table when a voice exploded across the room.

"Well, shit on a biscuit, if it ain't Will Hawkson! The man who breaks furniture and hearts in equal measure!"

Will didn't even need to look to know. That voice hadn't changed one bit in all the years he's been coming here.

"Corben," he said with a lopsided grin, turning toward the bar. The man behind it was built like a forge, thick arms, full head of floppy wavy, brown hair with blonde highlights, and blue eyes that sparkled like he was halfway through a joke. He met Corben and his twin brother Zane on his first merchant ship crew that he worked. They spent the better part of seven or so years getting into so much mischief together, until they finally saved up enough money to buy their first tavern in Sarhan, then the second here.

again. Last time, your stunt had a table dancing the tarantella!"

Will chuckled. "That table was cursed before I ever touched it."

"Right," Corben drawled. "And I'm the bloody High Mage of Sarhen." He grinned wider, then added with surprising warmth, "Glad to see you alive, Hawk. I thought you said you were stopping the transport gig..." Mid-sentence, he seemed to notice Malin wrap her arm around Will's waist, "Oh... I see... Well... Bring the kidlets and the stunner over when you're ready. First rounds on me."

Will nodded his thanks, glancing toward Ellie and Zane. They were both watching him now, Zane with guarded curiosity, Ellie with open fascination.

Great. One more legend to live up to.

The alcove Malin had chosen was a cozy nook, cushioned benches embracing a sturdy wooden table. As they settled in, the children's attention was soon captivated by a small dog; a terrier mix with boundless energy and an uncanny ability to perform tricks for scraps. Laughter bubbled up from their little circle, innocent and carefree, as the dog fetched a tossed piece of bread and brought it back with a wagging tail.

Malin watched them for a moment before turning her gaze to Will. The flickering candlelight cast dancing shadows over her features, giving her an almost otherworldly appearance. Her eyes, those remarkable pools of icy blue, met him with such an intensity it made electricity run up and down his spine.

"Will," she began, her voice low, hinting at conversations past and secrets yet to be shared. "We've been through a lot, and I have no doubts about you, but I must be seeing a different you, this rogue Will Hawkson I keep hearing about."

Her words hung in the air, a delicate invitation to delve into memories long guarded. In the quiet corner of the inn, with the comforting scent of roasting meat filling the air, the stage was set for confidences to unfurl.

Will took a slow breath, feeling the weight of stories unspoken settling on his shoulders. He looked at Malin, acknowledging the past they shared and the future that might yet weave their lives together more tightly.

"Indeed," he replied, his voice barely above a whisper as the noise of the inn continued unabated around them. "And tonight, perhaps, some shall be told."

The children laughed again, the sound mingling with the crackle of the hearth and the soft murmur of conversation. For a moment, the world outside; with its dangers and uncertainties; faded away, leaving only the intimacy of shared histories and the promise of revelations to come.

Will felt a large hand on his shoulder. Corben stood there with a lively gleam in his eyes. He had a tray of bowls of food on the other hand that he set on the table. He pulled a chair up to the table and settled in. When Zee and Ellie noticed, they also joined and began digging into their food. Corben, between bites of steaming stew and sips of mulled cider, telling tall tales of their shenanigans from their youth. He had to correct some facts and had to remind him more than one time that some tales were not acceptable from the kids' ears. The air grew thick with laughter, rich and full, they pried him for more and more details. The stories were full of cockeyed plans and reckless feats, some of them incriminating enough to make Will and Corben exchange knowing glances, that some details were omitted for other reasons.

simple cargo run turned into a high seas chase, because of a misread map, to another tale of a night that began with a lark and ended with the transport's entire crew drunkenly locked inside the cargo hold.

Will watched Malin's reactions intently. It was the way her eyes rounded in surprise at some of the more dangerous, or reckless feats, but didn't look disgusted or upset about how different his life was from hers. Through it all, he had the barmaids bringing over drinks, the kids getting Corben's personal brew of root beer. He knew he needed to keep his wits with him, so he limited himself, but the drinks kept coming.

Watching Ellie and Zane also made his heart warm. They were wide-eyed, hanging on to each word as if watching a movie. Zane inched closer to Corben. He sat transfixed with an intensity that made him seem older than his years. Ellie bounced in her seat, alternately giggling and asking questions that had Corben blinking with surprise. "Then what happened?" she gasped, her eyes bright with wonder. "Did you get away? Did they catch you?"

Will marveled at the ease with which the Ellie embraced this world, a world he had never truly left.

The stories kept coming and with Corben, Zane and Will's friendship, there were plenty of them to cover. They would never finish all of them in one night. Finally, with a booming laugh and a wink at Malin, Corben declared Will guilty of all charges and took a generous sip from his mug. "But you know the best part, the very best part?" Corben leaned in, stage-whispering to the two children now leaning across the table, "He wasn't even drunk when he did most of this. Just crazy!" Laughter erupted, genuine and infectious, more revealing than any confession.

begin their trek the next day. It was time to head to bed. He noticed how quickly Ellie and Zane were yawning, he guessed they wouldn't complain too much about leaving. He glanced at Corben, not missing the warmth in the other man's smile, the silent acknowledgment that this was more than just a tavern, more than a safe harbor. It was family. There was a comfort in that thought, a welcome respite from the pressures that had been building around them all day; all month; all year.

Meanwhile, Will retrieved a small container filled with humm worms, offering them to Malin, Zane, and Ellie.

"Sir. I already got one. Lysa wanted to make sure I wasn't being cheated by some of the traders," Zee corrected.

"It really don't feel like nothing," he assured Ellie.

Both girls put their worms carefully near the back of their mouths and held their breath. Will watched intently, amused by the variety of expressions that played across their faces, disgust, surprise, and a hint of reluctant appreciation.

Ellie said, "You're right. It didn't hurt, but yuck!" She took a swig of water.

"Now that is out of the way, I think it is time for us to get some sleep. We need to be up early." Will turned to Corben, "I'm guessing you have a room we can have for the night," Will asked.

"Of course. It only has one bed, but room for two cots. Will that work?" Corben asked.

Will and Malin agreed, and Corben fetched the key from behind the bar and handed to them, giving Will a huge bear hug before they headed up the stairs to the room.

The first fingers of dawn had barely brushed the windows of the inn when Malin's eyes blinked open to the curious sensation of being wedged tightly between two bodies. One was warm and muscular, undeniably Will. The other was smaller, lighter, and pressed against her arm like a very determined kitten. Ellie.

She groggily recalled a whisper in the night, a tear-streaked face, and her own half-asleep instruction: *Climb in, sweetheart.* Apparently, Ellie had taken that as an open invitation to cocoon herself fully into her mother's side. Malin's arm was half-asleep beneath her daughter's head, but her heart softened at the sight.

At her first motion, Will stirred. His hand slid instinctively along her thigh before pausing, fingers tensing slightly when they encountered the unexpected second presence. He pushed up on one elbow and peered over her shoulder.

"Good morning, beautiful," he murmured, a crooked grin tugging at his mouth. "I see we had a stowaway."

Malin gave him a mock glare but smiled. "Ellie, honey," she whispered, brushing hair from her daughter's face. "Time to get up."

Ellie groaned and stretched like a cat, blinking slowly before burrowing her face into Malin's arm one last time. Malin gently slid her arm free and winced at the pins and needles. Will took it wordlessly and began rubbing it back to life, his touch deft and purposeful.

Once the tingling faded, Malin stood and crossed the room to wake Zane. He was curled up under the windowsill on his cot, Chitter, his chipmunk companion, nested contentedly in his wild

complaint.

In the cool hush of morning, each took their turn in the washroom down the hall. Malin moved efficiently, repacking their things and checking supplies, but her attention kept drifting back to Will.

He was inspecting his weapons with the quiet devotion of a ritual. Malin's eyes narrowed. She'd known he carried a blade or two. She hadn't realized he was practically a walking armory.

Two curved blades strapped to his back beneath the pack. A crossbow folded at his side with a quiver of bolts tucked neatly beside it. A sleek handgun holstered within a worn leather harness on his hip, freshly checked and reloaded. Twin boot knives. Smaller throwing blades strapped to his thighs.

The sheer amount of steel made her eyebrows arch.

"Are you expecting a war?" she asked dryly.

He glanced up, his smile twitching at the corners. "Sparks," he said, using the nickname like a caress, "I'd rather carry too much than risk one hair on your head."

She rolled her eyes, lips twitching. "With that much weaponry, you're basically a walking hazard."

He tugged her close with one arm and murmured, "Good thing you like danger."

She huffed, but her lips twitched with reluctant amusement.

Once they were packed, dressed, and fully geared, the four of them made their way downstairs to the tavern, each step taking them further from safety, and deeper into whatever waited in the wild.

floorboards as he approached, a folded parchment in one hand and the weight of worry draped across his shoulders like an old cloak. The morning meal was half-eaten bread, cold meat, and lukewarm tea gulped between glances toward the door. Tension clung to everything: the air, their silence, even the corners of the inn that no longer felt like safety.

"Will, here is the map we discussed," Corben murmured, his voice low and rough as he slid the parchment across the table. "There's more than one way to get to Seaborn from here, but none of them come easy."

Malin's fingers brushed the aged paper, unfolding it with more care than she expected. She traced the lines with her eyes before her fingers followed. Each path looked like a scar across the wilderness, a history of choices carved into the land.

Corben leaned in and pointed with a calloused finger. "The main trade road bends south through Windmere Hollow and hooks around the ridge. It'll take longer, but it's well-traveled and easier terrain. Safer for kids."

Her eyes flicked toward Ellie and Zane, their heads close together over a shared biscuit. Safe. That word had never carried more weight.

Corben continued, tapping another route. "This one cuts through Redroot Crossing. The bridge is still intact, but last I heard, a bandits holed up there. Might talk your way through… might not."

Malin's stomach twisted. She didn't need to look at Will to know what he was thinking. The shortest distance wasn't always the best choice. She had seen enough injuries and broken bodies caused by shortcuts that turned out to be traps.

line that carved an unsettling path straight through the forest's heart, "is the hidden route. It cuts nearly half a day. But there's a reason it's not marked well. Steep climbs, unstable terrain. Creatures, some old, some angry. The forest in there… doesn't forgive easily."

Her heart knocked against her ribs. The idea of saving time was tempting, every hour mattered. But not at that price.

She met Will's eyes across the map. No words. Just the tight, quiet agreement between two people who understood the cost of mistakes.

Not today.

Will straightened. "We'll take the main path," he said. "It'll be longer, but we're not risking them on bandits or beasts."

Corben gave a slow nod. "That's the way I'd go, with young ones in tow." He slid the map back toward her but didn't fold it. "Keep it. As you know, plans sometimes need to change."

Malin tucked the map into her satchel. Her fingers lingered on the edge for a moment longer than necessary.

Just in case.

As they stood, Corben clasped each hand in turn. His grip was warm and brief, a gesture that said, *You were missed, and I look forward to the next time.*

She smiled as she saw Ellie and Zane walking ahead of them. They were sharing what was left of the sweet roll Ellie had in her hand. They were laughing and looked full of energy. Dawn had started the day and the world around them stirred to life, oblivious to the gravity of their mission.

the forest's hush, the scent of pine and damp earth filling her lungs. Each breath tasted wild and untamed, unlike the sterile metallic tang of Media's corridors. Moss clung to stones like soft armor, and underfoot, the soil gave slightly, alive and yielding. Here, even the silence breathed.

Will walked ahead, quiet but purposeful, his figure moving through the trees like he belonged to them. Malin watched the way he moved, head tilted slightly, shoulders tight, always listening. Always aware. He didn't just walk; he *scanned*, his eyes darting toward the shifting underbrush, his hand flexing by instinct near his hip. The way he kept watch for threats made her spine tense and her heart settle at the same time.

She found herself mirroring him, listening. Not just to the breeze brushing the canopy, or the occasional creak of a branch, but to the *layers* beneath it. Her eyes spotted a squirrel, maybe, darting across the dry leaves. She heard a crow caw from somewhere up ahead. Familiar forest noises. But still... she felt it too, that instinctive coil of awareness that something could go wrong at any moment. That something *could* be watching.

She didn't need to be told what Will was thinking. She could read it in his posture. In the slight pause when the wind shifted. In the way his hand lifted, silent signal to stop.

Each time, Malin froze mid-step, with her breath held. Her eyes swept the thicket just ahead, where one bush stirred against the stillness. The others were still. Her pulse quickened, tension prickling along her arms. She waited... counted.

Just the wind.

She exhaled slowly. When Will resumed walking, she followed.

It wasn't just the forest that hummed with hidden energy. Her nerves had been on edge since they left the inn, stretched taut

his, her wide eyes soaking in every shifting leaf and speck of light. Malin's gaze drifted to Ellie as they walked, her hand tucked into Zane's with a quiet familiarity that didn't belong to a child anymore. Eleven. *Almost twelve,* Malin reminded herself, causing an ache pressing against her ribs. Not quite a little girl. Not yet a woman. But something was shifting in her daughter, something just on the edge of becoming.

Ellie walked with more confidence now, her steps steady even over the uneven ground, her chin slightly lifted as though daring the forest to challenge her. The way she moved reminded Malin, painfully, of herself at that age. Still soft, still innocent, but already carrying more than she should.

When did her daughter start standing so tall? When had her shoulders begun to square like someone preparing for a world that wouldn't go easy on her?

Malin swallowed hard, watching as Ellie bent to inspect a leaf clinging to her boot, brushing it off with a quiet laugh. Her smile still held that spark of mischief, but even her laughter had matured, richer somehow. There were fewer giggles now, more knowing smiles. Less clinging, more independence. She didn't ask to hold Malin's hand anymore, apparently not even when she was scared, as she thought back to the train. That alone made her throat tighten.

She'd missed it happening. Between change happening all around her, her little girl had been growing into herself, step-by-step. And now, walking ahead of her, Ellie looked like she belonged to this wild place. Not a child to be protected, but something braver. More becoming.

She's not my baby anymore, Malin thought, the words striking harder than expected.

foreign world with a quiet strength, it came laced with grief. Grief for the lullabies that no longer soothed, for the toys abandoned on the shelf, for the bedtime stories traded for whispered secrets shared with Zane.

Malin reached out instinctively and brushed a strand of hair from Ellie's collar. Ellie didn't flinch, but she didn't lean in either. Just a flick of a smile, a brief acknowledgment of the gesture before she turned back to the path.

That was enough.

But Malin's hand lingered at her side, fingers curling once in empty air before falling still.

Her gaze drifted back to Will's broad shoulders as he led them forward, and a realization settled over her like mist: he wasn't just walking ahead. He was *guarding* them. Every move he made had a purpose. She had always relied on her own vigilance, her own control – Just her and Ellie. But now... part of her let him carry that weight, just a little. Just for now.

As the shadows lengthened, stretching into twisted shapes across their path, the deeper parts of the forest whispered secrets older than cities. And Malin listened, not just to the sound of the woods, but to her own pulse, to her thoughts spinning quietly behind her eyes.

They were walking through danger. But they were walking through it together.

And somehow, that made it bearable.

As they pressed forward, Malin noticed Will slow his pace. He'd been leading with quiet confidence all morning, but now his posture had changed, it was slight, but she had noticed. His

listening to something only he could hear.

"Will?" she called quietly, matching his pace. "What is it?"

He didn't answer right away. Instead, he scanned the tree line to their left, then without a word, shifted direction, off the main path and into a dense thicket where the canopy grew thick enough to dim the daylight. She hesitated for half a second before following, motioning for the others to stay close.

The air grew cooler as they moved through the shaded brush, the soft scent of moss and old bark replacing the bright sunlit air of the path they'd abandoned. Malin kept glancing at Will, reading the tension in his jaw, the flick of his gaze. He wasn't guessing. He was *following* something. But there were no tracks. No obvious threat.

What are you seeing that I'm not?

Just as she was about to ask, the trees thinned, revealing a narrow clearing—and beyond it, a jagged sinkhole carved deep into the earth, veiled by ferns and vines. The forest had swallowed the trail whole. She took a sharp breath and stepped to the edge, heart thudding as she realized how close they'd come.

A few more minutes. A few more paces on that path, and they could have walked straight into it.

She turned to Will, her voice low but laced with alarm. "How did you know?"

He looked down at the ruined path, then back at her, clearly struggling to name whatever instinct had pulled him aside. "I didn't... not exactly. It just felt wrong ahead. Like something was waiting."

"Waiting?" she echoed, brows lifting.

together himself. "The forest... sometimes it gives you that feeling. A pressure. A quiet push. You learn to listen."

Malin studied him, trying to decide if that was superstition or some kind of magic he hadn't told her about yet. Either way, it had saved them.

"You sure it wasn't luck?"

He offered her a half-smile, more tired than cocky this time. "Luck doesn't usually feel like a voice in your chest."

That gave her pause.

She turned again to the jagged sinkhole, its maw still and waiting. A reminder of how quickly the wrong choice could end everything. Then her gaze drifted to the path they'd chosen instead—winding, longer, but stable underfoot. Safer... for now.

But safety came at a cost.

They would have to move faster. Cover more ground. Push harder than they planned, with children in tow.

Malin exhaled slowly. The forest wasn't done testing them. And this path might be safer, but only if they could outrun whatever else was waiting in the dark.

She caught Will's eye, and this time, she didn't need to say it out loud.

Could they make it on time?

The wind shifted, and the trees didn't answer.

ill had seen a lot in the wilds, but watching a twelve-year-old boy try to train a deer with his mind was a first. He leaned against the moss-covered trunk of a broad oak, arms crossed, one boot propped against the roots and couldn't take his eyes off the kid growing into his power. Lady Anariel was an amazing teacher; it surprised him how quickly Malin and the kids were coming along – all while they walked.

The break was well earned, Zane had started limping twenty minutes ago but hadn't said a word about it, and Ellie's eyes had gone glassy from focus and fatigue. They all needed the pause.

Across the small clearing, Zane stood with Lady Anariel at his side, the two of them facing a sleek brown deer that had wandered near without fear.

"Focus your intent, not your fear," she said softly from the edge of the trees. "The forest listens best when you're certain of what you're asking."

Zane's jaw tightened. The deer blinked once but didn't run. Will wasn't sure who was more tense, Zane, or him.

Zane's brows furrowed in concentration, one hand extended, fingers trembling slightly as he focused. Not just communicating anymore. He was trying to guide the creature. Influence its movement. Command with intent rather than empathy.

Will watched in stillness, eyes narrowed. The kid was pushing himself, riding the edge of his talent. And Lady Anariel, patient as always, let him try. Her posture elegant, her eyes half-lidded, she watched Zane, measuring, teaching, all without interrupting.

sliding in beside him. Her arms wrapped around his middle from behind, head resting lightly on his shoulder.

"He's doing it," she murmured against his shirt, pride and wonder threading through her voice.

Will grunted softly, not looking away. "He's close. He'll figure it out."

It was only when she shifted slightly that he noticed Ellie by the stream. She stood a few feet from the bank, her palms up, eyes narrowed in concentration. Thirty stones, fist-sized and smooth, rose from the earth around her, hovering in a loose orbit. They weren't wobbling either. They spun, slow and controlled. She tilted her head, and the stones shifted with her, forming a spiral in the air before floating gently back down.

Will stared. "When did she learn *that*?"

"So powerful. So fast. Either Lady Anariel is that amazing of a teacher or she is truly gifted," he murmured back, his voice low. "I've seen mages train for years to do half of what those two are figuring out in days."

"Last night," Malin said, her voice tinged with awe. "She didn't want to tell you. Said she wanted to show you when she had it perfect."

Will huffed a laugh, arms sliding over Malin's where they rested across his chest. "Show-off," he muttered, but it was affectionate. The kind of pride that coiled warm in his chest and almost hurt to hold.

"Ellie turns twelve next month," Malin said, almost to herself. "She was just a kid... a little girl. I still see her sleeping with that dragon pillow."

anymore."

"She's going to be powerful," Will said quietly. "They both are."

Malin's hand tightened around his hand, just a little. "We just have to keep them alive long enough to see it," she said, her voice low. "I grew up hearing how dangerous the world was outside Media... especially the journey to Aloria. Please tell me that was all just government propaganda. Just something they made up to keep us in."

Will wanted to lie.

He wanted to smooth it over, say the stories were exaggerations, say things weren't as bad now.

But he couldn't. Not to her.

"I'd like to tell you that," he said quietly. "But the truth is, I've lost people on the way before."

He felt her stiffen beside him, caught the flicker of fear in her eyes. Regret twisted in his gut like a blade, but he couldn't leave it there.

He turned toward her, voice firm. "But none of them meant what you three mean to me. I would die before I let anything happen to you."

She looked at him, the fear still there, but so was trust. And something deeper he didn't feel like he deserved, but he'd die trying to earn.

Will's gaze drifted back to Zane, who stood motionless, his eyes still locked on the deer. The animal had finally bowed its head and taken a few cautious steps forward, crossing the boundary of uncertainty into trust. Zane didn't move, didn't flinch. He simply lowered his hand, and the deer followed, slow and deliberate, as if tethered by something unseen.

merely listening. But either way, something stirred in him. Something old. Something deep.

Respect, first.

Then perhaps a touch of envy. Maybe envy. His powers were so passive, how he had always wished he had a power that could be used for protection or control, anything more than simple – find people.

Zane, barely twelve, had already tapped into something powerful, something Will could never touch. His own magic felt so... passive. A locator. A seeker. Useful, yes. But never commanding. Never protective. Never felt like enough. Traveling with Malin, Ellie, and the elves, he just felt so useless.

How many times had he wished for more?

Not for glory. For defense. For control. For the chance to shield instead of just guide.

He exhaled slowly, a quiet weightlifting from his chest. Zane wasn't just finding his power; he was becoming someone the world would have to notice. Someone who could shape it, not just survive it.

And he couldn't be prouder, especially to call him his son. He thought about that and let is sink in. He was really looking forward to telling Zee, but he wanted to give him a chance to get to know him.

"Come on," Malin said softly, her fingers brushing his arm. "We should keep moving. Time's getting away from us, and progress only matters if it gets us closer to where we need to be."

Will cast just the smallest twitch of a smile. The danger ahead still loomed, the forest still held its secrets, but for now. They were moving forward. Together.

They had steadily made pace and though they had been going slower lately, they had made good progress.

"Watch your step here," Will said softly as they neared a brook, the water singing over smooth stones. He gestured toward a more stable crossing.

"Thank you," Malin replied, the sound of the stream mingling with the timbre of her gratitude. As the day aged and shadows stretched, the group continued their vigilant march, bound by a common purpose and a bond forged in the crucible of shared trials. In the silent communion of their journey, each member found their place, their strengths interwoven into a tapestry of resolve, ready to face whatever lay ahead.

As they walked beneath the towering canopy, each step muffled by fallen leaves and moss, Anariel moved among them like a gentle current of wind, silent but guiding. She had gifted each of them with a new focus. Zane was whispering to the trees now, his voice low and sure, learning how to summon not just one creature, but many. Ellie floated a few inches off the ground, her arms stretched wide for balance, a determined crease in her brow. Malin's flames had grown. They were beautiful and wild, curling through the air like living ribbons as she practiced shaping them to her will.

Anariel was truly an exceptional teacher. Patient. Perceptive. Demanding in the kindest way.

Then she turned to him.

"Will," she said with that quiet authority that always managed to get his full attention. "Did you not want training?"

"I would love to do more," he replied, scratching the back of his neck, "but my powers aren't exactly... exciting." His tone came out more dismissive than he meant it to. "I can sense other

maybe a cup if I concentrate hard enough. Nothing that can actually protect anyone."

She didn't laugh. She didn't even frown. She just tilted her head slightly, eyes studying him as if his soul were a knot she intended to untangle.

"You sense power," she said slowly. "You know what it is, where it is, how strong it is?"

He nodded.

"Then why not learn to redirect it?"

Will blinked. "Redirect?"

"Or block it," she continued, as if the idea had always been obvious. "If you can identify and isolate magic, especially in others, then you may be able to suppress it, channel it, or even bend it slightly, given the right training. Your power isn't passive, Will. You've just been using it passively."

He stared at her, silent.

"Lodestone magic is rare," she went on. "And rarer still in someone with your instincts. You don't need fire or force to be formidable. Imagine walking into a fight and stripping the magic from your opponent before they can even lift a finger. Imagine protecting your people by stopping harm before it's cast."

Will felt something unfurl in his chest. The idea was wild, strange... but it resonated. Like the magic itself had just heard her words and started to hum in response.

"I've never thought of it like that," he admitted.

She gave him a small, knowing smile. "That's why I'm here."

He gave a single nod, more to himself than to her. "Alright then. Where do we start?"

your influence."

As the others practiced their flashier gifts around them, Will took his first steps down a new path, one of subtlety, strategy, and, perhaps for the first time, real power.

The group paused at the forest's edge, breath misting in the cooling air as the trees finally gave way to the low hills ahead. The sky burned orange and indigo, the last fingers of sunlight dragging across the land like a warning flare.

Will scanned the horizon. He hadn't expected much trouble on this stretch, but he knew what lie ahead for tomorrow.

Nar appeared beside him, silent as smoke. "Few travelers use this trade road anymore," he said, eyes narrowing toward the west. "Not since the Norlan began keeping to themselves." He recalled that the Norlan were a race of half-elf/half-dwarf people that preferred animals and nature to humans. It didn't help that Media had tried wiping them from existence a few times, so they were understandably wary.

Will nodded. "Still... it's too empty. Barely a soul all day. Just snares and that orc band."

Khelek joined them, brushing pine needles from his bracers. "They were scouts. The main force camps near the southern ridge. If we pass that way tomorrow..." His voice trailed off; his implication was clear.

"We'll be in range of their raiding parties the closer we get, they do love to loot the traders passing," Will finished for him.

Nar gave a slight nod. "They favor the deeper cut in the ravine, ambush territory. If we stay on the path, they'll smell us before dawn."

from the south. That faint bite of sea air told him they weren't far now. Close enough to taste it. But not close enough to relax.

"We didn't make as much ground today as I hoped," he admitted. "We'll have to push hard tomorrow to reach Seaborn by nightfall."

Khelek didn't flinch. "We've had easier days. This was a gift."

Will gave a dry laugh. "You call evading orcs and traps a gift?"

"For what comes tomorrow?" Khelek met his eyes. "Yes."

Will let the silence stretch between them a beat longer, then turned to face the rest of the group. Zane and Ellie sat by the edge of a small clearing, sharing dried fruit. Malin was tending the fire pit with practiced efficiency.

He squared his shoulders. "Let's set camp here," he called out, loud enough for all to hear. "It's not ideal, but we've got enough cover and space. It is safer here then passing by orcs at night or camping too close to them."

Nar raised an eyebrow. "And tomorrow?"

Will's jaw tightened. "Tomorrow, we walk harder. I know a few shortcuts, they'll cut time, but they're steep. We'll be hugging the edge of orc territory. No stops unless it's life or death."

Khelek slung off his pack with a grunt. "Nar and I will keep patrol through the night."

Will nodded, casting one last glance toward the dark ridge looming in the distance. "Must be nice," he muttered, half to himself. "Only needing four hours of sleep."

Khelek gave a faint smirk. "It helps."

The three of them exchanged a quiet look, one forged in shared battles and unspoken trust. For now, they were safe. For now.

through the clearing. His fingers twitched toward his blade.

Tomorrow would be harder.

He was glad Nar and Khelek were here to help.

The night wasn't done with them yet.

H er boot skidded against the gravel-laced rock face, sending her sliding several feet before she caught herself with a grunt, skin tearing raw across her palm. *That will be yet another cut to heal later*, she though. Another damn reason to hate this climb.

Will had told her there were some gentle climbs.

Gentle my ass. I hate to imagine what he thinks hard climbs are like.

She flattened herself against the craggy incline, forehead pressing to the stone as her lungs heaved. Apparently, today was the day she discovered she was afraid of heights. That, or this mountain had a personal vendetta.

Ellie was excelling at the whole levitation thing and had basically floated her way up the rocks. Zane and Will climbed up like the goats they had passed earlier.

She had even heard of a goat before today, but her world had changed so dramatically in the last week.

Malin clung to the rock; her fingers burning, thighs shaking, utterly wrecked. Three hours of relentless uphill had hollowed her out. She had always prided herself on staying fit, but this was a different beast. She was tired, hungry, and far too close to crying. Eyes closed; she hung there from the steep rock incline trying to gather the courage to keep going.

She squeezed her eyes shut, willing herself not to lose it.

Not here. Not now. Not in front of...

Arms wrapped around her waist.

with concern... and infuriating amusement.

She wanted to snap back. She wanted to laugh. Instead, all she could manage was a weak smile.

Then she noticed the rope.

It dangled beside her. She looked up to the other side of the rope, where Khelek's strong arms anchored it above. Relief surged. She looped it around her waist and clung to it like salvation.

As the rope tightened and began to pull her upward, Will's breath warmed her neck.

"I gotta say," he murmured with a smirk, "this view's a lot better from here. I should've stood below you the last climb too."

She groaned, but she didn't stop climbing.

They had stopped for a short lunch break after the climbing ordeal, to allow her to calm down but that had been at least two hours before. The day's journey had been relentless, and she could feel every step weighing upon her. Her sun-kissed hair, usually held in a twist by ornate chopsticks, now clung to the nape of her neck with the damp kiss of exertion. To pass time, they discussed scenarios of how they might work together to fight, if needed.

"Something isn't right," Will muttered, his voice was so low it seemed to meld with the forest. His eyes scoured the underbrush, searching for signs of life where none appeared.

"Agree," Nar said in his low voice.

"Could it just be animals in the area? Zee. Do you notice anything?" Malin asked, focusing on their assets and skills. Her

in the familiar shapes of the woodland.

"Maybe," Will conceded, though his posture remained taut, a strung bow ready to release at the slightest provocation.

"There are a few larger creatures, a bear and some elk in the area, but I can't tell how far yet," Zane responded.

"But this silence... it feels too still."

The way Will said it sent a cold ripple through her spine. Not fear, *anticipation.* Like something had just changed, and her body sensed it before her brain could catch up.

The forest wasn't breathing. No rustling leaves, no birdsong, no hum of insects. Just a dense, unnatural quiet that pressed in on her eardrums until her own heartbeat was the loudest thing she could hear.

Malin scanned the trees. Shadows sprawled across the mossy floor like fingers trying to drag her under. The light that remained was fractured through the canopy in sharp golden slashes, gorgeous in that fleeting, doomed sort of way.

She hated how beautiful it was.

"Let's keep moving," she said, trying to keep her voice steady. *Authoritative. Capable.* Like she used to sound in the infirmary when everything was chaos and people needed her to be calm. "Whatever it is, maybe we can move away from it."

She didn't believe it. Not really. But no one argued, and that was enough for now.

They moved, but the light didn't follow. It dimmed behind them, the sun bleeding out through the trees like it was trying to stay but couldn't quite hold on.

The headache hit without warning.

around her skull and squeezing. She closed her eyes for just for a second.

Her mother's voice dropped into her mind like a knife.

"We just intercepted their transmission. It's urgent. They know where you are and are in-route. Meet me on the boat. Please be safe."

The connection snapped, gone as fast as it came.

Malin stumbled a step before catching herself. "My mother just reached out," she said aloud, not sure how her voice was so calm. "She says they're on their way. And they know where we are."

No one asked who *they* were. They all knew.

Will's head snapped toward her, his eyes narrowing. Already on alert, now sharpening like a blade. He didn't speak, but he didn't have to. His whole body was tuned to danger now.

Malin fell in step beside him, her pulse ticking in her ears. The kids moved quietly between them, Zane guiding Ellie with a hand on her back. Malin could feel the tension radiating off everyone, Khelek and Nar somewhere just beyond her vision, part of the forest and watching it all.

Something was coming. She didn't know what, but the woods knew. They felt different. *Charged.*

And she couldn't shake the feeling that something out there was already watching.

The silence shattered.

A barked command ripped through the underbrush, sharp and jarring, fracturing the uneasy calm like glass under a boot.

forest like they'd been grown in its shadows. Metal and menace fused into living machines. Their matte-black armor absorbed the light. Laser rifles gleamed at their hips. The kind of men who didn't hesitate. The kind of men who made people disappear.

Her breath caught. She knew those insignias, Media's elite enforcement squad. Not just guards. Hunters.

They were here for Ellie, and her.

"Malin and Ellie Neldoreth, you will come with us," the lead soldier ordered, his voice cold and mechanical, like it had been engineered for intimidation. "Resistance will only bring trouble."

She knew *trouble,* really meant death.

Her mind raced. Seventeen, no, eighteen soldiers. They were in some tactical formation. The glint of reinforced implants on their arms and legs. The low hum of powered exosuits. These weren't scare tactics. This was a capture operation. Efficient and brutal.

Ellie's hand found hers.

Her hands were shaking, but the look in her eyes said she was not going to stand by and accept their answer.

Malin pushed her behind her instinctively shielding her. She felt the heat rise in her chest, a slow, searing boil. Her vision flickered yellow and green at the edges, something she has now learned to be her magic itching to be used. Not fear. Not this time. Rage. The kind that came with fire and ash and teeth.

From the corner of her eye, she caught the shift, Lady Anariel and the elven guards melted upward into the trees, silent as wind. Hidden. Waiting. Deadly.

log, with his crossbow up. His gaze locked with hers. That look. Like a silent oath. They would not be taken. Not without a fight.

She turned, her voice came out low and even, a growl of steel barely held in check. She called out to the guards, "I don't know if you have been properly briefed, but we are not planning on going quietly."

The guard leader made a signal. From the confused look in his eyes, they had not expected that answer. *What had they been told about this operation?*

Malin's eyes scanned the field. Calculating. Fire at the edges of her thoughts. She could feel the magic building, hot and volatile. The air itself seemed to charge in anticipation. One move, one twitch, and everything would ignite.

They would not be going easily.

They weren't ready. They weren't safe. But she'd be damned if they would go quietly into the hands of a government that treated magic like a disease.

Let them come.

Ellie's eyes turned a tempestuous green with anger overshadowing the calm blue. They shimmered with an inner fire as she raised her palms to the sky. With a furrow of her brow, she focused her will upon the elements around them. Leaves rustled and twigs snapped underfoot as the air began to swirl, coalescing into a fog that rose like specters from the forest floor, followed by a pelting of rocks and stones. The smoke screen billowed forth, obscuring Malin and her companions from the soldiers' cold technological gaze but thinned after a few moments. Her move had given Nar and Khelek the advantage they needed, to pick off several guards, with their elven eyesight.

whispers, each breath tasted of earth and rebellion. Ellie ducked behind the rock, which belied the strength within her. Malin noticed the air around her became thick, like the barrier at Stoneholds. Ellie could only hold it for a time, but it might be the time she needed.

Through the haze, she saw Zane nearby. He stood tall behind a tree, out of sight of the guards, his hazel eyes locked with those of an elk paused at the edge of the clearing. He extended his hand, and his fingers trembled ever so slightly. She watched in awe as the huge elk bowed its great antlered head in assent before turning to face the shrouded threat.

With a thunderous bellow, the elk charged, hooves pounding the verdant carpet with primal fury. The soldiers, momentarily taken aback by the unexpected ally, scattered their laser fire into the mist, red beams slicing through the haze in search of targets.

Will was pinned behind a large tree. With practiced ease, he loaded the bolts into his crossbow, each movement a quiet promise of lethal intent. His eyes, sharpened to the minutiae of battle, spied the chinks in the soldiers' gleaming armor; the soft underbellies where technology yielded to human frailty. The guards' weapons were so close to hitting him. So dangerously close to hitting him, and they were not holding back.

In the heartbeat between chaos and silence, Will's bolt flew.

It sliced through the air, clean and final, burying itself in the narrow gap at a soldier's throat. It was a punctuation mark in a sentence written in death. Two more followed in quick succession, silent and sure. Thuds softened by moss. Motion halted mid-charge.

Above them, Lady Anariel vanished from the treetops like smoke curling into dusk, only to reappear behind two soldiers. Her blades whispered through the air, one smooth and one

crack of sound. A laser. She staggered, violet eyes flaring as the shot grazed her ribs and continued through a third guard behind her. The starlight in her expression dimmed. She blinked, breath catching, then vanished again, appearing beside Nar and Khelek, who already had the high ground pinned with deadly precision.

Malin saw it all. The threat. The blood. The pain.

And she couldn't stand still anymore.

I must do it, she thought

She raised her arms and Ellie dropped the barrier she had raised.

Heat surged from her.

The air around her warped as she raised both hands, and the blue fire exploded from her palms like a dam breaking. It wasn't just fire. It was fury. Years of being lied to, of fearing her powers, of hiding what should have been *hers*. Her father's betrayal. The guards' arrival. The threat to Ellie. To Zane. To Will.

They would burn, if it meant she could protect those she loved.

The flames tore across the clearing like summoned wrath, licking across armored limbs and melting visors to faces. Screams cut the night. Guards scrambled, but the polymer of their suits fused to skin in the blaze. They were not prepared for this, not for her.

Malin's ice-blue eyes locked forward, glowing now with the same wild, brilliant blue of the inferno. She could feel it. It wasn't *just casting the fire, but she was becoming it.* It curled around her like armor. It didn't hurt. It *loved* her.

bend the fire's edge away from the trees, directing it down paths of less destruction. Beside her, Nar joined her, unleashing his own fire like twin dragons dancing across the battlefield.

And still, it wasn't enough.

The fire surged hotter. Brighter. Faster.

It wanted vengeance. It knew what these men stood for, the erasure of magic itself. This wasn't just *her* fury anymore.

This was magic exacting revenge.

And she couldn't stop it, so she gave in.

Malin let it take her. Her mind opened wide, and her world went black.

ill's jaw went slack, as a few of the guards stopped shooting at him at that moment also, it is likely they did also. The fire he expected. Malin throwing flame like a trained battlemage? Sure. But *this*?

She was on fire.

Not burning, but fully engulfed.

Her entire body was wrapped in brilliant blue flames, her form a silhouette against a seething inferno. The air shimmered around her. She moved like the heart of a wildfire, she was deadly, graceful, and untouchable.

And she was magnificent.

The guards that hadn't already fled were melting in place, armor warping, weapons clattering uselessly to the ground as they tried to run. Will forced himself to look away.

Zane.

He spotted the boy hidden behind the twisted roots of an old cedar, hazel eyes wide, bow drawn with practiced tension. Fear rippled across his young face, but so did something else, a determination. Power. *Control.*

The elk came crashing through again. He was amazed it kept going.

The huge elk, coaxed into service by Zane charged headlong into the fray. Its cry split the air as it gouged its racks through the ranks for its third pass. Metal shrieked. A soldier flew like a ragdoll, impaled on antlers slick with blood. The beast buckled

thud that vibrated in Will's spine.

Zane cried out, pain flashing across his features as if he'd been struck himself.

The bond, Will thought, chest tightening. He didn't have time to dwell on it.

He saw the shimmer of an energy weapon leveling toward Zane.

Will ran.

Angled his steps through roots and loose stone, heart hammering with a single goal—*get to him first.*

The energy weapon pulsed. Will saw the flash.

But the guard never got the shot off.

Nar's dagger slammed into his neck and dropped him like a sack of grain. The bolt still fired, reflex and wild.

It hit Will.

A pulse of heat tore through his side just as he collided with Zane, knocking the boy to the ground and shielding him with his body.

Pain ignited in his hip like a branding iron buried in flesh. He gasped. The scab forming over the cauterized wound throbbed with every heartbeat, a tight, blistering coil that refused to be ignored.

"You saved me," Zane whispered, voice quaking.

"Of course I did." Will forced the words out through clenched teeth, one hand pressed hard over the charred hole in his jacket. *Could've been worse.* He was still breathing.

Zane's eyes widened suddenly. "Behind you!"

guards breaking through the tree line, weapons raised.

He didn't have time to lift his crossbow.

Then something massive stepped between them.

A bear. No. Not just a bear. It was a beast of a bear *larger* than any bear Will had seen. It roared into the clearing, tearing into the guards with terrifying efficiency, claws flashing, metal screaming under the weight of raw magic and fury.

Will's breath caught.

He turned back to Zane, who now sat, arms raised, his eyes blank-white with focus.

It then dawned on him that Zane hadn't just asked the bear to act, as he had the elk. This time, he was wielding the power of the bear.

No command, no begging.

Just *power*.

Awe struck him. This was not just a boy with magic.

A force.

And right now? That force was fighting for *them*.

The bear, an avatar of Zane's desperation, roared with primal rage, its massive paws swiping through the air with deadly precision. Two soldiers, their technological superiority rendered moot against nature's fury, were caught in the creature's relentless assault, their cries swallowed by the forest's indifferent embrace.

Ellie, her ice-blue eyes were a mirror to the sky's deepening hues. She stood resolute amidst the chaos. The soldiers, emboldened by the thinning veil of concealment, advanced with

reached for her, his fingers grazing the hem of her cloak, but Ellie moved like water; fluid and unpredictable.

With a grace that belied her tender years, she pivoted, her blonde hair a golden whip in the fading light. She extended her hand, palm side outward. The soldier's weapon jerked free from his grasp, dancing through the air as though caught in an unseen current. Ellie leapt in a silent symphony of martial discipline; a high kick here, a sweeping leg there; each motion augmented by the invisible push and pull of her telekinesis. When did she learn that?

The man stumbled backward, his comrades halting their advance, their expressions masked yet their hesitation evident.

"Just get her! She's a little girl," one said charging.

Will took that moment to send a well-placed crossbow arrow directly into a weak spot in his armor. He crashed to the ground. Of course, the arrow was small, so from their vantage point and without seeing Will, they assumed it was her.

Confusion spread through their ranks like a whisper through the leaves, their orders clashing with the unforeseen prowess of a child who wielded power with the poise of an ancient mage.

He held his breath worrying for her. In the waning light, the forest seemed to hold its breath, the very air charged with the latent force of Ellie's resolve, but there were so many of them. Her gaze, now tinged with the verdant shade of determination. He sighed with relief when he saw her rise, high into the tree canopy then she disappeared.

At this point, only three or four guards remained upright, and that wouldn't last long. The leader had dropped early, and now the tide was irreversible.

down herself, clean, efficient. The others fell to Anariel, Nar, and Khelek like dominos toppling under fate's hand.

And then the fire within her vanished.

She crumpled like a marionette with its strings cut, the flames flickering out around her as if the very forest stole them back into its roots. A final wave of heat pulsed outward from her body, *a shimmer in the air,* like the mirage of pavement on a scorching day. Steam hissed off her skin where the fire had kissed her, and for a heartbeat, Will swore he saw her glow. Then even that faded.

He froze.

Panic clamped around his chest like a vice. "No, no, no…"

He stumbled forward, pain lancing through his side, but he barely felt it. The only thing that mattered was her.

But she was breathing.

Relief dropped him to his knees beside her. Burns be damned, he gathered her into his arms, heedless of the fire-warmed skin or the tremble in his own hands. He'd almost lost her. *Again.*

She stirred.

Slow. Dazed. Her lashes fluttered, and then those storm-swept blue eyes blinked up at him, unfocused, searching.

"Don't you ever do that to me again, Sparks," Will said, voice frayed at the edges. A thousand unsaid things clung to those words, but he still managed a crooked grin.

Her lips tugged into a faint, lopsided smile. "What? Be a badass and save your life again? Did it look as cool as it felt?"

"You nearly killed me. Not from enemy fire, just from sheer panic."

She was still trying to blink herself into coherence, but the sass was back, and that was all he needed. He pressed his forehead gently to hers, letting the warmth of her skin settle the last of his shaking nerves.

"Turns out I've got a weak spot," he murmured, voice low and rough. "It's a Firestarter with a reckless streak and an infuriatingly smart mouth."

Her eyes sparkled despite the exhaustion. "Takes one to know one."

"I'm serious," he added with a lopsided smile. "Next time, give me a little warning before you go full inferno goddess. I didn't exactly plan for that heart attack."

She gave a quiet laugh, soft as kindling catching flame. "You practice that line, or was that off the cuff?"

He smirked, eyes crinkling. "Please. I'm naturally charming under even the most extreme situations."

"Still," she murmured, teasing creeping back into her voice, "on a scale from one to epic...how cool did I look?"

"Oh, definitely epic." He shifted to sit up, but the motion pulled a sharp gasp from his throat as he clutched his side.

Her smile vanished. "Will?"

Her hands began to glow just as the world tilted slightly around him. He tried to wave her off, even as his knees started to go soft.

"I said you were epic! This doesn't feel like the time for violence..."

back as she peeled his shirt up with brisk precision.

"Trying to undress me out here?" he rasped, grimacing. "I mean, I'm flattered, but I don't think I'll perform my best with all these people watching…I won't perform my worst, but…"

She shot him with a glare, her brow arched. "Flattery won't close the hole in your side any faster. Now hold still and let me fix you."

"You're so hot when you're bossy," he muttered, wincing as her magic began to pulse through him.

She didn't even blink. "And you're hotter when you're not bleeding everywhere."

He grinned, a little dazed. "So, you think I'm hot. Good to know…. Still hoping this earns me a second kiss."

She rolled her eyes, but her hand lingered against his skin just a moment longer than necessary. The air between them shimmered with the quiet hum of her magic, tendrils of golden light seeping into him like sunlight through cracks in a wall. It wasn't just healing, it was *restoration*, a warmth that threaded through his bones, softening every edge, lighting every nerve with the hum of life renewed.

He exhaled slowly; a peace settled into him that felt almost foreign. Every cell felt like it buzzed, alive and awake.

Then small footsteps pounded toward them.

"Will!" Ellie's voice rang out as she and Zane rushed over, eyes wide with worry.

Malin's magic faded, but her hand didn't move from his chest. Not yet.

now just a ghost of memory. A thousand unspoken words passed between them in the hush before the children arrived, carried in the catch of a breath and the press of her palm.

So, of course, he joked.

Because that was easier than admitting just how close he'd come to breaking.

"Hey, look who's still in one piece," he said, his voice rough but light, flashing them a crooked smile. "Not exactly how I wanted to impress you two, but I'll take what I can get."

Zane gave a huff of disbelief, half-smile creeping in despite himself. "Are you okay?"

"You scared me," Ellie said throwing her arms around him. "Don't do that again."

Will met his gaze. "Yeah. Hey there Bright Eyes. It will take more than this to take me away from you."

His eyes flicked to Malin. "But I'll try harder, now that I've got some really good reasons to stick around."

He meant every word.

Sure, he'd nearly died. Probably lost his standing with the Resistance, might never see Gorek or Lysa again... hell, he was running through a list of people who'd kill him on sight if they found out he was still breathing.

But none of it compared to this. To them. To *her*.

He let the thought linger a heartbeat longer, then pushed to his feet with a groan, brushing the dirt from his palms. It wasn't pain he felt exactly, only the deep ache that came after too many battles, too many close calls. The kind of weight that wasn't physical.

chaos. Magic left its scent on the air, like the scent of burnt ozone, scorched bark, and the bitter tang of blood. But it was over. For now. The clash had faded into silence, the kind that settled on a place only after something irreversible.

Zane stood a few feet away, chest heaving, his eyes locked on the bear still pacing near the tree line. The creature's massive frame was streaked with blood, not all of it its own. Its breath fogged in the cool air, slow and deliberate.

"Easy, friend," Zane murmured. He took a step forward, his hand out, letting the last bit of dried meat drop to the forest floor.

Will watched, silent. Awe stirring in his chest.

The bear dipped its head. A gesture that felt... knowing.

It hadn't been chance. Not instinct. The boy had called it. Guided it.

Commanded it.

Will's throat tightened. *His son.* His son had bent a creature of raw strength to his will with nothing but empathy and a gift he was only beginning to understand.

The bear shifted, revealing a deep gash along its ribs. Will saw Zane's expression crumple.

"Can she help it?" he asked, voice small again, twelve again.

Will turned toward Malin. She was already moving.

"If it will let me," she said, and Will heard the warmth in her voice, the healer's calm, the mother's steadiness.

Malin knelt beside the bear. Her hands began to glow, soft and strong, light blooming from her palms like the embers of a fire not ready to go out. The bear didn't flinch. It allowed her to come close, to let her heal.

Not exhaustion.

Hope.

When the wound had closed, when the bear no longer swayed with pain, Zane stepped forward.

"Go now," he whispered.

The great beast turned. It caught Zane's gaze one final time, acknowledging something between equals, then it lumbered off into the trees, dragging the elk carcass with it.

And just like that, it vanished. Back into the wild.

Back into the quiet.

Ash clung to the moss like frost. The scent of burned polymer and scorched earth lingered, sharp and metallic, overlaying the usual damp green of the forest. Bodies lay strewn like forgotten tools, broken and still.

The forest had fallen still again, but not in peace.

Will's gaze swept over the smoking remnants of the ambush; his jaw set hard. "This would've drawn attention. Orcs, if not worse. We can't hang here long," he said, voice clipped and flat. "Grab what you can. Fast. We don't have the luxury of being picky."

Sunset bled across the canopy in molten streaks, painting the trees in fire and shadow. They hadn't made half the distance they needed today, and now they were burning daylight standing in the wreckage of a fight that was bound to bring predators sniffing.

He moved quickly, instincts kicking in. *Prioritize. Don't linger.*

gear, kneeling only long enough to retrieve what counted. Bolts first, he hated losing those. Then hands through armor seams and tech ports. A sidearm with half a charge, a couple of energy clips, one cracked but functional comm crystal, into his satchel.

The guards' weapons were solid but cumbersome. Built to intimidate, not survive a forest war. Still, parts could be scrapped or bartered. If they made it to Seaborn.

He crouched next to one more body, yanked a clean blade from a thigh holster, and wiped the blood on the soldier's own sleeve before slipping it into his belt.

Every second spent here was another second something might track them.

He straightened and called out quietly, "Let's move. Two minutes. That's all we've got."

Nearby, Malin knelt beside Lady Anariel, hands glowing with that soft, fierce light of hers. Will watched the way her brow furrowed in focus, how her fingers moved gently but with purpose over the gash along Anariel's side.

Nar hovered like a flame barely held in check, his normally unreadable expression etched with concern. Khelek stood behind them, arms crossed, but even from a distance, Will could see the tension in his jaw, the way his eyes never left Anariel.

Will crouched beside a fallen soldier, scavenging in silence, but his focus had shifted.

It wasn't just concern on their faces. It wasn't just duty that kept them poised at her side, weapons lowered, breath held. It was deeper than that. Older.

It was love.

puzzle piece he hadn't known he was missing.

They loved her.

Both of them.

He'd heard the whispers. *Double Bonds.* Rare, sacred. Especially among the elves. Even the idea of soulmates was uncommon, something most races scoffed at as romantic myth. But among elven births, twins or multiples were rare. The idea that soulmates could be formed… there were stories of triads. A connection so profound it defied magic, blood, or time itself.

He had never seen it. Until now.

Anariel had called them her protectors. Said they'd taken a vow. But this… this was something more. Something fierce and sacred, something woven through with lifetimes of choice and devotion.

And somehow, it reminded him of her and their tattoo.

His eyes drifted back to Malin. The woman who had changed everything. Who made every breath heavier and lighter all at once.

His chest tightened. He looked away before the thought could dig in too deep.

Whatever bond those three shared… it wasn't his place to question. But he understood it. More than he ever thought he would. When it was clear she would be fine, their demeanors changed and they began preparations to leave.

They were survivors, each bearing scars seen and unseen, their resilience a beacon in the encroaching night. And as they stood there, united by a bond stronger than blood, the whispers of the

entwined with the inexorable march of stars across the heavens. He took account of the team, pulled the map out to review how far they had gotten.

They were tired. Battered. But still standing.

Will crouched over the map, tracing their progress with a finger smudged by ash and dirt. Nar, Anariel, and Khelek knelt beside him, their faces grim and drawn with fatigue. The sun had long since vanished, and exhaustion clung to them like mist.

"We're not going to make it if we stay on this path," Will muttered, not needing to say it louder. They all knew it. "We've got two options now: the shortcut, with dangerous terrain and the strong likelihood that we will have to do at least one more battle like this, or the bridge with the bandits. Before you make your decision, I have been thinking about the later. I am not saying I have that many nefarious friends and enemies, but depending on who the bandits are, we might have an easier... or harder time. Either way, if we grab enough of these supplies, we may be able to use them for bartering across the bridge."

Khelek rubbed a hand along his jaw. "Shortcut's faster, but only if we survive it."

"Bridge might let us barter," Will added, motioning toward the recovered tech and gear they'd scavenged from the guards. "Worst case, we fight. Best case, we pay our way through."

"I vote bridge," Malin said, rising to her feet, the firelight casting a halo around her. "The ship leaves in two mornings. We need to be on it."

Nar and Anariel exchanged glances before nodding. Khelek agreed with a grunt. "If the bandits are the right kind, we might make it out with lighter pockets but intact limbs. If not, it could be a longer path. I put my odds on the bridge."

away from the trade path, away, hopefully, from being found.

They walked until the weariness in their bones refused to be ignored. Another forty-five minutes of hard journey gave them just enough distance to make camp without leaving a trail too easy to follow.

Malin sparked the fire with a casual flick of her wrist, Will never stopped being awed by how effortlessly she wielded her magic now. He tried not to look too closely, but he noticed the elves bedded down together, Anariel nestled between Nar and Khelek, an unspoken bond holding them in quiet formation.

Will took first watch beside Zane, while Malin curled around Ellie a few feet away. The night was cold, and the hard earth gave no comfort, but it was enough. For now.

Zane sat close, stroking Chitter's back while watching the treeline. After a while, he looked up. "The wolves will warn us," he whispered.

Will frowned. "Wolves?"

Zane nodded toward the woods. "There's a pack nearby. I... talked to them earlier. Told them we'd share our rations if they'd keep watch while we sleep."

"You bartered with wolves?" Will blinked.

Zane gave a small, sheepish smile. "They're smarter than people think. And they like jerky."

Will snorted softly, not sure if he was more amused or impressed. "You really are full of surprises."

Zane grinned, then sobered. "They'll howl if anyone gets close. They promised."

"maybe they're on first watch." He clapped a hand on Zane's shoulder, then gestured toward the sleeping forms by the fire. "Go on. Lie next to Ellie. You earned it today."

Zane didn't argue. He slid down beside her, and Ellie shifted instinctively, curling toward him. Within seconds, they were still.

Still, long after the others had surrendered to dreams, Will's gaze drifted eastward. Toward the path they'd abandoned. Toward the blood and ash they'd left behind.

Whoever had sent those soldiers would find the aftermath.

And they'd follow.

The wreckage they'd left behind wouldn't go unnoticed for long. Not by orcs. Not by Media. Not by whoever had tracked Malin and Ellie this far into the wilds.

He tightened his grip on his crossbow and let his eyes scan the shadows beyond the flickering firelight.

Will eased down beside Malin, her warmth already working its way into his bones. He didn't expect to sleep deeply, not tonight, but it felt good to close his eyes, even for a little while.

They had bought themselves a night. Maybe.

But someone would be coming.

And Will wasn't sure they'd be ready.

They'd packed up at first light. The air was sharp with the morning chill and the scent of moss and ash still lingering faintly from the battle. After a quick breakfast and leaving a generous share of jerky for the wolves, Will had to admit he was impressed. Everyone had moved with purpose. No complaints. No dragging feet. Just quiet determination. They were ready to reach that boat.

The forest trail sloped downhill, flanked by towering evergreens whose canopies filtered the sun into shifting gold patterns across their path. The silence between them had settled into something easy. Peaceful.

"Come on," Will said after a stretch of quiet. "Tell us about the bear."

Zane glanced up, a flicker of surprise in his eyes, like he hadn't expected the interest. Will kept his tone casual, but his curiosity was real.

"It was amazing," Zane said, his chest puffing a little. "I did what Lady Anariel showed me. I didn't just call it... I... I kind of joined with it. Took over, but not like forcing it. It was like... sharing. Like the bear and I were one. I felt everything it felt. Its strength, its fury, but also its calm. There was understanding."

Will nodded, genuinely impressed. "That's powerful, Zane. Really powerful. You've found something that most mages spend decades chasing. Your connection to nature, it's more than talent."

The words had slipped out before he could stop them, "*I think leaving the city's been good for you.*"

Will opened his mouth to backtrack, but Ellie beat him to it.

"Mom always says everything happens for a reason," she said, skipping over a root without breaking stride. "Even the bad stuff. If you're patient, the reason shows up. Eventually."

Zane's eyes flicked toward the trees again. His voice was softer this time. "Maybe. But... I do appreciate you. For protecting me. Back there, I didn't see it coming. I've never had someone do something like that. Not for me."

Will's heart pulled tight. The kid was trying so hard to be a man, to stay composed. But Will saw through it. He remembered what it felt like to be twelve and already carrying the weight of survival.

"I know you're not used to this," Will said gently. "Honestly? I'm not either. But these two," he nodded toward Malin and Ellie ahead, "they bring something out in us. Something good. We're a family now, Zee. That's what family does—we show up for each other. And you? You're pretty damn amazing. I'm proud to know you."

Zane didn't respond with words. He just threw his arms around Will in a sudden, tight hug, burying his face in his jacket. Will blinked hard, arms wrapping around the boy automatically. A few tears slipped free before he could stop them. He didn't wipe them. Just let them fall.

When they finally pulled back, Will ruffled Zane's hair, then gently wiped the tears from his cheeks.

"Hope," he said, voice low, "is a powerful ally. And with your gift... we might just stand a chance."

They didn't speak after that. They didn't need to.

And still, Will's thoughts drifted.

But for now, they had each other.

And for now... that was enough.

He glanced toward Malin just in time to see her stagger and bring a hand to her temple.

Will was beside her in a heartbeat, steadying her with a hand at her elbow. "Malin?"

She blinked, wincing, but didn't collapse. "Mother just reached out again. I think I'm starting to get used to it. It wasn't as bad this time." She drew in a breath. "She said we need to reach the boat before dawn. She made arrangements to keep us safe at the footbridge."

He let out a slow breath. "Good thing we're already headed that way."

Malin gave a weary nod, and Will turned back to the others.

"I know you're tired," he said, his voice pitched for quiet strength. "We've had a long day. But once we're on that boat, we'll have rest. The first leg's a week on water. Then three more weeks on the second."

He paused to let that settle, then added, "We're a few hours from the bridge. There's an inn near Seaborn; we can eat there. But if we miss the ship, the next isn't for another week. And by then, they'll find us. Tonight, is our shot."

They continued on, each step muffled by moss and soft earth. The air carried weight, but it was expectation, not dread.

Will led the way, every instinct on alert. At the forest's edge, they came upon the valley, with a view of the great chasm that split the land like a scar. In the distance, stretched across it, was the footbridge. They were close.

his face in shadow. Two guards stepped forward, cautious but not overtly hostile. He didn't recognize them, which wasn't surprising. He hadn't worked in this territory in over a year.

His eyes flicked over their gear. No visible tattoos. No insignias. They had their weapons raised in concern, he guessed the fact that their clothing was a blood-soaked and filthy, and they were well armed probably screamed red flags. If he were them, he'd be on edge.

Will kept his voice low and steady. "We're here to cross. Told we were expected."

One of the guards raised a brow. "Wait here." He ducked into the Tollhouse.

Will shifted, hand brushing the hilt of his blade out of habit. Seconds passed. Too many.

Then the door burst open again. The guard jogged out, panting, his grip tight on the shaft of his spear. "Sorry. There's... been a complication. Someone placed a new bid on your crossing. They want an additional fee."

Will exhaled and tugged down his hood. "That so?"

Recognition hit the guard like a slap. His eyes widened. "Mr. Hawkson. Sorry, sir. Didn't realize..." He spun on his heel and disappeared back inside.

Sometimes reputation can be a good thing, he thought.

This time, when the Tollhouse door opened, four broad-shouldered men stepped out. The biggest among them had arms like tree trunks and a grin to match.

"Do I hear Hawk's slinking around my bridge?" The voice boomed, half menace, half mirth. Will could have recognized that gravel-coated chuckle anywhere.

"How's the wife? Kids still keeping you honest?"

"You bastard," Harmire laughed, clapping a meaty hand to Will's shoulder. "She's still ugly as ever, but... Umm... Can't get enough of her...." He caught sight of Ellie and Zane and cleared his throat. "...her cooking. Her cooking's top notch."

Will let out a deep laugh at that, as he knew what he was going to say. How Harmine married the ex-whore Ume, he didn't know, but word had gotten out about her skills and cooking wasn't one of them, last he remembered hearing the rumors.

He unhooked the two rifles strapped to his back and handed them over. "Picked these up from some Media soldiers we crossed west of here. Might be more if you've got a horse and move fast."

Harmire's eyes lit up like a kid on solstice morning. "Oho... now you're speaking my language."

Then the grin faded. "Official word is I am supposed to shoot you. Some brown-eyed bureaucrat from Media, real slick type, really pissed me off, even flirted with Ume. He offered good coin to make sure you didn't leave this canyon."

Will didn't flinch. "Let me guess. Andrew?"

"Could be," Harmire said, his expression sobering. "But I remember the day you saved my baby Emman. I owe you for that." His voice dropped to a gruff whisper. "This makes us square, Hawk. You come back through again, I might not be able to help you."

"I understand," Will said, nodding. "Thanks, Harmire. Looks like you've built yourself a proper empire."

Harmire's chest puffed slightly. "We took over from Vernon about a year back. It's solid. Keeps the boys busy. Media started

convenience."

Will smirked. "Always knew you had a head for enterprise."

He turned and motioned for the others to follow. The guards stepped aside.

One misstep, and the whole thing could still come crashing down.

The bridge groaned under their weight, each board a gamble and each gust of wind a whisper of disaster. It swayed in lazy arcs over the chasm, a ragged line strung between two cliffs and the sharp promise of a fall.

Khelek had carried Zane across already, his long strides graceful, somehow making the precarious rope bridge look like solid ground. Nar followed, Ellie clutched easily in his arms, both giggling like this was a carnival ride.

Will paused at the midpoint, glancing back to check on Malin. He found her frozen at the edge.

She hadn't moved.

Her fingers clutched the rope rail like it was a lifeline, her knuckles white. The wind whipped her hair across her face, but she didn't flinch. She wasn't blinking.

Well. Shit.

He turned around and strode back across the boards, careful not to bounce them too much.

"You need some help, Sparks?" he asked, his voice low and warm.

wind.

"You can. I'm here. I'll be here the whole time. What do you think would be easier? If I go behind you, or stay in front?" When she wouldn't or couldn't decide, he made the decision to get behind her.

She didn't move. Just a frantic little shake of her head.

The footbridge loomed ahead, it was narrow, swaying, and stretched across the fading light like a dare from the gods. The canyon yawned wide below, shadow swallowing the depths.

Will's jaw tightened.

They were too close now. Too close to fail.

He wrapped his arms around her and whispered in her ears. "We are going to take one step at a time until we get to the other side."

They started moving. Will pressed closer, lowering his voice to a teasing murmur. "Okay, look. Would it help if I listed all the things more terrifying than this bridge?"

Her eyes narrowed at him. "This is not the time."

"Incorrect. It is *exactly* the time. Let's see... that soup Lysa made that one time, it moved. That was terrifying. You didn't eat it, but I promise it was pretty terrifying."

She gave a tiny snort.

"Or that time I walked in on Gorek singing opera in the forge. Still have nightmares."

He leaned in, pressing his chest lightly to her back, wrapping his arms around her waist. "One step at a time," he whispered. "I'll be right here the whole way. Behind you. Watching your every move. Definitely *not* staring at your ass."

"Will..." she muttered, but she was moving.

But if the wind shifted, even slightly...

They were almost halfway across when he could feel the wind build quickly. He stopped, and told her to turn around to face him, while his arms immediately dropped from around her waist. He grabbed the rope railings on either side, planting his feet wide to steady them both.

A sharp gust barreled down the canyon like it had a vendetta, slamming into the bridge with a creaking groan. The ropes twisted. Boards beneath their feet shifted with a sickening lurch.

"Whoa. All right, this is fine," he muttered, teeth clenched as the bridge swayed like a drunk in a storm. "Totally fine. Just the forest's way of giving us a good ol' wake-up call."

Malin made a strangled noise, not quite a scream, but not far off. She looked up at him, her eyes wide, lips pressed into a thin line.

"Don't move," he said quickly, adjusting his grip as the wind howled. "You're okay. Just look at me."

"I am looking at you," she hissed. "You're the only solid thing on this damned bridge!"

"Well, lucky you," he said with a tight smile. "Most women have to pay extra for this kind of full-body panic bonding."

Her hands were firmly wrapped around his chest, and he leaned in just slightly, keeping his tone light even as the wind kept tugging at them. "Alright. Eyes on me. Don't look down, don't look behind. Just my charming, rugged face and this ridiculous situation."

The bridge rocked again.

threat. "If we die because you made a joke, I'm haunting you forever."

Will grinned. "Promise? I've always wanted a hot ghost girlfriend."

The wind began to settle.

Gradually, the swaying slowed, the ropes creaked as they regained some tautness. Will kept one hand on the rope and reached the other to brush a strand of hair out of her face.

"There we go," he said quietly. "Still breathing. Still gorgeous. Still here."

She gave him a look. It was tired and slightly murderous, but also grateful.

He reached back for her hand. "Ready to finish this? I'll shut up for the last part."

"You better not," she muttered, letting him turn her back around. "That was the only thing keeping me upright."

He tucked her in close again, arms back around her. "In that case... let me tell you the story of the time I tried to wrestle a goat. Spoiler: I lost."

They walked again.

One step at a time.

"That's my girl," he murmured.

Together, they took the next step.

And then another.

"So," he murmured as they took another step, "I've decided if we survive this, we're starting a bridge-building business."

"I'm serious. We'll call it *Spanning Sparks.* Custom rope bridges. Structurally questionable. Emotionally traumatic. Guaranteed to test your relationship—or strengthen it. No refunds."

She groaned softly. "You're the worst."

"Wait, there's more," he went on cheerfully. "We'll offer matching panic cloaks. Embroidered with *'At least we didn't die'* in tasteful thread. And maybe complimentary vomit bags."

"You're actually trying to kill me."

"Oh, come on, I'm being supportive. Emotional support with a side of architectural humor."

Another step. The wind gave a small tug, and she flinched.

Will tightened his hold, voice softening just a bit. "You're doing great, Sparks. Honestly. Way better than me the first time I crossed this thing. I cried. Twice. And sang sea shanties. It was a low point."

She huffed again, but the tightness in her shoulders lessened.

"I'm also thinking of inventing levitating shoes. For people with, you know, *excellent taste in danger and terrible taste in men.* You could be the brand ambassador."

"You're lucky I'm too scared to push you off right now."

He grinned. "I'm counting on it."

By the time they reached the other side, her legs were trembling, and she was breathing like she'd run a marathon, but she was upright.

Still standing.

And when she turned to him, there was a faint, exhausted grin tugging at her mouth.

He offered her a bow, one hand over his chest. "And I shall pay you… in sarcasm and unwavering devotion."

He leaned in and kissed her temple. "But you made it. Sparks."

At the end of the footbridge, they quickly got far enough away from the bridge to feel some semblance of safety. Malin reached for Will's hand. "You are an enigma," she smiled.

alin's stomach grumbled as she looked back at the tavern they had chosen not to eat at. The tavern owner had a thing against elves and wouldn't let them in, so they chose to all leave. The tavern food didn't really smell all that good, but her dried fruit was gone, and the bread was stale. They turned a corner on the path from the footbridge and the town of Seaborn came into view. They decided to stop here to eat what was left of their food and come up with a plan to get to the inn. The elves were not burdened with needing to eat as frequently and chose to scout ahead, as it was unlikely that their presence would be noticed. It was quite a sprawling town, not at all what she expected.

From their view, they could see some details, the neon signs flickering, the spectral glow on weathered stone buildings, juxtaposing the old with the new in a haphazard mosaic of progress and decay. Salt-laden breezes danced up the cliffside, carrying the scent of brine and industry, while below, the constant rhythm of waves crashing against the seawalls provided an ominous soundtrack.

There were so many ships of various sizes all moored on docks jutting from the coastline. Engines hummed faintly from the technological district, where Will explained the Media docks were. Past all of this, the waters, which had no end. Somewhere in the shadows, the splash of unseen creatures reminded them of the dangers lurking beneath the surface. Somewhere within was the Shantness Inn. It would be on the far side of town opposite the technological district, and next to the docks where a large four-mast sailing ship stood, its sails tucked neatly in port. She could see the ship from here, it was the largest sail ship there.

controlled gates. Technically they were town-controlled gates, but Will said it was highly likely if they had paid off the footbridge, they would have paid off the guards also. They would be looking for their group.

Her icy blue eyes mirrored the steel hues of the churning seas below, as she scanned the distant streets, brainstorming ideas.

They had been sitting in silence, not wanting to interfere with any planning. Ellie was the first to speak up, "I'm so excited to get to finally see the ocean. The real ocean, not just in stories or dreams?"

Was that a sea or an ocean beyond the town? She had never seen either, so no matter, she could appreciate the excitement.

Malin turned, softening at the sight of Ellie, head tilted in childlike wonder, her wide eyes reflecting the glimmering hues of the sea like polished glass. Despite everything, risk of death, the battle with the guards, the chaos, her daughter still found wonder. She still dreamed.

"Patience," she whispered, brushing a lock of hair behind Ellie's ear. Her throat tightened, but she kept her voice even. "Tomorrow. Let's just get through tonight."

Ellie nodded. That shy, hopeful smile. Eleven, on the brink of the spark of childhood and entering the teen world.

Then Khelek appeared beside her like a shadow parting from the trees, his low voice barely a ripple. "Seaborn stirs with unease. Patrols have tightened. There are mercenaries at the docks. It will not be easy."

Malin's stomach dropped. It sounded ominous.

"Thank you, Khelek," Will answered, calm and steady. How he managed that, she didn't know.

"What if we split up?"

Malin blinked, instinct screaming *no* before her logic caught up. But his tone wasn't casual, it was careful. Intentional.

Will nodded, pulling his jacket tighter. "Hear me out. I might be able to reach an old contact. He owes me a couple of really big favors. I couldn't get him to help with all of us, but he would probably help with me and my daughter? Maybe. It was he and his daughter that I saved."

Her arms folded on instinct. "And we're just hoping he's still willing to help?" She kept her voice even, but she could feel the steel threading through it.

He met her gaze, not flinching. "No guarantees in this world, Sparks. But it's better than walking through the main gate with a target on our backs."

She turned to the flickering lanterns of Seaborn in the distance, each one like a heartbeat. "If it gets Ellie there safely," she murmured, "I can be okay with that, but then we have to figure out Zane and I."

She turned away from him, but not in anger. Just to breathe. Just to *think.*

The logic held. Fewer people. Smaller profiles. More chances.

Her gaze lifted to Ellie, who stood watching them with quiet trust, and then to Zane, who stood so still it almost hurt. Not a boy. Not yet a man. But brave.

"If we separate," she said softly, "we increase our odds. I get it. We should go in different entrances."

Zane caught her eye and nodded.

me, but we will need to know where we are going… We meet at the inn at first light."

Will bent and scratched a rough city map into the dirt, walking them through both sides of the plan until no detail remained untouched.

Dawn was too close.

And they were not nearly close enough to where they needed to be.

Farewells were brief. They had to be. No long looks. No final words. Just a few nods, a shared breath of trust. They would meet again in a few hours—*they had to.*

Malin watched them disappear into the thickening twilight, one by one, their silhouettes swallowed by distance and the rustle of salt-touched wind. The silence afterward felt deafening.

She exhaled slowly—only then realizing how tightly she'd been holding her breath. Her hand found Zane's shoulder, grounding herself in motion. No more watching. No more waiting.

Time to move.

They kept a steady rhythm, matching steps as they skirted toward the far eastern gate. The narrow back lanes of Seaborn loomed ahead. They were quiet now but pulsed with potential threats. As they passed a crooked little house, laundry still hanging limp from its line, Malin paused.

A heavy robe that was long and oversized, swayed in the wind like an invitation.

tugging the hood low. A handful of coins clinked onto the stone porch. *Payment. Fair is fair.*

At the next puddle, she dropped to her knees, plunging her fingers into the cold, dirty water. Her reflection vanished under the ripples as she slicked back her hair, muting the bright blonde into a muddled, forgettable brown.

Zane eyed her critically. "Yeah. You don't look like you."

She offered a tight smile. "That's the goal."

They kept moving.

"Stay close," she whispered, not because he needed the reminder. She just *needed him close.*

The gate they aimed for was less guarded but more dangerous for how *quiet* it was. Secrecy always came with its own risks.

Zane slowed, his head tilting as if catching a sound she couldn't hear. "The mice say it's clear. And… they found a spot."

He led her to the wall, low and old, nothing like Media's impossible heights. One of the boards near the foundation had come loose. Zane knelt, pulling it aside gently, reverently, like it was a secret meant only for them.

"Well done," she murmured, crouching to slip through. "Tell them thank you."

Zane nodded, scattering what was left of their bread for the unseen watchers. "They're happy. I think," he added, eyes flicking to her. "They say… it's their job. To help the ones who help."

Malin blinked. Her throat tightened. *Little hearts, doing big work.*

"Can they lead us?" she asked. "Help us navigate?"

city. They can tell what's near... but not where we are."

"That's okay," she said gently. "That's more than enough."

They stepped into Seaborn like ghosts, cutting through alleys that smelled of brine and coal smoke, passing shuttered windows and crooked fences. Every step they took felt like a roll of loaded dice.

Malin glanced around for something, anything that might resemble the map Will had etched into the dirt. *A shop sign, a street name, a landmark... come on.*

Nothing yet.

She grabbed Zane's arm, her voice low. "Okay. New plan. I'll limp; you play the dutiful grandson. We keep heads down, and we find that inn."

She bent her knees, adjusted her stance, and leaned heavily on him. Her arm looped through his as if she were leaning on family.

Their eyes met.

"Keep me steady," she murmured. The pain in her voice was only half feigned. The exhaustion, the ache of worry, the weight of trust, it was all real.

Zane didn't hesitate. "I got you."

And together, they vanished into the city, walking the thin line between hunted and hidden.

A skittering warning from Zane's tiny allies sent their hearts thudding against their ribs: troops were approaching.

into the alley's shadowed embrace. The stench of refuse and swine wrapped around them like a second skin, masking their scent with the foul camouflage of the streets.

"Here," Zane whispered, motioning toward a sagging pig pen nestled against a crumbling stone wall.

They clambered in, the pigs snorting in protest. Mud and muck rose greedily, sucking at their boots and soaking through layers of disguise. Filth clung like betrayal.

Tucked in the rank enclosure, Malin pressed a trembling hand over her mouth. Her mind drifted, briefly, bitterly, to the clinical sterility of home. Her shower. Hot water. Clean tiles. A memory so distant it felt like someone else's life.

Through the slats, she watched boots march past. Clink, clink — metal on stone, a death drum. The patrol moved with precision, armor gleaming even in Seaborn's grime. Every footfall felt like a hammer to her chest, ready to smash through their fragile anonymity.

"Almost there," she breathed, voice barely audible. The promise gave her strength, even as she sank deeper into the filth.

The inn rose before them, its stone walls were sturdy, and it whispered like an invitation. A beacon of sanctuary, or perhaps just a softer sort of danger.

Malin and Zane shuffled forward, their movements weighed by damp fabric and exhaustion. The wooden sign above the door groaned in the wind, it creaked like a warning: *No masks once you're inside.*

The scent of roasted meat mingled with sea brine, beckoning them in.

They'd made it to the inn, but that didn't mean they were safe. Not yet.

Inside, the air buzzed with conversation, low and layered like a swarm of bees. Laughter flared in bursts, jagged and jarring, while the scent of old ale and smoke clung to everything.

Malin scanned the room to identify exits, angles, and threats. Her eyes cataloged each face, each hand too close to a weapon, each glance held a beat too long.

They moved toward the back, just as Will had shown her on the dirt map, only to find the hidden passage barred by a lock. Thick. Rusted. Solid.

Frustration prickled hot behind her ribs.

She turned to the barkeep, a heavyset man with tired eyes and the bearing of someone who'd seen too much and would die with it.

"We seek the drink *Angelis*," she said softly.

The man's gaze flicked to hers. Weighed her. Judged the dirt on her face, the fatigue in her spine, the fire still banked behind her eyes. Then he nodded, barely more than a twitch, and came around the bar without a word.

He had them follow him through the crowded room.

Behind the tapestry, the world shifted, as he opened the room, they had found locked.

The clamor of the tavern vanished. A quiet, dense and secretive room took its place, with cool stone walls, dim light, and a soft voice they recognized.

"You made it." Then she caught a whiff. "I'm sure there is a very good reason for that smell. I will stand over here."

unshaken, flanked by her ever-silent guardians.

Malin's breath caught. Relief, disbelief, gratitude—all tangling at once in her chest. They'd made it.

But only just.

"Finally," Malin breathed out, relief washing over her in a gentle wave. But as her gaze darted around, tallying allies, the knot of worry in her stomach twisted tighter. Will... Ellie... they were conspicuous in their absence.

"Will and Ellie should have been here by now," she murmured, the icy blue of her eyes darkening to a stormy green. Her hands clenched into fists at her sides, the need to protect, to envelop her daughter in safety, clawing its way up her throat.

"Patience, Malin," Lady Anariel counseled, her voice a melodic balm. "They possess their own cunning."

"Indeed," Malin conceded, though the gnawing anxiety remained. She glanced toward the wash bucket, the sight of clear water promising a semblance of cleanliness, a temporary armor against the grime of fear.

"My mother was to meet us here as well," she added, allowing just a sliver of hope to temper the edge of her concern. The prospect of reunion, however brief, was a star in the night sky, a guide, a comfort.

Lady Anariel explained, "We were told that she would meet us in the morning, perhaps the boat."

Together, they settled into a watchful wait, the silence stretching between them filled with unspoken fears and the echo of absent footsteps. Each passing moment was a thread pulled tight, the fabric of their plan straining at the seams.

rough against her fingertips. Hunger did battle within her with her unease as she forced herself to eat, sustenance a necessary ally in the shadowed game they played. For now, they were safe within the Inn's walls, but beyond, who knew what would happen.

The muted whispers of the inn's patrons seemed to slowly disappear, tightening like a noose with every tick of the clock above the bar. Shadows danced across her face as she sat in the back room, the dim glow of a single candle illuminating her furrowed brow. The subtle scent of salt and seaweed wafted through the open window, a cruel reminder of the ocean's proximity; a vast, unknowable expanse that paralleled the abyss of her worries.

She stared at the door, but it remained closed, and the night stretched on, endless and unforgiving.

They smeared coal into their hair in the dark predawn, the soot clung to Ellie's golden locks until they dulled to a dusty brown, closer to Will's now-darkened strands. It wasn't perfect, but it would do. Anything to avoid attention.

It had taken more than thirty minutes to find the right moment, a lull in the patrol rotations near Seaborn's southern gate. Now, as they approached, their footsteps were nearly silent against the uneven cobblestone, lit by a patchwork of electric lanterns and swaying oil lamps.

Will's eyes never stopped moving.

The guards were relaxed. Too relaxed. Their stances are loose. Their spears gripped lazily. A half-heard joke passed between them, followed by the easy rhythm of disinterest. A lazy shift.

He didn't stop walking, didn't even slow, but cataloged every detail. Their timing was lucky, or suspiciously so.

Still, walking in at this hour would get them flagged instantly, he wouldn't be able to get to his contact.

Then he saw it, a troupe of street performers preparing to enter the town, clustered around two rickety carriages, instruments and props strapped in bundles, their colorful garments barely shielding them from the chill. Several walked beside the wagons, chatting sleepily. The perfect distraction.

I might not need to call in that favor after all.

Will angled his path toward them, nudging Ellie gently with his elbow. She fell into step beside him. He found the troupe leader, a stout, red-faced man with a beard like an overfed squirrel, and offered a warm, casual smile.

"Mind a couple of quiet additions to your merry band? Looking to avoid a little… attention."

The man squinted at them, already suspicious. "Who are you?"

"Just travelers. Thought we might accompany your group into town unnoticed." Will slipped a handful of coins into the man's hand. "We're not looking for trouble. Just the gate."

The man stared at the coins, then at Will, then back at the coins.

Will leaned closer, voice low. "More when we pass safely."

The man grunted, greed winning out. "We could always use another pair of dancers," he muttered, then eyed Ellie. "But she'll need to cover that hair."

Will nodded and turned to Ellie, handing her a scarf he'd pulled from Malin's pack. "Wrap up," he whispered. "Like the other girls."

Ellie obeyed, tying the scarf tight with a small, nervous nod.

As they blended into the troupe's line, the gates loomed ahead. The guards stepped forward, spears angling slightly.

"Halt!" one barked. "We're searching for a group, three elves, a man, a woman, and two kids. Could be dangerous."

Will's heartbeat steadily, deceptively calm.

The troupe leader stepped forward, all showmanship. "You wound me, good sirs. Dangerous? We are performers! Jugglers, singers, flame-dancers. No elves here. Just actors and dreams."

The guard frowned and began scanning faces. Will kept his gaze low, stance relaxed, heartbeat climbing only when the guard's eyes briefly flicked his way.

annoyed. "Your hand! You comin' or folding?"

The first guard hesitated, then let out a long sigh. "Yeah, yeah." With a wave of his hand, he stepped aside. "Go. But no funny business."

Will didn't breathe until they were halfway into town.

The troupe leader gave him a nod and grinned. "Tomorrow. Town square. Don't miss the show."

"Wouldn't dream of it," Will replied, passing him the promised second stack of coins before guiding Ellie away from the group.

They turned off toward the inn, but Will didn't relax. Not even close.

He felt a shift in the air, it started as an itch between the shoulder blades. He glanced over his shoulder and caught movement near the edge of the square.

A group of men, that were too quiet, too focused, and not interested in the troupe. They were armed, organized, and watching them.

Not good.

He reached for Ellie's hand.

"Stay close," he murmured, smile never wavering.

Whatever happened next, it wasn't going to be part of the performance.

"We need to get past those guards," he murmured, calculating routes in his head as they crouched behind a stack of broken crates. The city was unfamiliar, but the patterns of patrols were

they slipped away from the troupe.

Ellie tugged his sleeve, her voice a whisper. "This way."

She darted toward a narrow window on the side of an abandoned building. Will followed, and together they hoisted themselves up and squeezed through, landing in a dark, musty storage room. Shelves lined the walls, stacked with crates and supplies thick with dust.

They crept to the rear of the building, but there were voices. At least three people were in the back of the building. Waiting them out proved futile. After nearly an hour, the voices didn't budge.

Will's eyes scanned the room. Rope. Good length, decent weight. An idea sparked.

With a grin, he nodded toward the rafters. "Up."

They climbed to the roof, boots silent on weather-worn shingles. Moving quickly and low, they navigated a series of rooftops until they were beyond the mercenaries' line of sight. At the edge of the final roof, Will tied off the rope and looked down.

"Ready?" he asked, mischief curling at the edge of his voice.

Ellie rolled her eyes. "I don't need it, silly." And with that, she floated down, feet touching the ground like a falling feather.

Will muttered, "Show off," and began his descent.

Once they were both on solid ground again, they darted down a narrow back alley that opened up near the edge of the town square. The scent of brine and oil hung heavy in the air, the silence between them speaking louder than words. Ellie's hand stayed in his, small, firm, trusting. He squeezed it gently.

Ahead, the inn's warm light glowed like a promise.

past.

Will's stomach knotted. As they stepped into the open street, one of the soldiers turned. His eyes landed on them. Narrowed, then broke off to head their way.

Will adjusted his cloak and angled away with an unhurried pace, steering Ellie toward a side path, threading through the sparse crowd.

Then he heard, "Names," a voice barked.

The soldier stepped in front of them, boots sharp on stone, hand resting casually on the butt of his weapon. His tone carried no threat, just certainty.

Will opened his mouth, but Ellie beat him to it.

"Jothan and Elara Tannen," she said brightly, her tone just the right mix of innocent and annoyed, like someone tired of travel and guards.

Will caught the brush of her thoughts in his mind. A soft, silent reassurance. She was good at this.

"Destination?" the soldier asked, frowning.

"Visiting family on Moore Street," Will replied smoothly. "Festival's got us nostalgic. It's been too many seasons since we seen kin."

The soldier studied them a second longer than was comfortable. Will met his gaze evenly, willing his heartbeat to slow.

Then, with a grunt and a dismissive wave, the soldier stepped aside.

Will didn't exhale until they were half a block away.

warming his fingers. Will gave her a faint smile without looking down.

"Nice name, Elara."

"That was fun," she said with a smirk.

"Bright Eyes, your mother is going to kill us, when she finds out."

"I don't have to tell her if you don't. I didn't tell her that you were the one chasing me in No Man's," she said innocently. "Nanna says there are somethings that are better if Mom doesn't know."

Will was solidly impressed with this little imp.

Once out of earshot, they slipped into the city's veins, the less-traversed alleys where the vibrant life of Seaborn gave way to hushed whispers and the quiet scuttle of rats. Here, the urgency in their steps became pronounced, each footfall a muted drumbeat against the cobblestones.

Will led with the assurance of one who had mapped every shadowed corner and hidden turn. The alleyways curled around them like dark ribbons, hiding their passage from the prying eyes of the world above. There was a rhythm to their flight, a cadence that pulsed with the thrumming energy of the town; a dance as old as time, etched into the stones beneath their feet.

Each turn took them deeper into the labyrinth, where the air grew heavier with the scent of damp earth and the promise of rain. The sky above was a distant memory, shrouded by the close-knit embrace of the buildings that rose on either side like silent sentinels.

Through it all, Will remained vigilant, his senses attuned to the slightest shift in the atmosphere.

Finally, the rear entrance of the Inn loomed ahead, an ancient edifice of timber and stone that whispered tales of bygone eras.

lidded gaze, promised sanctuary to those weary from the city's relentless pulse. Will's eyes, sharp as flint in the dim light, scanned the entrance where the glow of oil lamps spilled out onto the cobbled street. It cast a warm, amber hue across their path.

He nudged Ellie forward. They slipped through the doorway, and the atmosphere closed around them like a cloak, heavy with the scent of aged wood and the residue of countless stories etched into its grain. The low murmur of patrons formed a lulling backdrop, a stark contrast to the electric tension that thrummed through Will's veins.

With calculated steps, he navigated the dimly lit interior, where flickering candlelight danced with secrets held tight by the walls. The ambiance was a paradox; welcoming yet fraught with unspoken threats; and every sense was attuned to the delicate balance they now tread upon.

Their journey ended at a door tucked away in the far corner of the common room, unremarkable and easily missed by most. But not by Will; his gaze sharpened as he laid eyes on it, recalling its many previous uses. He had entered through this doorway countless times to save lives, but never before were those lives so precious as the ones he was about to protect now. His palm hovered over the latch, heart knocking once against his ribs, not from fear, but from the weight of what waited on the other side. Malin. Zane. Safety, if only for a breath. And beneath it all, the knowledge that this might be the last moment of quiet before the storm broke again.

A deft twist here, a gentle nudge there, and the lock yielded with a sigh, like an old friend tired of keeping secrets. Will eased the

or a fireball, depending on how Malin's night had gone.

He stepped into the dim room, struck immediately by the sight of her. Malin stood near the far wall, hair wild and loose like she'd just survived a windstorm or wrestled a small dragon. Her eyes locked onto him, and for a moment, his breath caught.

Then she raised an eyebrow. "Took you long enough."

He grinned. "You know how I like to make an entrance."

Their embrace was fast, fierce, and silent. It was the kind of reunion that required no words. Ellie shot up from where she'd been sitting and hurled herself into Zane, nearly toppling him to the floor. Dragging her with him, he followed with a slightly more dignified run into Will's arms. The four of them in an embrace.

It was then that the smell hit him.

Will pulled back and sniffed the air. "So... who brought the pig pen to the party?"

Ellie wrinkled her nose. "It's Zane's fault."

"The pig pen was the easiest place that they would not be looking," Zane muttered.

Ellie's eyes widened. "Eww!"

"No amount of water has helped yet," Malin said.

Will chuckled, dropping his pack with a wince. "Well, lucky for you two, with so long with no showers, I think we're all a full bouquet of travel disasters. I do think you win the prize though."

Malin rolled her eyes, but her fingers lingered on his arm. "If we get caught, we'll be remembered as the stinkiest rebels to ever smuggle a child."

possibly in local health code violations."

The laughter that followed was soft, but real, a brief bloom in the soil of exhaustion and fear. It was exactly what they needed.

It didn't take long for them to get tired enough that they were ready to get sleep.

Dawn waited just beyond the window, brushing the horizon in shades of warning. The ship, their ship, would only be in port a few precious hours longer. If they missed it, there wouldn't be another for days. And days… they didn't have.

Will lay back, arm draped over his eyes, his thoughts spinning. He wasn't worried about getting on the boat.

He was worried about *who might be waiting for them* when they boarded.

Malin crouched just behind Will, breath shallow, watching the guards with the kind of intensity she once reserved for triage rooms. Every step was a risk, every movement calculated. The air felt electric; things were too quiet. She could feel Zane's nervous fidgeting behind her, hear the soft scrape of Ellie's boot against stone. When Will finally signaled, she was already moving.

The hinges groaned under his push, the door creaked open just wide enough to let the predawn air in, a breath of salt and steel, full of both promise and threat. Malin stepped through first. As her eyes adjusted, her instincts sharpened. She swept the alley like a scanner, eyes cataloguing everything: blind corners, rusted crates, the gleam of rain pooled in uneven stone. The city was waking.

The ship was in sight.

The sea wind caught her hair, and for a second, she closed her eyes, grounding herself. They were so close.

Cobblestones still shimmered with morning drizzle, turning puddles into fractured mirrors of the fading night sky. Every step forward brought the ship into sharper focus. Four masts stretched into the sky like fingers daring the gods. The Dawn's Beacon.

She'd read about ships like this. Rumors only. A hybrid of magic and engineering. No two were ever made alike.

Will moved beside her. "She's a beauty," he murmured.

Malin nodded once, curt. "As long as she gets us to the next port safely, that's all I need."

at the sight, her daughter caught in the in-between, still a child, but quickly becoming a teen. She clutched the cloth doll in her arms tight. It was ridiculous, really, that the thing survived this long. But somehow, it had. And Malin had come to view it not as a weakness, but a small rebellion. One piece of innocence they hadn't taken.

Zane hovered behind her. She loved seeing all the same signs of protectiveness in him that she loved about Will. He didn't once give her grief about her having her doll, as little boys always did when she was a kid. She surmised that he had lost too much of his own childhood to want her to lose a piece of hers. Malin's pulse skipped. She wanted to protect him so badly, so that he could have the childhood he deserved.

"We need to stick to the shadows," she whispered, pressing a hand lightly to Zane's shoulder as they moved into the narrow space between buildings. No one spoke. No one needed to.

The harbor buzzed ahead, more alive than she'd expected for such an early hour. Dockworkers barked orders. Crates thudded against wooden planks. The scent of fish and diesel mingled with damp sea air. Everything looked so ordinary. Then why did it feel so *wrong*. She scanned the perimeter. Too many guards. Too much movement.

Will's voice came low, close to her ear. "Those two are the ones I suspect. They aren't loading and the just keep looking at the other people around them. I think they are waiting for us."

She didn't flinch. Just shook her head once. "Well, what do we do?"

The Dawn's Beacon loomed ahead like something out of myth, its hull a fusion of dark timber and gleaming alloy, metal chased with ancient runes and rivets like veins of silver. It wasn't just beautiful. It was safety.

clipped. "The ship's almost done loading. Once it leaves, so does our last shot. We need to be on that deck."

He scanned the dock, eyes narrowing on the two unassuming workers that weren't working. They were watching.

"Nar. Khelek." Will's voice dropped lower. "Think you can take them out quietly?"

The brothers shared a look. Then a grin.

"Yes," Khelek said, already moving.

"Quietly?" Nar echoed with a smirk. "Always."

Malin's gaze flicked back to the guards. It hadn't even been a full minute before she saw the first slump forward, chin tucked to chest like he'd nodded off. The second leaned back as if simply dozing.

No fuss. No sound. Just **gone.**

Now was the moment.

Malin squeezed Ellie's hand and whispered, "No mistakes. Just one quick run. We get to that ship."

Ellie gave a sharp nod. Zane exhaled. They moved.

They kept to the edges of the dock, their footsteps swallowed by the hiss of steam and the sharp cry of gulls overhead. Pipes dripped condensation in a rhythmic *plink-plink-plink*, like a metronome counting down their seconds. A blast of vapor erupted from a valve, briefly engulfing them in warm, metallic mist before dissipating into the chill dawn.

The ship loomed larger with every step. Up close, it was a beast, impossibly massive, with rigging that reached like skeletal arms into the sky. The closer they came; the more Malin felt the pulse of urgency inside her ribs. *We're almost there.*

glinted in the first kiss of sunlight.

Will moved ahead, his gaze darting to the crew. Activity hummed around the vessel. Dockhands hauled crates aboard with brisk efficiency. The gangplank was wide and sturdy, with handrails, much like the footbridge; it made her heart race. The ship was already halfway loaded. The yawning groan of its timbers echoed across the water like a warning bell.

They reached a man with a clipboard, his oil-stained fingers curling around the edge as he eyed them warily.

"We're supposed to be on this ship," Malin said quietly, stepping forward. "Can we board?"

The man's eyes narrowed. "Name?"

She hesitated, heart pounding, then responded, "Malin Neldoreth."

A pause. It felt like it was too long. *Maybe they don't have us on the list, as planned.* Then…

"Yes, ma'am," he said in a graveled voice. "You're cleared. Come aboard."

Relief surged so sharply through her chest she almost stumbled.

They climbed the gangplank one by one, the bounce of the boards beneath their feet both reassuring and nerve-wracking. Will once again stood behind her, his presence providing the calm she needed. She was determined that she was going to do this without incident. She didn't exhale fully until her boots hit the deck, but she did it.

She glanced over her shoulder, there were no alarms. No shouts. The docks behind them remained the same tapestry of organized chaos.

One of the deckhands motioned them toward the top deck. "Captain's up that way," he muttered without looking up.

The stairs to the upper deck were practical and efficient, this was a ship designed for transport and people were not the main purpose. Around them, the crew worked with machine-like precision, they were tying off lines, adjusting rigging, and securing cargo. They didn't stare. They didn't question. Either by policy or survival instinct, they simply didn't see.

And that, more than anything, made Malin believe they had a real shot.

Zane and Ellie had reached the deck just ahead of her and now stood near a large brass compass housing. Malin had seen it before, on school field trips, public tours, but to Ellie, this was a whole new world. The little girl spun in slow circles; her eyes wide as she tried to memorize everything at once. A burst of delighted giggles spilled from her lips, her joy unfiltered and infectious.

Zane, by contrast, simply stood in awe, mouth agape, staring up at the vast sails like he was witnessing magic incarnate.

Malin caught Will watching them from the rail, one hand braced against the wood. There was something soft in his expression. Not quite amusement. Not just pride. *Wonder*, maybe. The kind of awe that came from seeing possibility reborn.

"Hey," he called gently, not taking his eyes off the kids. "I know this is exciting and all, but maybe keep it low-key, yeah? Let's move inside soon."

He didn't push them, though. Not yet. He seemed just as reluctant to interrupt the moment as they were.

There stood a woman, her back to them, silhouetted against the rising sun. Tall black boots. Tightly tailored leathers and linen. A lightweight jacket draped over one arm, simple but expensive. Her silver-streaked blonde hair was swept into a perfect twist, not a strand out of place despite the salty wind.

It took Malin a heartbeat to place her.

Mom?

Gone were the flowing council robes, the severe bun, the air of prim detachment. This version of Elowen Neldoreth looked... formidable, comfortable in her own skin, and effortlessly cool.

Will came up behind her, whispering low in her ear as he wrapped an arm around her waist.

"I can see where you get your body from," he murmured. "Shame, she kept that under wraps for so long. I mean... you've clearly got the upgrade, but damn. Momma's got some ouch to her."

Malin sucked in a breath to suppress a laugh. She hated how right he was. Her mother looked... incredible.

And when Elowen turned, her whole face lit up, not with the tempered warmth Malin expected, but with *honest joy*. There was no judgment in her expression, no tight-lipped disapproval. Just light.

Malin couldn't reconcile this woman with the one who'd raised her. She didn't *look* like *the* councilwoman. She looked like *the* Resistance leader Malin had only heard about in whispers.

"Welcome aboard," Elowen said, her voice low, perfectly pitched to carry only to their small group. She stepped forward, sweeping them all in with a look. "You made it."

pulling her into a quick, fierce hug, but quickly pulled away with a look of disgust on her face.

"I'm so glad you made it. There's a shower in the passenger quarters, thank the stars. What did you two get into?" Her nose wrinkled slightly at the scent. "We'll be casting off soon. I was afraid you'd be late."

"We had our challenges," Will said lightly, watching her greet Ellie next. "But we're here."

"You've been doing beautifully with Lady Anariel," Elowen told Ellie, brushing a strand of hair behind the girl's ear. "Your progress is... extraordinary."

Then, to the group: "You're all making significant progress. Let's continue this inside, away from wandering eyes. And let's get these two cleaned up."

Just then, a nearby speaker crackled and died, the interruption brief but jarring. The silence that followed was too sudden. Loaded.

A man passed nearby, uniformed and armed, but the crest on his shoulder bore the symbol of a private security firm, not the Media government. He glanced their way... and kept walking.

"What was that?" Malin murmured to Will, barely turning her head. "Why didn't he stop?"

He leaned in. She felt the heat of his breath against her cheek. "Likely because your mother paid him not to notice." Then his voice dropped, rough and warm. "Ugh. I agree with your mother. Shower. Now. That pigpen stink is... still happening."

He drew in a mock breath. "That said, I'm *very* happy to volunteer to scrub your back. Wouldn't want you to miss any places."

embarrassment.

They were halfway to the interior stairwell when the captain intercepted them.

"Welcome aboard," he said, his voice smooth and clipped with authority.

He stood just inside the doorway, framed by the soft glow of the ship's interior light—as if he'd been waiting for them. Everything about him projected readiness. Command. Expectation.

His uniform was crisp, tailored to flatter his average frame, though he stood a little taller than Malin's mother. Not quite Will's height. Curly black hair framed a square jaw, his olive-toned skin catching the amber lanternlight with a warm, healthy sheen.

Without further pleasantries, he launched into a tour—efficient and practiced.

He showed them the cargo hatches and passenger companionways. The quarterdeck rose at the ship's rear, dominated by the wide wheel and gleaming navigation panels. Belowdecks, crates of merchant cargo filled the hold in carefully arranged rows. Amidships held a modest galley and common area for passengers, its clean lines and brass fixtures revealing a captain who took pride in the comfort of his crew.

Then came the passenger cabins.

A single hallway housed them: eight doors in total—four on each side—with the captain's own quarters situated prominently at the stern, its tall windows wrapping the rear of the ship like a panoramic frame.

theirs—just a step away. Will noted the layout automatically. Two of the cabins had already been claimed by the elves: one for Nar and Khelek, the other for Lady Anariel. Elowen would've taken the largest. That accounted for five rooms. Another, it turned out, was the small but functional head—compact, with a modestly enchanted water timer mounted to the wall. The First Mate occupied a sixth.

That left one unaccounted for.

Malin's fingers brushed the wall absently as they walked. The wood was smooth and cool beneath her fingertips, polished but not ostentatious. The lanterns cast golden pools along the corridor, warm and steady despite the ship's subtle, constant sway.

She noticed it then—faint lines of glyphwork woven into the baseboards and worked into the sails outside. Not ostentatious, but deliberate. Hidden enchantments. Reinforcements, perhaps?

And the room dimensions felt... off.

Either the ship's blueprints were unconventional... or there were hidden compartments. Contraband holds? Smuggler's caches? Pirate protections?

She filed it away for later.

When the others peeled off to settle into their quarters, the captain turned to her and Will. His nose crinkled slightly, and Malin braced herself.

"Showers are available in the passenger quarters," he said, tone clipped. "Water is limited. Use it wisely."

The way he said it made it sound like a personal attack.

Then his gaze cut to Will.

free, shall we?"

Will blinked, clearly offended. "That wasn't me. That was your hotheaded first mate who couldn't handle losing at cards."

The captain arched a brow. "And the other time?"

"Okay, *that* time was my fault. But come on, he was rich. He was not going to miss those rings. How did I know he knew how to fight too? And those rings were *ridiculous.* I don't think anyone who saw them could blame me for trying to take them."

"Third time?"

Will winced. "Also, me. Well, I'm definitely not going to be hitting on the wrong woman this time and to be fair, she didn't tell me she was seeing the cook also," he defended.

"Just don't let it happen this trip," the captain said as he left.

Malin tilted her head, with mock seriousness. "You know, the more time I spend with you, the more I think the *rogue* is your default setting and the Will I met at the bar was you playing me."

"Oh, Sparks. I am a rogue who's only mark is you from now on," Will grinned, pulling her in for a kiss before abruptly recoiling. "Okay... nope. We're burning these clothes."

They showered quickly. The water was tepid at best and there was a timer on the faucet to ensure that showers were not too long, but it was the intimacy they needed.

The ship had set sail while they were in the shower, and it was *exactly* what she needed. With each mile they put between themselves and the shore, the tension in her shoulders eased. It wasn't just about distance, it was about forward motion. About finally being off the grid, untraceable.

didn't count as a full meal.

They made their way to the dining room, the warm scent of baked bread and something roasted drifting through the corridors. Zane was already there, but he didn't look well. He was pale, greenish, and clutching his midsection like a storm was brewing inside.

Will fished into his pocket and pulled out three narrow bands of copper. "These might help," he said, handing one to Zane and keeping one for himself. "Sea sickness. Old trick. We will be on this ship for about a week. We will transfer to the *Qenya Stin Haven* when we reach Sarhan. From there, we catch another to Aloria. A few stops along the way."

Malin nodded, grateful for any method that didn't involve hiking through forests, dodging drones, and hiding in pig pens. This was still going to be a long trip, but at least they weren't walking it.

Across the table, Ellie sat very still.

"Nanna," she said suddenly, her voice carrying a strange confidence. "You didn't just leave because he found out. You took something, didn't you? What did you take?"

The shift in her mother's posture was minuscule, but Malin caught it. A slight tension in the shoulders. Not fear. Calculation.

"Perceptive little minx," Elowen said, tone fond but edged. "Just like me at that age."

With a practiced flick, she adjusted her jacket, just enough to reveal the glinting edge of a data storage device tucked into an inner lining. Sleek. Government-issue.

"Nothing he'll notice is missing until it's far too late, but information Aloria needs."

She hadn't just left. She'd committed *theft,* possibly the kind of theft that triggered full-scale manhunts. What had been a dangerous escape because they were leaving her well connected father, had just tipped into something *treasonous.* Having magic was one thing. *Stealing government secrets* was something else entirely.

"We're not just running," Will said quietly, reading the shift in the air. "We're in the middle of something bigger, aren't we?"

Elowen didn't answer. She didn't need to.

Will's attention drifted to Zane again. The boy wasn't as exuberant as Ellie, his shoulders were hunched, his hand fidgeting with the cuff of his sleeve. Will remembered that look from his youth. That anxiety that buzzed just under the skin, always scanning for danger.

"Will there be dragons?" Zane asked, voice small and his eyes were wide.

Will let the corner of his mouth lift. "We'll be passing between Draco and Zmaj, in the Draconian Mountains. There's a good chance we'll see one. From a distance, if we're lucky."

Ellie perked up instantly, eyes shining. "I *hope* we see them. Dragons are just the beginning, there are so many new creatures to meet."

Zane looked uneasy. Will was about to say something comforting when Malin cut in.

"He might not feel the same way about dragons as you do," she said, voice dry but not unkind.

Zee. I won't let anything happen to you. You can talk to them, remember? I bet they *won't* hurt you, cause you can."

Zane gave a shy nod, his cheek pressed against her shoulder. They'd grown nearly inseparable since leaving Media. It was sweet. And, if Malin was being honest, it was a tiny bit concerning. That kind of closeness could either anchor them... or become a liability when things got harder.

But that was a problem for another day.

Right now, they were safe. Together. And on the open sea.

Will's hand trembled slightly as he guided Zane away from the others, his palm hovering just above the boy's shoulder without quite making contact. He had been dreading this conversation for the past hour, but now was the time. Each step toward the quiet alcove felt heavier than the last, his legs somehow aware of the gravity before his heart was ready.

They moved into the recessed pocket of space near the ship's stern, partially hidden by canvas-covered crates and thick coils of rope. The air here was still, carrying only the scent of salt and the rhythmic creak of the hull.

Zane looked up at him with those hazel eyes, so familiar they hurt to look at.

"Did I do something wrong?" the boy asked.

Will gave a soft shake of his head. "No. Definitely not." His voice cracked. He cleared his throat and tried again. "There's something I need to tell you. Something important."

Zane nodded, his stance squaring instinctively, braced for disappointment. That posture alone nearly broke him. Will instinctually reached out and placed his hand on his shoulder to steady both of them.

He crouched, bringing them eye to eye. "Zane," he said softly. "I found out that I'm your father."

The words landed between them like a dropped stone, it was simple, but enormous.

searched Will's features as if trying to reconcile the information. His lips parted, but no sound came.

"Remember I told you I knew your mother?" Will went on, careful to keep his tone steady. "We were in love. I was going to propose, but I waited too long. When she found out she was pregnant… she didn't tell me. She just disappeared. I never even knew you existed until Lysa told me."

Will's hand stayed steady on the boy's shoulder. "If I had known, I would've moved mountains to be there."

Zane looked down, jaw trembling. "My mom… I had a dad. They killed him."

Will nodded gently. "Lysa told me what really happened. He *was* your dad, in every way that a dad should be, except blood. He loved you. Wanted you. He chose you. I couldn't have picked a better man to raise my son, if I couldn't."

Will paused, his voice catching.

"I'm not here to replace him, Zane. But I *am* still your father."

Zane was quiet for a long moment. Then his expression cracked open into a smile, so sudden and radiant it made Will's throat tighten.

"Ellie told me and I didn't believe her," Zane whispered. "She said the world believes in me so much, it gave me two dads and brought us together."

A heartbeat passed. "I couldn't ask for a better one."

Will didn't answer. He couldn't. But when Zane reached for his hand, Will closed his fingers around it, anchoring them both.

"When did you know?" Will asked. "Did you know about me the whole time?"

sure... not until that fight. That's when I *felt* it. When you saved me, I knew."

He smiled crookedly. "My dad... your grandfather... taught me everything I know about survival, picking pockets, finding marks, and most importantly... about how to be the kind of man you need to be. How to love a family. I lost him too young. Like you lost yours. I had lost hope that I would ever be able to find a family of my own, but we're not alone anymore."

Zane leaned in. "Does this mean... we'll stay together? In Aloria?"

Will nodded without hesitation. "If you'll have me... I'll never leave you again, Aloria or wherever. You are stuck with me."

Zane threw his arms around him. "You're not allowed to leave. Ever."

Will held his son tightly, the moment sinking into his chest like an oath.

Then Zane pulled back slightly, eyes glinting. "Do we get to keep Malin and Ellie too?"

The question carried all the hesitant hope of a child who had learned not to expect permanence. Will felt something crack inside him; a fissure in the careful composure he'd maintained through years of separation and loss.

Will gave a crooked grin. "If they'll have *us*? I'd be the luckiest man alive. If they do, yes," he said firmly. "We stay together. From now on. I don't think I could ever let you go, now that I know you are out here."

Zane smiled again, broader this time, revealing a gap in the back of his mouth where a tooth had recently been lost; a mundane childhood milestone that Will had missed among so many others. The boy moved forward then, closing the short distance

Thin arms wrapped around his neck in an embrace that felt both fragile and fierce.

Will returned the hug carefully at first, then with growing conviction as Zane pressed closer. He closed his eyes, memorizing the feeling of his son in his arms; the weight of him, the scent of his hair, the slight tremor in his shoulders that suggested he might be fighting tears. Will's own eyes burned, but he held himself together, wanting to be the strength his son needed at this moment.

From a few yards away came the soft sound of fabric shifting. Will opened his eyes without releasing Zane, his gaze finding Ellie standing half-hidden behind a ventilation shaft. Her small hands clenched around her doll as she watched the exchange, her expression, a complex mixture of emotions too nuanced for her young face.

Something in her posture; perhaps the slight tilt of her head or the stillness with which she observed them; reminded Will of Elowen. "I told you!" She then threw herself into the hug with a squeal of delight.

He looked up from the hug to see Malin, a slight tear running down her face. Their eyes locked and she smiled.

Will smiled and nodded back, acknowledging her presence without breaking the moment, motioning that she should huddle with them. Malin joined with overjoyed feelings.

Zane pulled back slightly, his eyes bright with tears and newfound determination.

Will nodded, rising from his crouched position with a slight grimace as his knee protested. He kept one hand on Zane's shoulder, unwilling to break physical contact now that it had

touch.

Zane looked up at Will, a question forming in his expression. "Are we family now? All of us together?"

The question contained layers of meaning that Will wasn't sure the boy himself fully understood; about belonging, about safety, about the complicated bonds that had brought them all to this moment of escape and possibility.

"Yes," Will answered, the word was a commitment, and a hope rolled into one. "We're family now."

Ellie pulled Zane to their room to show him that she had made both her bed and his bed, leaving Will and Malin alone in the hallway. He pulled her close, the emotions thick and needing her stability. They parted slightly, not letting go, gazing into each other's eyes. He tucked a strand of blonde hair behind her ear.

With a slight nod toward the children now safely settled, Malin turned and moved toward the aft section of the ship. Will followed her into their room.

The cabin was compact but thoughtfully arranged, with every element designed to maximize the limited space. A narrow double cot with neatly folded blankets occupied one wall, while a small desk and chair were secured to the opposite side. A compact trunk sat open on a low table beneath a porthole that admitted a circle of strengthening sunlight. The floor was bare wood, worn to a smooth texture by countless passengers before them, and the walls featured built-in hooks and small shelves for personal belongings.

It wasn't luxurious by any measure, but it felt remarkably like sanctuary. Will stepped inside after Malin, closing the door behind them. The sound of the latch falling into place created a curious shift in the atmosphere as if they had entered a pocket

here.

"Home for several days," Malin said, her voice soft but steady. She moved to the porthole, glancing out at the distant harbor they had left behind. The water beyond the glass rippled with early morning light, the surface broken occasionally by the wake of smaller vessels.

Will remained by the door, watching as she oriented herself to the space with methodical precision. There was something mesmerizing about her movements; economical yet graceful, each action serving a clear purpose. She removed her jacket and laid it on the bed, then reached up to release her hair from its severe twist. The chopsticks that had held it in place were set carefully on the desk's edge, and blonde waves tumbled down her back in a sudden cascade that caught the sunlight, just the way he liked it.

The transformation was striking; from the fierce firewoman, who had single-handedly taken on some of Media's toughest guards, to someone vulnerable, more human. Will felt privileged to witness this private ritual, this shedding of armor that few were allowed to see.

He moved to his bag, kneeling before it to examine the contents and dig items out. Their possessions were few; necessity had forced them to travel light, bringing only what could be carried inconspicuously.

"Zane had asked about if we would be staying together as a family. I know we hadn't really talked about it, but I would like to," he said honestly, trying to keep the absent-minded tone in his voice as he readjusted items in his bag.

He extracted his spare shirt and placed it on the bed beside Malin's jacket, then reached down to smooth a wrinkle absently. "I know I'm not a perfect man, but I can say that I always mean everything in my power to show you that I want to be," he pulled her into his embrace and looked her deep in her eyes. "I love you, Sparks."

Will reached into his inner pocket and removed a small package wrapped in soft cloth. He unwound the protective covering to reveal a bracelet; a simple band of braided silver threads interspersed with tiny blue stones that caught the light from the porthole.

Without comment, he held it so that it would capture the light, where the sunlight struck it directly, it sent scattered blue reflections across the cabin walls. "Malin, This bracelet belonged to my mother. It is one of the few possessions I have left of her. I carried it for years. I wanted to wait for the right moment, the right person." he shuffled nervously, looked away, and swallowed hard.

He looked up to find her watching him carefully, cautiously. Her expression revealing nothing yet somehow acknowledging everything. The soft clicks of metal and the shuffle of cargo from adjacent cabins filtered through the walls, creating a soundtrack of ordinary activities that felt extraordinary under the circumstances.

She didn't respond. He wanted to look her in the eyes to try to figure out what she was thinking but he was afraid of what he would see.

His hands were clammy and trembled ever so slightly as he nervously stroked her back with the other hand. His heart pounded in his chest like a drum, and his breathing came in short, uneven bursts. Beads of sweat gathered on his forehead, and he swallowed hard, trying to steady himself.

Why didn't she answer? he thought.

her face and the other on his hand holding the bracelet.

"It's Sparks," Malin stated with a wicked smile, "and I love you."

Then he realized in his nervousness... He had forgotten to actually ask the question.

"What I said out there to Zee, about us being family and being together forever," he paused again, the lump in his throat needing him to take a beat. He then bent down on one knee and looked up at her. "I want to make it official. I don't have a ring, and I don't have jewels, but I do have this.... Malin Neldoreth... would you do me the honor of being my wife?"

Her face was a canvas of raw astonishment, eyes widening to their fullest and mouth parting in silent awe as she held her breath, grappling with the surreal reality unfolding before her. In that electrifying heartbeat of disbelief, the tension shattered as she erupted into a brilliant smile, her voice quivering with an overwhelming blend of joy and certainty as she cried out, "Yes. Yes! A million times yes!"

He carefully wrapped the bracelet around her wrist and pulled her close. He didn't think he could breath. She said, Yes!

A tear of joy creeped down his chin, as he was drawn to her lips. They parted eagerly, as they sealed the decision.

Sunlight slanted through the porthole, catching dust motes that danced in lazy spirals. The air smelled of beeswax polish and the faint saltiness that permeated everything aboard ship. These sensory details registered in his mind with unusual clarity, as if he body sought to memorize every aspect of this moment.

She looked down at the bracelet. She hadn't expected this. The metal was cool against her skin, the weight unfamiliar, yet somehow right. Her fingers closed around it, feeling its texture like a promise.

Malin moved first, reaching for the top button of her blouse. The motion was deliberate, unhurried. They had spent days in constant motion, through alleys and back rooms, fleeing authority, chasing hope. But now, with the ship carrying them swiftly from danger, time seemed to slow, offering an unexpected breath of calm.

Will followed her lead, his movements just as measured. His fingers, so precise in the way they methodically worked down the row of buttons. The warm light of the cabin played along the line of skin he revealed.

He slipped the shirt off and draped it over the back of the desk chair. Malin's eyes traced the lean strength of his torso, shaped by necessity more than vanity. Scars marked his skin, in silent reminders of close calls and hard-won survival.

She continued undressing, each button a choice, not just a step. The way he watched her made her feel like it was not just appreciation for her body, but for the woman she was, all the parts of her: magical, brilliant, and resilient.

Her blouse parted to reveal a plain cotton undergarment, functional, unadorned. Yet in his eyes, she saw reverence. Even the simplest things felt precious under that look.

He stepped closer. The floorboards creaked beneath his feet, joining the sounds of the ship, the soft thrum of engines, the call of distant voices, the splash of water against the hull.

jaw with such gentleness it stole her breath. She leaned into the touch, allowing herself the rare luxury of vulnerability.

"Malin," he said, her name barely more than a breath, part question and part vow. She loved to hear him say it, but that silly nickname she thought was a joke was the one she liked to hear the most.

"It's Sparks," She answered as he smiled. She kissed the corner of his lip, as punishment for answering wrong.

The air in the cramped quarters was thick with the scent of salt and sweat, a heady mix that clung to their skin like a third presence. Will's beard was coarse against her jawline, the rough scrape of it sending jolts of electricity down her spine. His lips, warm and insistent, traced a path from her jaw to the soft hollow of her neck, his breath hot and ragged against her skin. She shivered, her hands clutching at his shoulders, her nails digging into the fabric of his shirt as if she could pull him closer, fuse them together.

His hands were everywhere; they were skimming her sides, gripping her waist, sliding up to cup her breasts through the thin fabric of her blouse. Each touch was deliberate, reverent, but there was a hunger there too, a raw need that had been building for days. She could feel it in the way his fingers trembled, in the way his breath hitched when she arched into him.

His lips left a trail of kisses down her collarbone, his tongue darting out to taste the salt on her skin. She gasped, her head falling back as he licked and teased her nipples, the fabric sliding off her shoulders to pool on the floor. His shirt followed a moment later, discarded in a heap with hers, then both their pants, their bodies finally bare against each other laying next to each other on the small double cot.

brushing against her nipples as he pressed her back against the wall. She could feel the tension in him, the way his muscles clenched and shifted as he fought to keep control, to keep quiet. But there was something wild in his eyes now, something she'd hadn't seen before, and it made her ache for him in a way that was almost painful.

His hands slid down to her hips, fingers slipping into her in one swift motion. His cock pressing insistently against her stomach. She could feel the heat of him, the way he throbbed with need, and she reached down to wrap her hand around him, stroking him slowly, teasingly, until he groaned against her neck.

"Fuck," he muttered, his voice low and rough with desire. "I need you. Now."

She didn't need to be told twice. She lay back and guided him to her entrance, her breath catching as he pushed into her, inch by slow inch, filling her completely. They moved together in a rhythm that was frantic but somehow still tender, their bodies fitting together like they were made for each other. His thrusts were deep and deliberate, each one sending waves of pleasure crashing through her, until she was trembling on the edge of release.

He kissed her then, hard and desperate, their tongues tangling as he drove her to the edge of desire. She could feel the pressure building inside her, coiling tighter and tighter until it finally snapped, her orgasm washing over her in a flood of heat and light. He followed her over the edge a moment later, his hips stuttering as he came inside her, his manhood pulsing with each wave of his release.

They stayed like that for a long moment, bodies pressed together, hearts racing in sync. And then he was moving again, pulling out of her with a groan and sinking to his knees before licked and sucked and teased her back to the edge. She bit her lip to stifle a moan, her fingers tangling in his hair as she came again, her knees buckling as pleasure tore through her like a storm.

He lay next to her, pulling her into his arms. She knew that wherever he was would be home, not the ship, not Aloria, but him. She held her wrist up, admiring the bracelet, the delicate design and the stones that almost matched her eyes. She couldn't help but smile at the thought of knowing that he felt the same.

In this small cabin, with its sparse furnishings and narrow bed, with blue reflections dancing across worn walls and the promise of an uncertain future waiting beyond the porthole, she felt something she had not experienced in years; a sense of rightness, of belonging that transcended location. Not safety, exactly; they were far from safe; but a foundation upon which safety might eventually be built.

As the sunlight slowly shifted from gold to amber through the porthole, they realized that they were expected at dinner.

"We will be expected at dinner. We should clean up," she said.

Malin straightened the collar of her top as she followed Will into the dining area, conscious of the faint mark his lips had left just below her collarbone, a private reminder of their afternoon together, barely hidden now. The air here felt different from the quiet intimacy of their cabin; cooler, heavier, filled with unspoken expectations.

The dining room occupied a section of the mid-deck, more polished than the utilitarian corridors they'd just walked. Dark

patina of years. Brass fixtures curled into decorative patterns along the ceiling beams, catching and scattering the warm light from a series of clever mechanical lanterns. There was no visible flame, just a steady, diffuse glow that softened edges and eliminated harsh shadows.

A broad table dominated the center of the room, its surface marked by faint scratches, heat rings, and patches where the varnish had worn away, evidence of countless voyages and stories exchanged over shared meals.

Ellie and Zane were already seated, heads bent together, Zane gesturing animatedly with his hands. Malin noticed how his usual reserve had eased in her presence. His posture was loose, and his face more expressive.

Across from them, her mother watched with her usual silent intensity. Nothing escaped Elowen's notice, she had no doubt she already knew what the news was, but was being polite and would not say anything until it was news.

It was then that she felt the knock within her head, of her mother's presence in her head. *"Yes. I know your news, but it isn't for the reason you think. He asked me for your hand. I gladly gave it."*

Her jaw opened in shock. Will looked at her with a quizzical look.

"Mom told me you got permission," she smiled. He responded with a sheepish smile.

At a side table, the elven guards dined with the crew, while Lady Anariel sat beside Elowen. That didn't feel right. She would have to say something to the captain about that. They deserved to sit with the rest of them. They wouldn't be here without them.

The table had been laid with practical elegance. Sturdy dishware bore faint floral etchings at the rim. Bowls of steaming fish stew warm enough to steam the cooler air. A platter of pastries waited at the far end, their flaky crusts hinting at unexpected delicacy from the ship's galley. Garlic, herbs, and fresh bread perfumed the space with something close to comfort.

Will guided her to an empty seat beside Ellie, his hand brushing the small of her back in a gesture both protective and claiming. A quiet warmth followed the touch, one that had nothing to do with temperature. She caught her mother's raised eyebrow across the table and ignored it.

Footsteps sounded in the corridor; it was two men. The first was the Captain, broad-shouldered and relaxed in his authority. The second was leaner, sharper, with the quiet readiness of someone used to watching and waiting. The cut of his vest and shirt suggested precision, not vanity. Where the captain's gaze was open, the first mate's was more reserved, his attention sweeping the room before resting, narrowing slightly, on Elowen.

"Lady Neldoreth," the captain greeted, voice rough from years barking orders into salt wind. "Your guests are settling in, I see."

Elowen inclined her head with the precise measure of acknowledgment, neither deferential nor dismissive. "Captain. Your accommodations are, as always, impeccable."

Malin clocked the familiarity between them, the easy rhythm of shared history. Her mother's resistance work was far more extensive than she'd realized.

The captain took his place at the head of the table, gesturing to the first mate to sit opposite. The lean man shook Will's hand with a firm grip before lowering himself with the ease of repetition.

"No fights tonight," the captain warned both men, handing Will a carved wooden mug.

Your engineer admitted the device was experimental."

"Experimental doesn't mean 'test its durability against the wall,'" the captain replied, dry but amused.

Laughter rose around the table, light and genuine. Malin felt something inside her ease, tension she hadn't even realized she'd been holding.

The first mate began serving the stew with efficient movements, filling bowls and passing them around the table without ceremony. Malin watched how he deferred to the captain in most matters yet maintained his own authority, particularly when his gaze swept toward the corridor as if mentally tracking the ship's operations even while seated at dinner.

"We'll reach the transfer point in only three days if the winds hold. It is on our side," he informed them, his voice quieter than the captain's but carrying a similar note of unquestionable competence. "Weather reports suggest favorable conditions, assuming there are no other variables, it should be smooth."

Her mother nodded, accepting both the information and a bowl of stew. "And the Qenya Stin Haven? She remains on schedule?"

"As of the last transmission," the captain confirmed. "Ahlgren's punctuality is legendary, if nothing else."

Malin observed the exchange while absently noting how Zane sat slightly straighter whenever Will spoke, the boy's attention shifting to catch every word. The transformation in their relationship from strangers to father and son had occurred with remarkable speed, yet there was nothing artificial in their growing bond. Zane had the look of someone who had found an answer to a question that had been bothering him for months.

gaze occasionally lingering on the mechanical light fixtures overhead. Malin recognized her daughter's expression; the slight furrow between her brows indicated she was working through some problem or observation. When those ice-blue eyes shifted toward a slight green color, she knew she was working her magic in some way, though her powers had been growing so quickly, it was hard to say what she was up to. Ellie's color-changing eyes were the most visible manifestation of her magical abilities.

"The bread is exceptional," Will commented. He broke a piece from the crusty loaf, releasing a fresh cloud of aromatic steam. "Your cook has outdone himself, Captain."

The captain nodded his acknowledgment, "Janik has been with us fifteen years. Claims he was trained in Aloria's finest kitchens before deciding the sea offered better opportunities."

"I ain't never gonna complain about someone who has abilities that enhance cooking so well. We is lucky to have 'em," the first mate added quietly, the comment serving as both information and reassurance. This was a vessel where magic was not feared.

Malin felt something tight in her chest loosen slightly at this confirmation. She had known the Dawn's Beacon operated outside Media's rigid anti-magic strictures; her mother would have arranged nothing less; but it did feel good to know that it had been stated out loud.

The conversation continued as they ate, flowing between practical matters of their journey and more general topics that allowed them to become acquainted without venturing into potentially sensitive areas. The captain proved to be a skilled host, sharing tales of unusual cargo and peculiar passengers that had Zane leaning forward with undisguised interest and even drew reluctant smiles from Mom.

table with a doctor's analytical eye. Her mother remained composed as always, but Malin noticed the occasional glance toward the porthole, measuring their progress away from Media's receding coastline. Will, meanwhile, made a point of drawing Zane into conversation. Nothing overt, just quiet affirmations and well-timed questions that bolstered the boy's confidence.

The captain and first mate moved in a kind of seamless tandem, their communication requiring few words. It was the ease of long partnership, battle-tested, and unburdened by ego.

Amber light from the mechanical fixtures gleamed against the dark-paneled walls as evening deepened into night. The clink of cutlery against dishware, the low hum of voices, and the occasional burst of laughter formed a rhythm both mundane and remarkable. In this borrowed quiet, a sense of camaraderie bloomed.

Malin found herself watching Will's hands as he spoke. They were animated as he described a particularly intricate lock he had picked. The same hands that had touched her with reverence only hours earlier moved with precision and life. She glanced at the captain, who listened with unfeigned interest, and recognized the look of someone who valued skill, regardless of its origin. Will wasn't just a rogue or a smuggler, he was someone others trusted to fix things.

As plates were cleared, crew members brought out cups of a rich, dark beverage, spiced with notes of chocolate and something citrusy. Malin wrapped her hands around the warm ceramic, letting herself sink into a rare moment of cautious optimism. They had escaped. The ship was moving. The children were adjusting, Zane's laughter still rang in her ears, Ellie's curiosity was satiated. It filled her with pride and love.

there, it felt so good to see the real person she had hidden from her for all these years. She would have rather had known the truth and had the relationship. She could read minds, why couldn't she have read hers to see that she could be trusted. If she had known the truth, would that have made her make different choices? Malin decided to acknowledge that choices were made, risks taken, paths diverged and now the choice was made to them to repair the relationship.

The captain raised his cup in a subtle gesture, stopping short of a formal toast, anything too ceremonial might tempt fate, given how much still lay ahead.

"To safe passages," he said simply.

The company echoed the words, their voices blending in a moment of quiet harmony. Malin's cup touched Will's, the clink soft and deliberate, their eyes locking over the rim. There was a promise there, warm and unspoken, cutting through the uncertainty that still waited outside the ship's wooden walls.

Beyond the hull, Media's forces would surely have noticed their absence, and the absence of the files Mom took. Orders would be issued. Names would be spoken aloud in rooms full of serious men. The sea crossing to Sarhan held its own perils, and Aloria, on the other side of the world, even with all its whispered promises, remained a distant shore.

But here, in the circle of shared warmth and quiet conversation, Malin let herself believe. Not in perfect safety, she was too practical for that, but in the possibility of something better. A place where Ellie could grow without fear. Where Zane could reclaim what he'd lost. Where she and Will might build something real from the fragile beginning they'd been handed.

felt something she'd almost forgotten. It wasn't happiness exactly, but it's quieter, steadier cousin, contentment. It might not last. But it was hers now, and she clung to it like a lifeline.

Then Will stood, his voice rising above the hum of the gathering.

"A few hours ago, Malin accepted my offer to be my wife."

The room erupted in cheers, like a thunderclap, echoing off the walls and into the bones of the ship. Ellie and Zane's faces lit with joy, their hands clasped tightly, eyes wide with unfiltered glee.

Will grinned, letting the laughter crest before adding, "Captain, I was hoping you'd do the honors. I'd like to hold the ceremony before she changes her mind."

More laughter followed, loud and full of warmth.

The captain stood; his expression was amused but touched. "I'd be honored. It's a simple ceremony. Are you sure you wouldn't prefer something grander, perhaps something to match your stature?"

Malin answered with quiet certainty. "Everyone I would want to attend is already here."

The captain nodded, pulling a worn leather book and a brilliant hand-fasting ribbon from his jacket. "Then how about now?"

Another cheer erupted, this one less surprised and more celebratory.

She was impressed. He had been a busy man since boarding.

Will reached out a hand to Malin, that boyish glint in his eye tempered by something deeper. She took it without hesitation.

He guided her through the sea of smiling faces, past clapping hands and wide-eyed children. They came to a stop before the

received in return was unlike any she had seen from her, wide, unguarded, and utterly full of love. It struck Malin with a surprising force, like discovering treasure in a place she hadn't thought to look.

Zane and Ellie stood close, their fingers laced, their faces radiant with hope.

The captain conducted the ceremony with quiet reverence. Each word felt precise and deliberate, marking not just time, but love. The ship seemed to hush with him, as though the walls and water knew the weight of this moment. When he placed the ribbon over their joined hands, a braid of deep blue, silver, and gold, the fabric shimmered in the lantern light.

The moment came for vows. The captain inclined his head toward Malin.

She swallowed hard. Her mouth was dry, her heart too full. Public speaking had never been her strength, too many eyes, too many feelings. But this wasn't for them. It was for him. Her voice trembled slightly as she began.

"I don't have the right words," she admitted, eyes locked on Will's. "But I know this: since you walked back into my life, I've felt more like myself than I ever have. You challenge me, steady me, and somehow... you make me believe in good things again. I don't know where this road leads, but if you're walking it with me, then I'm home." She smiled, a little crooked, a little shy. "That's all I have. Just... me. And I'm yours."

Will squeezed her hands, his smile tender, eyes shimmering with unshed emotion.

The captain turned to him. "And your vow?"

her chest tightened in warning.

"Right. My turn. I had something written, of course. I've been tinkering with it like a pocket watch for days, turning it over, tightening the words, trying to find the perfect gear to make it run smooth." He paused, voice softening. "But standing here… Sparks, none of it seems big enough."

She blinked, already overwhelmed, and he took a breath, continuing.

"I vow to keep you safe, even when you insist you don't need protecting. I vow to stand beside you, even when you're being impossibly stubborn, especially then. I vow to hold your hand when the road is clear and carry you when it's not. I promise to laugh with you, to fight for you, and when needed, to shut up and let you win… occasionally."

Soft laughter bubbled through the crowd, but his voice never wavered.

"I love your fire. Your brain. Your impossible beauty. But mostly I love that you're the kind of woman who sets the world on fire… both literally and figuratively… and still makes room in it for someone like me. I love you, Sparks. Every version of you. And I promise I will never stop trying to deserve the miracle of you saying yes."

By the end, her tears were slipping down freely, and she made no effort to stop them.

The captain gave them a small, knowing smile.

"You may seal your vows," he said, his voice hushed and reverent.

Will leaned in and kissed her, a kiss that wasn't about passion, though it held plenty. Will's hand slid to her cheek. The kiss stole Malin's breath. Her toes lifted off the deck, the ship swaying gently beneath her feet as the cheers swelled once again, as if the very sea was celebrating with them. It was about promise. Permanence. A future that might be built on shifting seas but would always be navigated together.

Cheers erupted from the crew, Ellie squealed, Zane whooped, and Malin felt something she never expected to find again.

Joy. Whole and unshattered.

A few hours later, Malin stood at the starboard railing, eyes turned skyward. The stars blinked like scattered diamonds across the dark velvet, and below them, a pod of sailfish danced through the waves, their silver fins catching the moonlight like living lanterns. The ship moved steadily through the water, a heartbeat in the vast open sea.

Will's strong arms wrapped around her from behind.

"The kids are tucked in," Will murmured against her ear. "They made me tell them a story."

A quiet laugh escaped her lips as she leaned into him. "Let me guess. You changed all the facts to make yourself the hero?"

"Absolutely," he said, without shame. "And you were a dangerous sorceress with a secret soft spot for roguish charm."

She smiled, the kind that settled deep in her bones.

They were sailing into a pirate-run port. Sea monsters were rumored to haunt the waters beyond. After that, the path would thread dangerously close to dragon-filled mountains. And somewhere behind them, Media's reach was stretching, growing colder and more determined by the day.

choices they might never be ready for.

But they had this.

Right now.

The ship, the stars, the warm circle of family waiting belowdecks.

She wasn't safe. She wasn't certain.

But for the first time in years, Malin Neldoreth was *free*.

And freedom… was only the beginning.

*J*ourney to Aloria is Book 2 in the Series, where Will, Malin, and Ellie will make their way to Aloria, with Media chasing after them, and the many dangers in their wake.

Will and Malin have made a commitment to each other, but when Will runs into an old flame and Malin finds her fiancé, Ellie's father is alive... How will that affect their relationship?

Physical dangers like the dangers of sea monster attacks, sirens, and Orc attacks, along with the continued pursuit of Media are dangerous. Through it all... can their love survive?

Brandy Stoker is a storyteller whose tales of love, resilience, and self-discovery captivate readers long after the final page. Growing up in Maryland, she draws inspiration from the charming landscapes and communities of her hometown to create relatable characters and vivid settings.

Blue Haven, her first published book, has taken off as a contemporary feel-good love story, but she felt compelled to switch back to her roots of fantasy.

Brandy has been writing since middle school and is a proud mother of three adult children. Life challenges, including health scares and a difficult divorce, led her to embrace independence and inspire others to do the same. Her books reflect her passion for personal growth and the beauty of real-life connections, offering readers examples of resilience and self-discovery.

When she's not writing, Brandy enjoys coffee, watching koi, and playing games with friends. By day, she works in statistics and finance, balancing her analytical work with her creative side. Recently, she's embraced new hobbies like painting and caring for her koi pond.

Brandy invites you to explore her heartfelt stories and encourages you to leave a review. She loves hearing from readers and values their feedback.

Facebook and Instagram - brandystoker.author

Her website is https://www.brandystoker.com

Check it out, to find some hidden treasures related to these stories.

The author would like to thank:

- Her family and friends for their encouragement to follow her dreams and persevere in her pursuit of happiness. Without their gracious feedback and support, I would not have been able to complete this novel.
- Brandy Over 40 for Publication support
- Brandy Jones and Angelee Van Allman for the Cover/Cover Art.
- Ben Cole providing the amazing Map of Media.
- A big thank you to Laura Holowitz, for her amazing talents in the Audiobook – expected to be available in December 2025.
- Special thanks to Mr. Nelson from Bel Air High School. He allowed me to create a personal class called – Creative Novel Writing that helped to cement my dream of one day being a full-time author. It has taken a few years, but I am finally working on my dream.